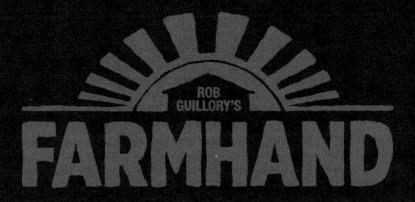

FARMHAND

ROB GUILLORY'S

VOLUME 4
THE SEED

Created, Written and Drawn by
ROB GUILLORY

Colors by
JEAN-FRANCOIS BEAULIEU

Letters by
KODY CHAMBERLAIN

Graphic Design by
BURTON DURAND

IMAGE COMICS, INC. • Robert Kirkman: Chief Operating Officer • Erik Larsen: Chief Financial Officer • Todd McFarlane: President • Marc Silvestri: Chief Executive Officer • Jim Valentino: Vice President • Eric Stephenson: Publisher / Chief Creative Officer • Nicole Lapalme: Vice President of Finance • Leanna Caunter: Accounting Analyst • Sue Korpela: Accounting & HR Manager • Matt Parkinson: Vice President of Sales & Publishing Planning • Lorelei Bunjes: Vice President of Digital Strategy • Dirk Wood: Vice President of International Sales & Licensing • Ryan Brewer: International Sales & Licensing Manager • Alex Cox: Director of Direct Market Sales • Chloe Ramos: Book Market & Library Sales Manager • Emilio Bautista: Digital Sales Coordinator • Jon Schlaffman: Specialty Sales Coordinator • Kat Salazar: Vice President of PR & Marketing • Deanna Phelps: Marketing Design Manager • Drew Fitzgerald: Marketing Content Associate • Heather Doornink: Vice President of Production • Drew Gill: Art Director • Hilary DiLoreto: Print Manager • Tricia Ramos: Traffic Manager • Melissa Gifford: Content Manager • Erika Schnatz: Senior Production Artist • Wesley Griffith: Production Artist • Rich Fowlks: Production Artist • IMAGECOMICS.COM

DEDICATION

For my friend Shane.

Special Thanks:

Ben Bender, for the good eye.

John Layman, for the encouragement.

And April, for putting up with the insanity of Comics.

CHAPTER 10

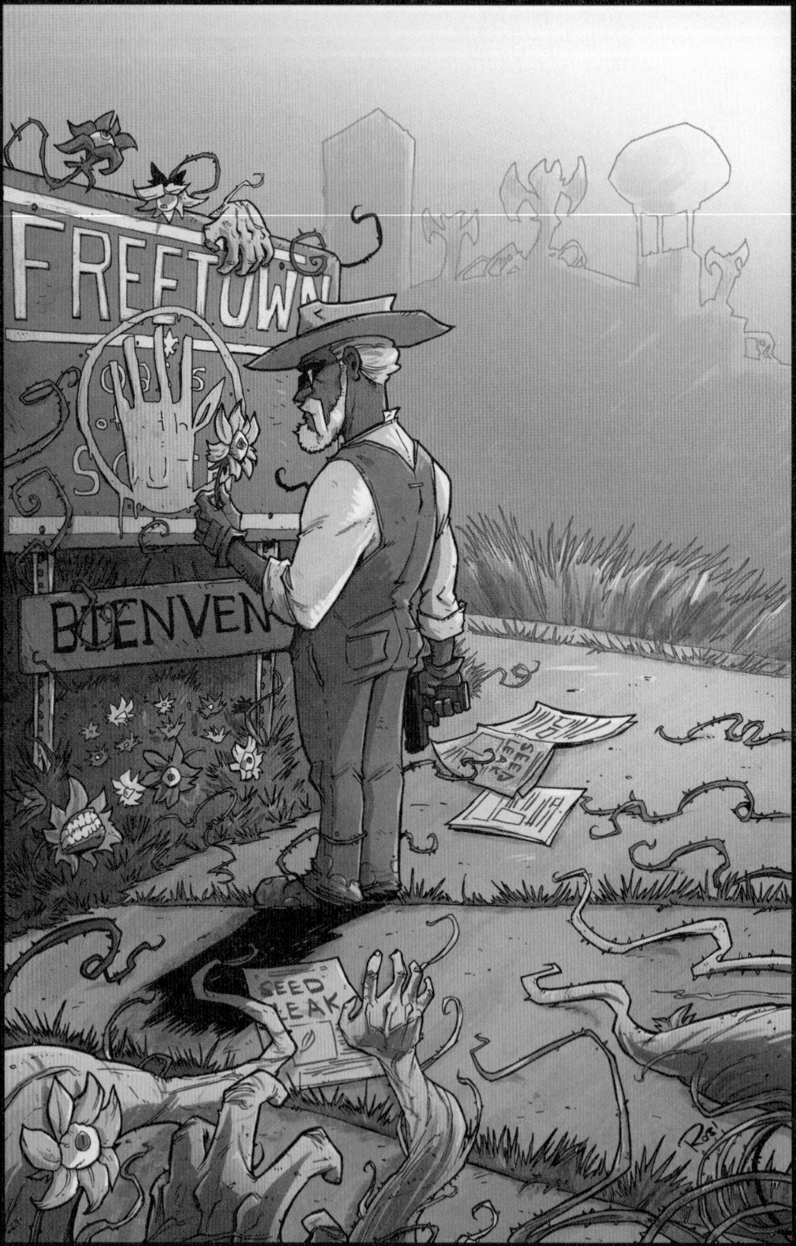

FREETOWN
BIENVEN
SEED LEAK
SEED LEAK

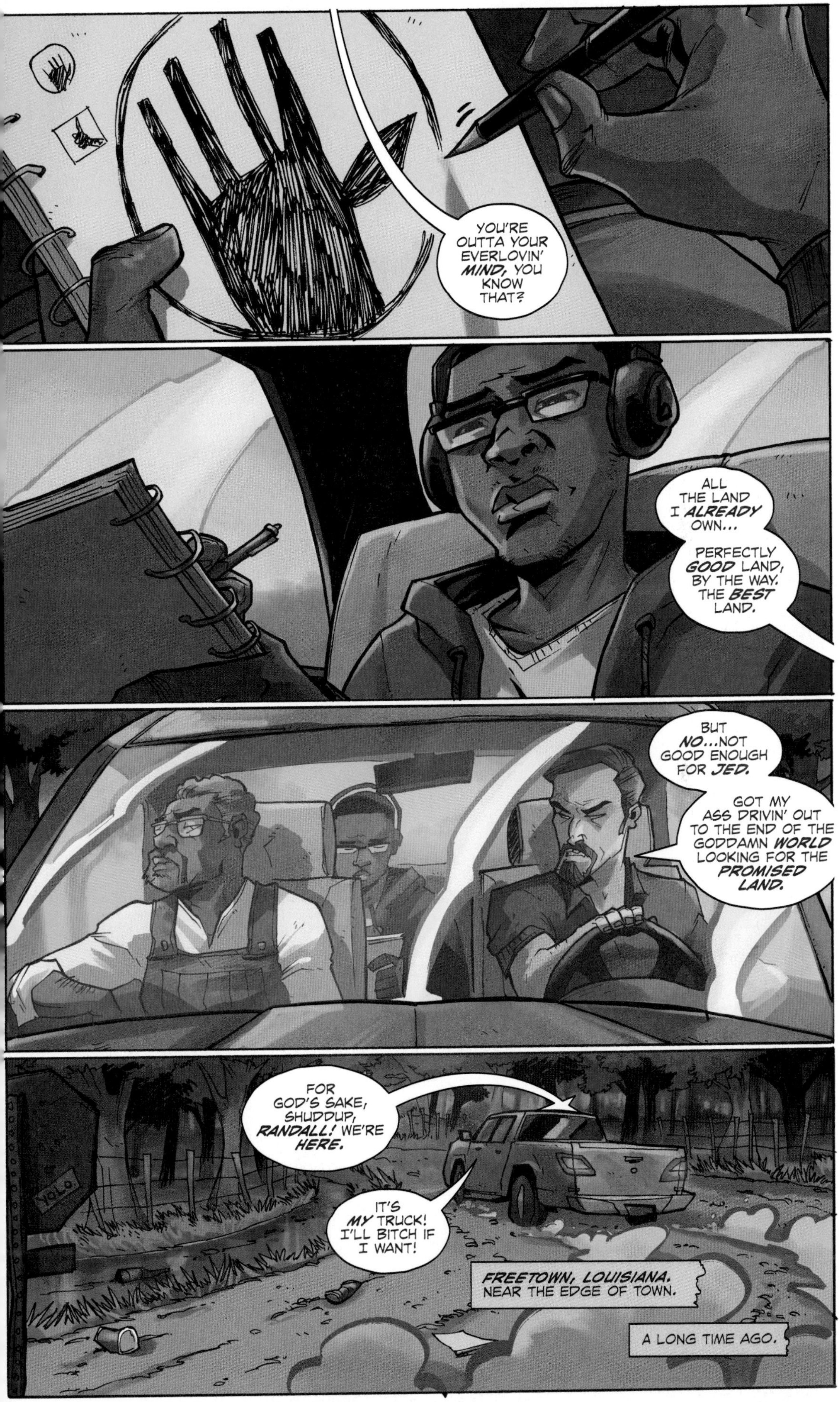
YOU'RE OUTTA YOUR EVERLOVIN' MIND, YOU KNOW THAT?
ALL THE LAND I ALREADY OWN...
PERFECTLY GOOD LAND, BY THE WAY. THE BEST LAND.
BUT NO...NOT GOOD ENOUGH FOR JED.
GOT MY ASS DRIVIN' OUT TO THE END OF THE GODDAMN WORLD LOOKING FOR THE PROMISED LAND.
FOR GOD'S SAKE, SHUDDUP, RANDALL! WE'RE HERE.
IT'S MY TRUCK! I'LL BITCH IF I WANT!
YOLO
FREETOWN, LOUISIANA. NEAR THE EDGE OF TOWN.
A LONG TIME AGO.

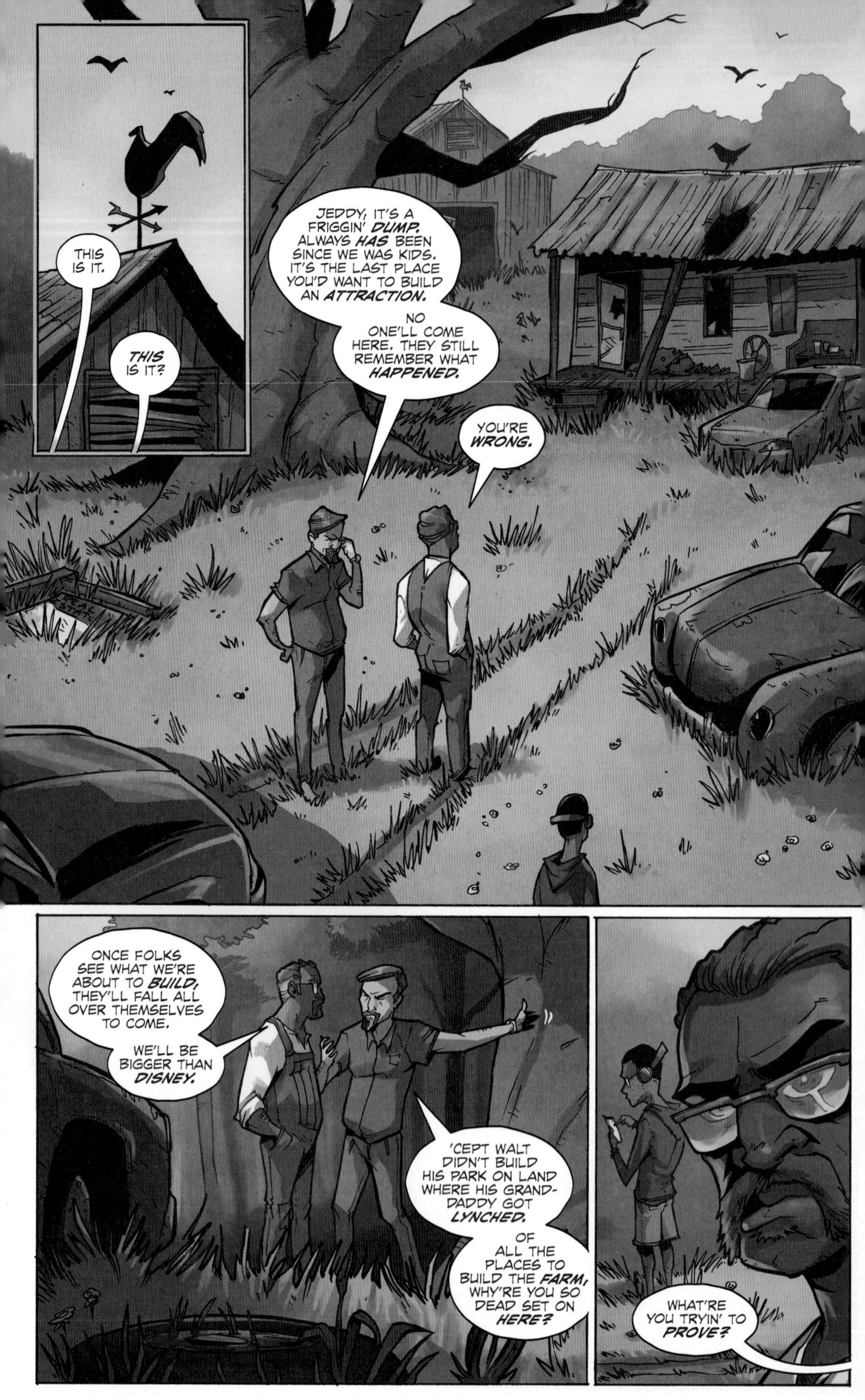
THIS IS IT.
THIS IS IT?
JEDDY, IT'S A FRIGGIN' DUMP. ALWAYS HAS BEEN SINCE WE WAS KIDS. IT'S THE LAST PLACE YOU'D WANT TO BUILD AN ATTRACTION.
NO ONE'LL COME HERE. THEY STILL REMEMBER WHAT HAPPENED.
YOU'RE WRONG.
ONCE FOLKS SEE WHAT WE'RE ABOUT TO BUILD, THEY'LL FALL ALL OVER THEMSELVES TO COME.
WE'LL BE BIGGER THAN DISNEY.
'CEPT WALT DIDN'T BUILD HIS PARK ON LAND WHERE HIS GRAND-DADDY GOT LYNCHED.
OF ALL THE PLACES TO BUILD THE FARM, WHY'RE YOU SO DEAD SET ON HERE?
WHAT'RE YOU TRYIN' TO PROVE?

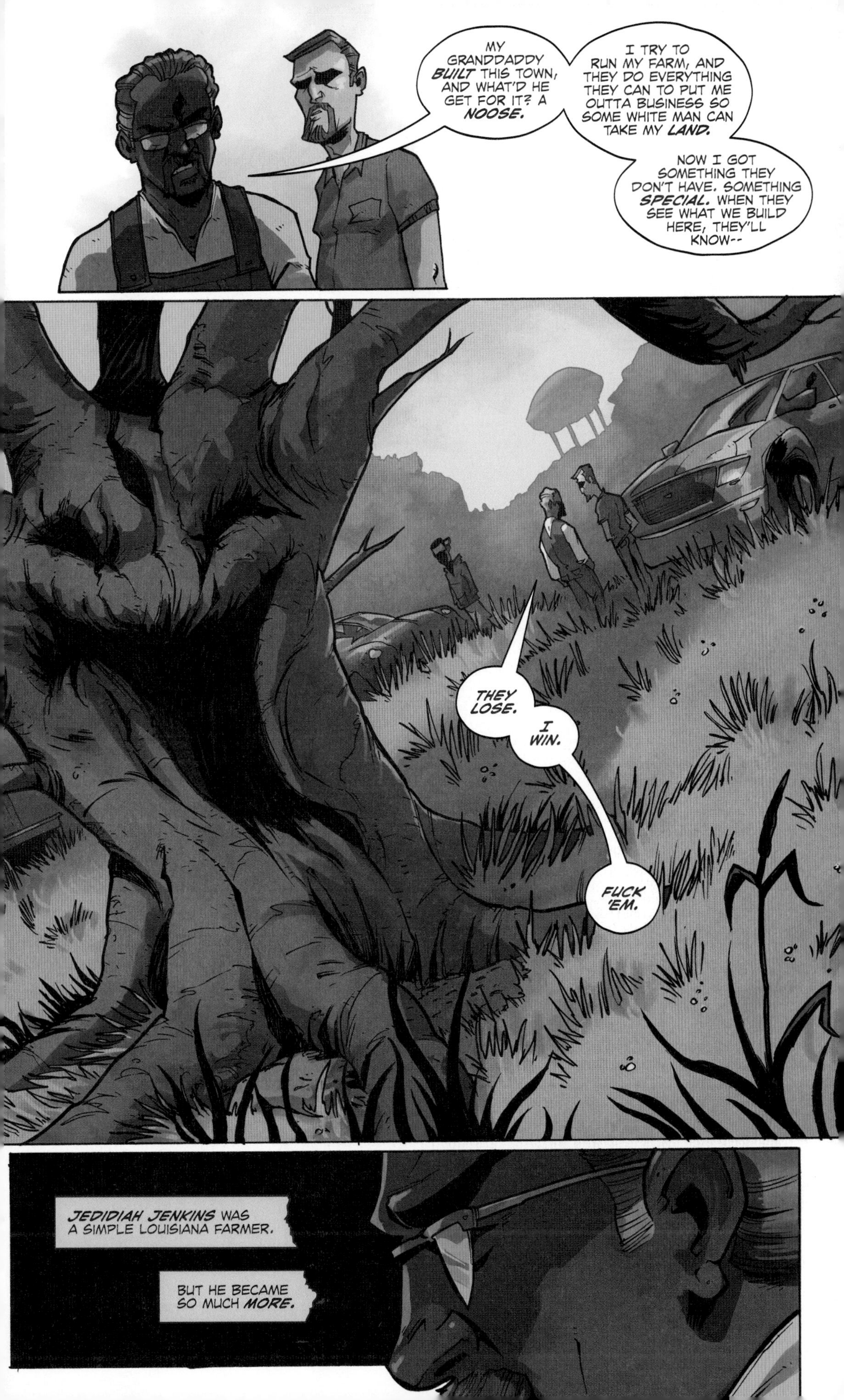
MY GRANDDADDY BUILT THIS TOWN, AND WHAT'D HE GET FOR IT? A NOOSE.
I TRY TO RUN MY FARM, AND THEY DO EVERYTHING THEY CAN TO PUT ME OUTTA BUSINESS SO SOME WHITE MAN CAN TAKE MY LAND.
NOW I GOT SOMETHING THEY DON'T HAVE. SOMETHING SPECIAL. WHEN THEY SEE WHAT WE BUILD HERE, THEY'LL KNOW--
THEY LOSE.
I WIN.
FUCK 'EM.
JEDIDIAH JENKINS WAS A SIMPLE LOUISIANA FARMER.
BUT HE BECAME SO MUCH MORE.

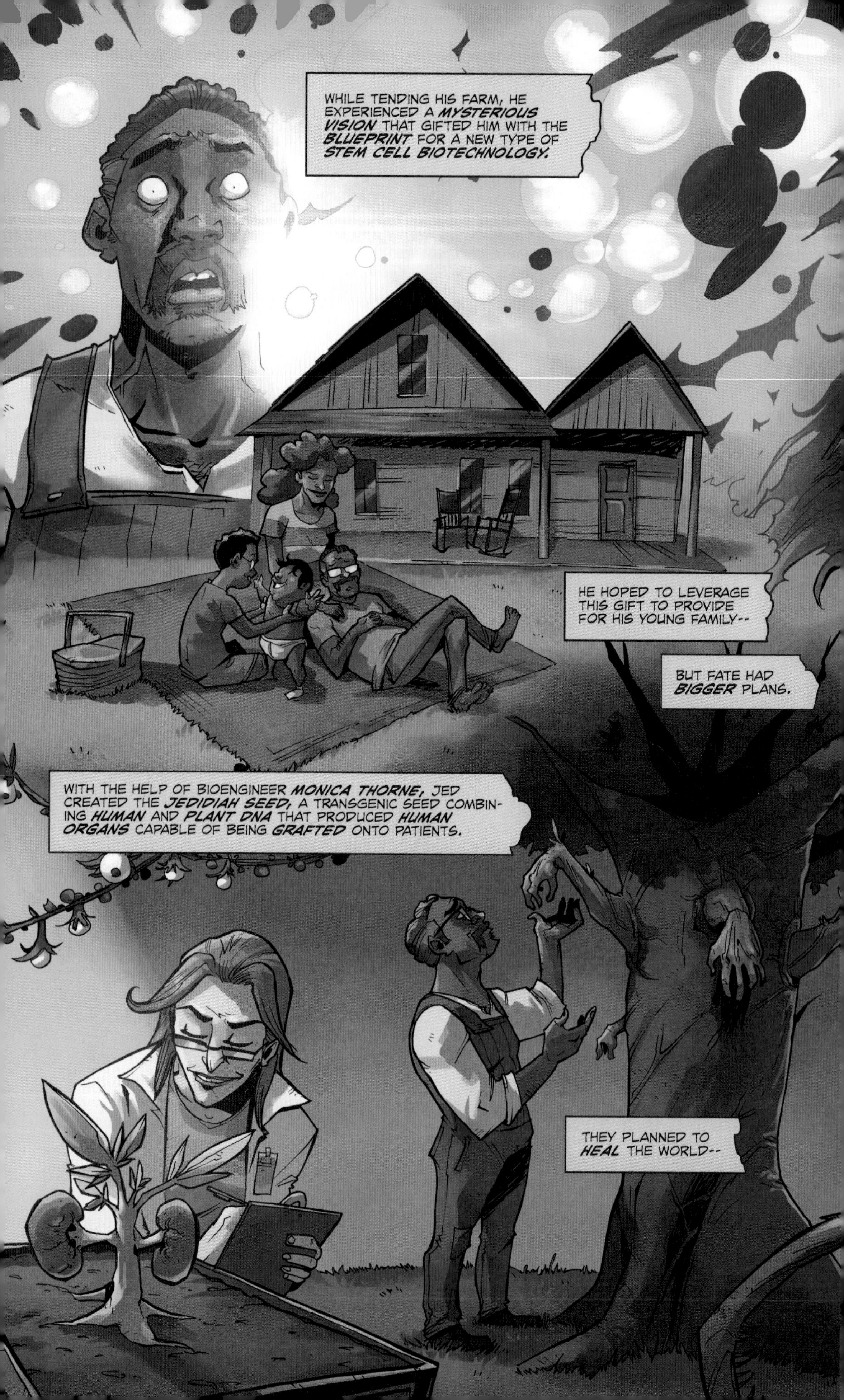
WHILE TENDING HIS FARM, HE EXPERIENCED A MYSTERIOUS VISION THAT GIFTED HIM WITH THE BLUEPRINT FOR A NEW TYPE OF STEM CELL BIOTECHNOLOGY.
HE HOPED TO LEVERAGE THIS GIFT TO PROVIDE FOR HIS YOUNG FAMILY--
BUT FATE HAD BIGGER PLANS.
WITH THE HELP OF BIOENGINEER MONICA THORNE, JED CREATED THE JEDIDIAH SEED, A TRANSGENIC SEED COMBINING HUMAN AND PLANT DNA THAT PRODUCED HUMAN ORGANS CAPABLE OF BEING GRAFTED ONTO PATIENTS.
THEY PLANNED TO HEAL THE WORLD--

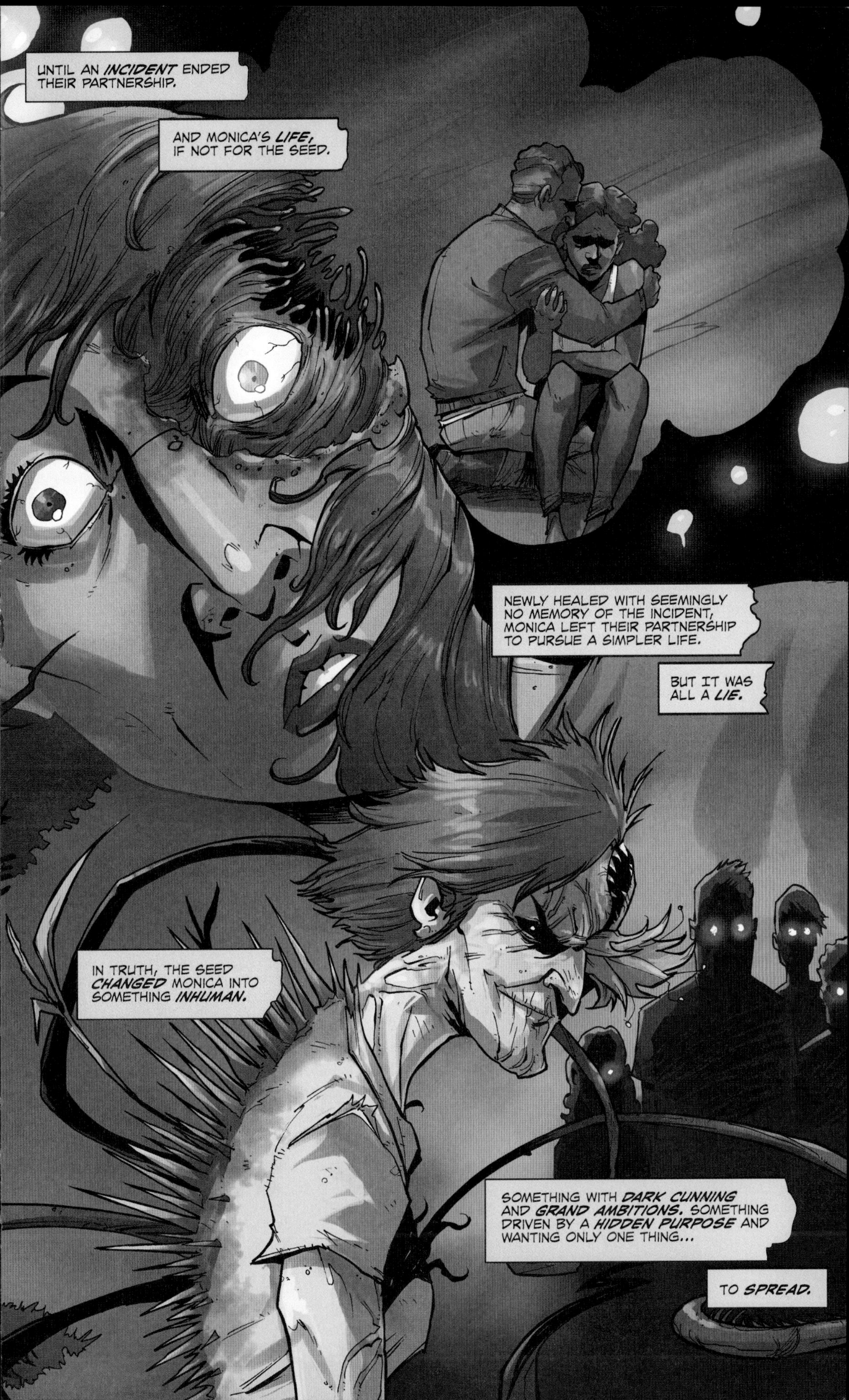
UNTIL AN INCIDENT ENDED THEIR PARTNERSHIP.
AND MONICA'S LIFE, IF NOT FOR THE SEED.
NEWLY HEALED WITH SEEMINGLY NO MEMORY OF THE INCIDENT, MONICA LEFT THEIR PARTNERSHIP TO PURSUE A SIMPLER LIFE.
BUT IT WAS ALL A LIE.
IN TRUTH, THE SEED CHANGED MONICA INTO SOMETHING INHUMAN.
SOMETHING WITH DARK CUNNING AND GRAND AMBITIONS. SOMETHING DRIVEN BY A HIDDEN PURPOSE AND WANTING ONLY ONE THING...
TO SPREAD.

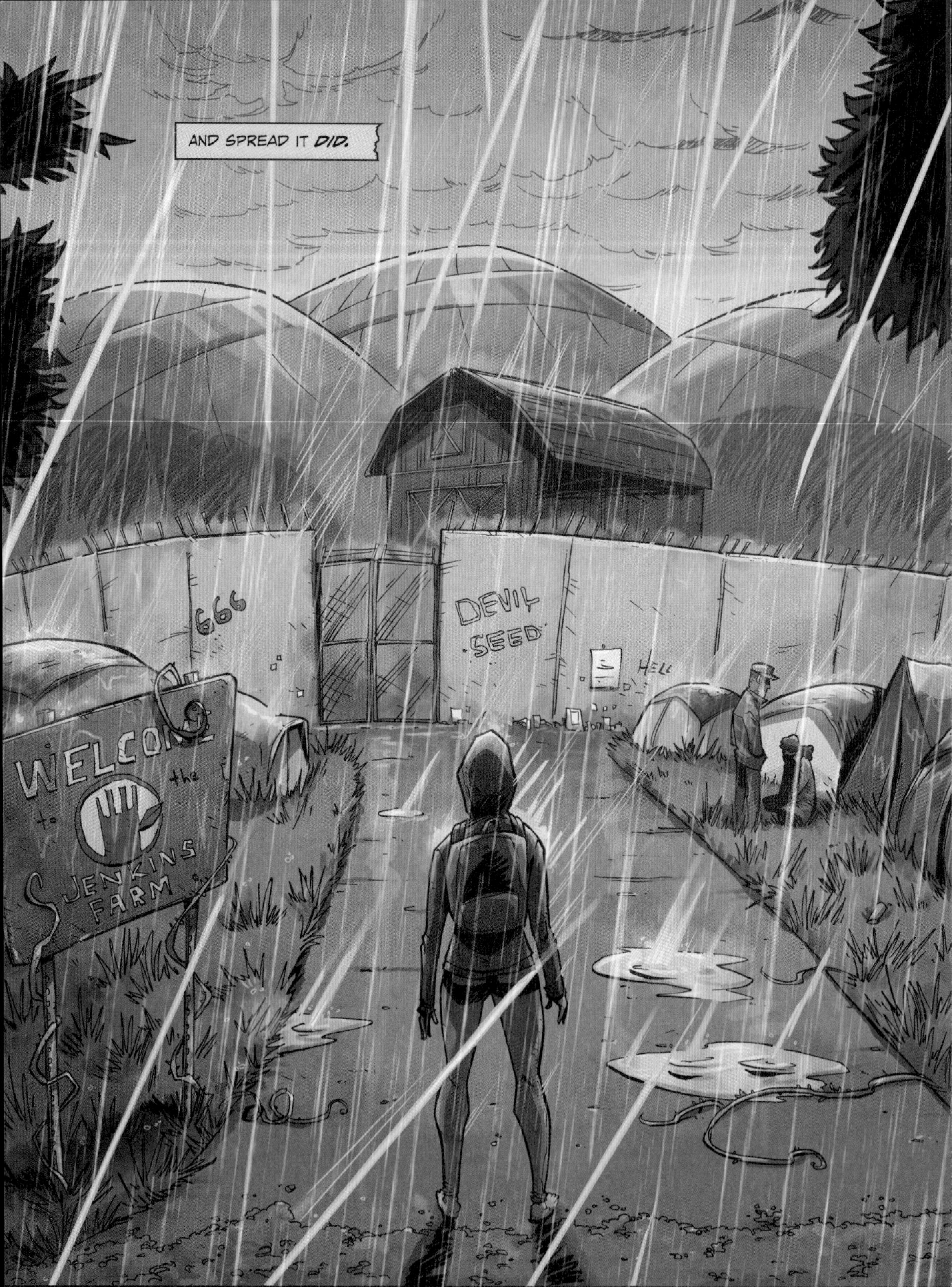
AND SPREAD IT DID.
666
DEVIL SEED
HELL
WELCOME to the JENKINS FARM

CHAPTER 16: **FALLOW EARTH.**

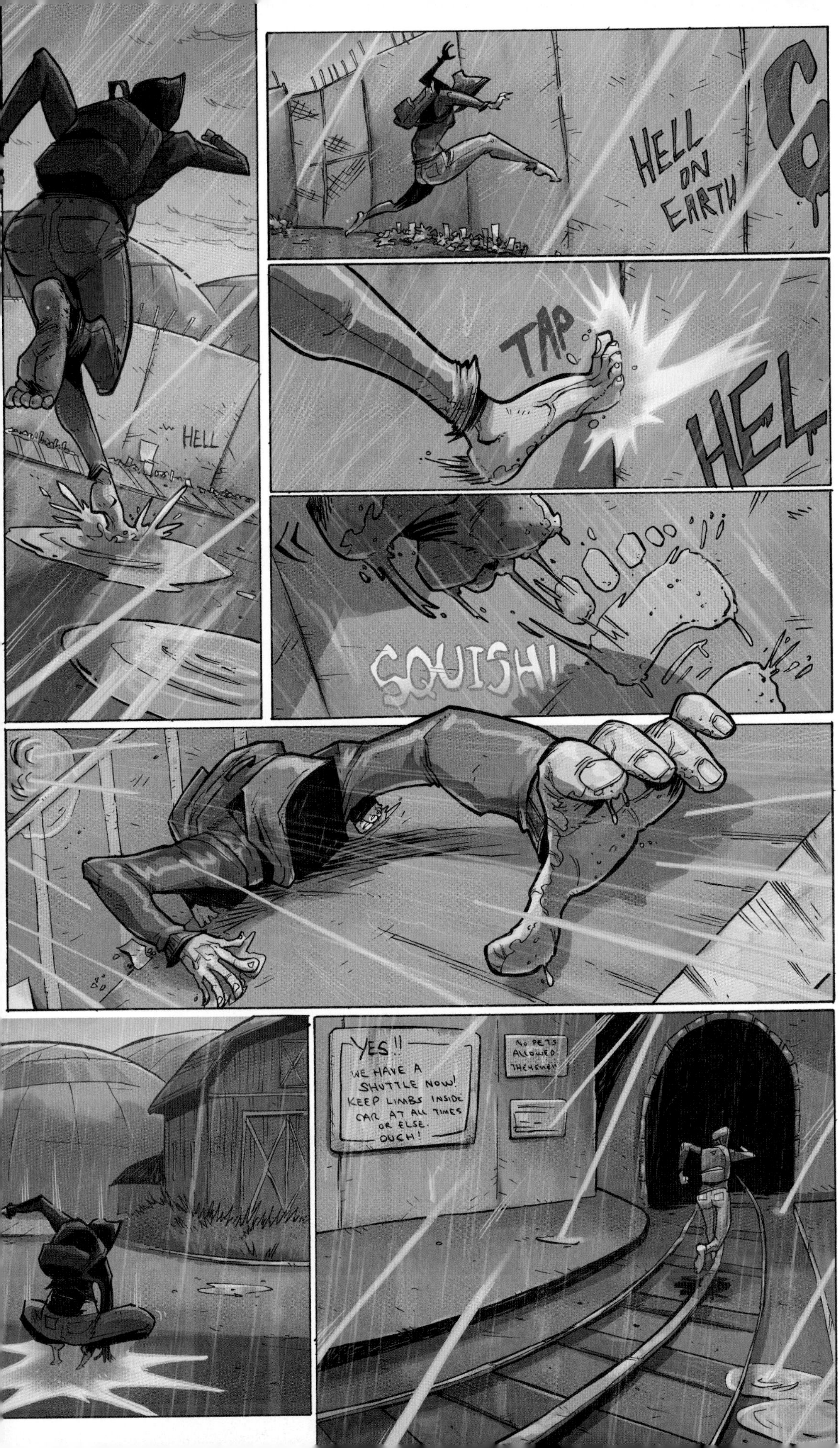
HELL
HELL ON EARTH
TAP
HEL
SQUISH!
YES!!
WE HAVE A SHUTTLE NOW! KEEP LIMBS INSIDE CAR AT ALL TIMES OR ELSE. OUCH!
NO PETS ALLOWED.

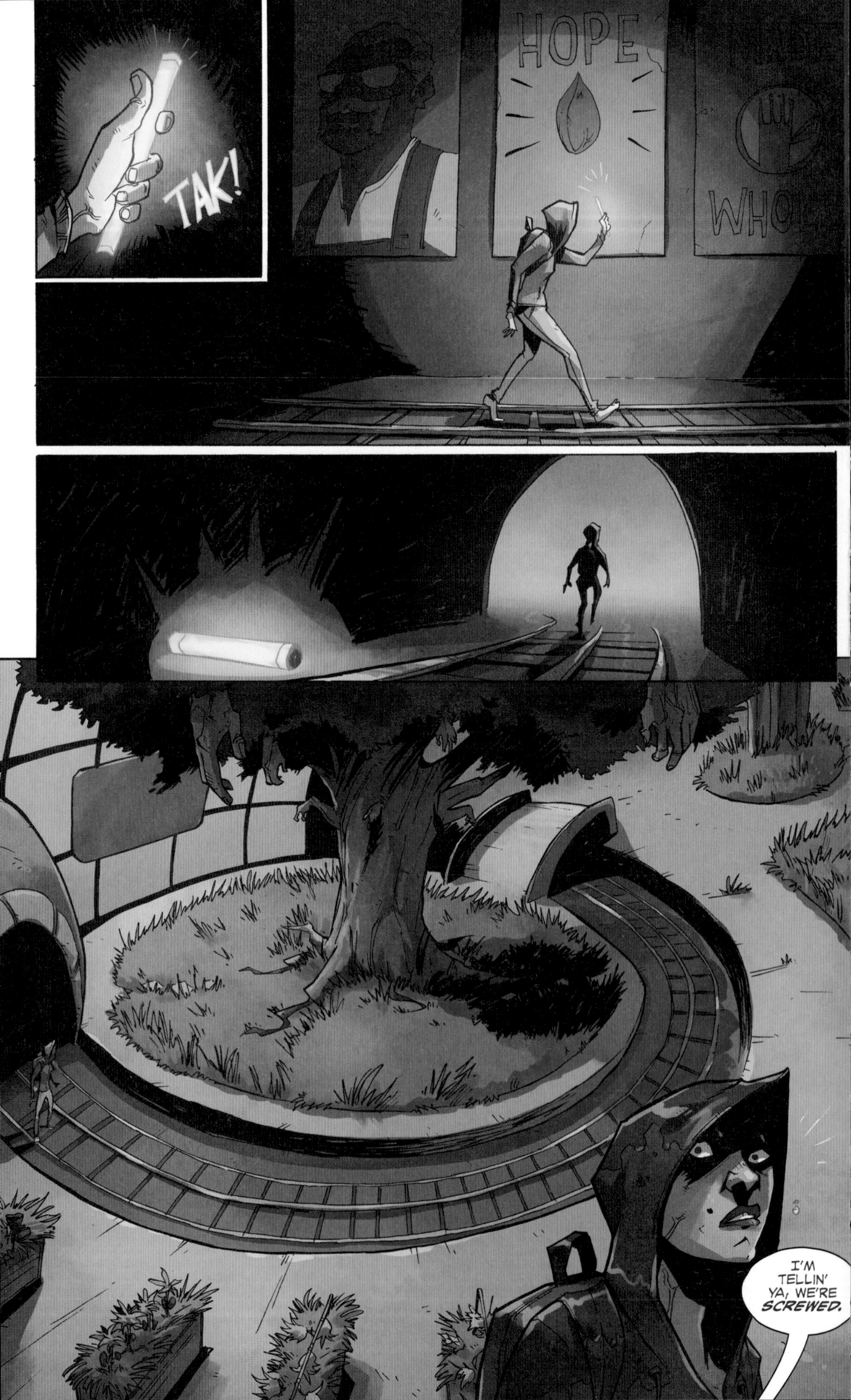
TAK!
HOPE
WHO
I'M TELLIN' YA, WE'RE *SCREWED.*

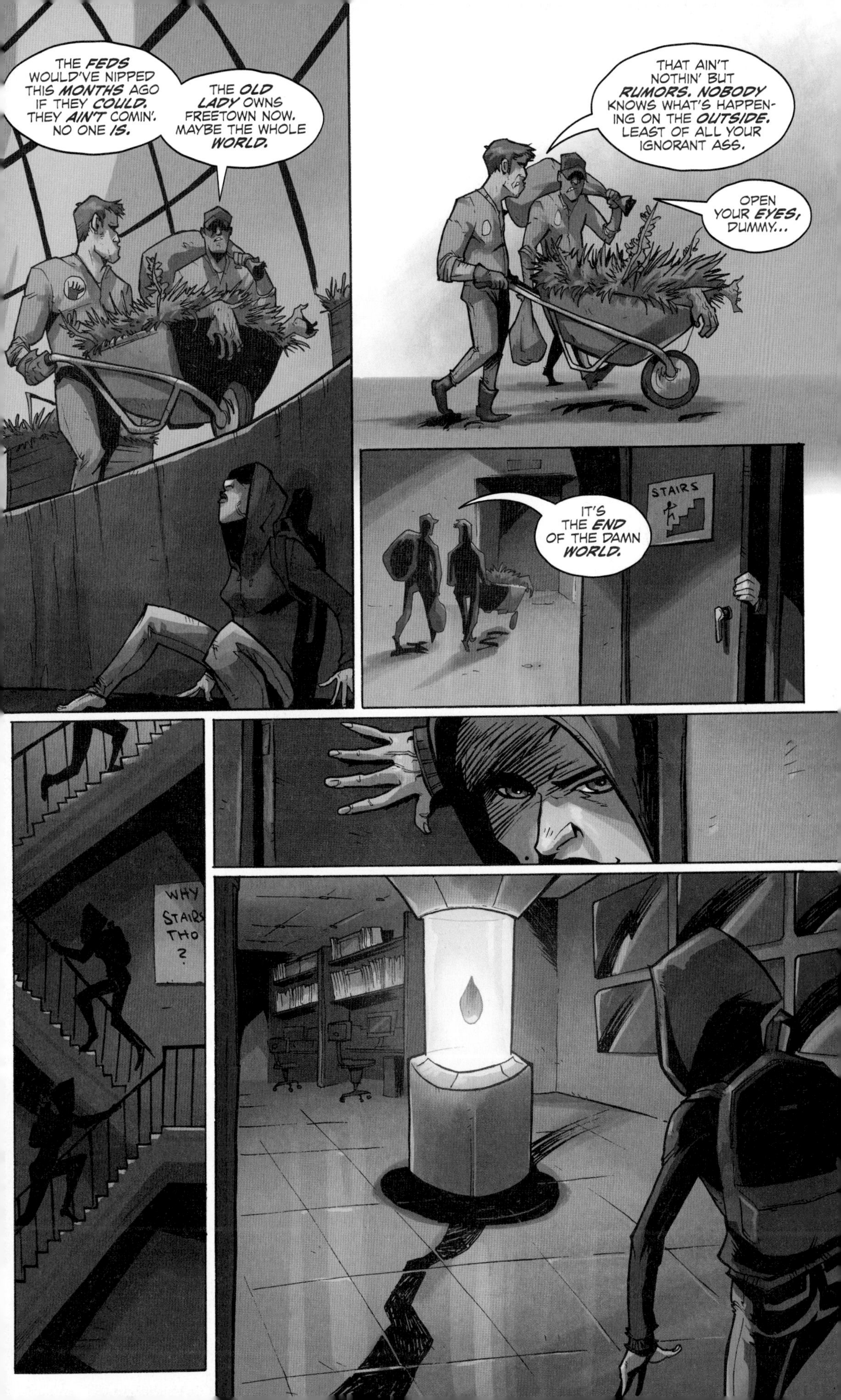
THE FEDS WOULD'VE NIPPED THIS MONTHS AGO IF THEY COULD. THEY AIN'T COMIN'. NO ONE IS.
THE OLD LADY OWNS FREETOWN NOW. MAYBE THE WHOLE WORLD.
THAT AIN'T NOTHIN' BUT RUMORS. NOBODY KNOWS WHAT'S HAPPENING ON THE OUTSIDE. LEAST OF ALL YOUR IGNORANT ASS.
OPEN YOUR EYES, DUMMY...
STAIRS
IT'S THE END OF THE DAMN WORLD.
WHY STAIRS THO ?

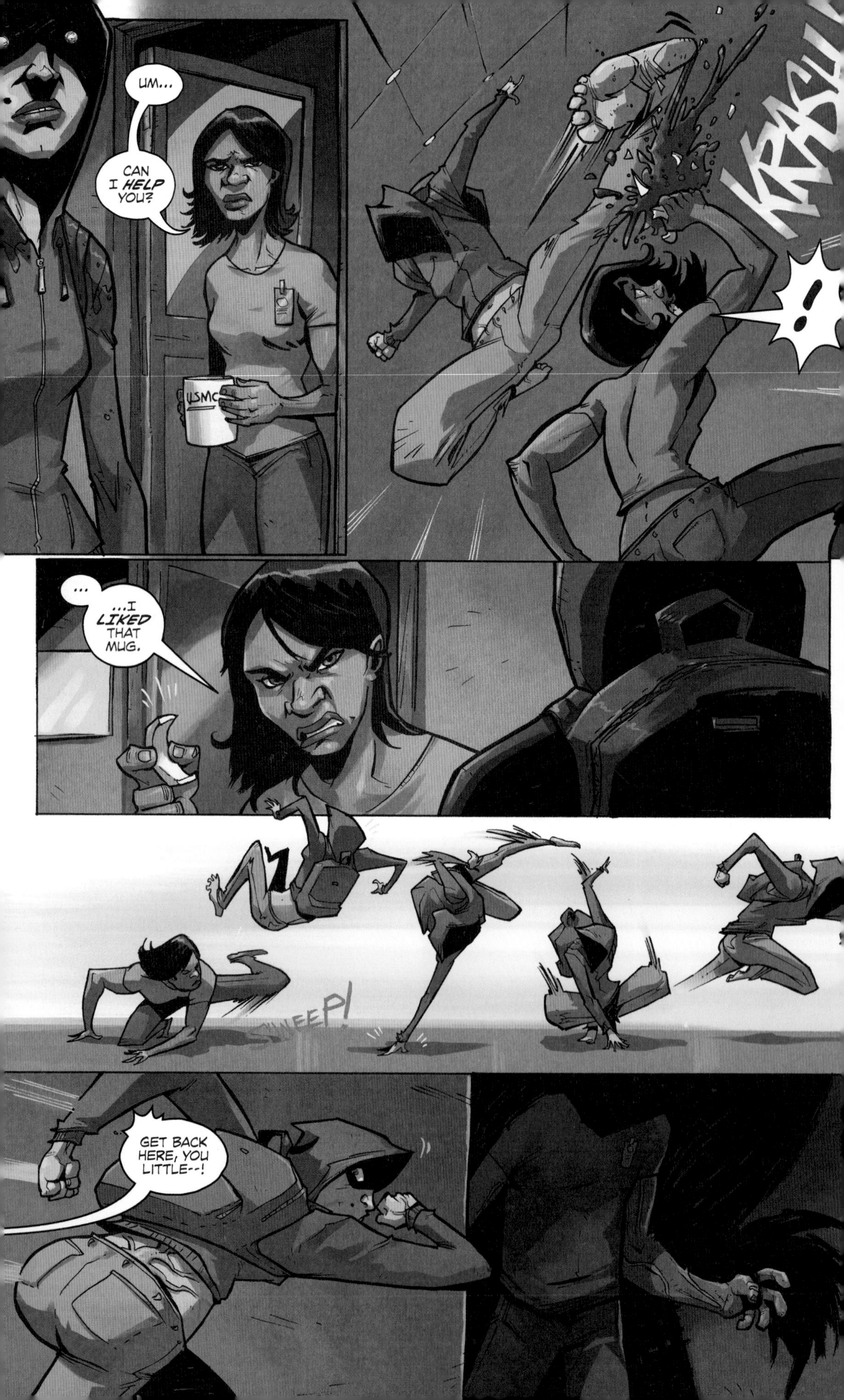

UM...
CAN I HELP YOU?
USMC
KRASH
!
...
...I LIKED THAT MUG.
SWEEP!
GET BACK HERE, YOU LITTLE--!

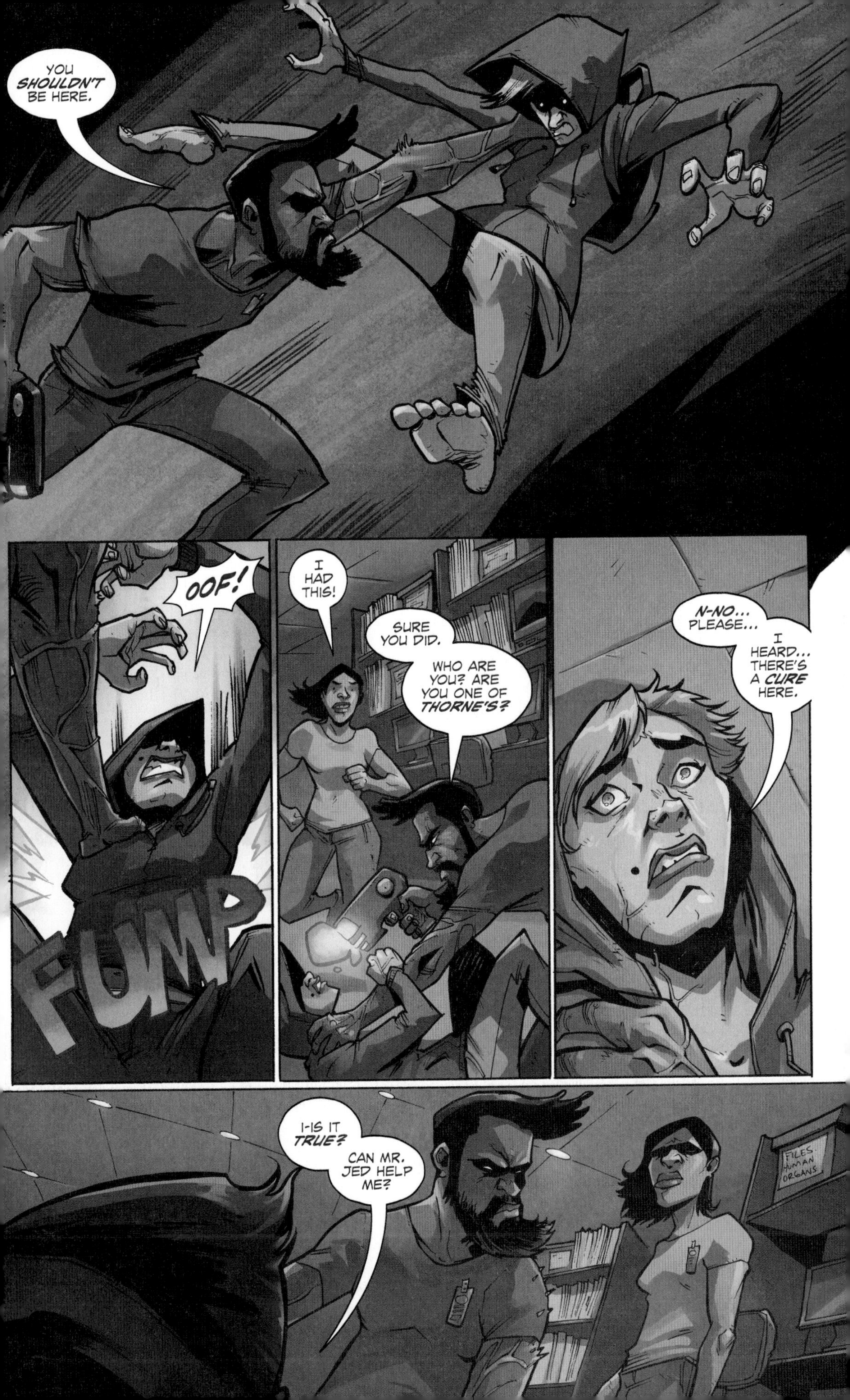

YOU SHOULDN'T BE HERE.
OOF!
FUMP
I HAD THIS!
SURE YOU DID.
WHO ARE YOU? ARE YOU ONE OF THORNE'S?
N-NO... PLEASE...
I HEARD... THERE'S A CURE HERE.
I-IS IT TRUE?
CAN MR. JED HELP ME?
FILES. HUMAN ORGANS

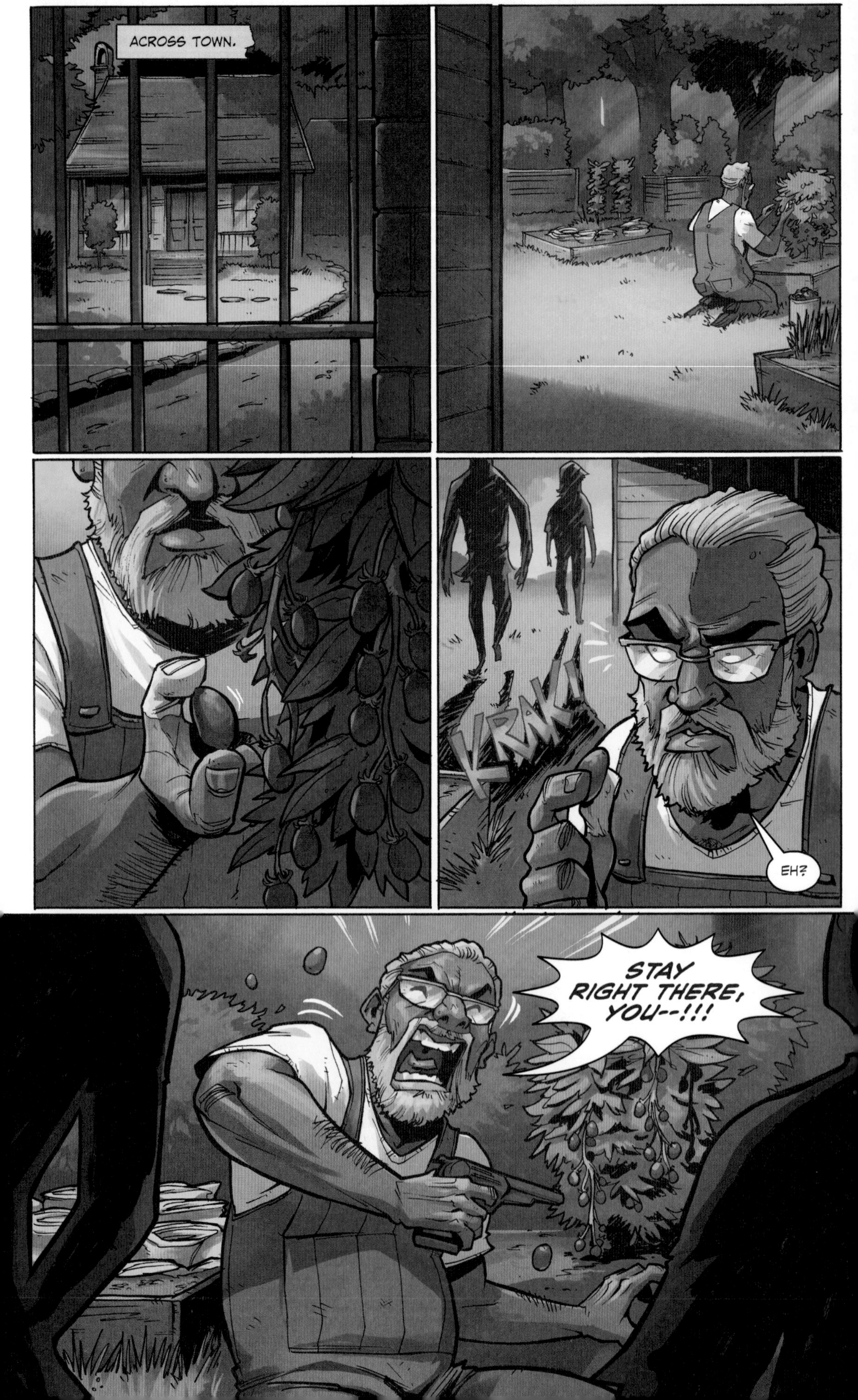
ACROSS TOWN.
KRAK!
EH?
STAY RIGHT THERE, YOU--!!!

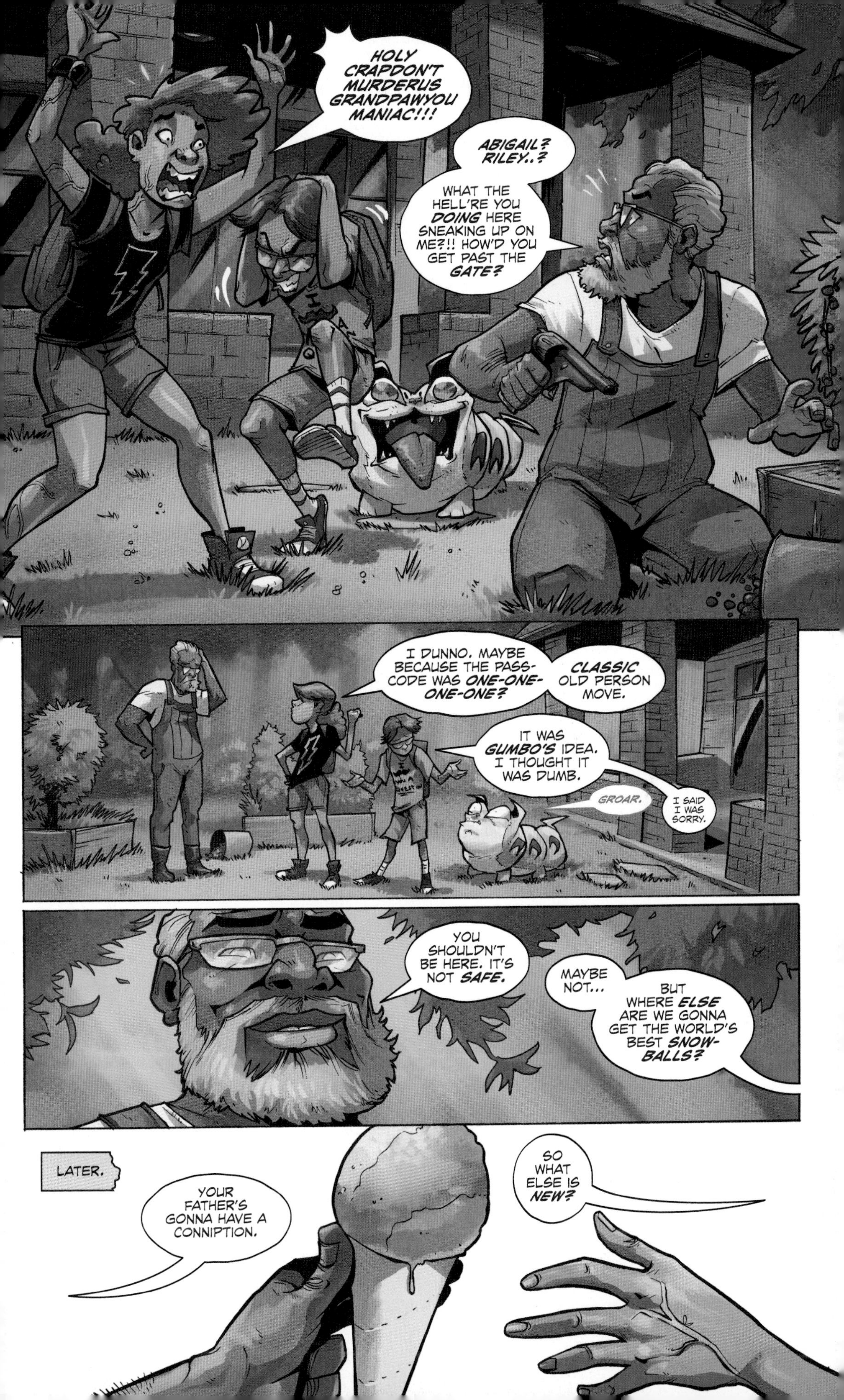
HOLY CRAPDON'T MURDERUS GRANDPAWYOU MANIAC!!!
ABIGAIL? RILEY..?
WHAT THE HELL'RE YOU DOING HERE SNEAKING UP ON ME?!! HOW'D YOU GET PAST THE GATE?
I DUNNO. MAYBE BECAUSE THE PASS-CODE WAS ONE-ONE-ONE-ONE?
CLASSIC OLD PERSON MOVE.
IT WAS GUMBO'S IDEA. I THOUGHT IT WAS DUMB.
GROAR.
I SAID I WAS SORRY.
YOU SHOULDN'T BE HERE. IT'S NOT SAFE.
MAYBE NOT...
BUT WHERE ELSE ARE WE GONNA GET THE WORLD'S BEST SNOW-BALLS?
LATER.
YOUR FATHER'S GONNA HAVE A CONNIPTION.
SO WHAT ELSE IS NEW?

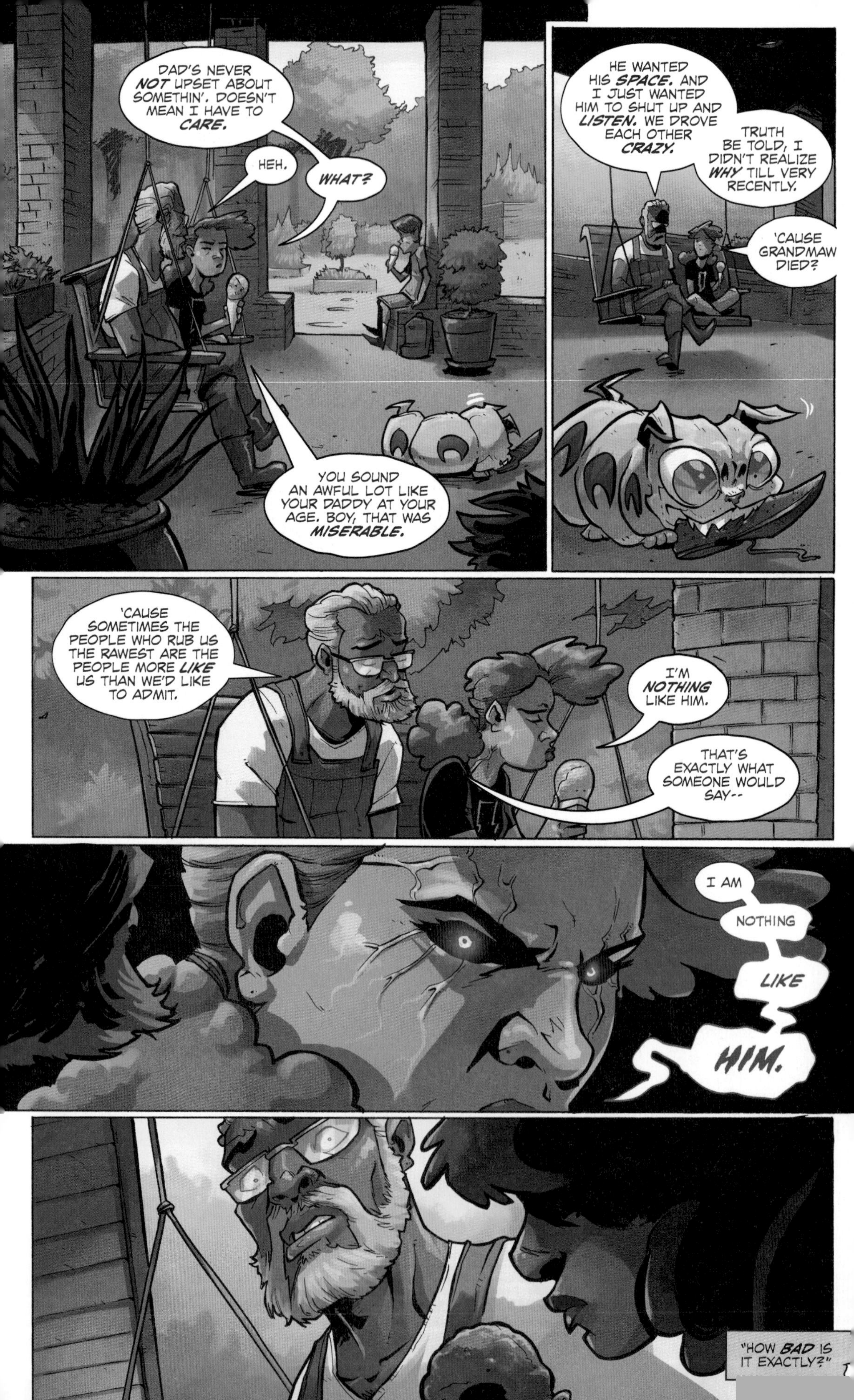
DAD'S NEVER NOT UPSET ABOUT SOMETHIN'. DOESN'T MEAN I HAVE TO CARE.
HEH.
WHAT?
YOU SOUND AN AWFUL LOT LIKE YOUR DADDY AT YOUR AGE. BOY, THAT WAS MISERABLE.
HE WANTED HIS SPACE. AND I JUST WANTED HIM TO SHUT UP AND LISTEN. WE DROVE EACH OTHER CRAZY.
TRUTH BE TOLD, I DIDN'T REALIZE WHY TILL VERY RECENTLY.
'CAUSE GRANDMAW DIED?
'CAUSE SOMETIMES THE PEOPLE WHO RUB US THE RAWEST ARE THE PEOPLE MORE LIKE US THAN WE'D LIKE TO ADMIT.
I'M NOTHING LIKE HIM.
THAT'S EXACTLY WHAT SOMEONE WOULD SAY--
I AM
NOTHING
LIKE
HIM.
"HOW BAD IS IT EXACTLY?"

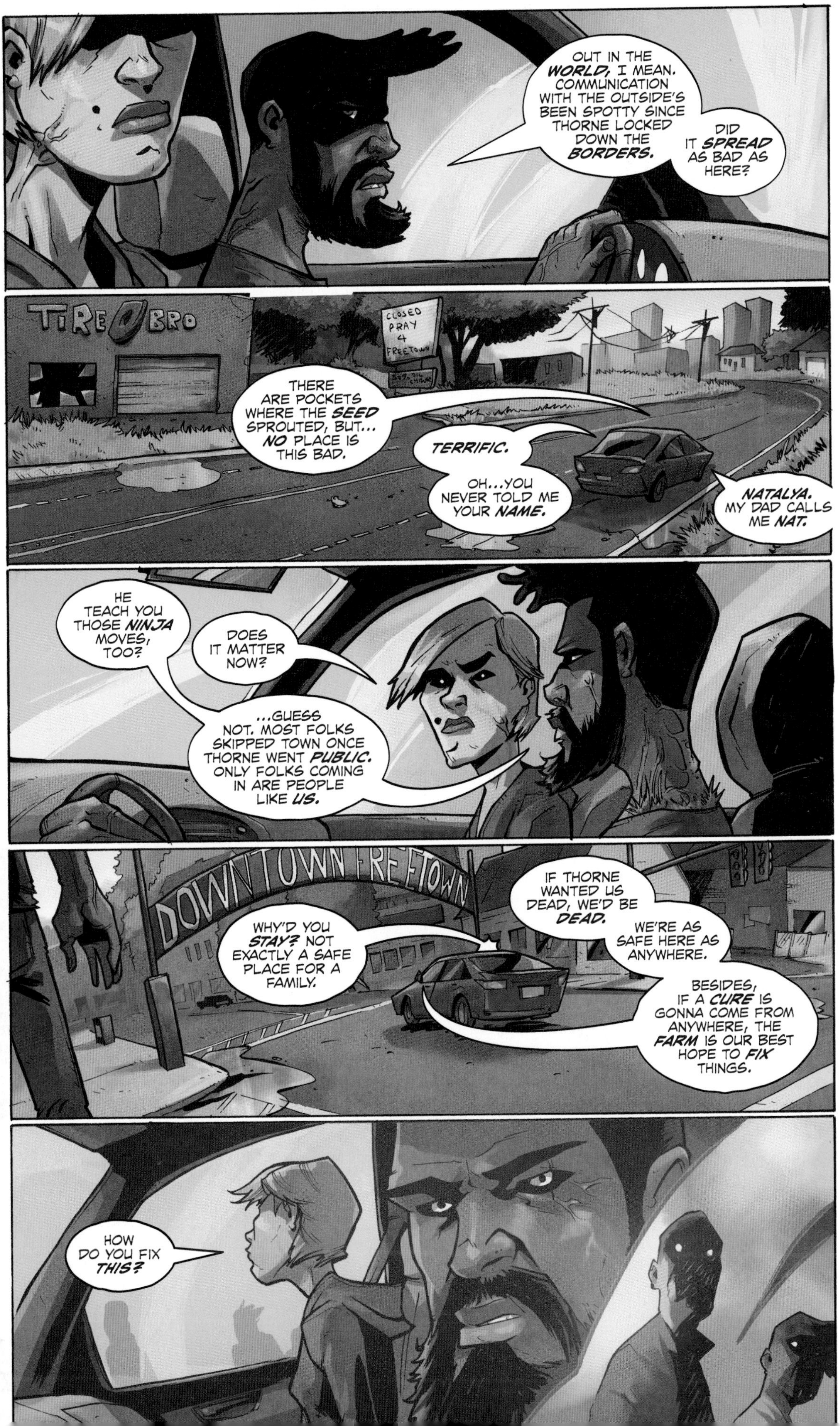
OUT IN THE WORLD, I MEAN. COMMUNICATION WITH THE OUTSIDE'S BEEN SPOTTY SINCE THORNE LOCKED DOWN THE BORDERS.
DID IT SPREAD AS BAD AS HERE?
TIRE BRO
CLOSED PRAY 4 FREETOWN
THERE ARE POCKETS WHERE THE SEED SPROUTED, BUT... NO PLACE IS THIS BAD.
TERRIFIC.
OH...YOU NEVER TOLD ME YOUR NAME.
NATALYA. MY DAD CALLS ME NAT.
HE TEACH YOU THOSE NINJA MOVES, TOO?
DOES IT MATTER NOW?
...GUESS NOT. MOST FOLKS SKIPPED TOWN ONCE THORNE WENT PUBLIC. ONLY FOLKS COMING IN ARE PEOPLE LIKE US.
DOWNTOWN FREETOWN
WHY'D YOU STAY? NOT EXACTLY A SAFE PLACE FOR A FAMILY.
IF THORNE WANTED US DEAD, WE'D BE DEAD.
WE'RE AS SAFE HERE AS ANYWHERE.
BESIDES, IF A CURE IS GONNA COME FROM ANYWHERE, THE FARM IS OUR BEST HOPE TO FIX THINGS.
HOW DO YOU FIX THIS?

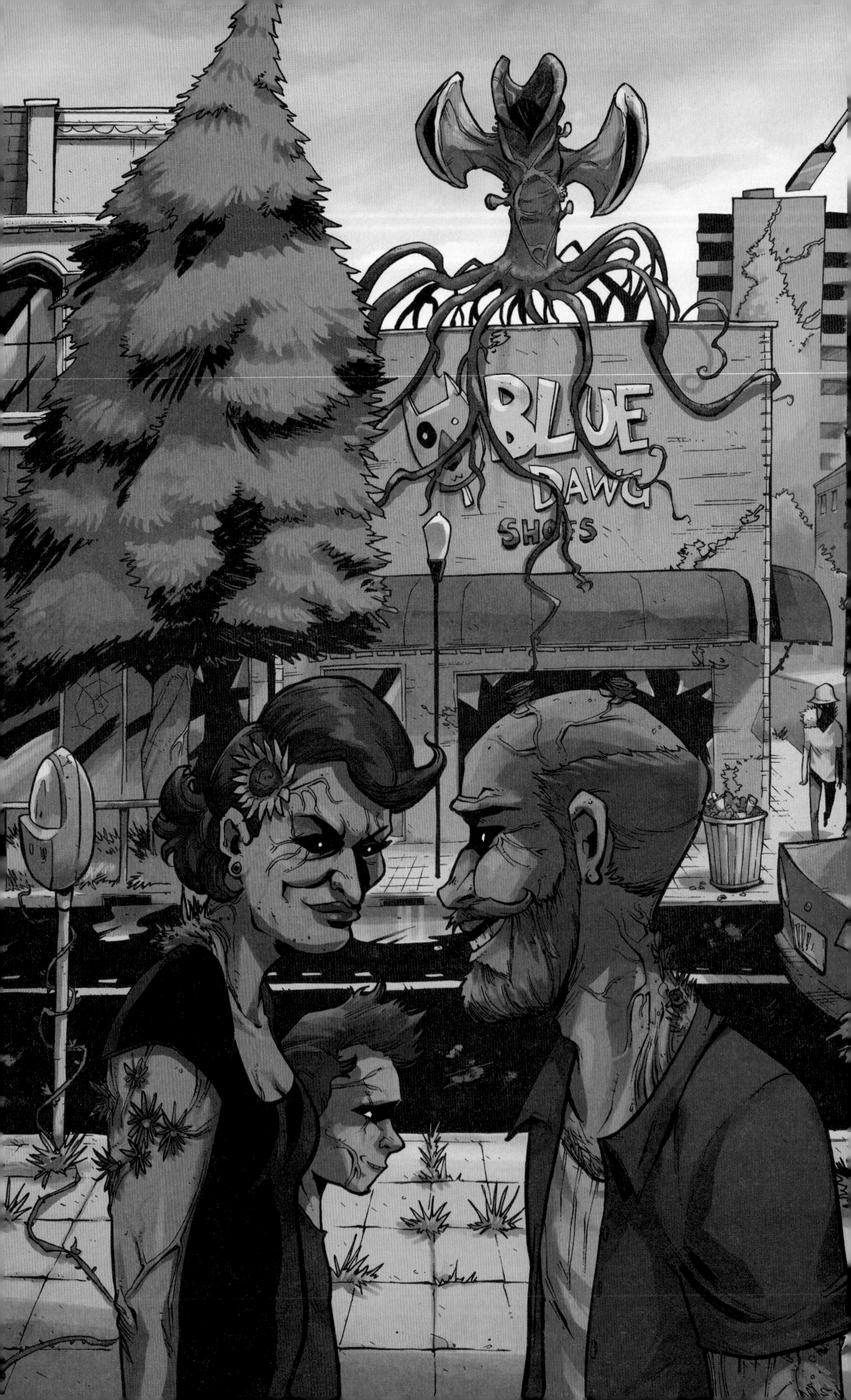
BLUE
DAWG
SHOES

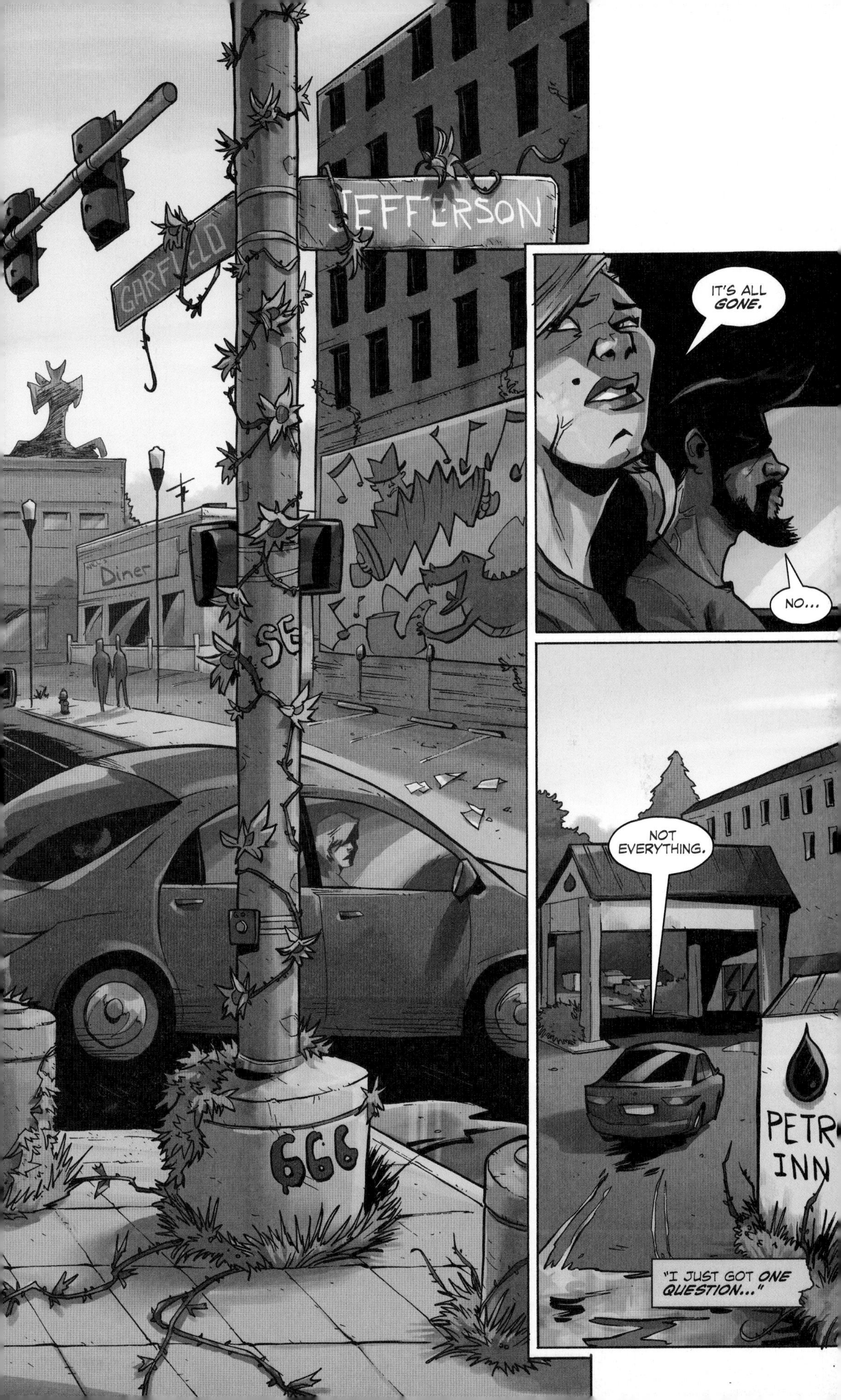
JEFFERSON
GARFIELD
Diner
IT'S ALL GONE.
NO...
NOT EVERYTHING.
PETR
INN
"I JUST GOT ONE QUESTION..."
666

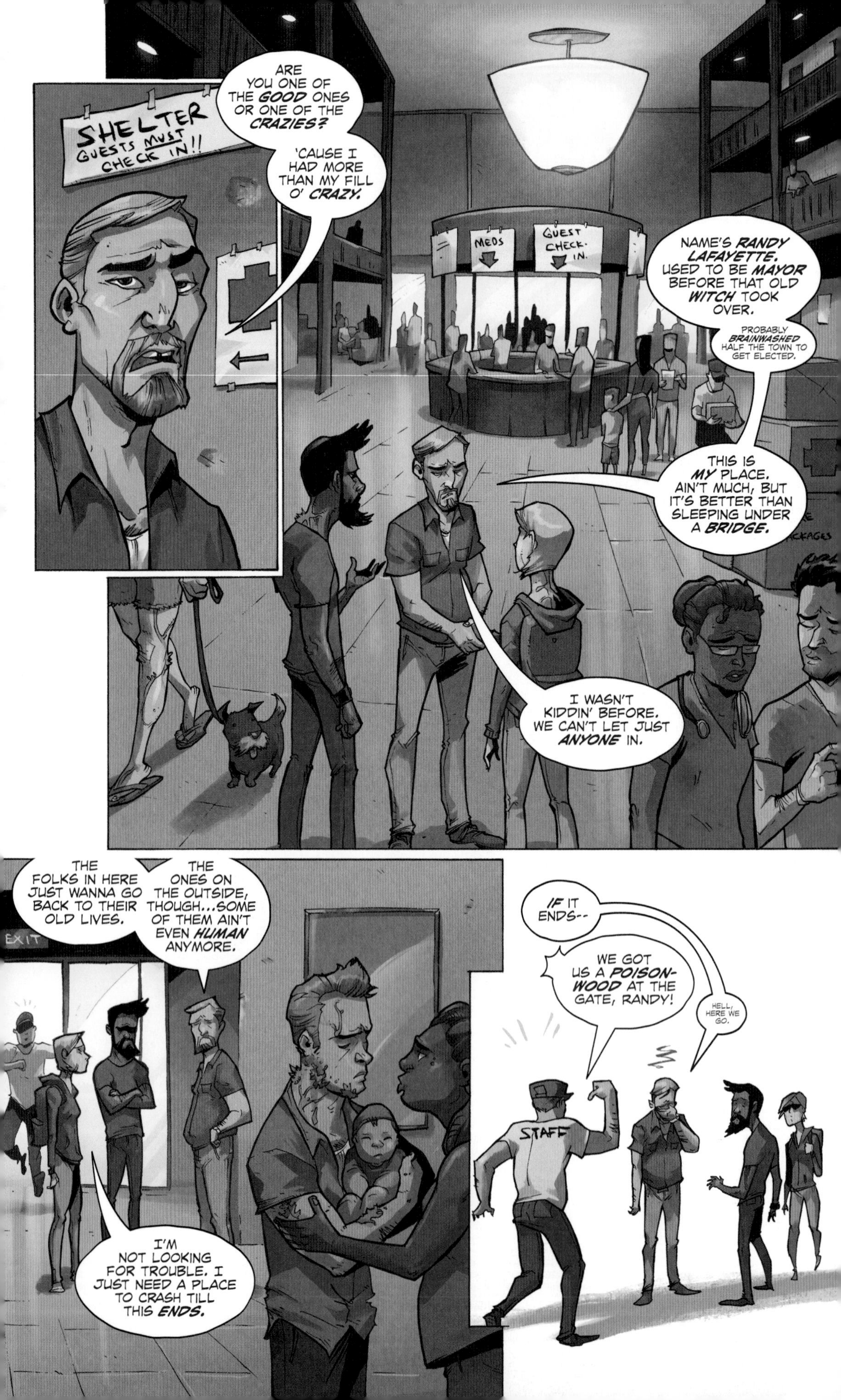
SHELTER
GUESTS MUST CHECK IN!!
ARE YOU ONE OF THE GOOD ONES OR ONE OF THE CRAZIES?
'CAUSE I HAD MORE THAN MY FILL O' CRAZY.
MEDS
GUEST CHECK-IN.
NAME'S RANDY LAFAYETTE. USED TO BE MAYOR BEFORE THAT OLD WITCH TOOK OVER.
PROBABLY BRAINWASHED HALF THE TOWN TO GET ELECTED.
THIS IS MY PLACE. AIN'T MUCH, BUT IT'S BETTER THAN SLEEPING UNDER A BRIDGE.
I WASN'T KIDDIN' BEFORE. WE CAN'T LET JUST ANYONE IN.
THE FOLKS IN HERE JUST WANNA GO BACK TO THEIR OLD LIVES.
THE ONES ON THE OUTSIDE, THOUGH...SOME OF THEM AIN'T EVEN HUMAN ANYMORE.
EXIT
I'M NOT LOOKING FOR TROUBLE. I JUST NEED A PLACE TO CRASH TILL THIS ENDS.
IF IT ENDS--
WE GOT US A POISONWOOD AT THE GATE, RANDY!
HELL, HERE WE GO.
STAFF

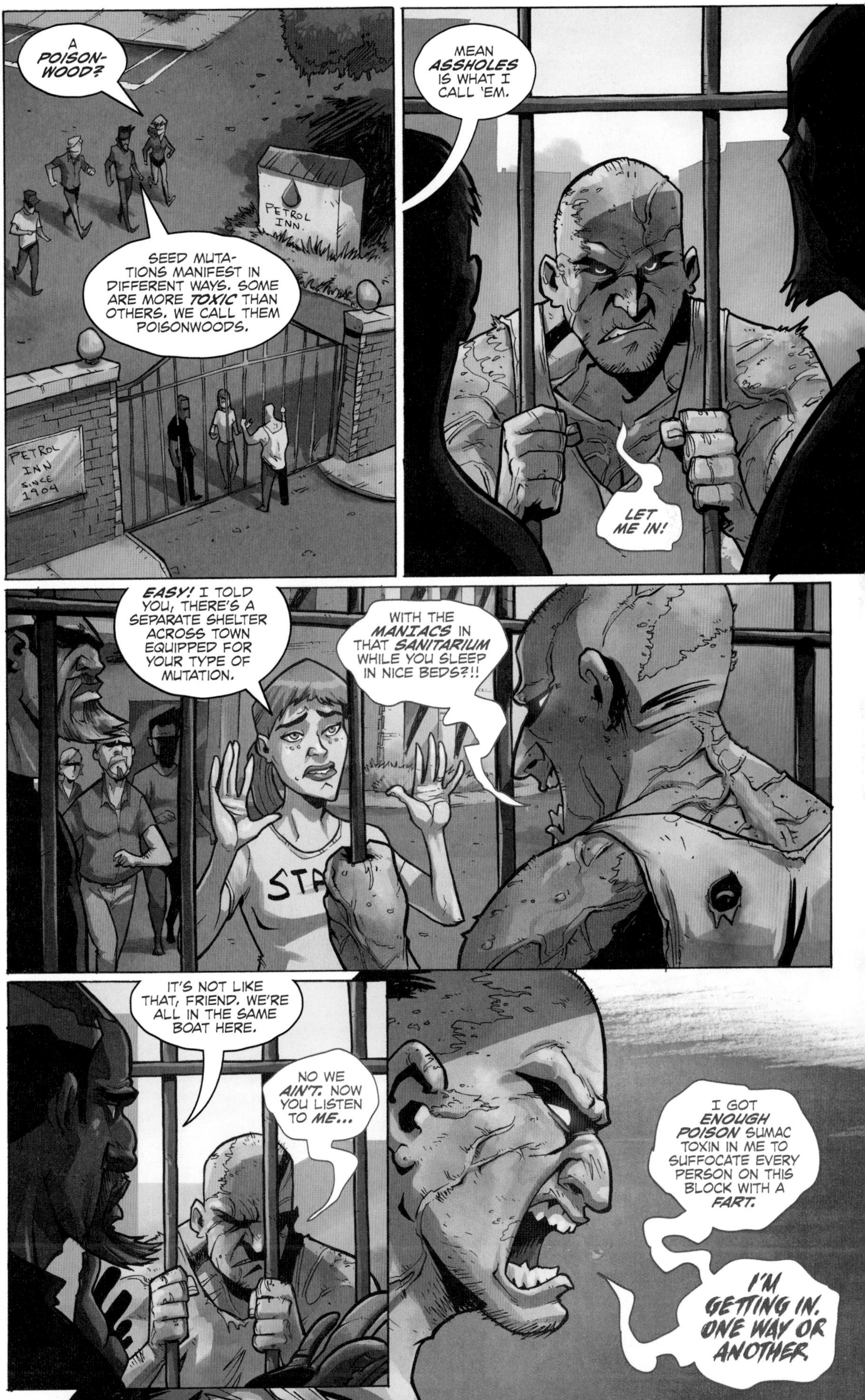
A POISON-WOOD?
SEED MUTATIONS MANIFEST IN DIFFERENT WAYS. SOME ARE MORE TOXIC THAN OTHERS. WE CALL THEM POISONWOODS.
PETROL INN.
PETROL INN SINCE 1904
MEAN ASSHOLES IS WHAT I CALL 'EM.
LET ME IN!
EASY! I TOLD YOU, THERE'S A SEPARATE SHELTER ACROSS TOWN EQUIPPED FOR YOUR TYPE OF MUTATION.
WITH THE MANIACS IN THAT SANITARIUM WHILE YOU SLEEP IN NICE BEDS?!!
STA
IT'S NOT LIKE THAT, FRIEND. WE'RE ALL IN THE SAME BOAT HERE.
NO WE AIN'T. NOW YOU LISTEN TO ME...
I GOT ENOUGH POISON SUMAC TOXIN IN ME TO SUFFOCATE EVERY PERSON ON THIS BLOCK WITH A FART.
I'M GETTING IN. ONE WAY OR ANOTHER.

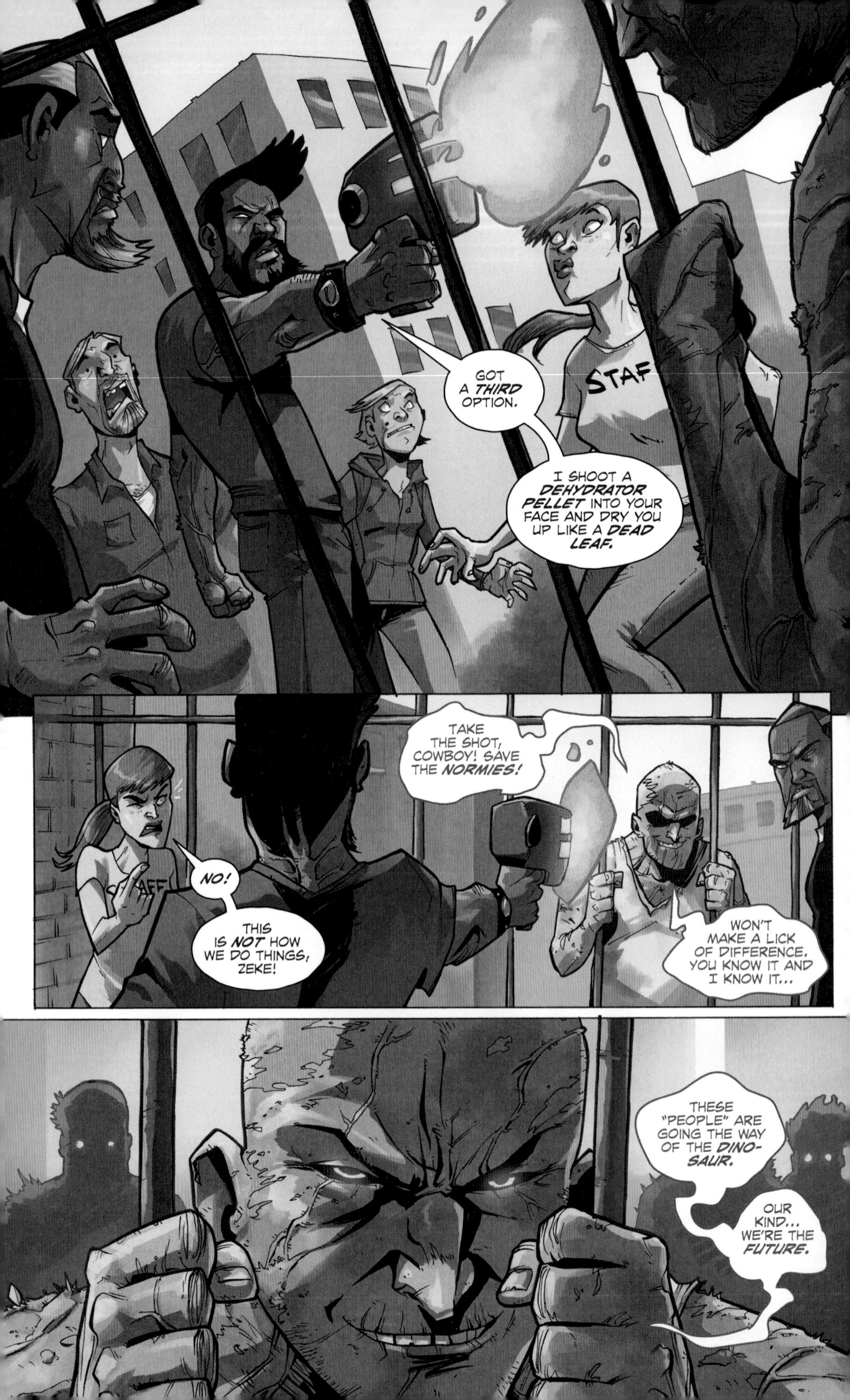

GOT A THIRD OPTION.
I SHOOT A DEHYDRATOR PELLET INTO YOUR FACE AND DRY YOU UP LIKE A DEAD LEAF.
STAF
TAKE THE SHOT, COWBOY! SAVE THE NORMIES!
NO!
THIS IS NOT HOW WE DO THINGS, ZEKE!
WON'T MAKE A LICK OF DIFFERENCE. YOU KNOW IT AND I KNOW IT...
THESE "PEOPLE" ARE GOING THE WAY OF THE DINO-SAUR.
OUR KIND... WE'RE THE FUTURE.

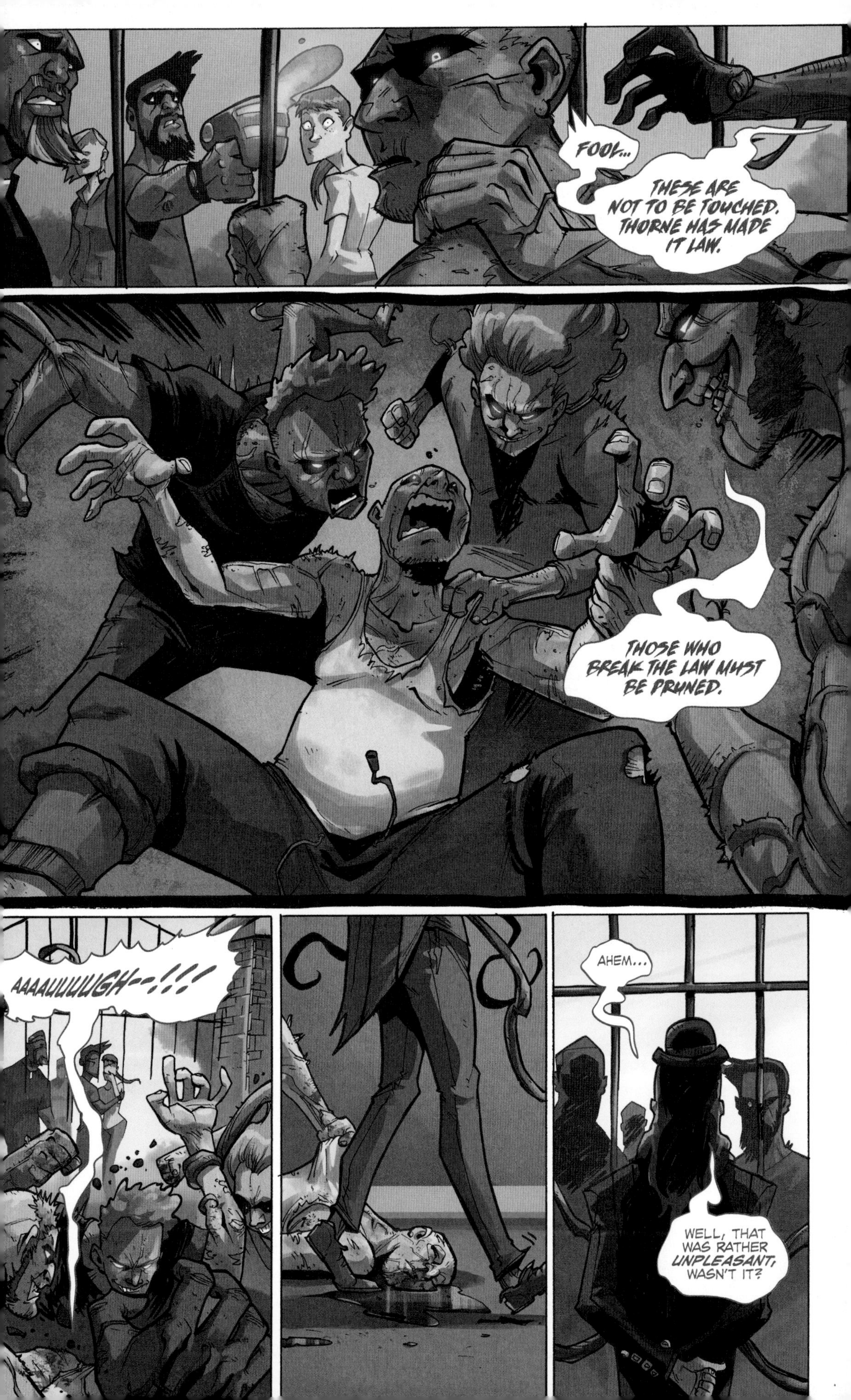
FOOL...
THESE ARE NOT TO BE TOUCHED. THORNE HAS MADE IT LAW.
THOSE WHO BREAK THE LAW MUST BE PRUNED.
AAAAUUUUUGH--!!!
AHEM...
WELL, THAT WAS RATHER UNPLEASANT, WASN'T IT?

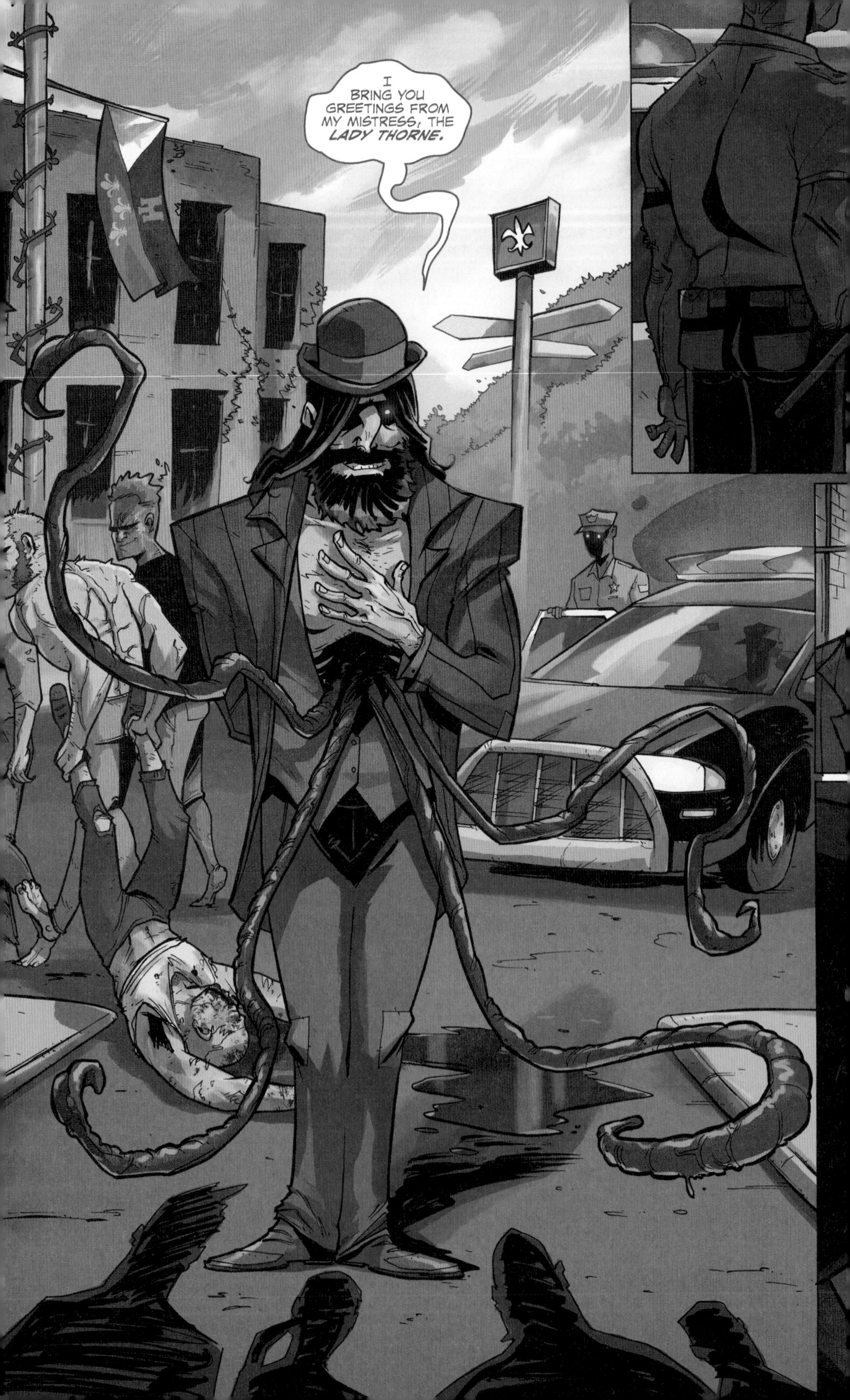
I BRING YOU GREETINGS FROM MY MISTRESS, THE *LADY THORNE.*

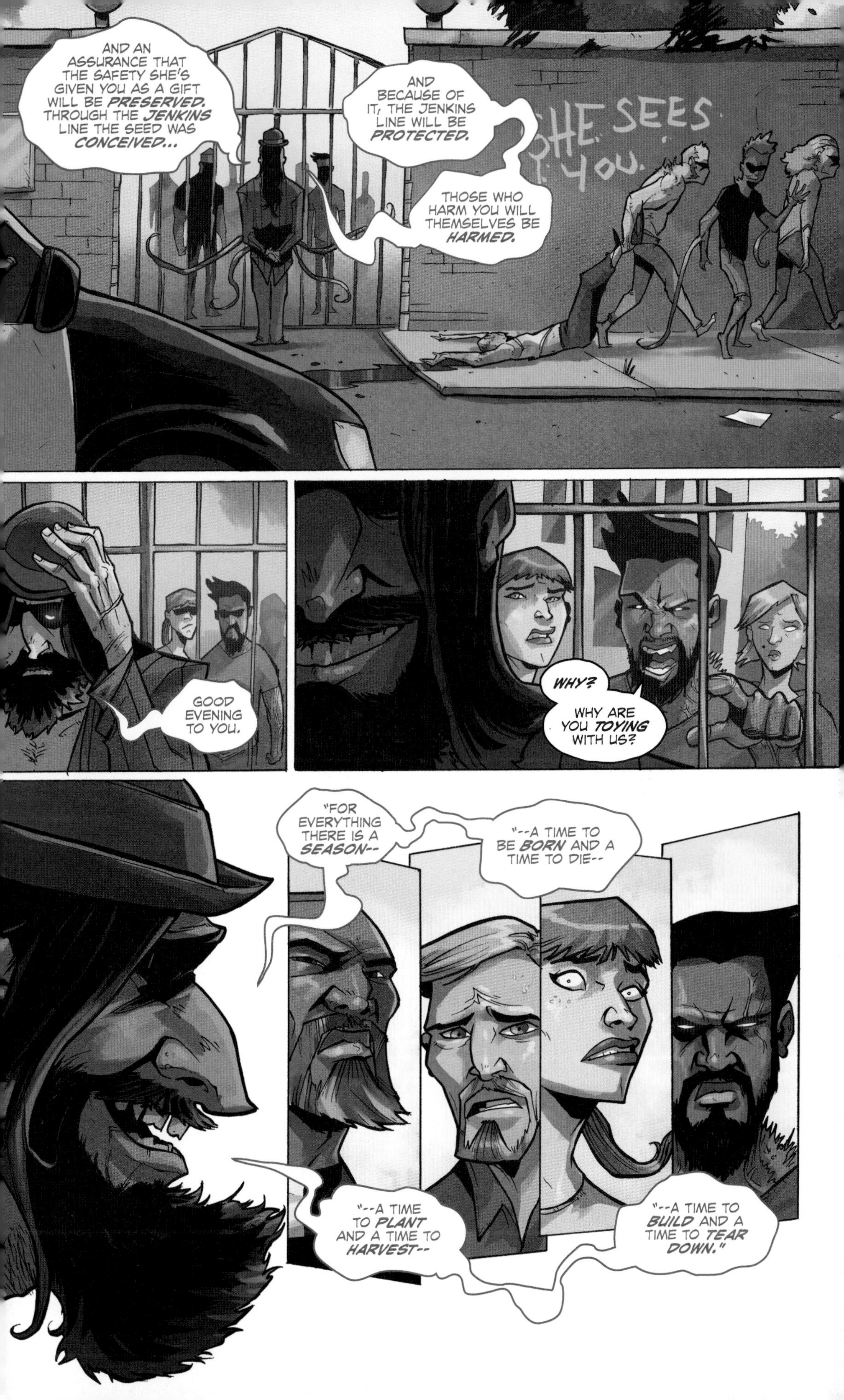
AND AN ASSURANCE THAT THE SAFETY SHE'S GIVEN YOU AS A GIFT WILL BE PRESERVED. THROUGH THE JENKINS LINE THE SEED WAS CONCEIVED...
AND BECAUSE OF IT, THE JENKINS LINE WILL BE PROTECTED.
THOSE WHO HARM YOU WILL THEMSELVES BE HARMED.
SHE SEES YOU.
GOOD EVENING TO YOU.
WHY?
WHY ARE YOU TOYING WITH US?
"FOR EVERYTHING THERE IS A SEASON--
"--A TIME TO BE BORN AND A TIME TO DIE--
"--A TIME TO PLANT AND A TIME TO HARVEST--
"--A TIME TO BUILD AND A TIME TO TEAR DOWN."

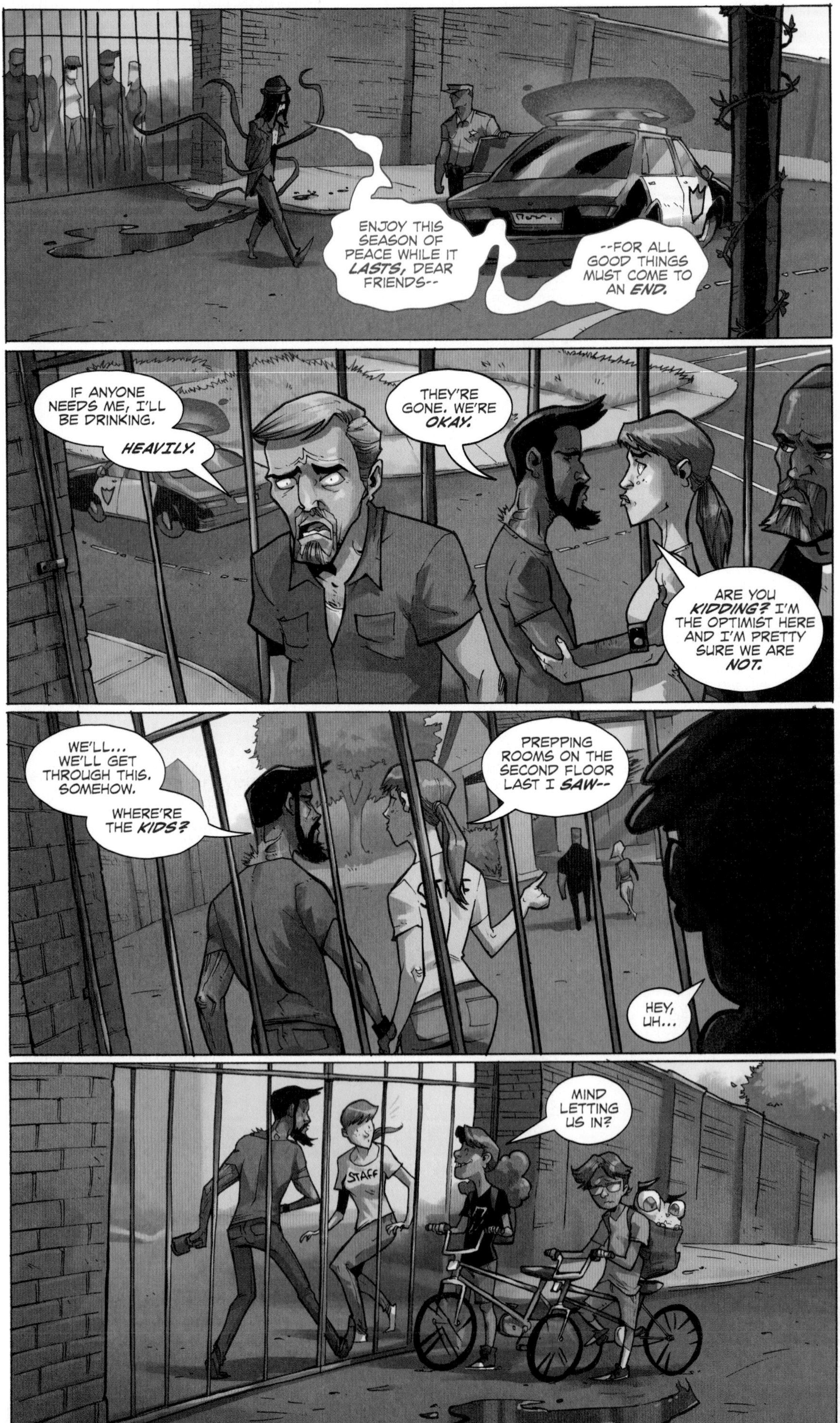
ENJOY THIS SEASON OF PEACE WHILE IT LASTS, DEAR FRIENDS--
--FOR ALL GOOD THINGS MUST COME TO AN END.
IF ANYONE NEEDS ME, I'LL BE DRINKING.
HEAVILY.
THEY'RE GONE. WE'RE OKAY.
ARE YOU KIDDING? I'M THE OPTIMIST HERE AND I'M PRETTY SURE WE ARE NOT.
WE'LL... WE'LL GET THROUGH THIS. SOMEHOW.
WHERE'RE THE KIDS?
PREPPING ROOMS ON THE SECOND FLOOR LAST I SAW--
HEY, UH...
MIND LETTING US IN?

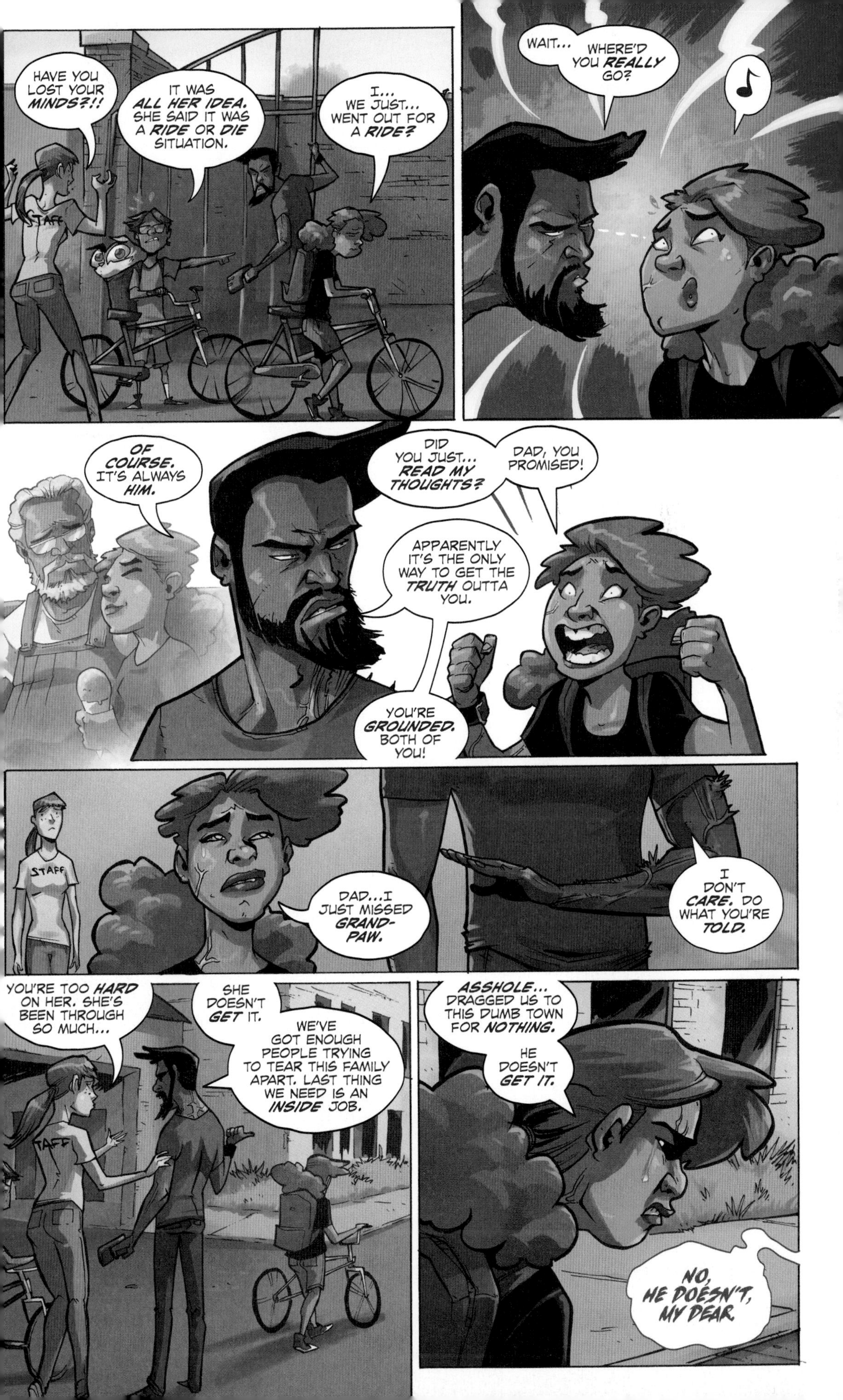

HAVE YOU LOST YOUR MINDS?!!
IT WAS ALL HER IDEA. SHE SAID IT WAS A RIDE OR DIE SITUATION.
I... WE JUST... WENT OUT FOR A RIDE?
WAIT...
WHERE'D YOU REALLY GO?
♪
OF COURSE. IT'S ALWAYS HIM.
DID YOU JUST... READ MY THOUGHTS?
DAD, YOU PROMISED!
APPARENTLY IT'S THE ONLY WAY TO GET THE TRUTH OUTTA YOU.
YOU'RE GROUNDED. BOTH OF YOU!
STAFF
DAD...I JUST MISSED GRAND-PAW.
I DON'T CARE. DO WHAT YOU'RE TOLD.
YOU'RE TOO HARD ON HER. SHE'S BEEN THROUGH SO MUCH...
SHE DOESN'T GET IT.
WE'VE GOT ENOUGH PEOPLE TRYING TO TEAR THIS FAMILY APART. LAST THING WE NEED IS AN INSIDE JOB.
ASSHOLE... DRAGGED US TO THIS DUMB TOWN FOR NOTHING.
HE DOESN'T GET IT.
NO, HE DOESN'T, MY DEAR.

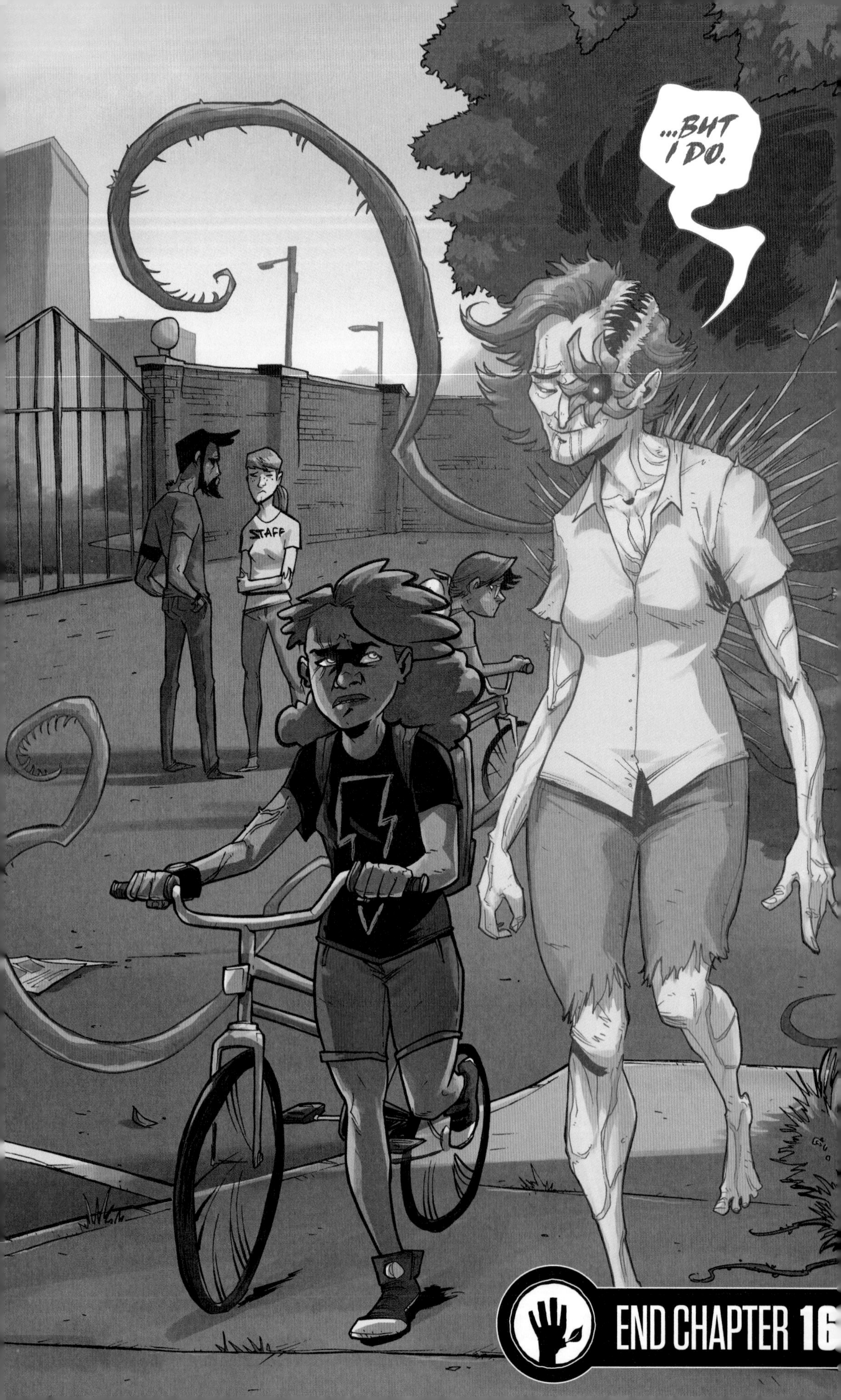
...BUT I DO.
STAFF
END CHAPTER 16

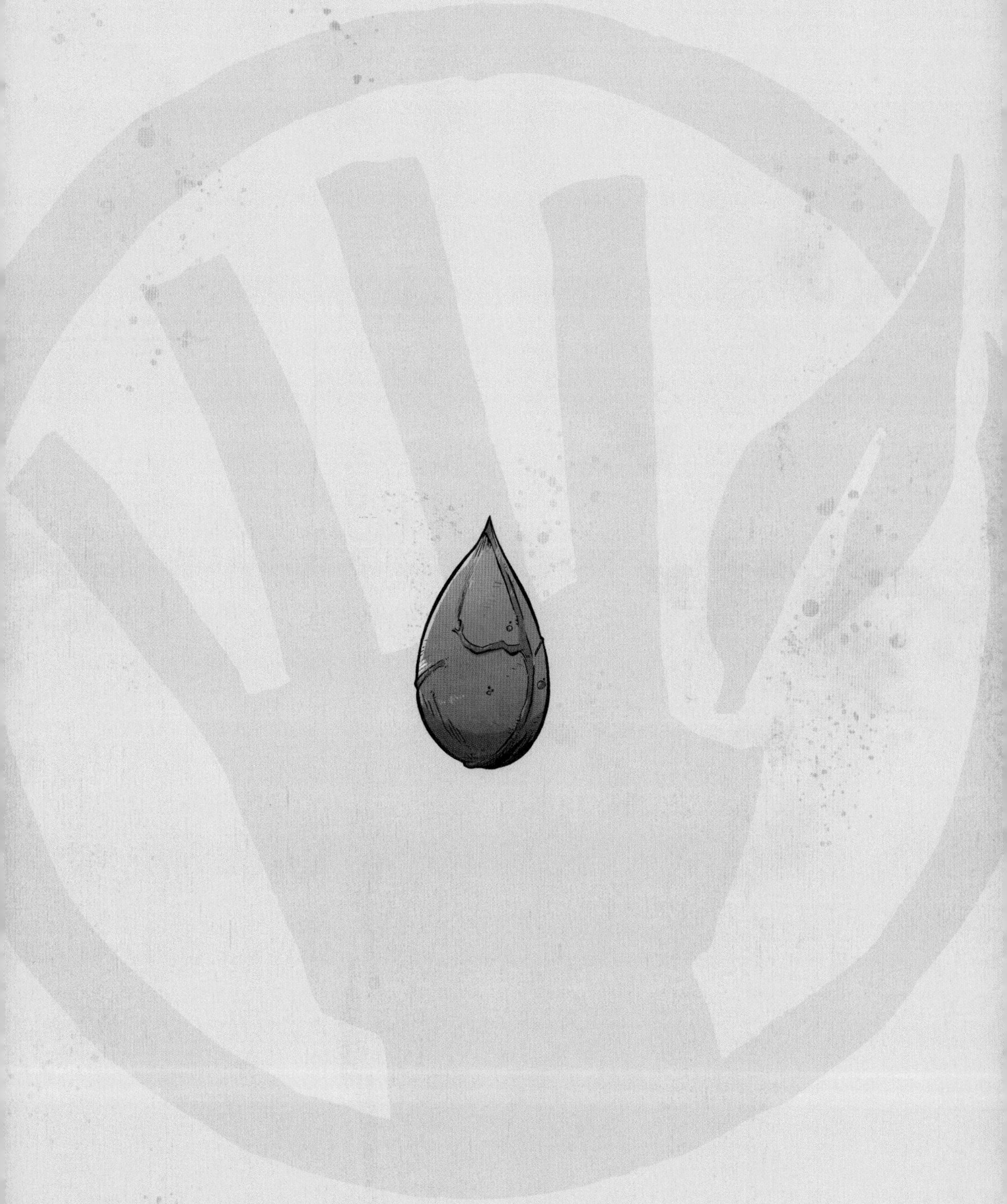

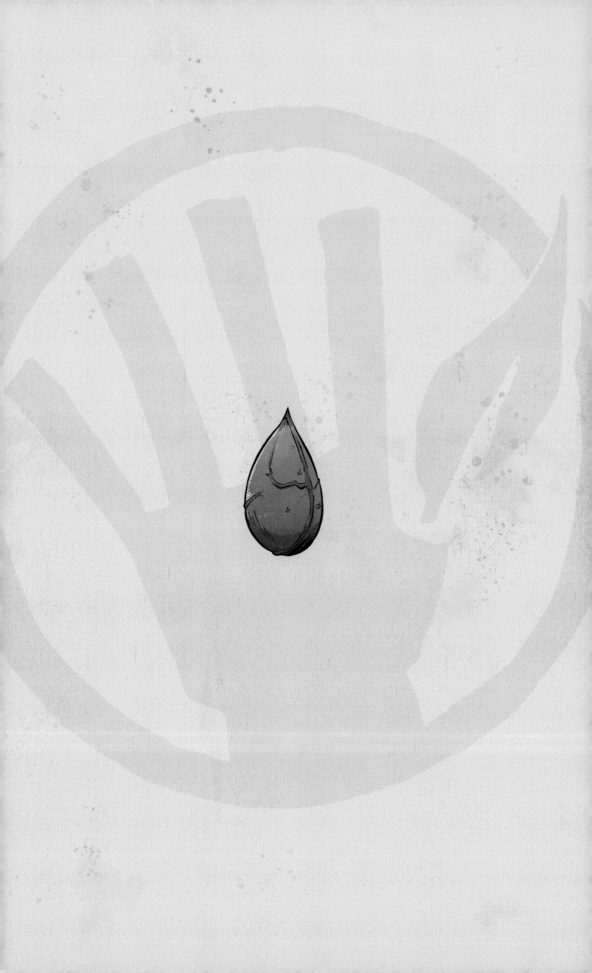

CHAPTER 17

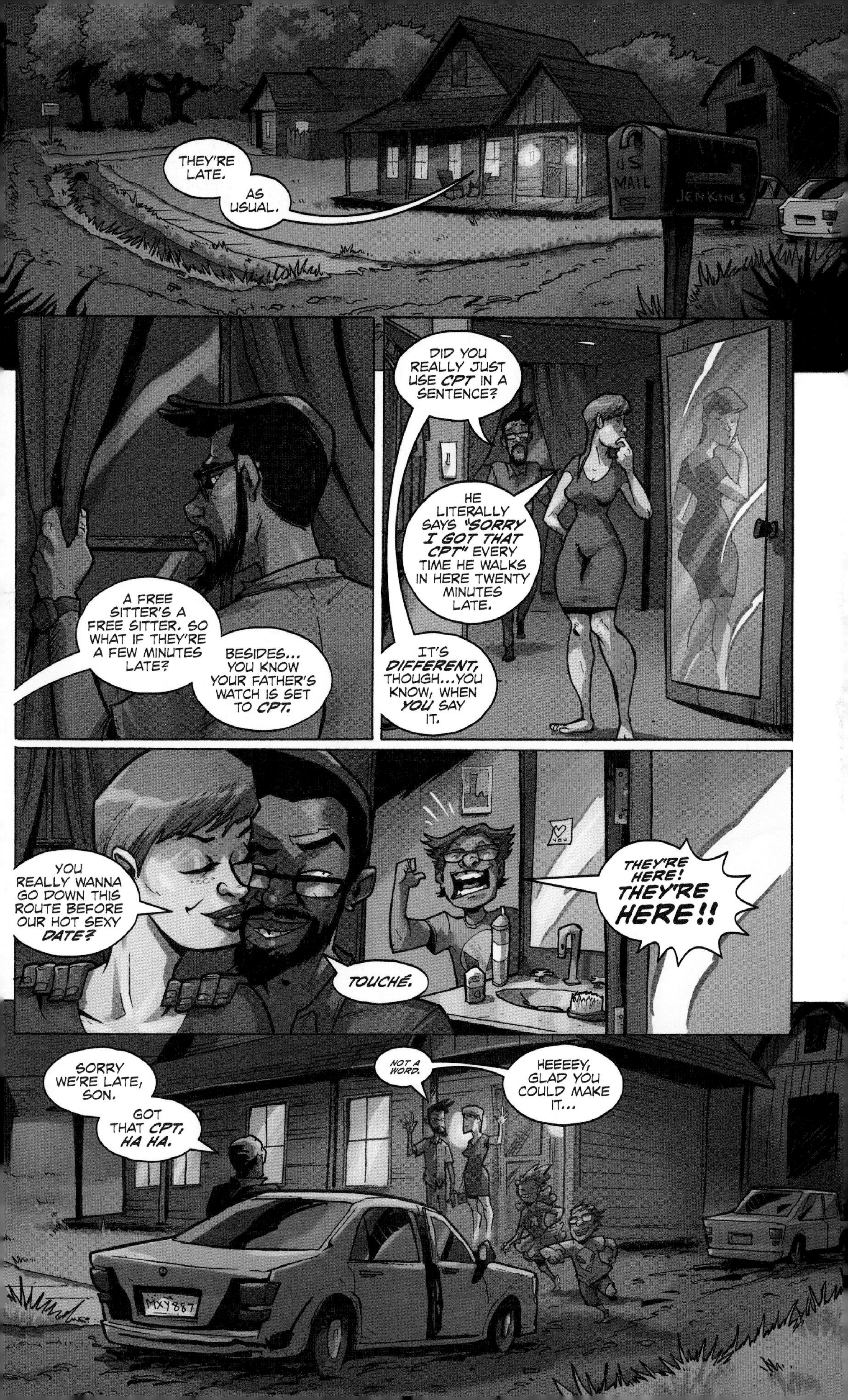

THEY'RE LATE.
AS USUAL.
U.S. MAIL
JENKINS
A FREE SITTER'S A FREE SITTER. SO WHAT IF THEY'RE A FEW MINUTES LATE?
BESIDES... YOU KNOW YOUR FATHER'S WATCH IS SET TO CPT.
DID YOU REALLY JUST USE CPT IN A SENTENCE?
HE LITERALLY SAYS "SORRY I GOT THAT CPT" EVERY TIME HE WALKS IN HERE TWENTY MINUTES LATE.
IT'S DIFFERENT, THOUGH...YOU KNOW, WHEN YOU SAY IT.
YOU REALLY WANNA GO DOWN THIS ROUTE BEFORE OUR HOT SEXY DATE?
TOUCHÉ.
THEY'RE HERE! THEY'RE HERE!!
SORRY WE'RE LATE, SON.
GOT THAT CPT, HA HA.
NOT A WORD.
HEEEEY, GLAD YOU COULD MAKE IT...
MXY887

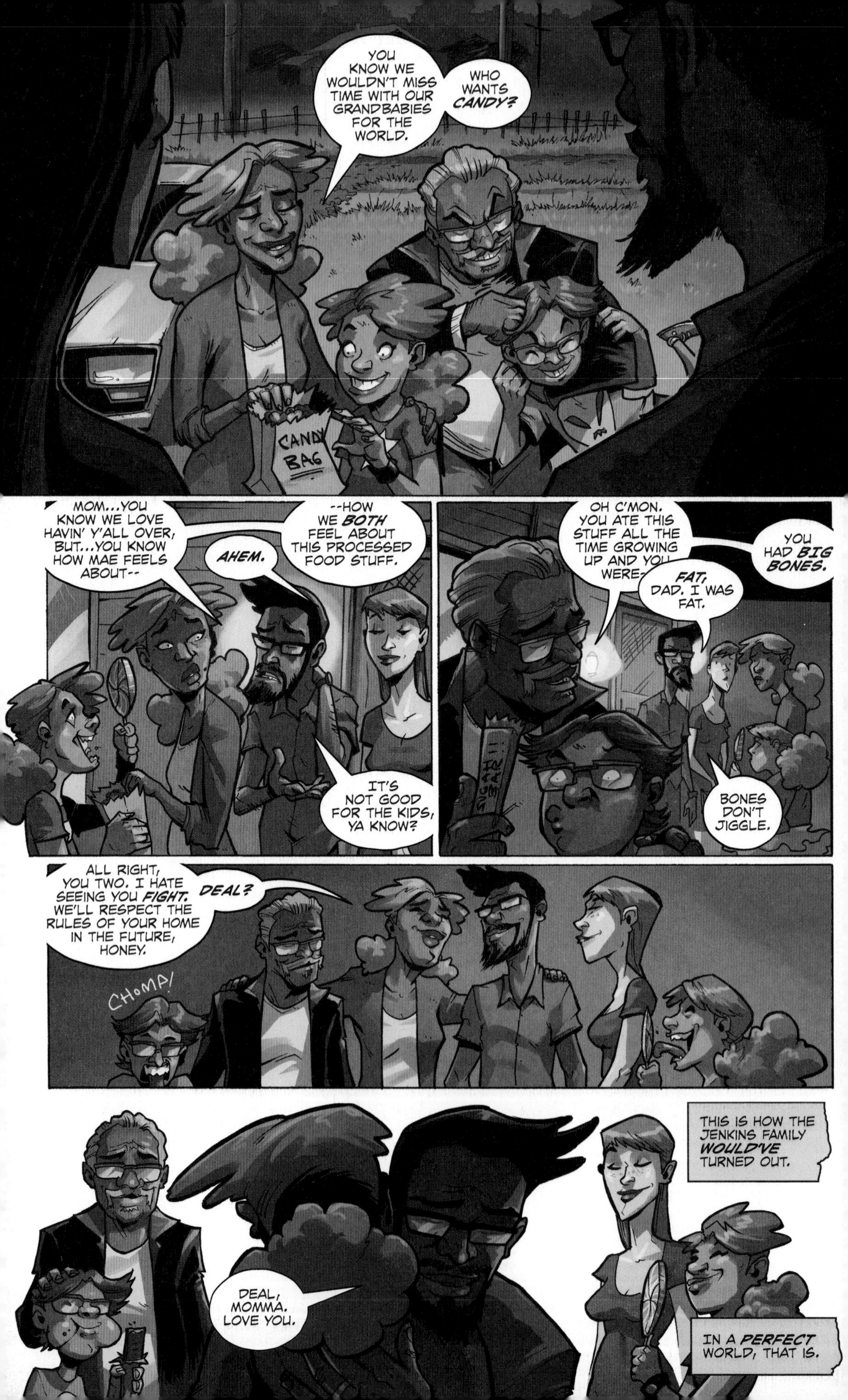
YOU KNOW WE WOULDN'T MISS TIME WITH OUR GRANDBABIES FOR THE WORLD.
WHO WANTS *CANDY?*
CANDY BAG
MOM...YOU KNOW WE LOVE HAVIN' Y'ALL OVER, BUT...YOU KNOW HOW MAE FEELS ABOUT--
AHEM.
--HOW WE *BOTH* FEEL ABOUT THIS PROCESSED FOOD STUFF.
IT'S NOT GOOD FOR THE KIDS, YA KNOW?
OH C'MON. YOU ATE THIS STUFF ALL THE TIME GROWING UP AND YOU WERE--
FAT, DAD. I WAS FAT.
YOU HAD *BIG BONES.*
BONES DON'T JIGGLE.
ALL RIGHT, YOU TWO. I HATE SEEING YOU *FIGHT.* WE'LL RESPECT THE RULES OF YOUR HOME IN THE FUTURE, HONEY.
DEAL?
CHOMP!
THIS IS HOW THE JENKINS FAMILY *WOULD'VE* TURNED OUT.
DEAL, MOMMA. LOVE YOU.
IN A *PERFECT* WORLD, THAT IS.

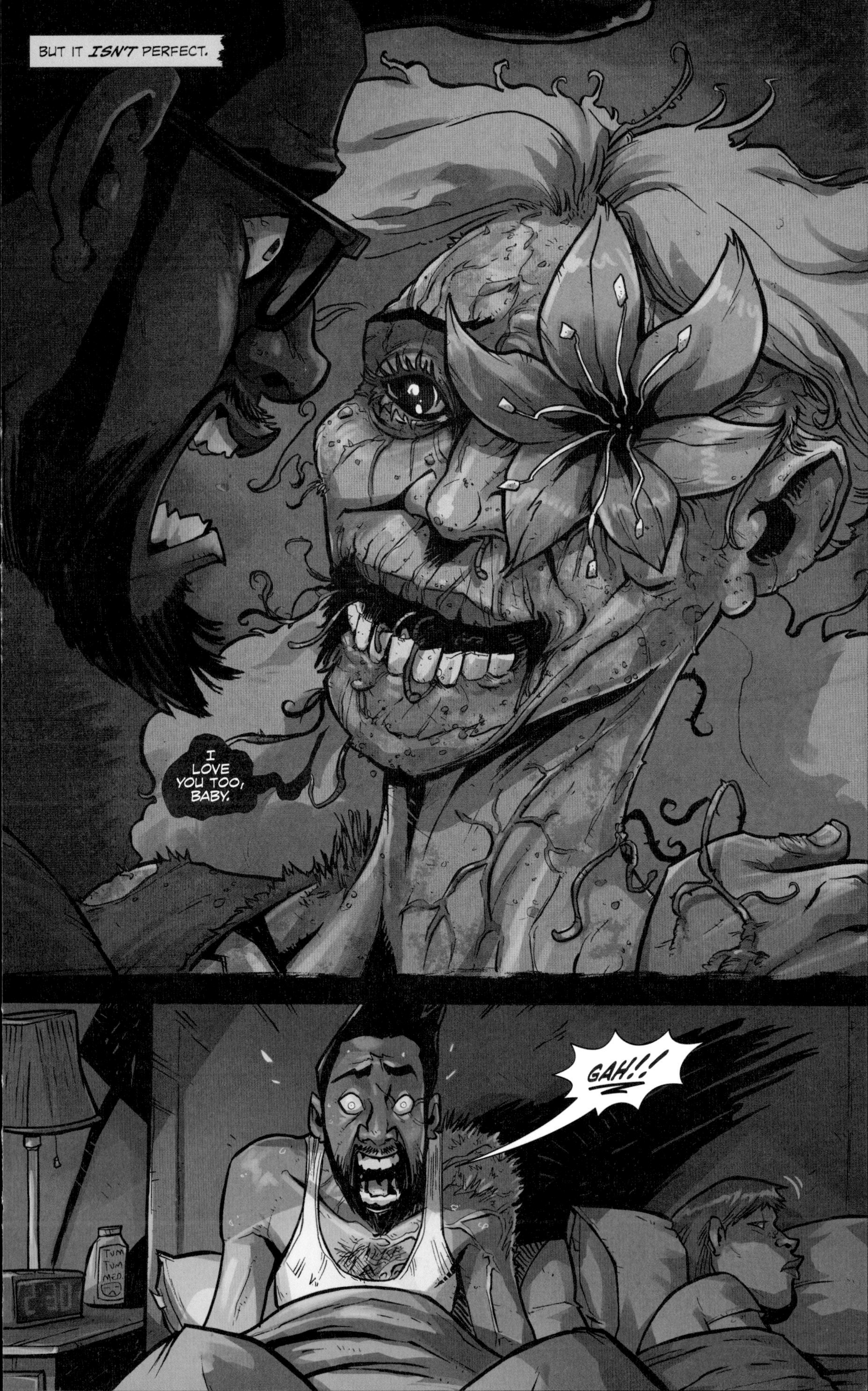
BUT IT ISN'T PERFECT.
I LOVE YOU TOO, BABY.
GAH!!!
TUM TUM MED

WHASSAT? WHAT'S WRONG? CAN'T SLEEP AGAIN?
...
SORRY...
S'OKAY. GET SOME SLEEP.
WHA... DAD?
COULDN'T SLEEP...
SSSHH. I KNOW, BABY.
ME NEITHER.

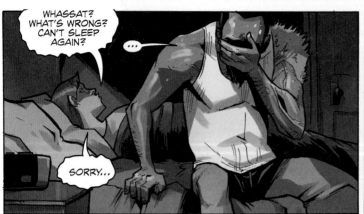

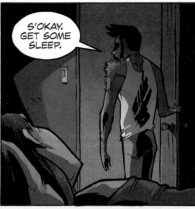

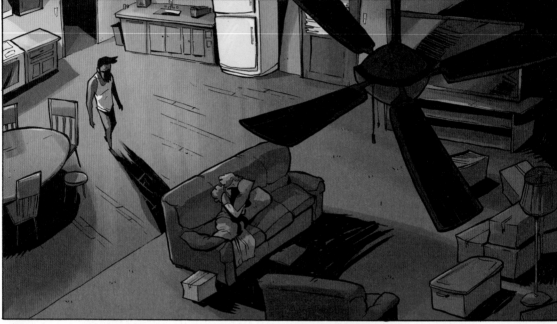

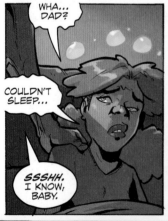

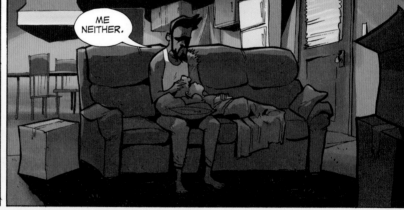

CHAPTER 17: **THE BRIDGE.**

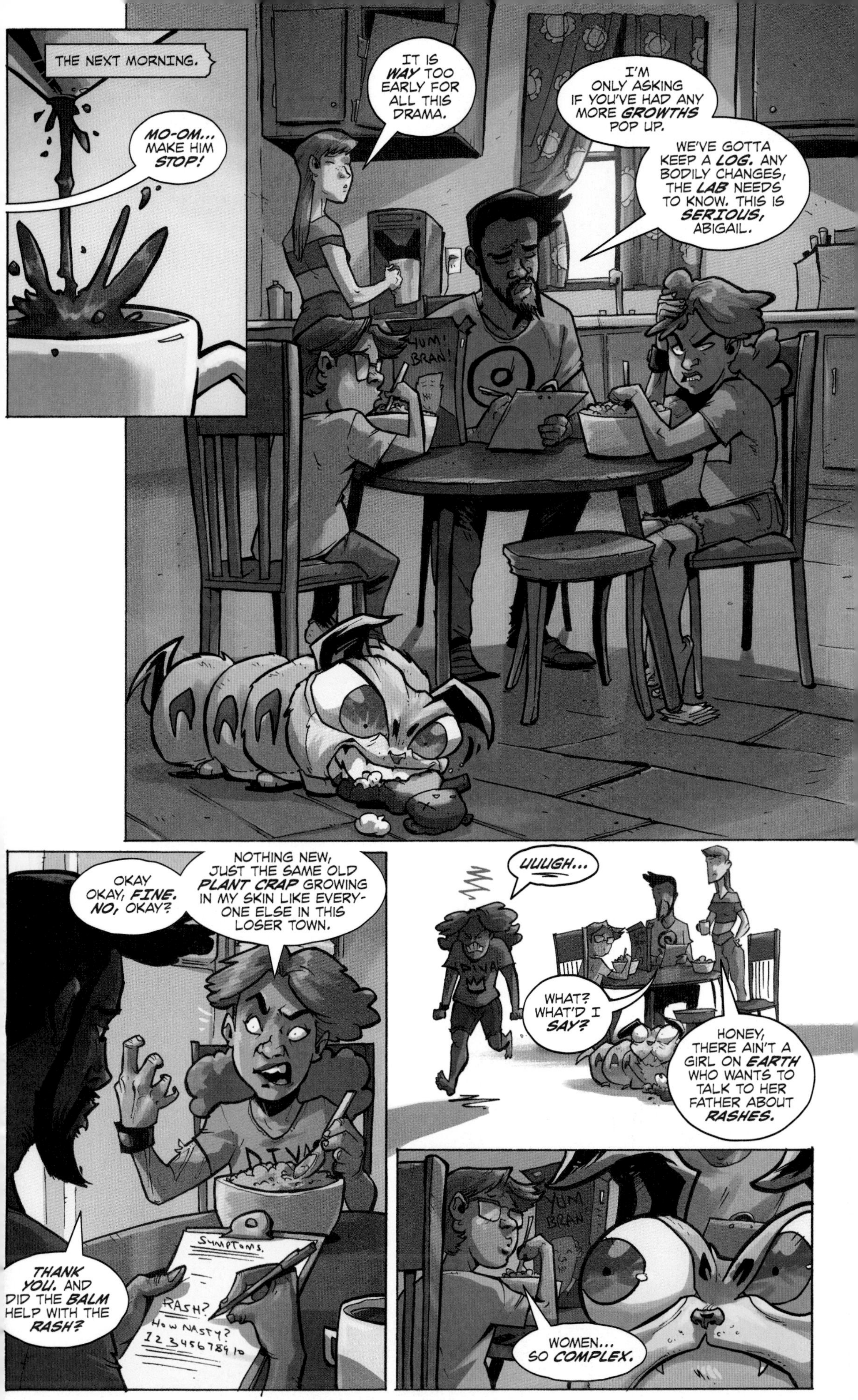

THE NEXT MORNING.
MO-OM... MAKE HIM STOP!
IT IS WAY TOO EARLY FOR ALL THIS DRAMA.
I'M ONLY ASKING IF YOU'VE HAD ANY MORE GROWTHS POP UP.
WE'VE GOTTA KEEP A LOG. ANY BODILY CHANGES, THE LAB NEEDS TO KNOW. THIS IS SERIOUS, ABIGAIL.
YUM! BRAN!
OKAY OKAY, FINE. NO, OKAY?
NOTHING NEW, JUST THE SAME OLD PLANT CRAP GROWING IN MY SKIN LIKE EVERY-ONE ELSE IN THIS LOSER TOWN.
SYMPTOMS.
RASH?
HOW NASTY?
1 2 3 4 5 6 7 8 9 10
THANK YOU. AND DID THE BALM HELP WITH THE RASH?
UUUGH...
WHAT? WHAT'D I SAY?
HONEY, THERE AIN'T A GIRL ON EARTH WHO WANTS TO TALK TO HER FATHER ABOUT RASHES.
YUM BRAN
WOMEN... SO COMPLEX.

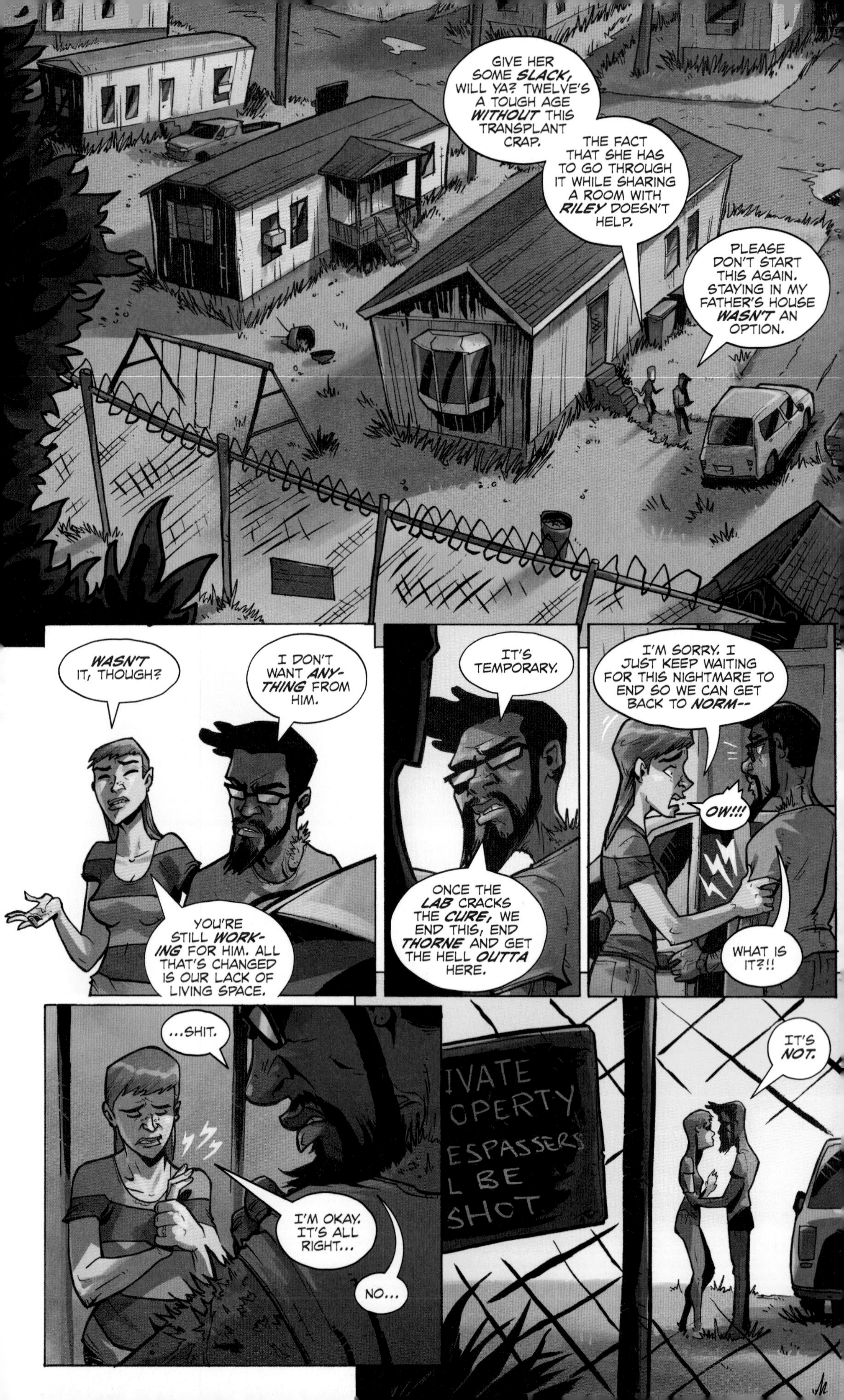

GIVE HER SOME SLACK, WILL YA? TWELVE'S A TOUGH AGE WITHOUT THIS TRANSPLANT CRAP.
THE FACT THAT SHE HAS TO GO THROUGH IT WHILE SHARING A ROOM WITH RILEY DOESN'T HELP.
PLEASE DON'T START THIS AGAIN. STAYING IN MY FATHER'S HOUSE WASN'T AN OPTION.
WASN'T IT, THOUGH?
I DON'T WANT ANYTHING FROM HIM.
YOU'RE STILL WORKING FOR HIM. ALL THAT'S CHANGED IS OUR LACK OF LIVING SPACE.
IT'S TEMPORARY.
ONCE THE LAB CRACKS THE CURE, WE END THIS, END THORNE AND GET THE HELL OUTTA HERE.
I'M SORRY. I JUST KEEP WAITING FOR THIS NIGHTMARE TO END SO WE CAN GET BACK TO NORM--
OW!!!
WHAT IS IT?!!
...SHIT.
I'M OKAY. IT'S ALL RIGHT...
NO...
IVATE
OPERTY
ESPASSERS
L BE
SHOT
IT'S NOT.

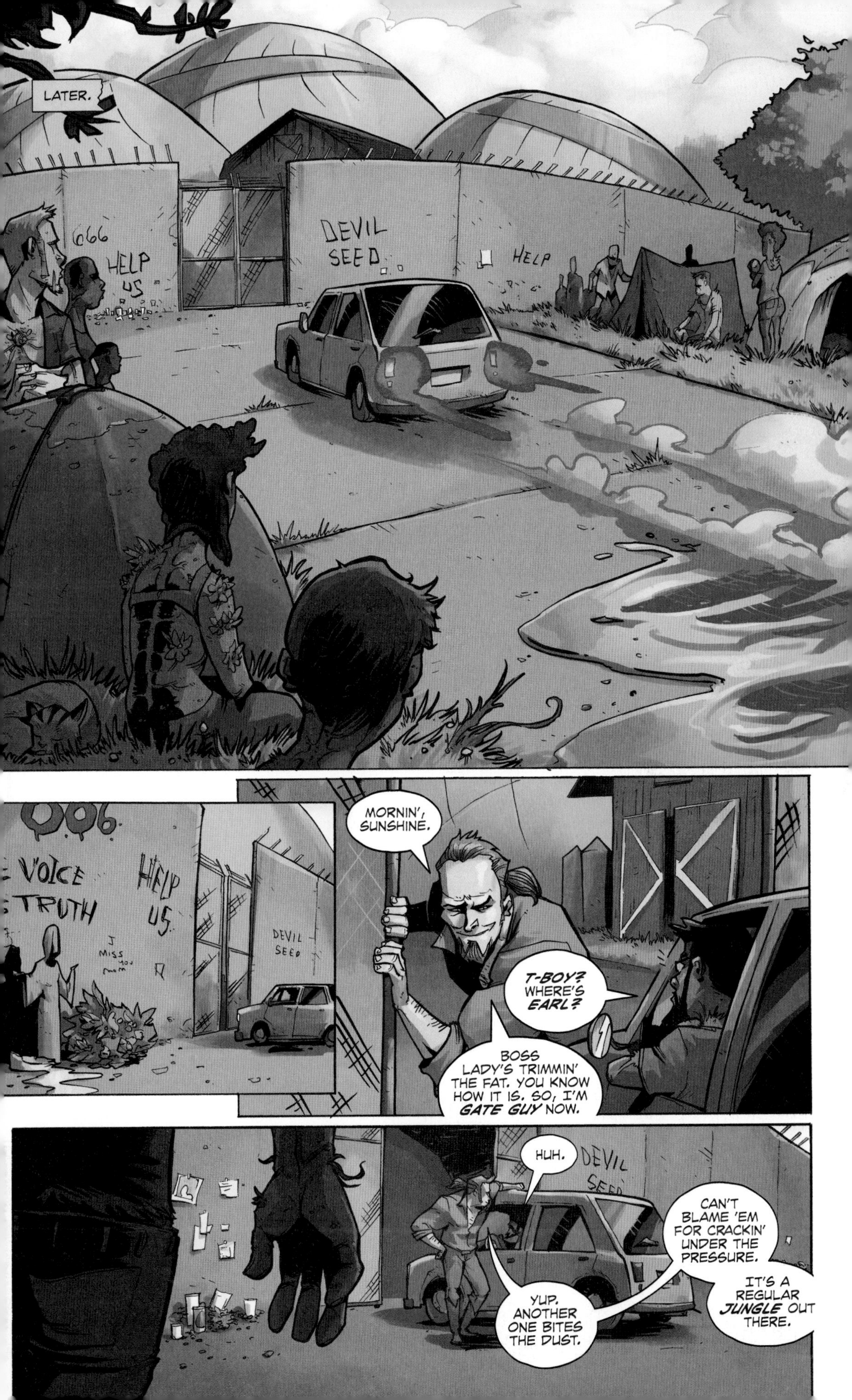
LATER.
666
HELP US
DEVIL SEED
HELP
VOICE
TRUTH
HELP US.
I MISS YOU MOM
DEVIL SEED
MORNIN', SUNSHINE.
T-BOY? WHERE'S EARL?
BOSS LADY'S TRIMMIN' THE FAT. YOU KNOW HOW IT IS. SO, I'M GATE GUY NOW.
HUH.
DEVIL
YUP. ANOTHER ONE BITES THE DUST.
CAN'T BLAME 'EM FOR CRACKIN' UNDER THE PRESSURE.
IT'S A REGULAR JUNGLE OUT THERE.

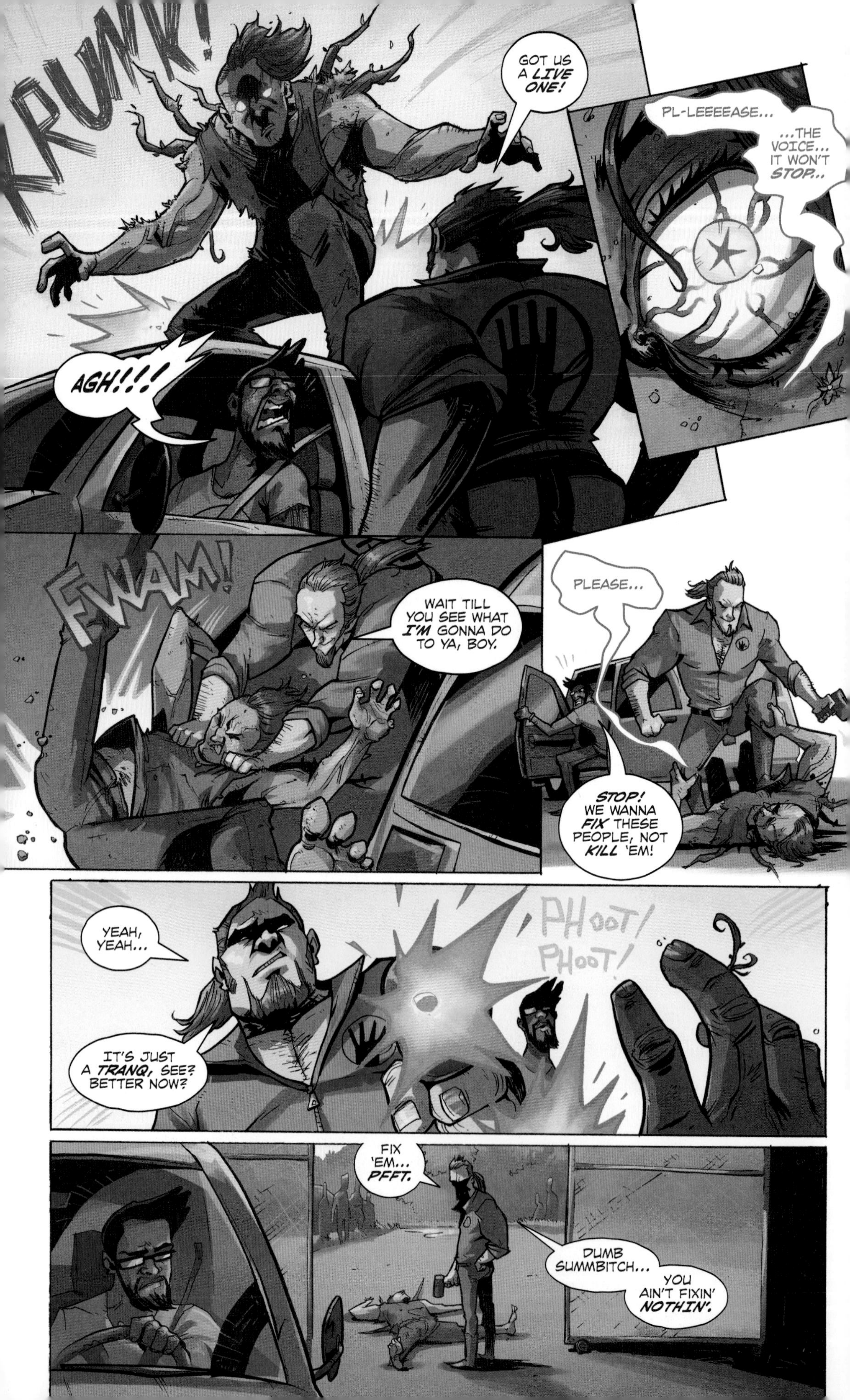
KRUNK!
GOT US A LIVE ONE!
PL-LEEEEASE...
...THE VOICE... IT WON'T STOP...
AGH!!!!
FWAM!
WAIT TILL YOU SEE WHAT I'M GONNA DO TO YA, BOY.
PLEASE...
STOP! WE WANNA FIX THESE PEOPLE, NOT KILL 'EM!
YEAH, YEAH...
PHOOT! PHOOT!
IT'S JUST A TRANQ, SEE? BETTER NOW?
FIX 'EM... PFFT.
DUMB SUMMBITCH...
YOU AIN'T FIXIN' NOTHIN'.

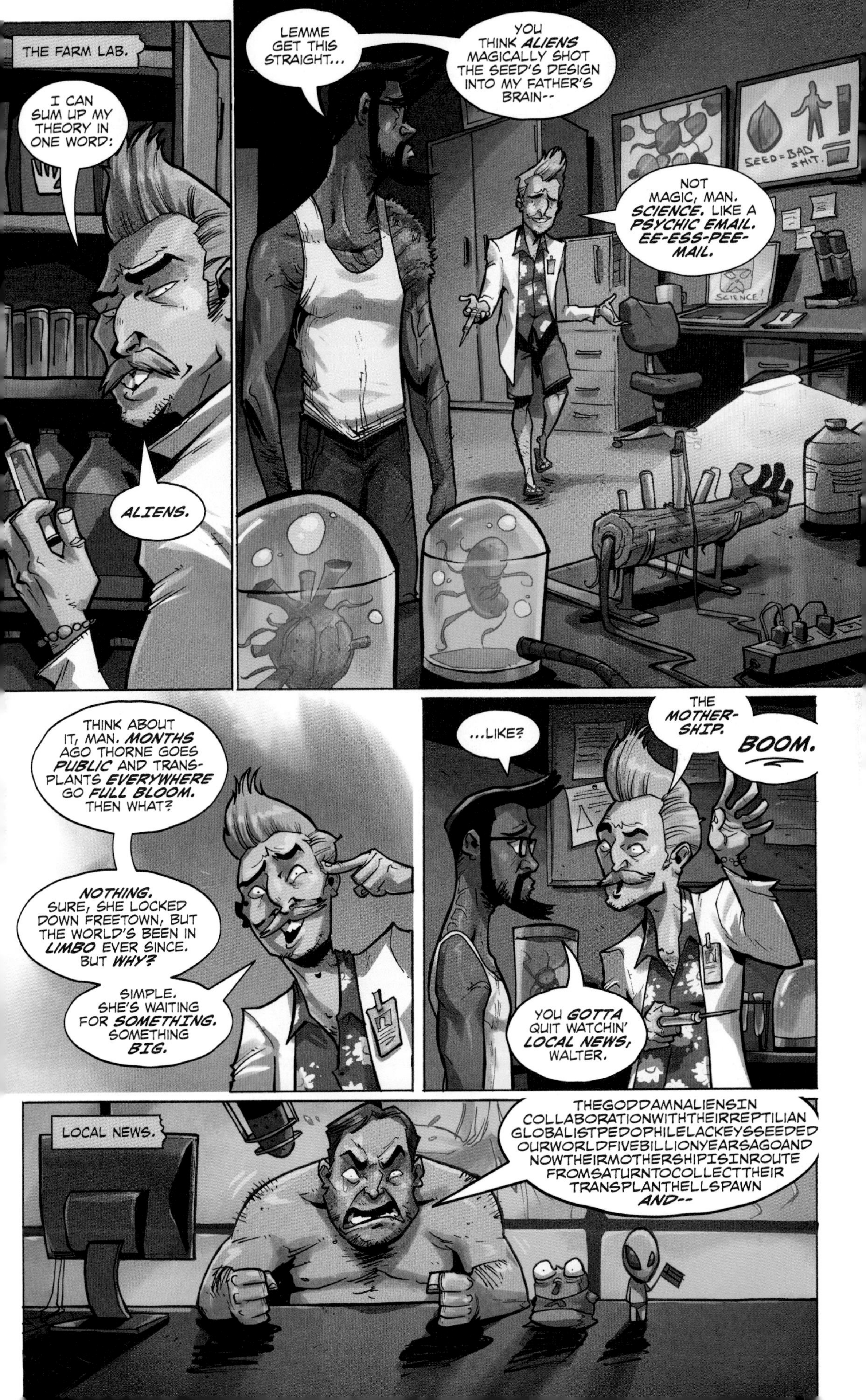
THE FARM LAB.
I CAN SUM UP MY THEORY IN ONE WORD:
ALIENS.
LEMME GET THIS STRAIGHT...
YOU THINK ALIENS MAGICALLY SHOT THE SEED'S DESIGN INTO MY FATHER'S BRAIN--
SEED=BAD SHIT.
NOT MAGIC, MAN. SCIENCE. LIKE A PSYCHIC EMAIL. EE-ESS-PEE-MAIL.
SCIENCE!
THINK ABOUT IT, MAN. MONTHS AGO THORNE GOES PUBLIC AND TRANS-PLANTS EVERYWHERE GO FULL BLOOM. THEN WHAT?
NOTHING. SURE, SHE LOCKED DOWN FREETOWN, BUT THE WORLD'S BEEN IN LIMBO EVER SINCE. BUT WHY?
SIMPLE. SHE'S WAITING FOR SOMETHING. SOMETHING BIG.
...LIKE?
THE MOTHER-SHIP.
BOOM.
YOU GOTTA QUIT WATCHIN' LOCAL NEWS, WALTER.
LOCAL NEWS.
THEGODDAMNALIENSIN COLLABORATIONWITHTHEIRREPTILIAN GLOBALISTPEDOPHILELACKEYSSEEDED OURWORLDFIVEBILLIONYEARSAGOAND NOWTHEIRMOTHERSHIPISINROUTE FROMSATURNTOCOLLECTTHEIR TRANSPLANTHELLSPAWN AND--

I'M JUST SAYIN'...I CAN'T SHAKE THE FEELING THORNE'S JUST THE FRONT FOR SOMETHING *BIGGER*.

FEELINGS AREN'T VERY *SCIENTIFIC*.

SAYS THE GUY WHO *ASTRAL PROJECTED* TWENTY YEARS INTO THE *PAST* TO CHAT WITH HIS DEAD MOTHER.

YOU'LL FEEL A *PINCH*.

INHIBITOR'S BEEN TAKING THE *EDGE* OFF?

A BIT. NOT HELPING THE *INSOMNIA*, THOUGH.

YEAH... ABOUT THAT...

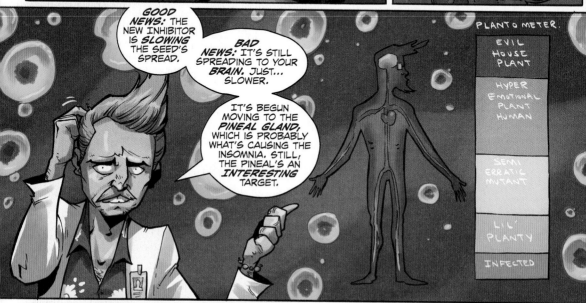

GOOD NEWS: THE NEW INHIBITOR IS *SLOWING* THE SEED'S SPREAD.

BAD NEWS: IT'S STILL SPREADING TO YOUR *BRAIN*. JUST... SLOWER.

IT'S BEGUN MOVING TO THE *PINEAL GLAND*, WHICH IS PROBABLY WHAT'S CAUSING THE INSOMNIA. STILL, THE PINEAL'S AN *INTERESTING* TARGET.

PLANTO METER.

EVIL HOUSE PLANT

HYPER EMOTIONAL PLANT HUMAN

SEMI ERRATIC MUTANT

LIL' PLANTY

INFECTED

I'M GLAD MY DEATH WILL BE *INTERESTING*.

THE PINEAL'S SORTA *MYSTERIOUS*. FOR YEARS SCIENTISTS BELIEVED IT WAS JUST SOME KINDA EVOLUTIONARY *REMNANT*. THEN PEOPLE STARTED THINKING IT MORE *VITAL*.

IT'S HAD DIFFERENT NICKNAMES. THE *THIRD EYE* OR THE *AJNA CHAKRA*. OR THE *SEAT OF THE SOUL*.

IT REALLY MAKES YOU WONDER, IS THAT WHAT MONICA'S *AFTER*?

TRIPPY SHIT, EH, ZEKE?

...ZEKE?

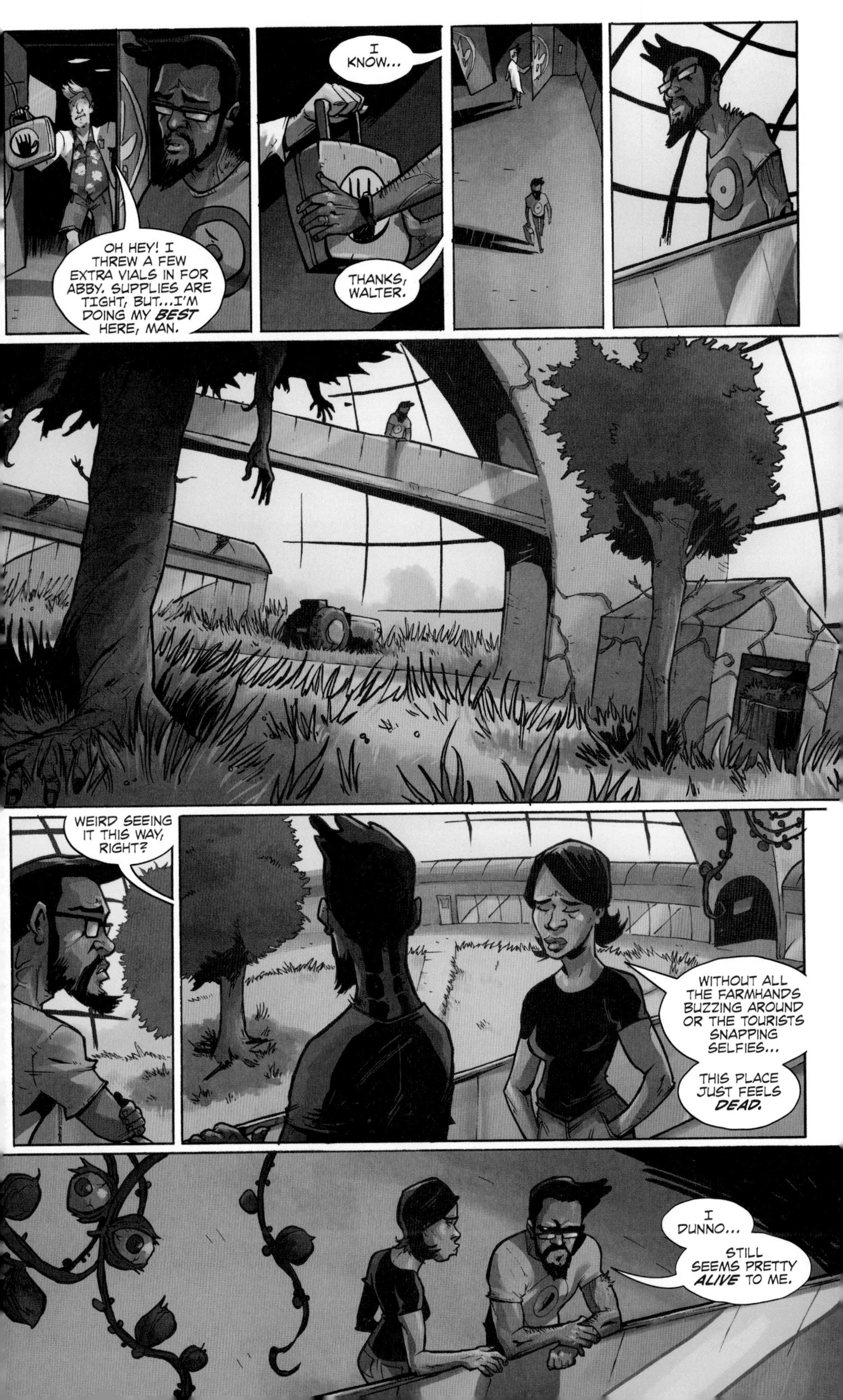
OH HEY! I THREW A FEW EXTRA VIALS IN FOR ABBY. SUPPLIES ARE TIGHT, BUT...I'M DOING MY BEST HERE, MAN.
I KNOW...
THANKS, WALTER.
WEIRD SEEING IT THIS WAY, RIGHT?
WITHOUT ALL THE FARMHANDS BUZZING AROUND OR THE TOURISTS SNAPPING SELFIES...
THIS PLACE JUST FEELS DEAD.
I DUNNO...
STILL SEEMS PRETTY ALIVE TO ME.

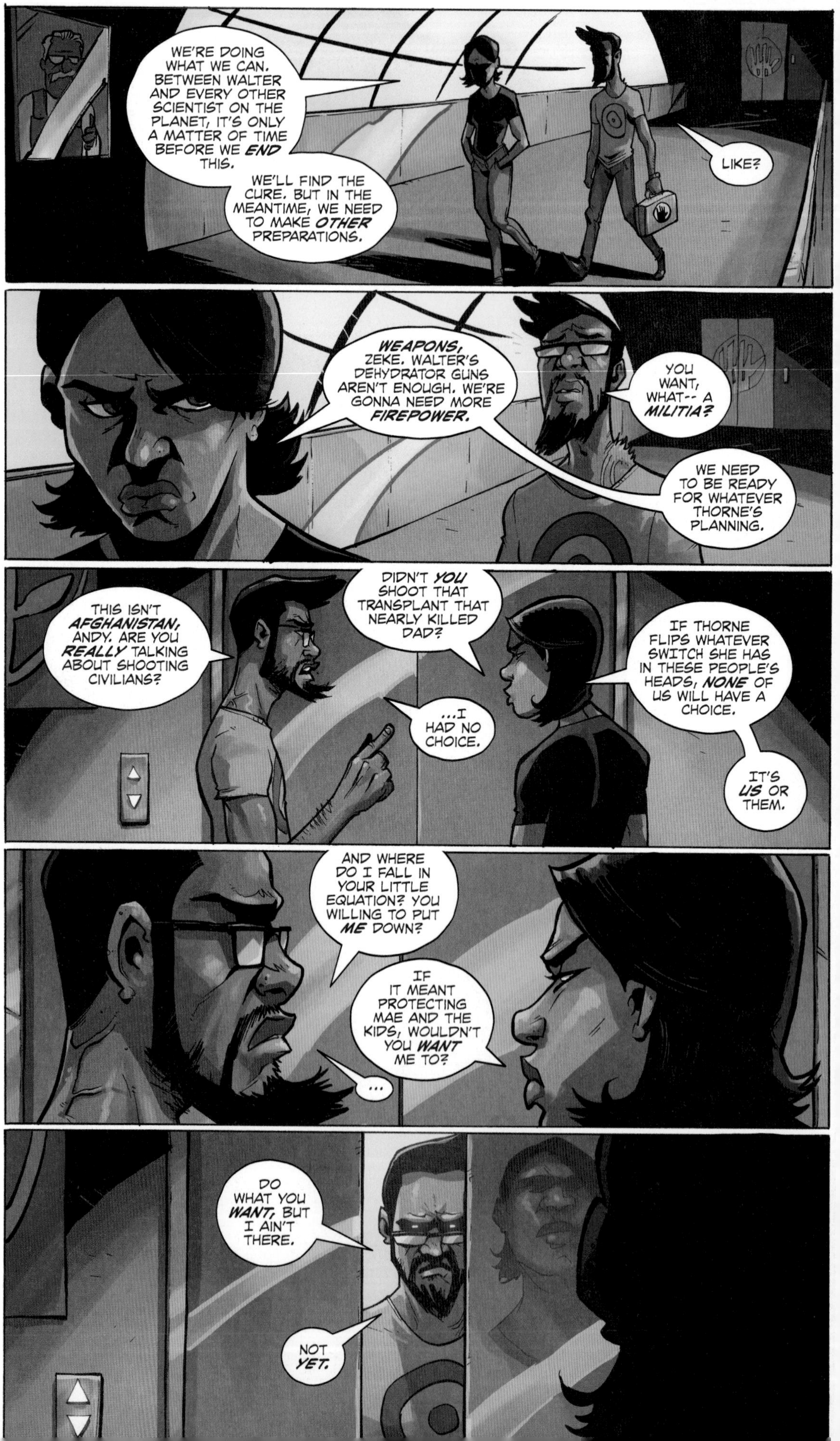
WE'RE DOING WHAT WE CAN. BETWEEN WALTER AND EVERY OTHER SCIENTIST ON THE PLANET, IT'S ONLY A MATTER OF TIME BEFORE WE END THIS.
WE'LL FIND THE CURE. BUT IN THE MEANTIME, WE NEED TO MAKE OTHER PREPARATIONS.
LIKE?
WEAPONS, ZEKE. WALTER'S DEHYDRATOR GUNS AREN'T ENOUGH. WE'RE GONNA NEED MORE FIREPOWER.
YOU WANT, WHAT-- A MILITIA?
WE NEED TO BE READY FOR WHATEVER THORNE'S PLANNING.
THIS ISN'T AFGHANISTAN, ANDY. ARE YOU REALLY TALKING ABOUT SHOOTING CIVILIANS?
DIDN'T YOU SHOOT THAT TRANSPLANT THAT NEARLY KILLED DAD?
...I HAD NO CHOICE.
IF THORNE FLIPS WHATEVER SWITCH SHE HAS IN THESE PEOPLE'S HEADS, NONE OF US WILL HAVE A CHOICE.
IT'S US OR THEM.
AND WHERE DO I FALL IN YOUR LITTLE EQUATION? YOU WILLING TO PUT ME DOWN?
IF IT MEANT PROTECTING MAE AND THE KIDS, WOULDN'T YOU WANT ME TO?
...
DO WHAT YOU WANT, BUT I AIN'T THERE.
NOT YET.

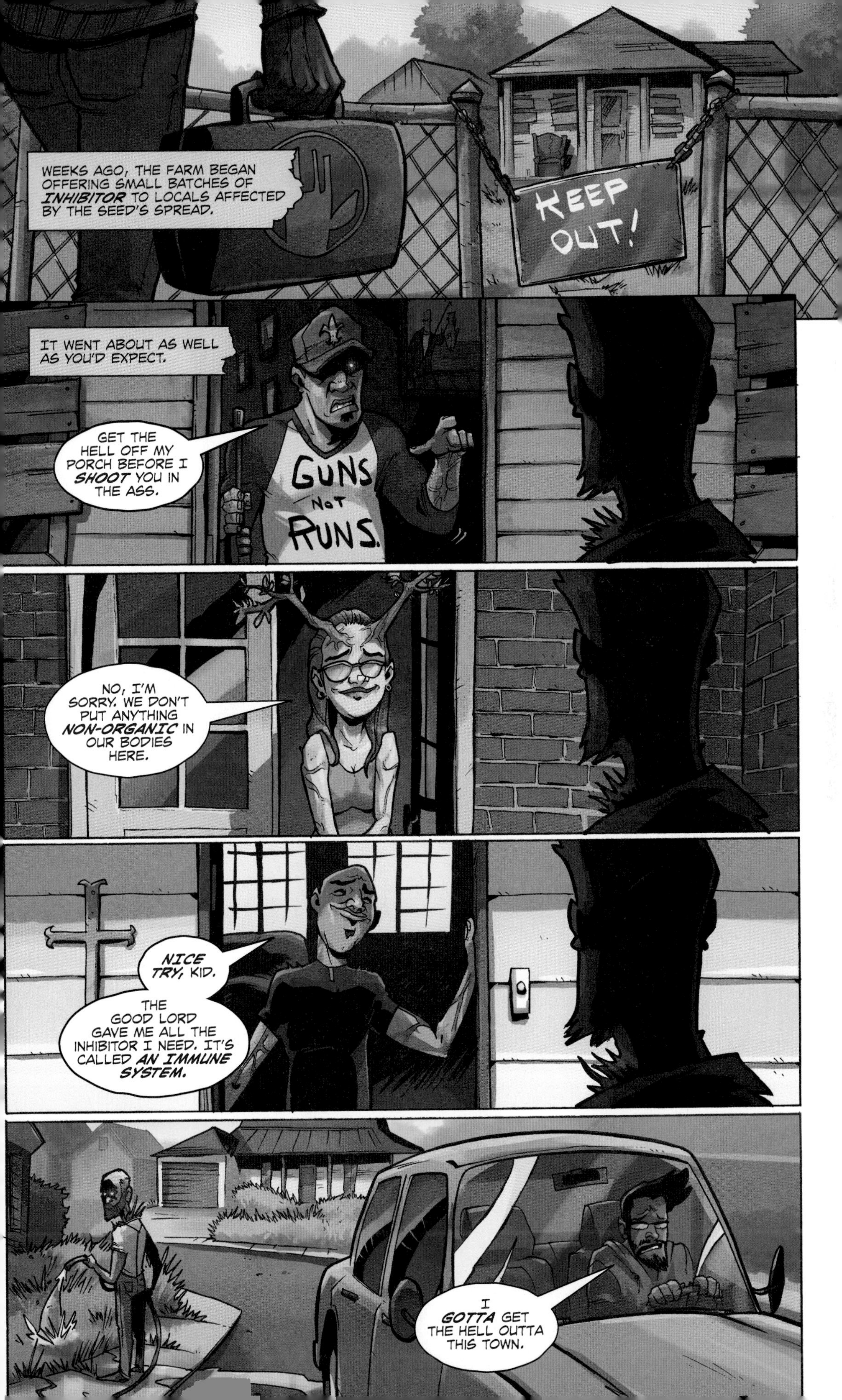
WEEKS AGO, THE FARM BEGAN OFFERING SMALL BATCHES OF *INHIBITOR* TO LOCALS AFFECTED BY THE SEED'S SPREAD.
KEEP OUT!
IT WENT ABOUT AS WELL AS YOU'D EXPECT.
GET THE HELL OFF MY PORCH BEFORE I *SHOOT* YOU IN THE ASS.
GUNS NOT RUNS.
NO, I'M SORRY. WE DON'T PUT ANYTHING *NON-ORGANIC* IN OUR BODIES HERE.
NICE TRY, KID.
THE GOOD LORD GAVE ME ALL THE INHIBITOR I NEED. IT'S CALLED *AN IMMUNE SYSTEM.*
I *GOTTA* GET THE HELL OUTTA THIS TOWN.

THE LAST STOP.

DING DONG!

PLEASE DON'T BE *CRAZY.*

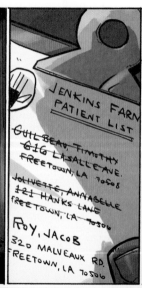

JENKINS FARM
PATIENT LIST

GUILBEAU, TIMOTHY
616 LASALLE AVE.
FREETOWN, LA 70508

JOLIVETTE, ANNABELLE
121 HANKS LANE
FREETOWN, LA 70506

ROY, JACOB
320 MALVEAUX RD.
FREETOWN, LA 70506

OH SH--

IS THIS ABOUT MY *HUSBAND?*

DID YOU FIND MY *JACOB?*

JACOB ROY.

UH...NO, MA'AM.

NOT YET.

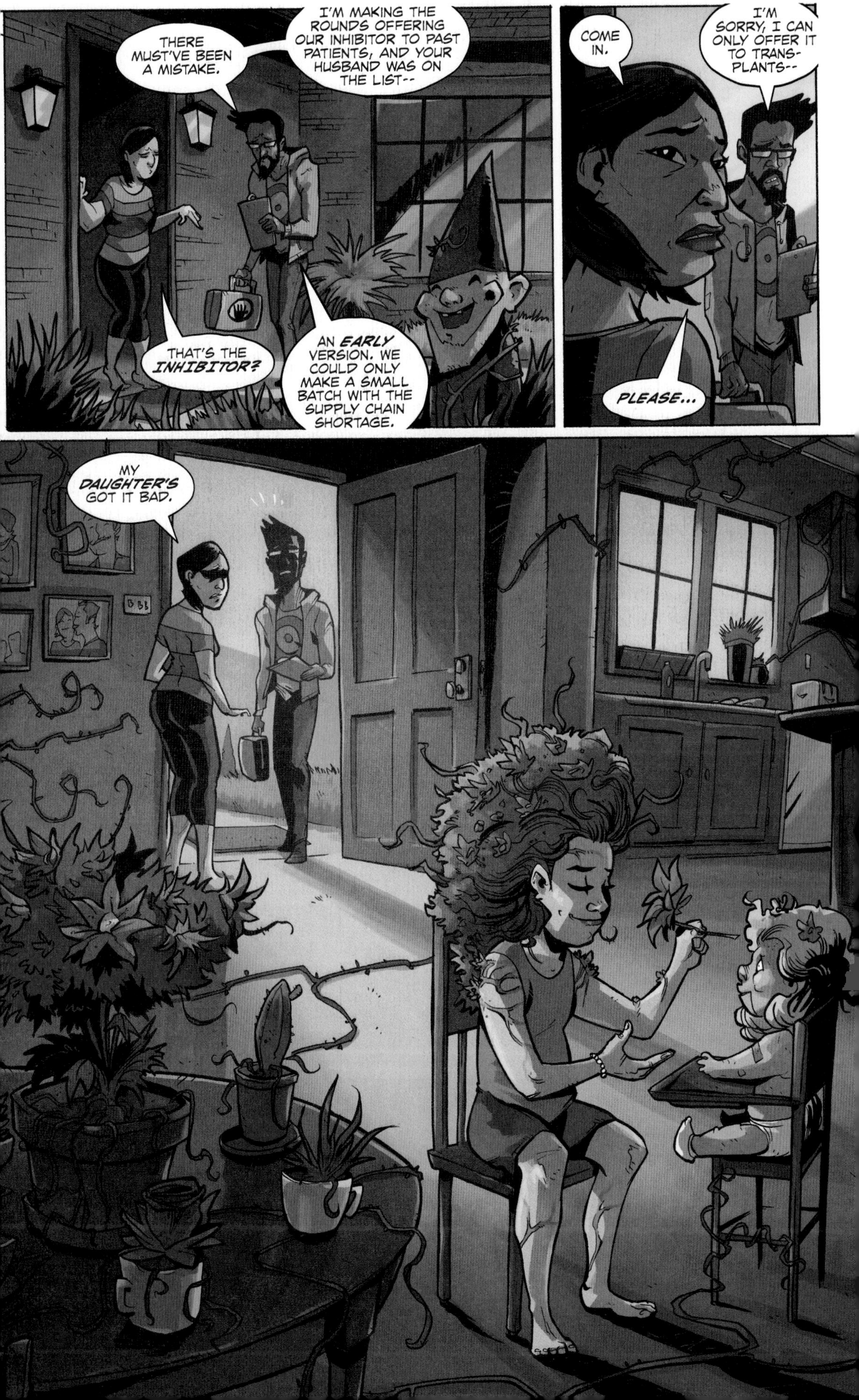

THERE MUST'VE BEEN A MISTAKE.
I'M MAKING THE ROUNDS OFFERING OUR INHIBITOR TO PAST PATIENTS, AND YOUR HUSBAND WAS ON THE LIST--
THAT'S THE INHIBITOR?
AN EARLY VERSION. WE COULD ONLY MAKE A SMALL BATCH WITH THE SUPPLY CHAIN SHORTAGE.
COME IN.
I'M SORRY, I CAN ONLY OFFER IT TO TRANS-PLANTS--
PLEASE...
MY DAUGHTER'S GOT IT BAD.

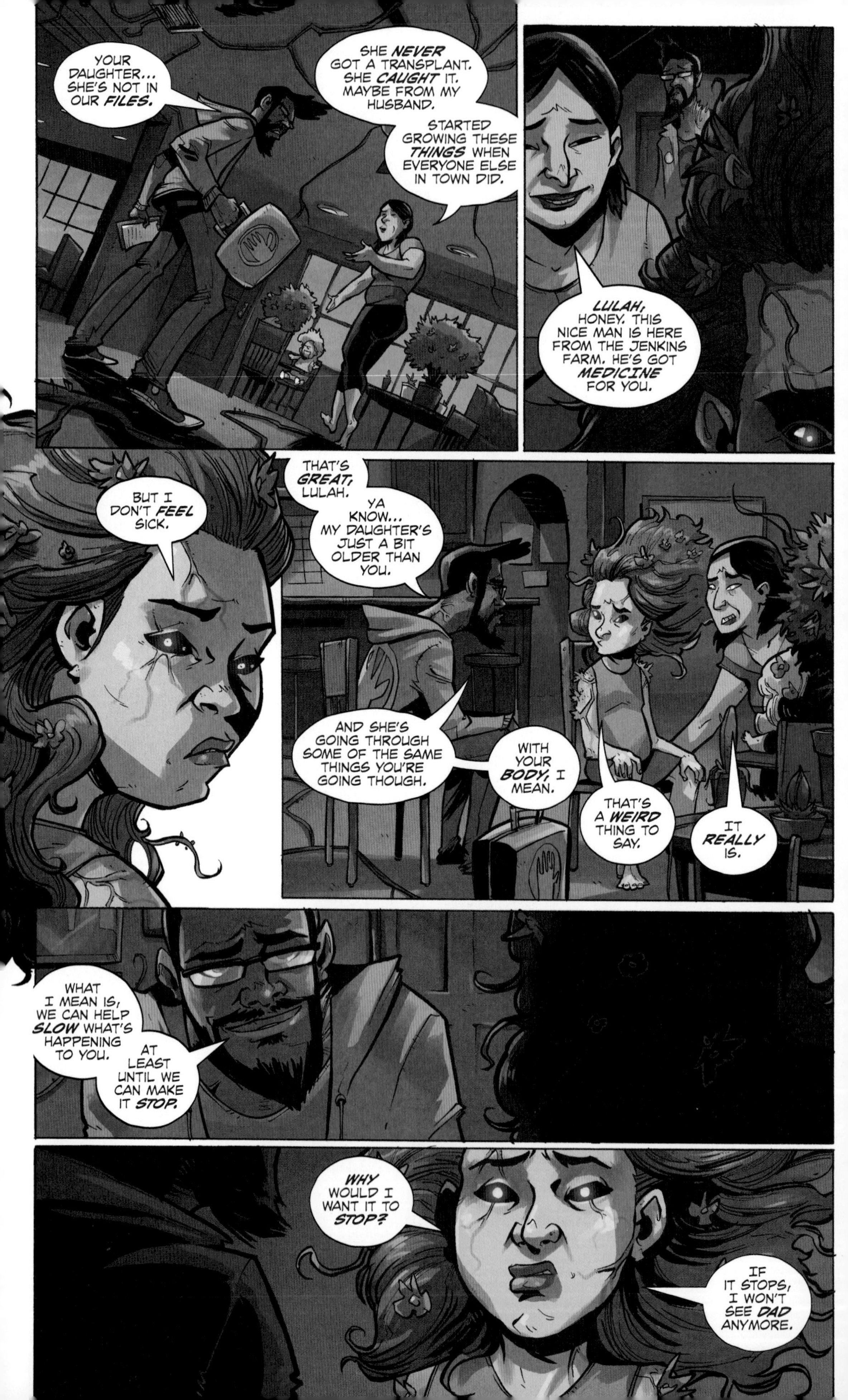
YOUR DAUGHTER... SHE'S NOT IN OUR FILES.
SHE NEVER GOT A TRANSPLANT. SHE CAUGHT IT. MAYBE FROM MY HUSBAND.
STARTED GROWING THESE THINGS WHEN EVERYONE ELSE IN TOWN DID.
LULAH, HONEY. THIS NICE MAN IS HERE FROM THE JENKINS FARM. HE'S GOT MEDICINE FOR YOU.
BUT I DON'T FEEL SICK.
THAT'S GREAT, LULAH.
YA KNOW... MY DAUGHTER'S JUST A BIT OLDER THAN YOU.
AND SHE'S GOING THROUGH SOME OF THE SAME THINGS YOU'RE GOING THOUGH.
WITH YOUR BODY, I MEAN.
THAT'S A WEIRD THING TO SAY.
IT REALLY IS.
WHAT I MEAN IS, WE CAN HELP SLOW WHAT'S HAPPENING TO YOU.
AT LEAST UNTIL WE CAN MAKE IT STOP.
WHY WOULD I WANT IT TO STOP?
IF IT STOPS, I WON'T SEE DAD ANYMORE.

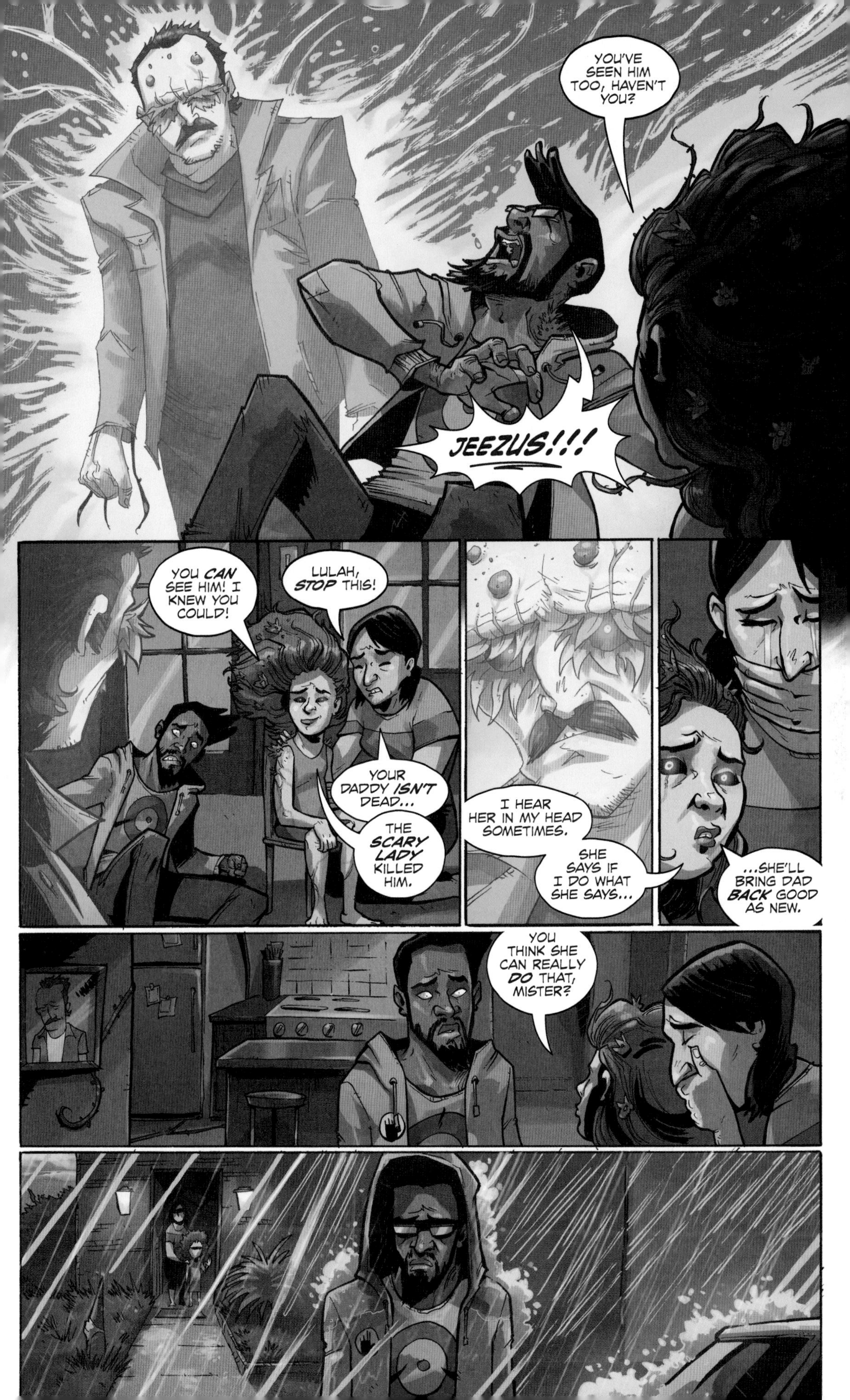
YOU'VE SEEN HIM TOO, HAVEN'T YOU?
JEEZUS!!!
YOU CAN SEE HIM! I KNEW YOU COULD!
LULAH, STOP THIS!
YOUR DADDY ISN'T DEAD...
THE SCARY LADY KILLED HIM.
I HEAR HER IN MY HEAD SOMETIMES.
SHE SAYS IF I DO WHAT SHE SAYS...
...SHE'LL BRING DAD BACK GOOD AS NEW.
YOU THINK SHE CAN REALLY DO THAT, MISTER?

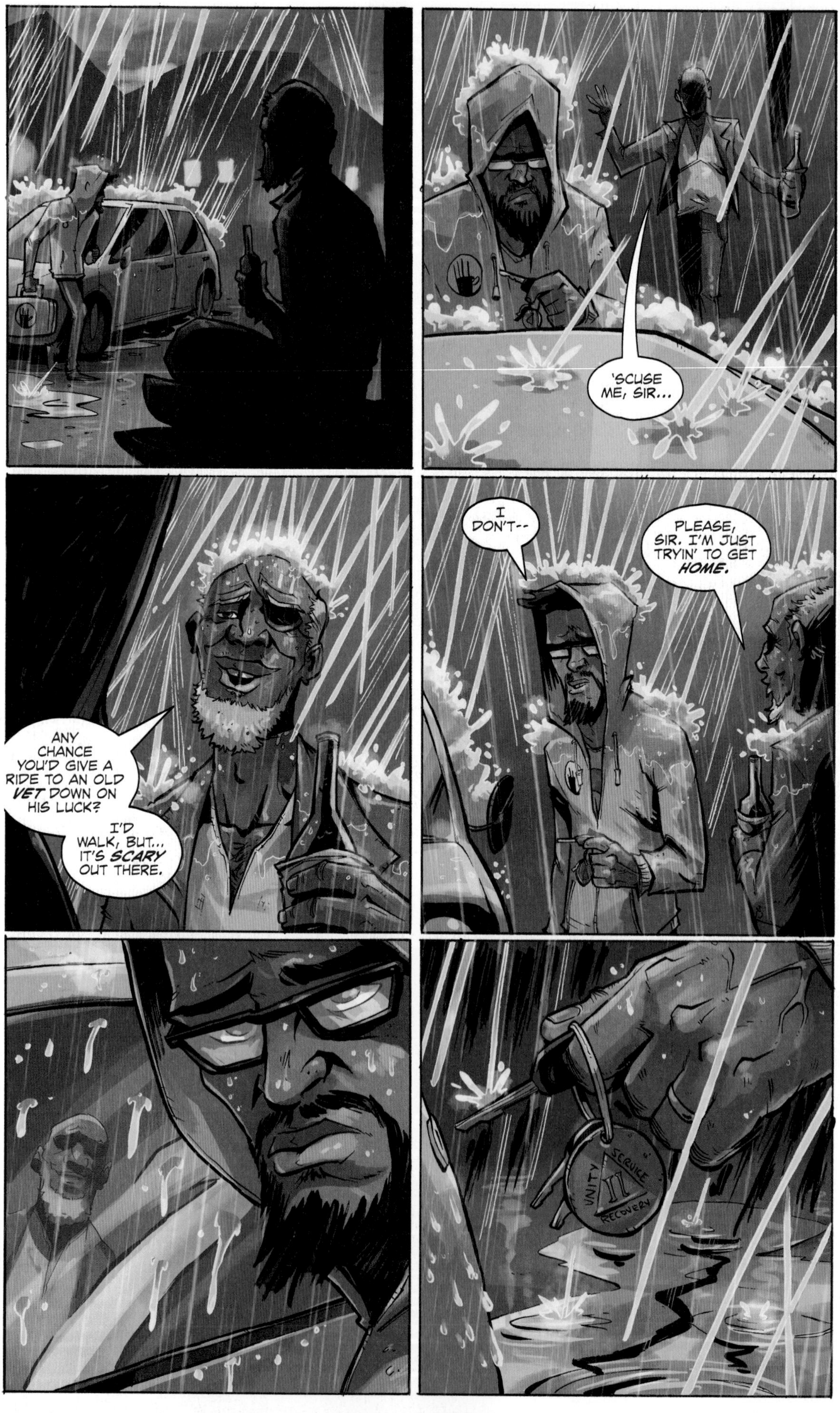
'SCUSE ME, SIR...
ANY CHANCE YOU'D GIVE A RIDE TO AN OLD VET DOWN ON HIS LUCK?
I'D WALK, BUT... IT'S SCARY OUT THERE.
I DON'T--
PLEASE, SIR. I'M JUST TRYIN' TO GET HOME.
UNITY SERVICE RECOVERY
II

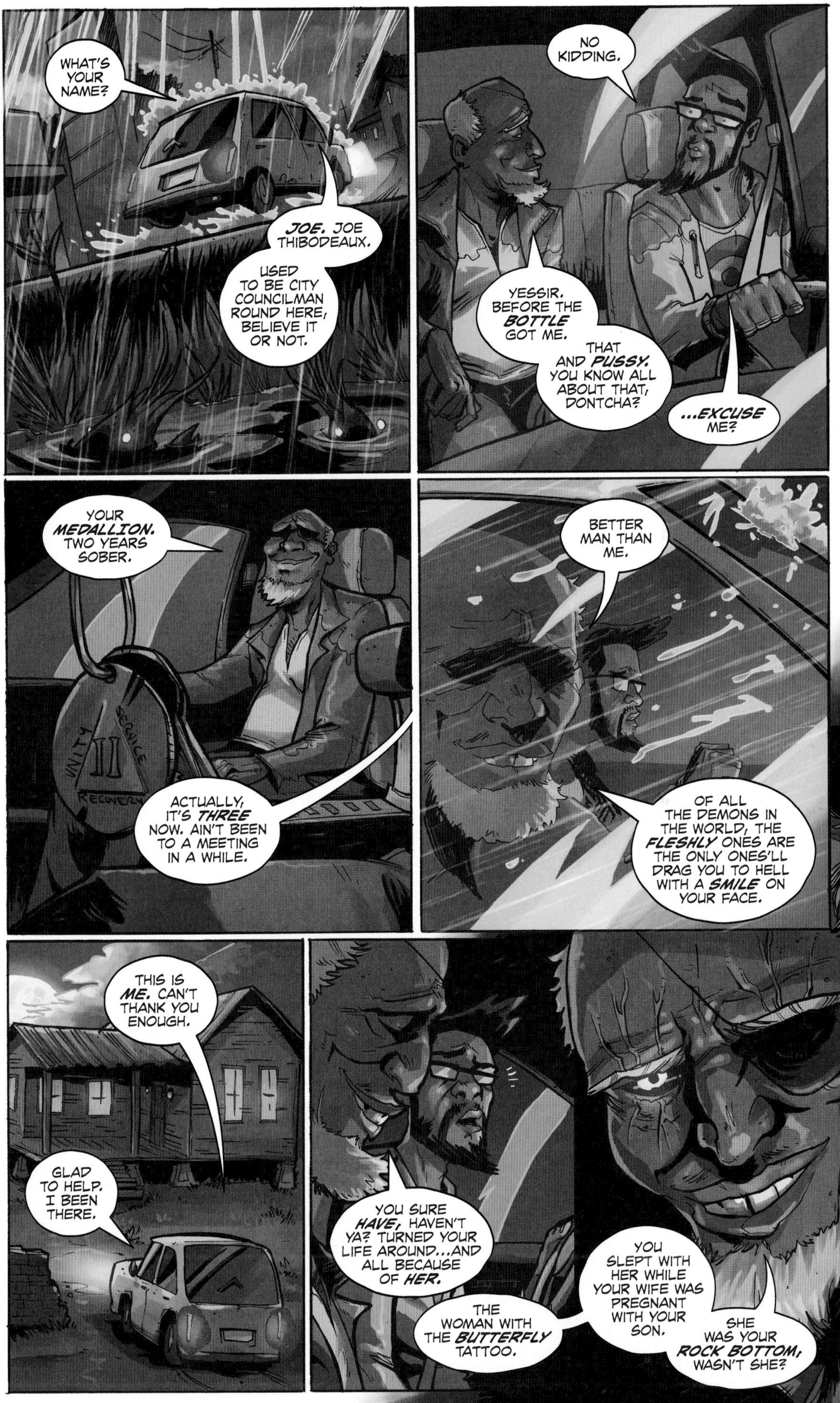
WHAT'S YOUR NAME?
JOE. JOE THIBODEAUX.
USED TO BE CITY COUNCILMAN ROUND HERE, BELIEVE IT OR NOT.
NO KIDDING.
YESSIR. BEFORE THE BOTTLE GOT ME.
THAT AND PUSSY. YOU KNOW ALL ABOUT THAT, DONTCHA?
...EXCUSE ME?
YOUR MEDALLION. TWO YEARS SOBER.
ACTUALLY, IT'S THREE NOW. AIN'T BEEN TO A MEETING IN A WHILE.
UNITY SERVICE II RECOVERY
BETTER MAN THAN ME.
OF ALL THE DEMONS IN THE WORLD, THE FLESHLY ONES ARE THE ONLY ONES'LL DRAG YOU TO HELL WITH A SMILE ON YOUR FACE.
THIS IS ME. CAN'T THANK YOU ENOUGH.
GLAD TO HELP. I BEEN THERE.
YOU SURE HAVE, HAVEN'T YA? TURNED YOUR LIFE AROUND...AND ALL BECAUSE OF HER.
THE WOMAN WITH THE BUTTERFLY TATTOO.
YOU SLEPT WITH HER WHILE YOUR WIFE WAS PREGNANT WITH YOUR SON.
SHE WAS YOUR ROCK BOTTOM, WASN'T SHE?

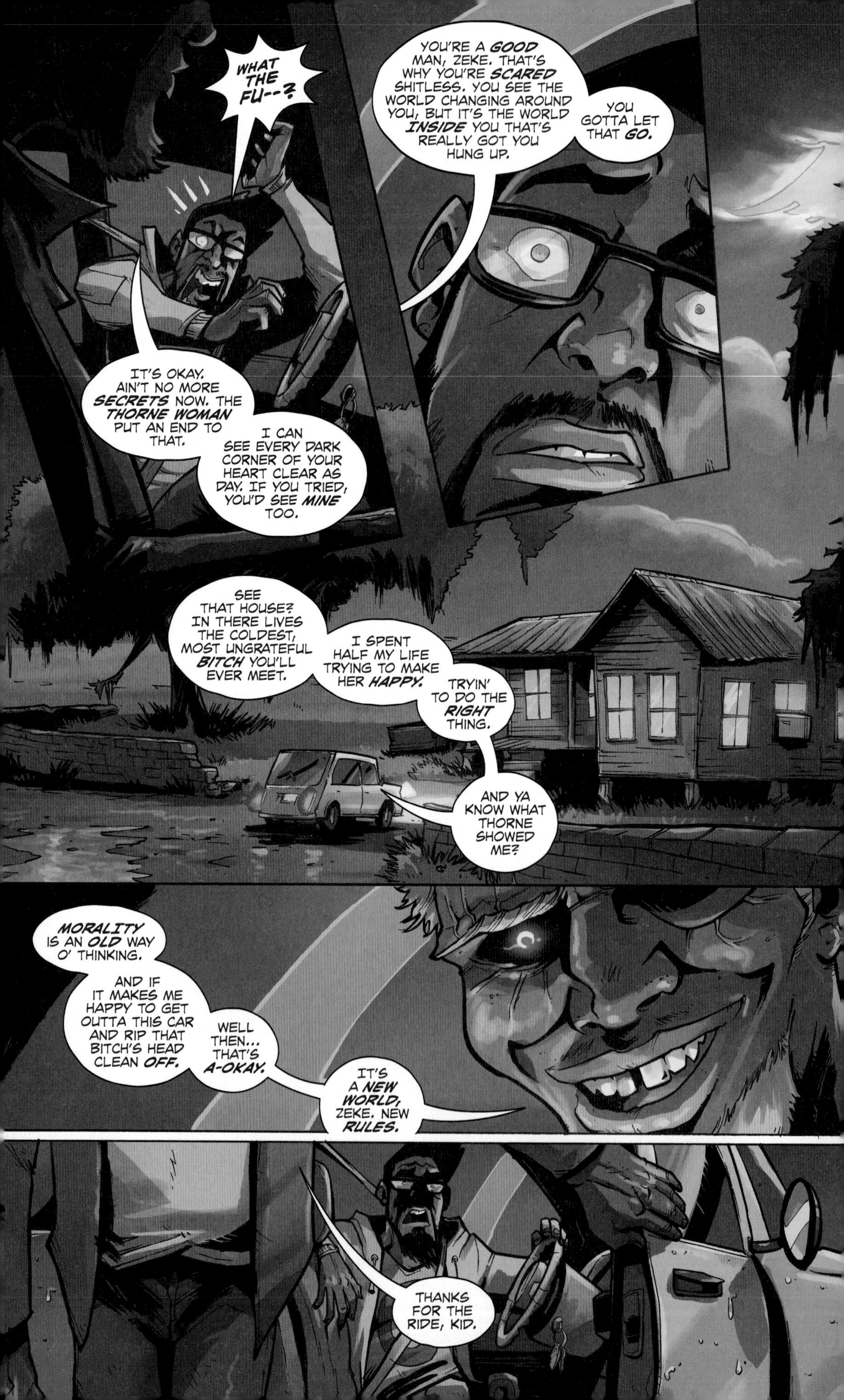
WHAT THE FU--?
YOU'RE A GOOD MAN, ZEKE. THAT'S WHY YOU'RE SCARED SHITLESS. YOU SEE THE WORLD CHANGING AROUND YOU, BUT IT'S THE WORLD INSIDE YOU THAT'S REALLY GOT YOU HUNG UP.
YOU GOTTA LET THAT GO.
IT'S OKAY. AIN'T NO MORE SECRETS NOW. THE THORNE WOMAN PUT AN END TO THAT.
I CAN SEE EVERY DARK CORNER OF YOUR HEART CLEAR AS DAY. IF YOU TRIED, YOU'D SEE MINE TOO.
SEE THAT HOUSE? IN THERE LIVES THE COLDEST, MOST UNGRATEFUL BITCH YOU'LL EVER MEET.
I SPENT HALF MY LIFE TRYING TO MAKE HER HAPPY.
TRYIN' TO DO THE RIGHT THING.
AND YA KNOW WHAT THORNE SHOWED ME?
MORALITY IS AN OLD WAY O' THINKING.
AND IF IT MAKES ME HAPPY TO GET OUTTA THIS CAR AND RIP THAT BITCH'S HEAD CLEAN OFF.
WELL THEN... THAT'S A-OKAY.
IT'S A NEW WORLD, ZEKE. NEW RULES.
THANKS FOR THE RIDE, KID.

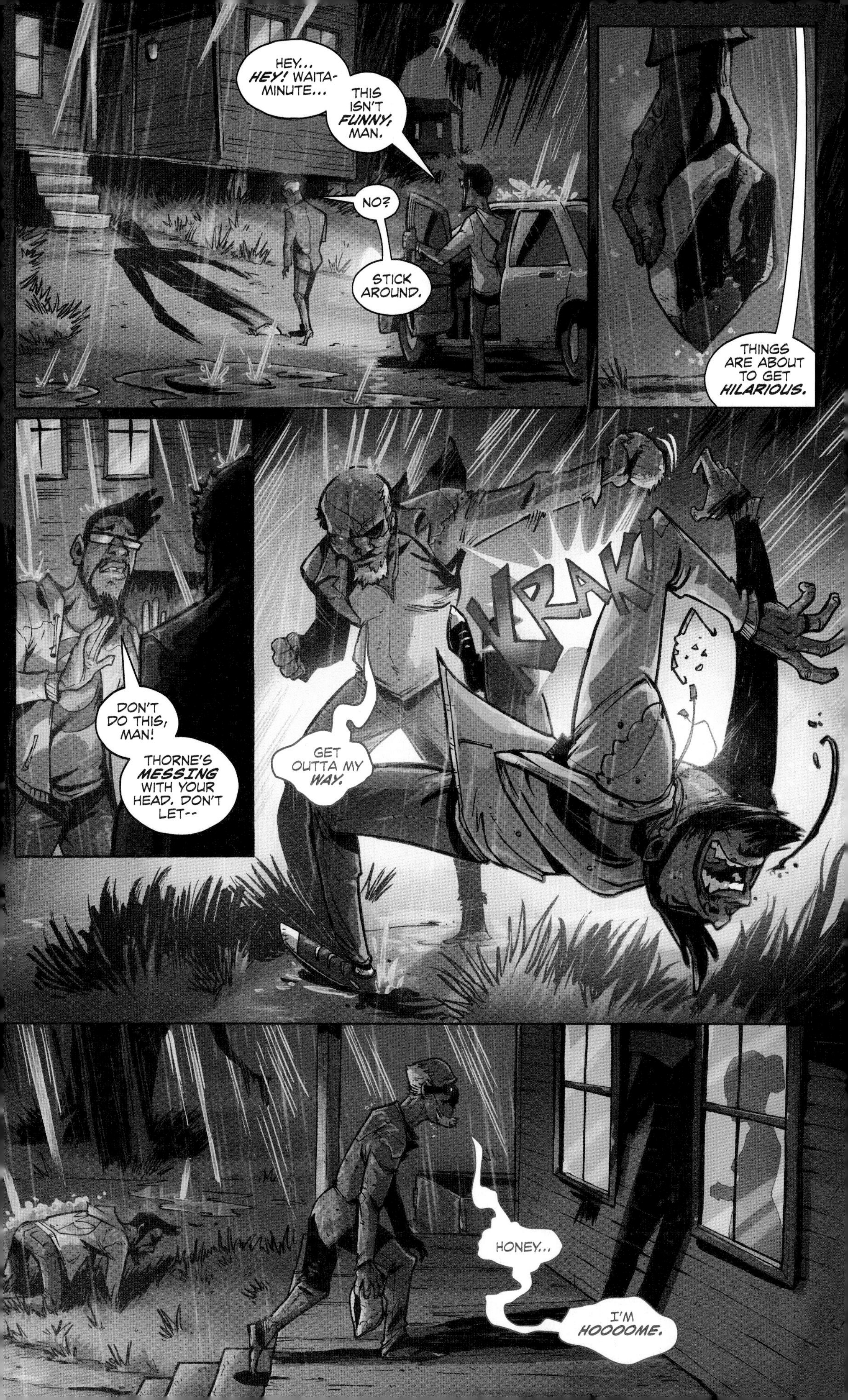
HEY... HEY! WAITA-MINUTE...
THIS ISN'T FUNNY, MAN.
NO?
STICK AROUND.
THINGS ARE ABOUT TO GET HILARIOUS.
DON'T DO THIS, MAN!
THORNE'S MESSING WITH YOUR HEAD. DON'T LET--
GET OUTTA MY WAY.
KRAK!
HONEY...
I'M HOOOOME.

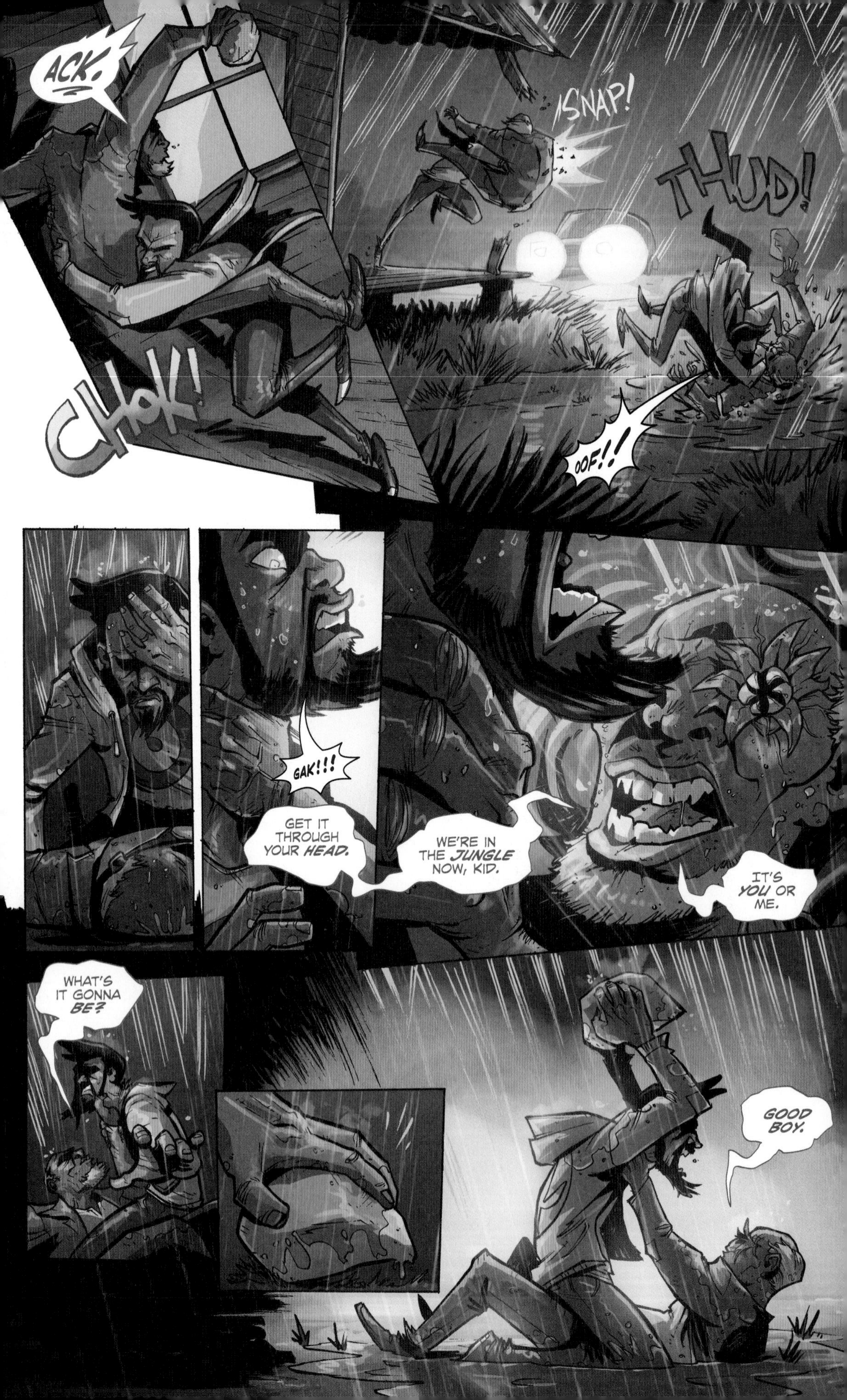
ACK.
SNAP!
THUD!
CHOK!
OOF!!
GAK!!!
GET IT THROUGH YOUR HEAD.
WE'RE IN THE JUNGLE NOW, KID.
IT'S YOU OR ME.
WHAT'S IT GONNA BE?
GOOD BOY.

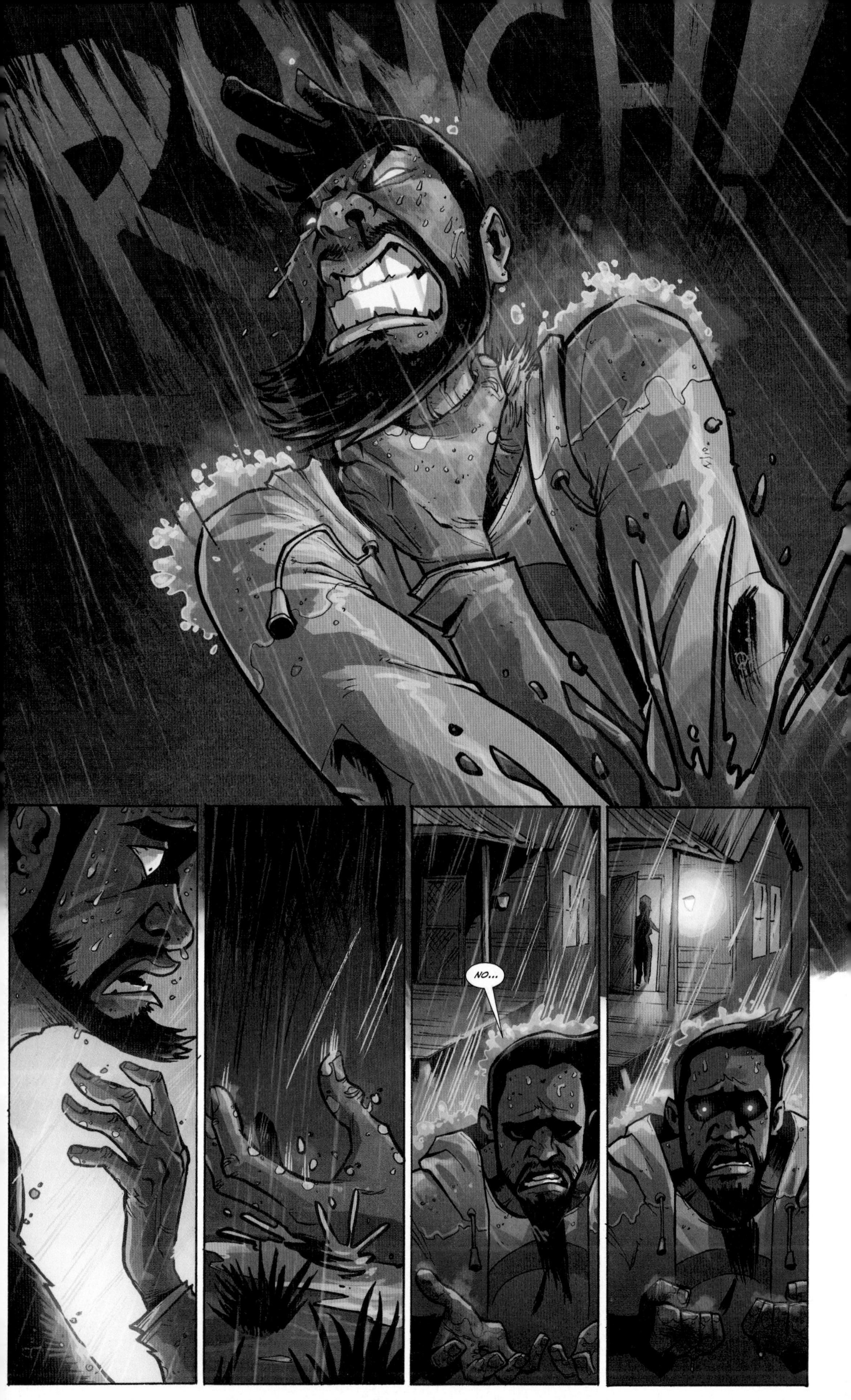
NO...

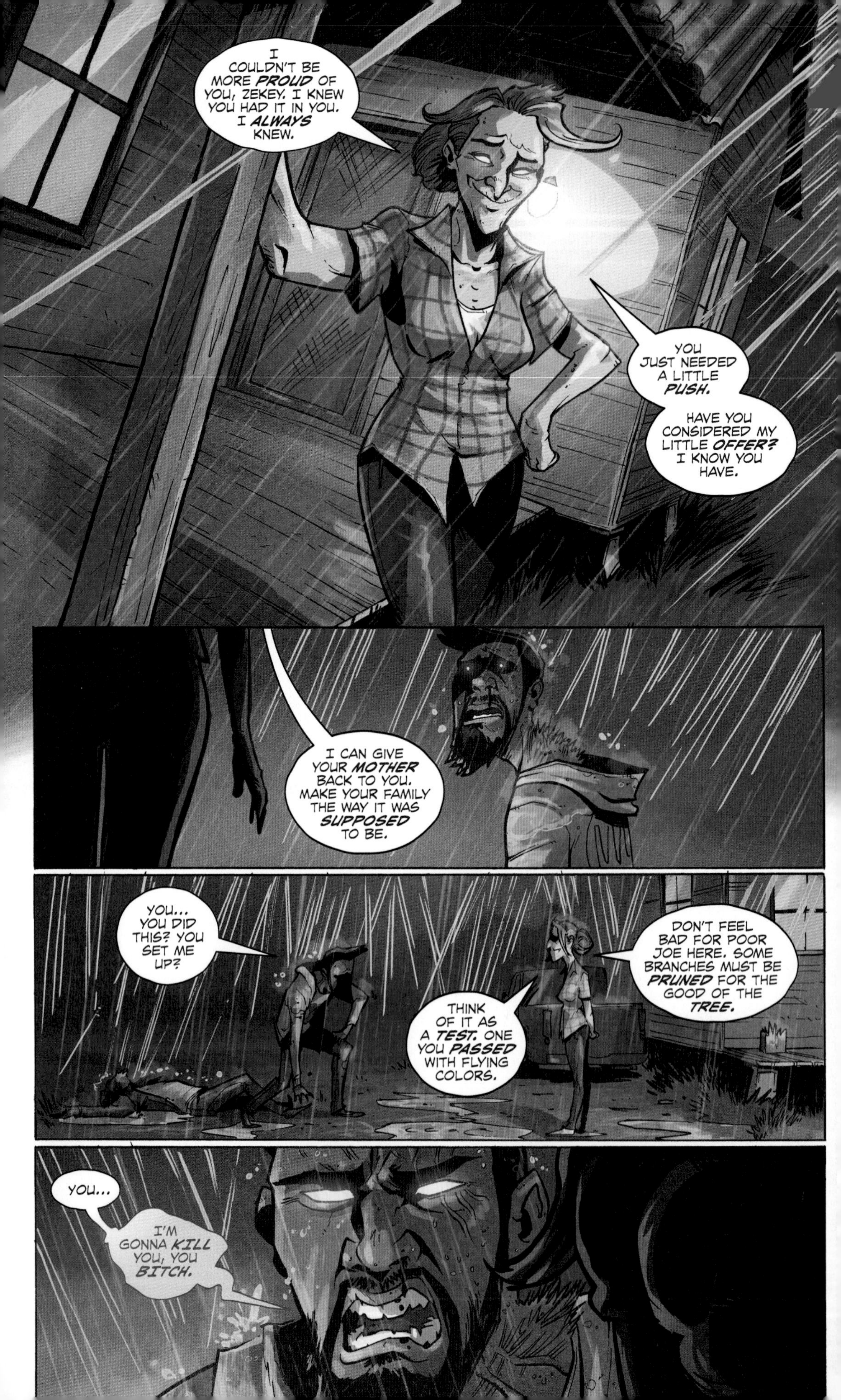

I COULDN'T BE MORE PROUD OF YOU, ZEKEY. I KNEW YOU HAD IT IN YOU. I ALWAYS KNEW.
YOU JUST NEEDED A LITTLE PUSH.
HAVE YOU CONSIDERED MY LITTLE OFFER? I KNOW YOU HAVE.
I CAN GIVE YOUR MOTHER BACK TO YOU. MAKE YOUR FAMILY THE WAY IT WAS SUPPOSED TO BE.
YOU... YOU DID THIS? YOU SET ME UP?
THINK OF IT AS A TEST. ONE YOU PASSED WITH FLYING COLORS.
DON'T FEEL BAD FOR POOR JOE HERE. SOME BRANCHES MUST BE PRUNED FOR THE GOOD OF THE TREE.
YOU...
I'M GONNA KILL YOU, YOU BITCH.

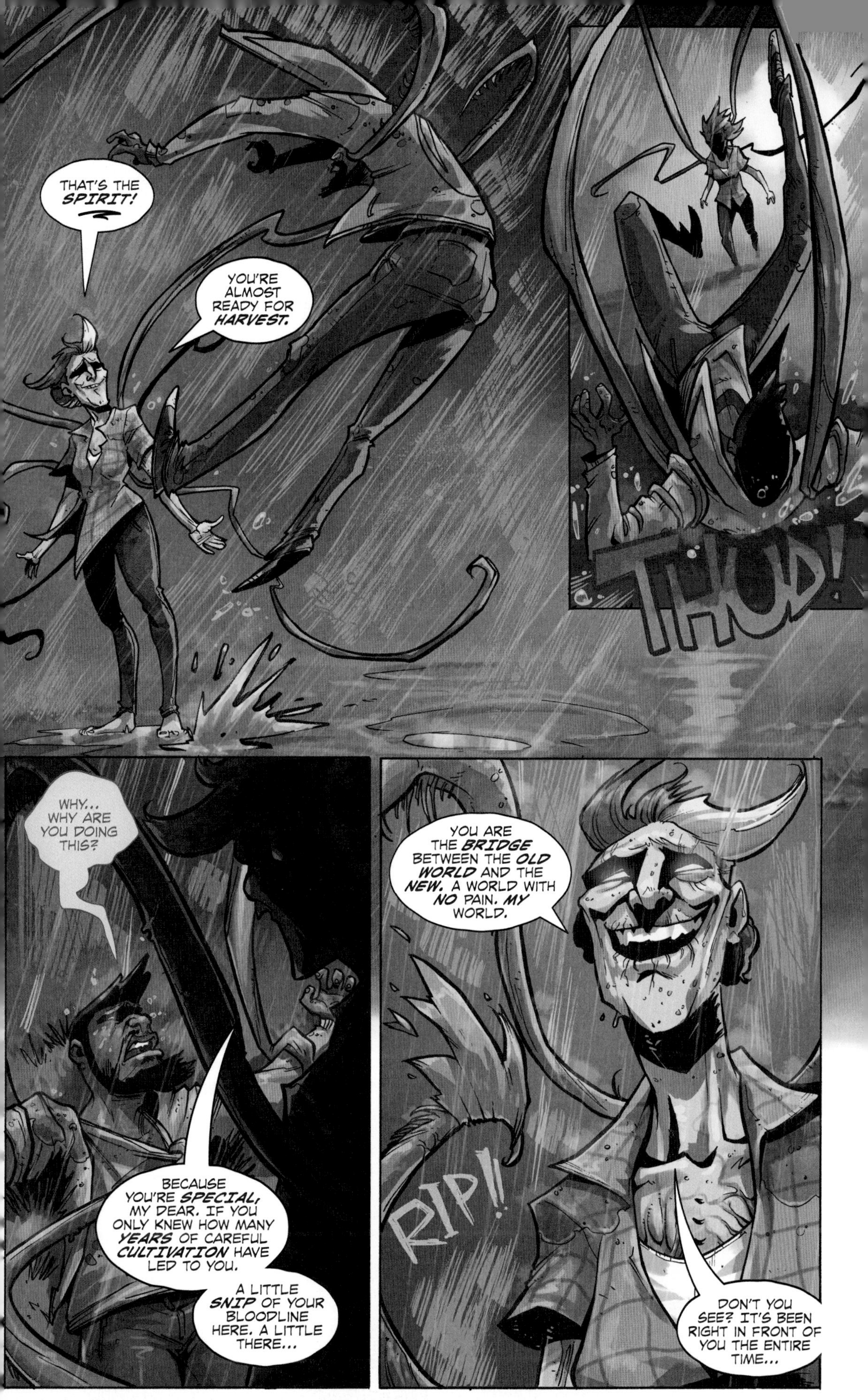
THAT'S THE SPIRIT!
YOU'RE ALMOST READY FOR HARVEST.
THUD!
WHY... WHY ARE YOU DOING THIS?
BECAUSE YOU'RE SPECIAL, MY DEAR. IF YOU ONLY KNEW HOW MANY YEARS OF CAREFUL CULTIVATION HAVE LED TO YOU.
A LITTLE SNIP OF YOUR BLOODLINE HERE. A LITTLE THERE...
YOU ARE THE BRIDGE BETWEEN THE OLD WORLD AND THE NEW. A WORLD WITH NO PAIN. MY WORLD.
RIP!!
DON'T YOU SEE? IT'S BEEN RIGHT IN FRONT OF YOU THE ENTIRE TIME...

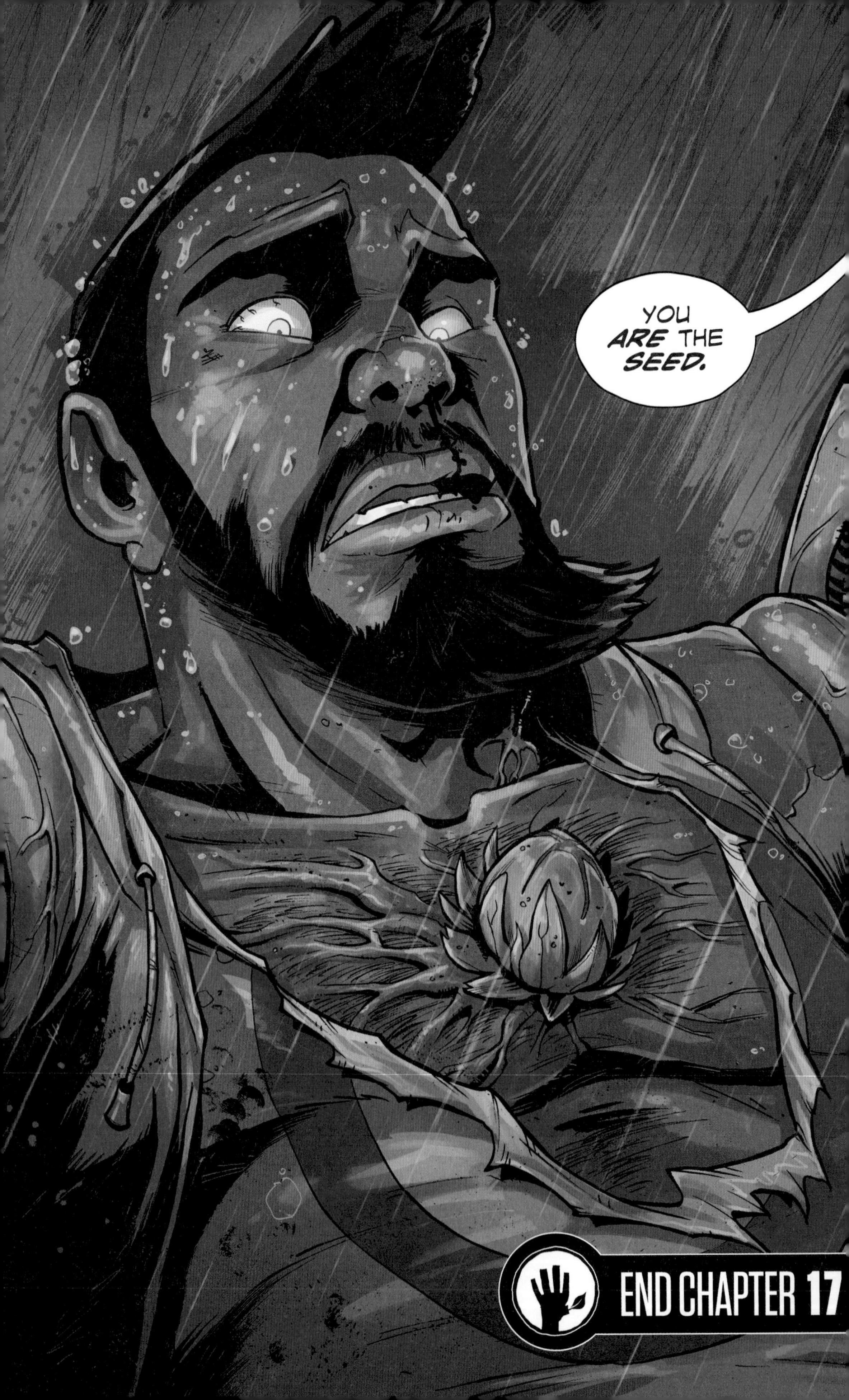
YOU ARE THE SEED.
END CHAPTER 17

CHAPTER 18

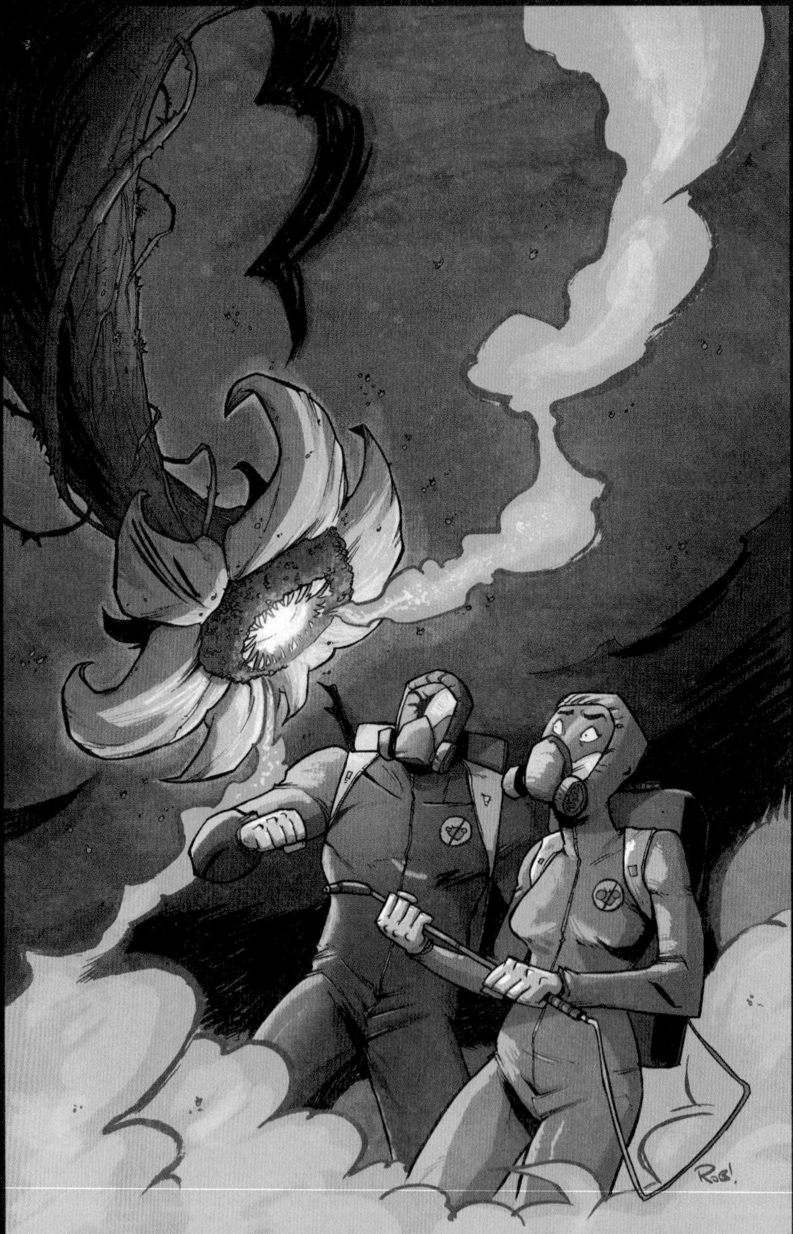
ROB!

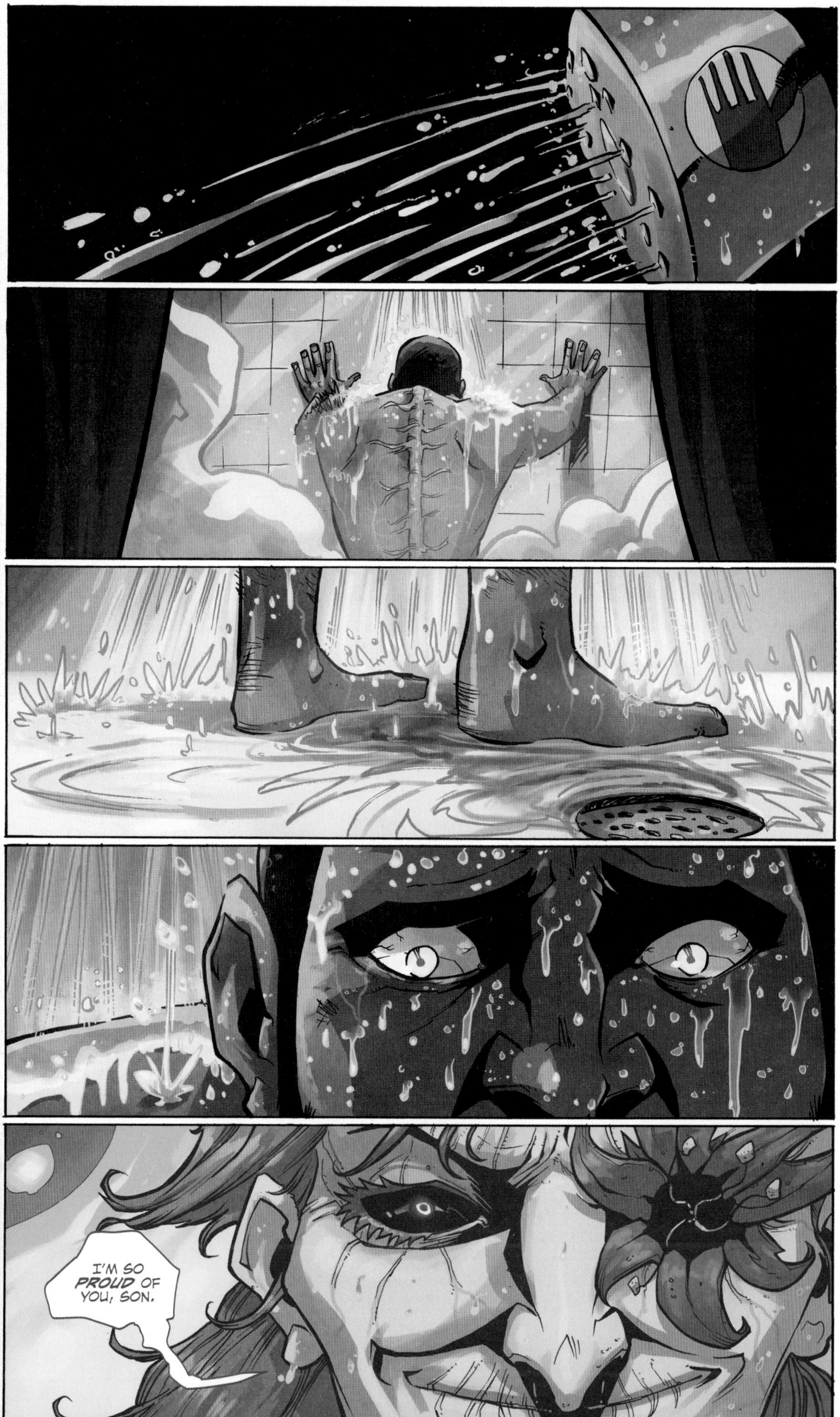
I'M SO **PROUD** OF YOU, SON.

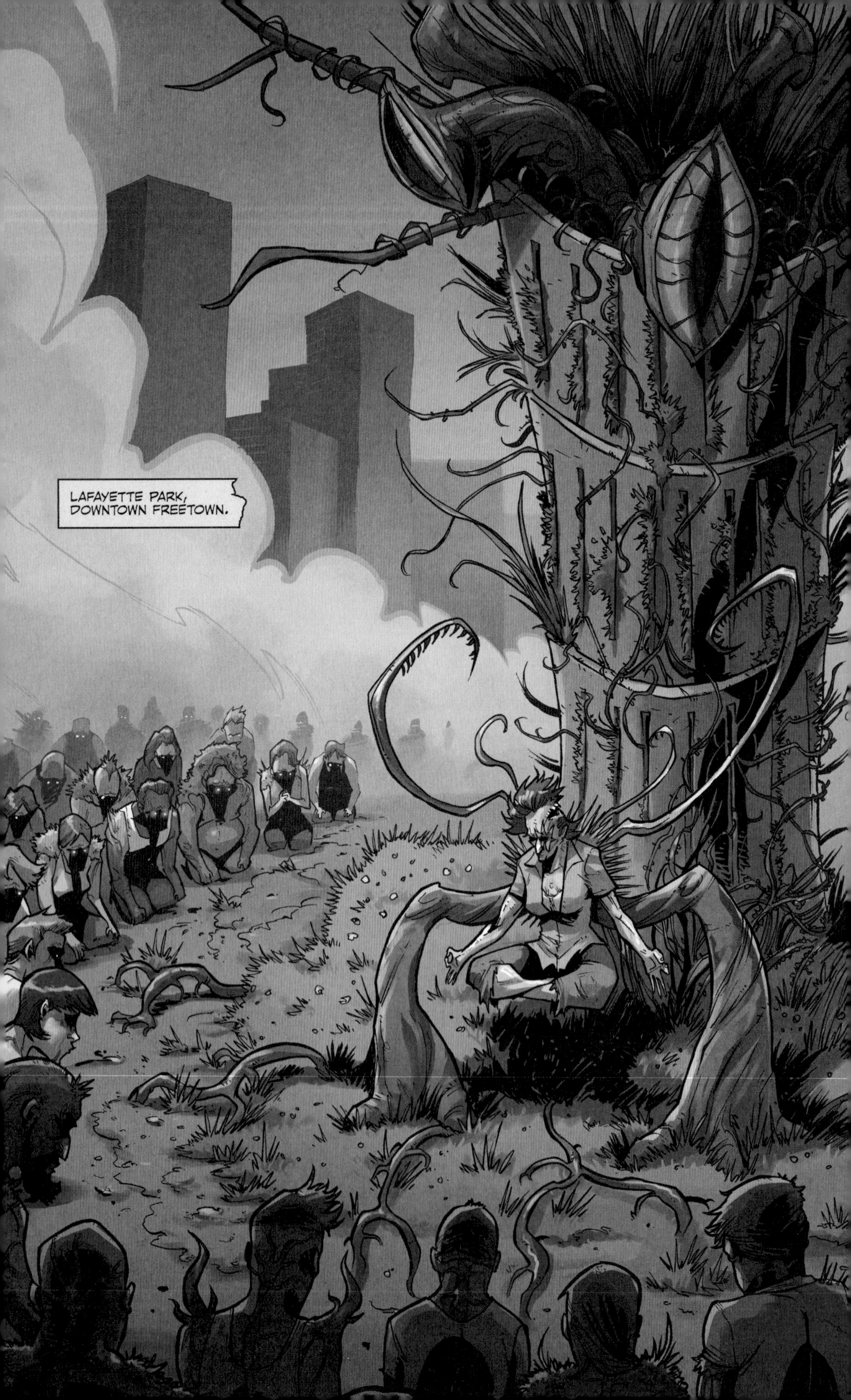
LAFAYETTE PARK, DOWNTOWN FREETOWN.

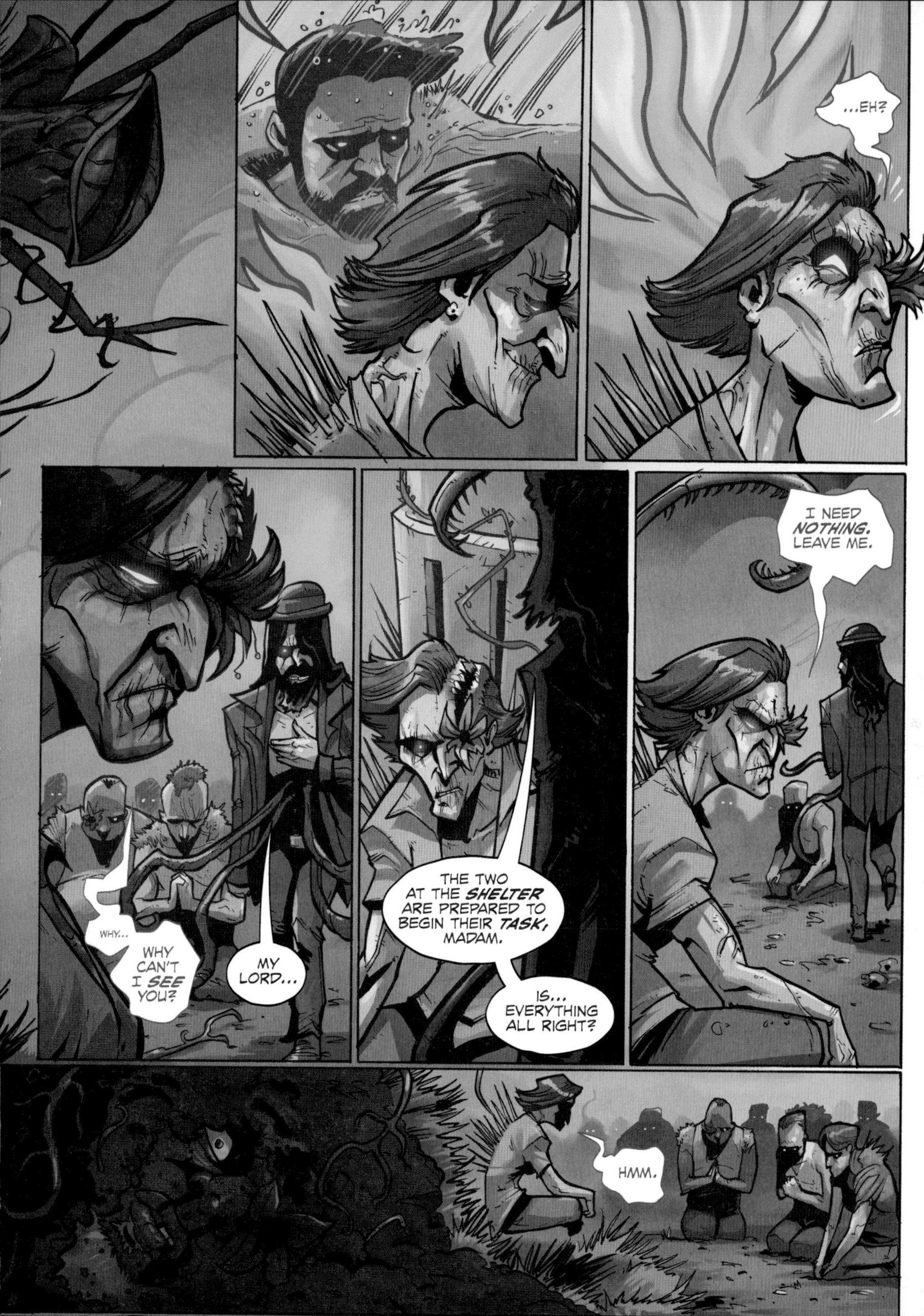

...EH?
I NEED NOTHING. LEAVE ME.
WHY...
WHY CAN'T I SEE YOU?
MY LORD...
THE TWO AT THE SHELTER ARE PREPARED TO BEGIN THEIR TASK, MADAM.
IS... EVERYTHING ALL RIGHT?
HMM.

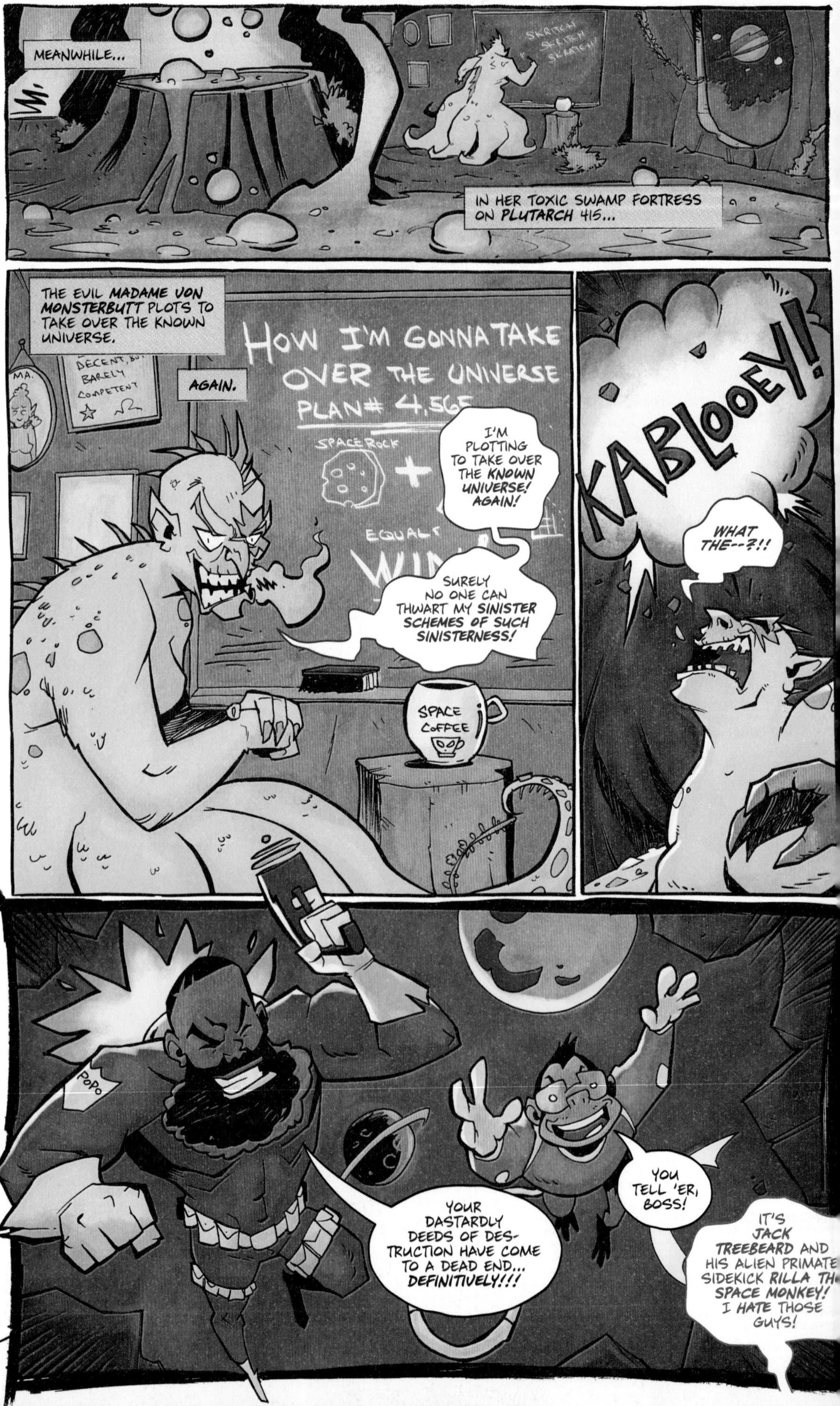

MEANWHILE...
SKRITCH SKRITCH SKRATCH
IN HER TOXIC SWAMP FORTRESS ON PLUTARCH 415...
THE EVIL MADAME VON MONSTERBUTT PLOTS TO TAKE OVER THE KNOWN UNIVERSE.
AGAIN.
DECENT, BUT BARELY COMPETENT
MA.
HOW I'M GONNA TAKE OVER THE UNIVERSE
PLAN# 4,56
SPACEROCK
EQUALS
I'M PLOTTING TO TAKE OVER THE KNOWN UNIVERSE! AGAIN!
SURELY NO ONE CAN THWART MY SINISTER SCHEMES OF SUCH SINISTERNESS!
SPACE COFFEE
KABLOOEY!
WHAT THE--?!!
POPO
YOUR DASTARDLY DEEDS OF DESTRUCTION HAVE COME TO A DEAD END... DEFINITIVELY!!!
YOU TELL 'ER, BOSS!
IT'S JACK TREEBEARD AND HIS ALIEN PRIMATE SIDEKICK RILLA TH SPACE MONKEY! I HATE THOSE GUYS!

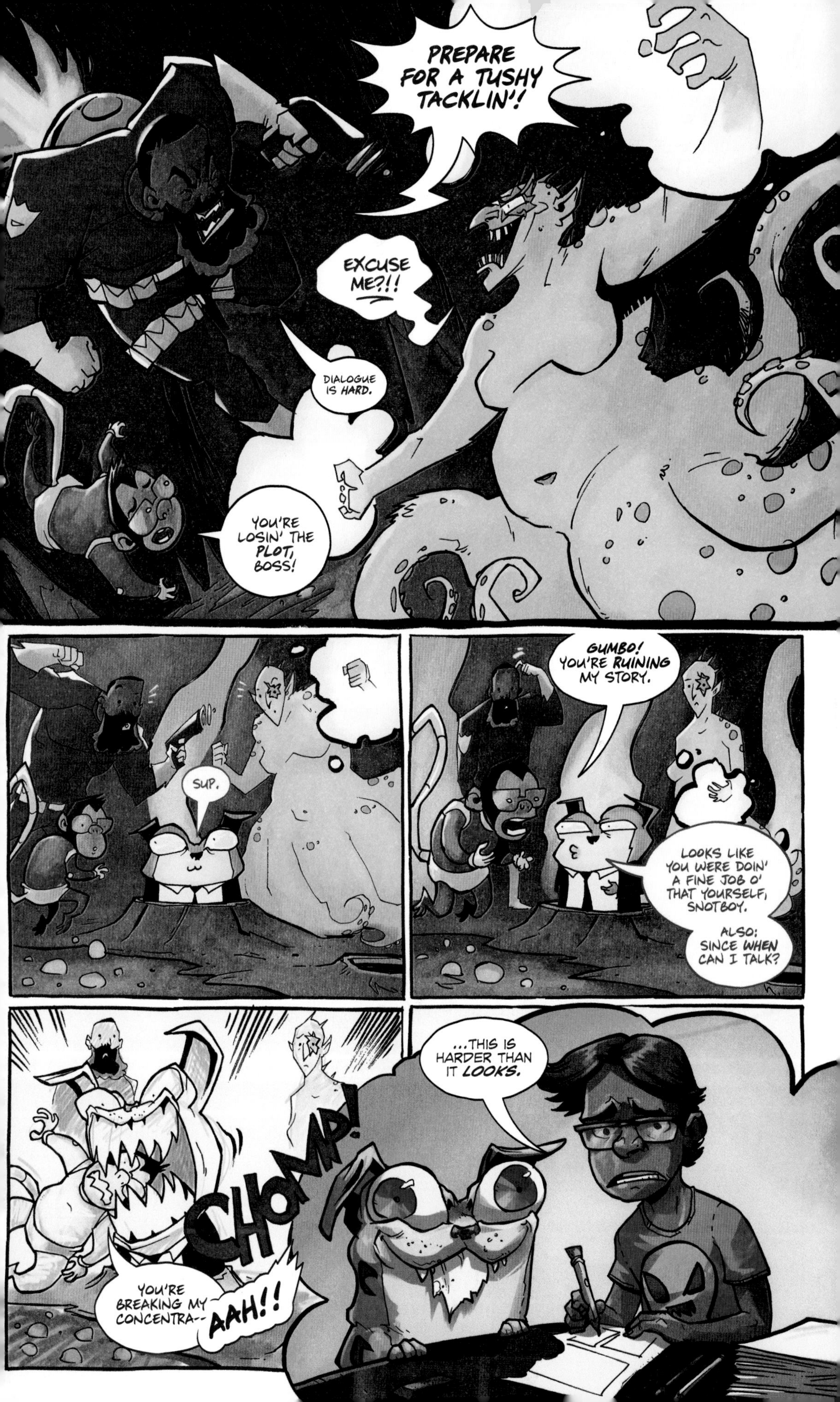
PREPARE FOR A TUSHY TACKLIN'!
EXCUSE ME?!!
DIALOGUE IS HARD.
YOU'RE LOSIN' THE PLOT, BOSS!
SUP.
GUMBO! YOU'RE RUINING MY STORY.
LOOKS LIKE YOU WERE DOIN' A FINE JOB O' THAT YOURSELF, SNOTBOY.
ALSO: SINCE WHEN CAN I TALK?
CHOMP!
YOU'RE BREAKING MY CONCENTRA--
AAH!!
...THIS IS HARDER THAN IT LOOKS.

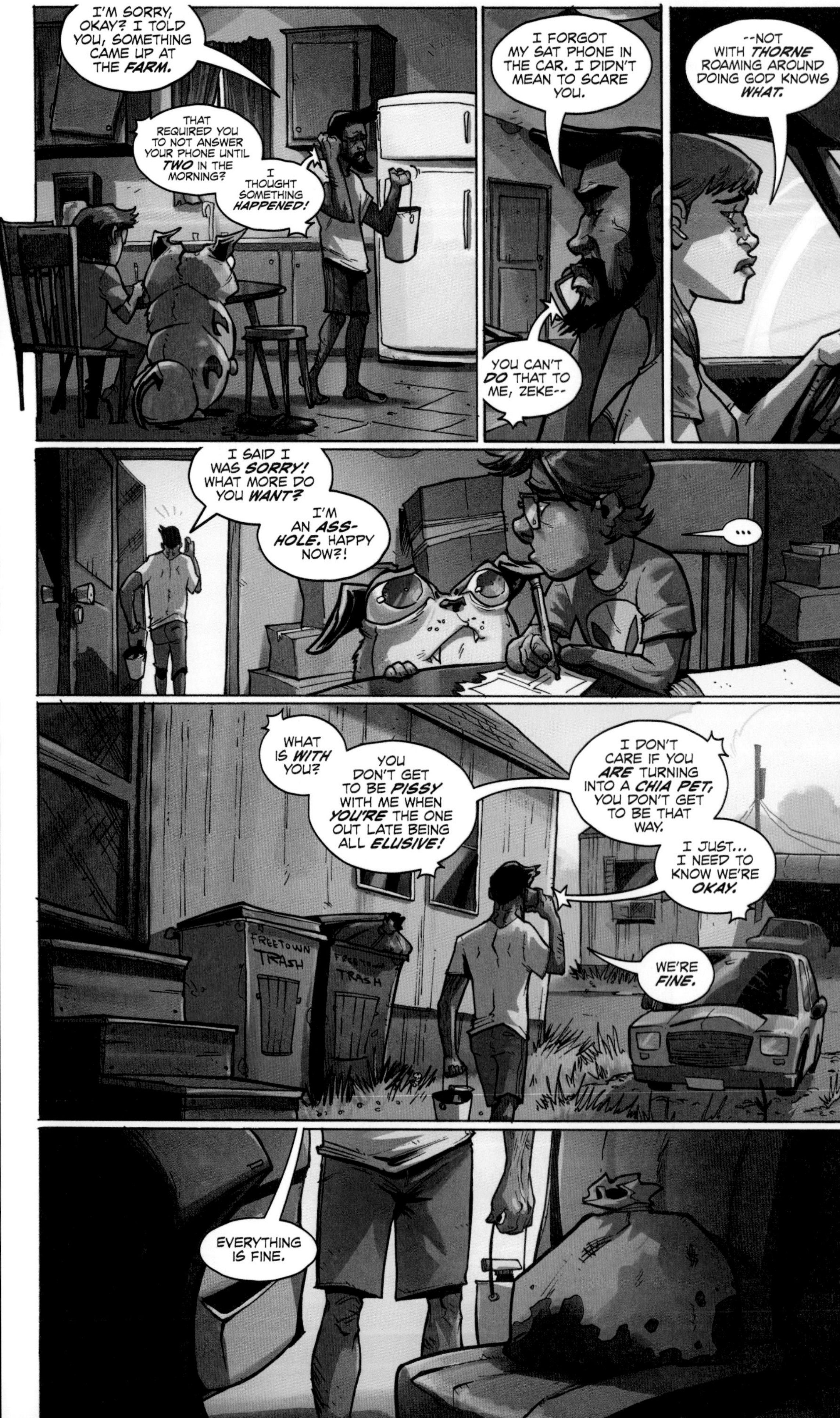
I'M SORRY, OKAY? I TOLD YOU, SOMETHING CAME UP AT THE *FARM.*
THAT REQUIRED YOU TO NOT ANSWER YOUR PHONE UNTIL *TWO* IN THE MORNING?
I THOUGHT SOMETHING *HAPPENED!*
I FORGOT MY SAT PHONE IN THE CAR. I DIDN'T MEAN TO SCARE YOU.
YOU CAN'T *DO* THAT TO ME, ZEKE--
--NOT WITH *THORNE* ROAMING AROUND DOING GOD KNOWS *WHAT.*
I SAID I WAS *SORRY!* WHAT MORE DO YOU *WANT?*
I'M AN *ASS-HOLE.* HAPPY NOW?!
...
WHAT IS *WITH* YOU?
YOU DON'T GET TO BE *PISSY* WITH ME WHEN *YOU'RE* THE ONE OUT LATE BEING ALL *ELUSIVE!*
I DON'T CARE IF YOU *ARE* TURNING INTO A *CHIA PET,* YOU DON'T GET TO BE THAT WAY.
I JUST... I NEED TO KNOW WE'RE *OKAY.*
FREETOWN TRASH
FREETOWN TRASH
WE'RE *FINE.*
EVERYTHING IS FINE.

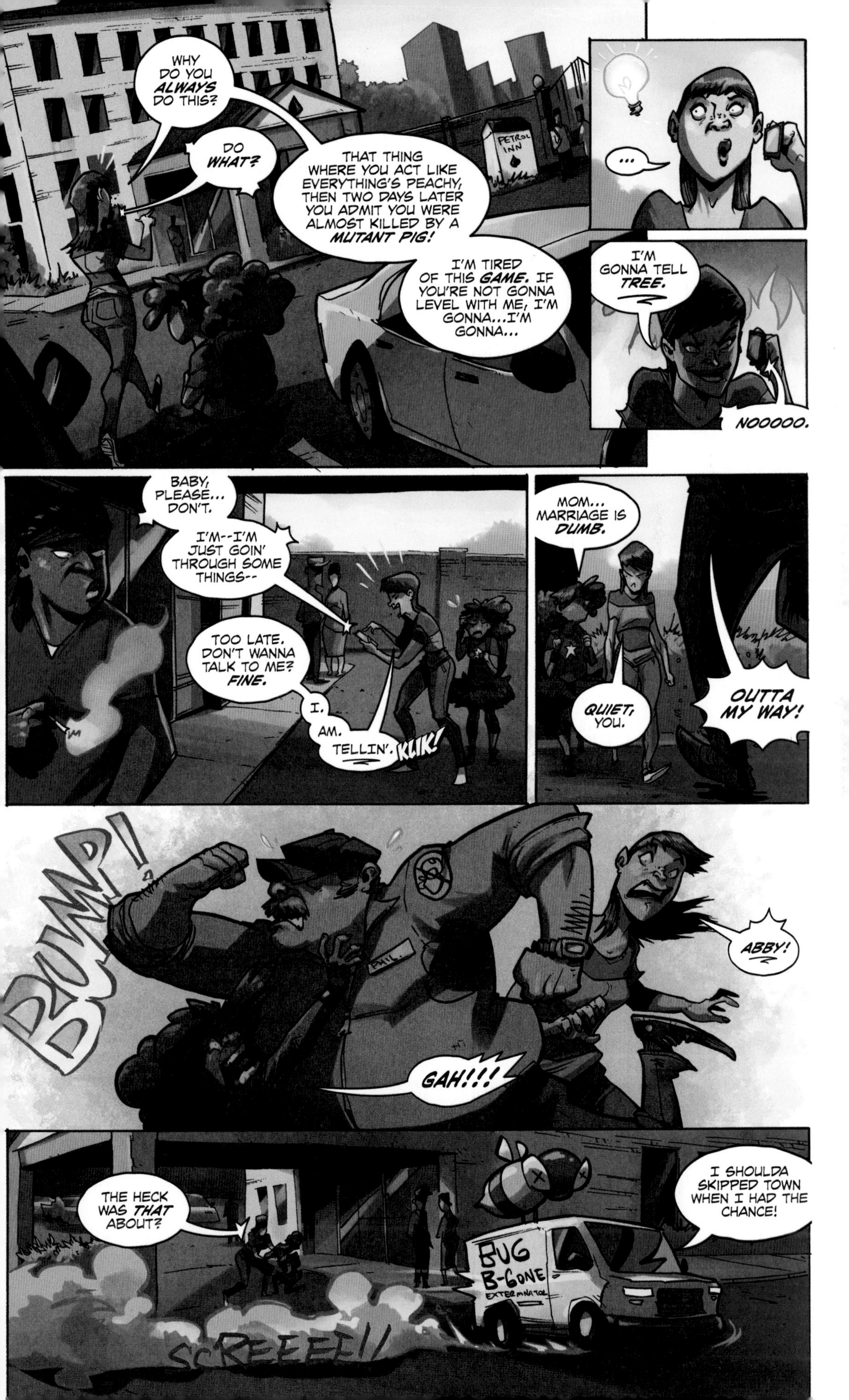
WHY DO YOU ALWAYS DO THIS?
DO WHAT?
THAT THING WHERE YOU ACT LIKE EVERYTHING'S PEACHY, THEN TWO DAYS LATER YOU ADMIT YOU WERE ALMOST KILLED BY A MUTANT PIG!
PETROL INN
I'M TIRED OF THIS GAME. IF YOU'RE NOT GONNA LEVEL WITH ME, I'M GONNA...I'M GONNA...
...
I'M GONNA TELL TREE.
NOOOOO.
BABY, PLEASE... DON'T.
I'M--I'M JUST GOIN' THROUGH SOME THINGS--
TOO LATE. DON'T WANNA TALK TO ME? FINE.
I.
AM.
TELLIN'.
KLIK!
MOM... MARRIAGE IS DUMB.
QUIET, YOU.
OUTTA MY WAY!
BUMP!
ABBY!
GAH!!!
THE HECK WAS THAT ABOUT?
I SHOULDA SKIPPED TOWN WHEN I HAD THE CHANCE!
BUG B-GONE EXTERMINATOR
SCREEEE!!

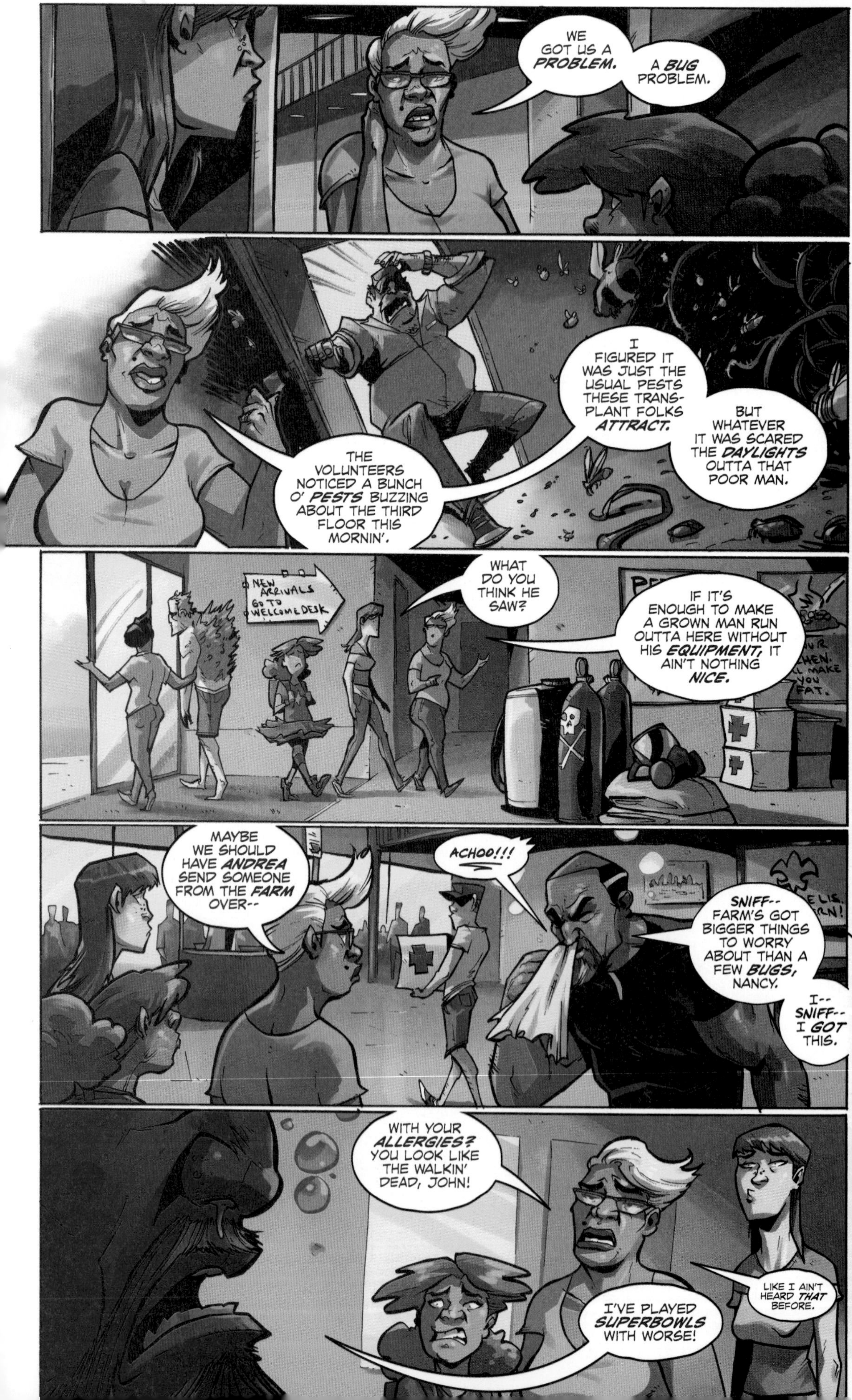

WE GOT US A PROBLEM.
A BUG PROBLEM.
THE VOLUNTEERS NOTICED A BUNCH O' PESTS BUZZING ABOUT THE THIRD FLOOR THIS MORNIN'.
I FIGURED IT WAS JUST THE USUAL PESTS THESE TRANS-PLANT FOLKS ATTRACT.
BUT WHATEVER IT WAS SCARED THE DAYLIGHTS OUTTA THAT POOR MAN.
NEW ARRIVALS GO TO WELCOME DESK
WHAT DO YOU THINK HE SAW?
IF IT'S ENOUGH TO MAKE A GROWN MAN RUN OUTTA HERE WITHOUT HIS EQUIPMENT, IT AIN'T NOTHING NICE.
MAYBE WE SHOULD HAVE ANDREA SEND SOMEONE FROM THE FARM OVER--
ACHOO!!!
SNIFF-- FARM'S GOT BIGGER THINGS TO WORRY ABOUT THAN A FEW BUGS, NANCY.
I-- SNIFF-- I GOT THIS.
WITH YOUR ALLERGIES? YOU LOOK LIKE THE WALKIN' DEAD, JOHN!
I'VE PLAYED SUPERBOWLS WITH WORSE!
LIKE I AIN'T HEARD THAT BEFORE.

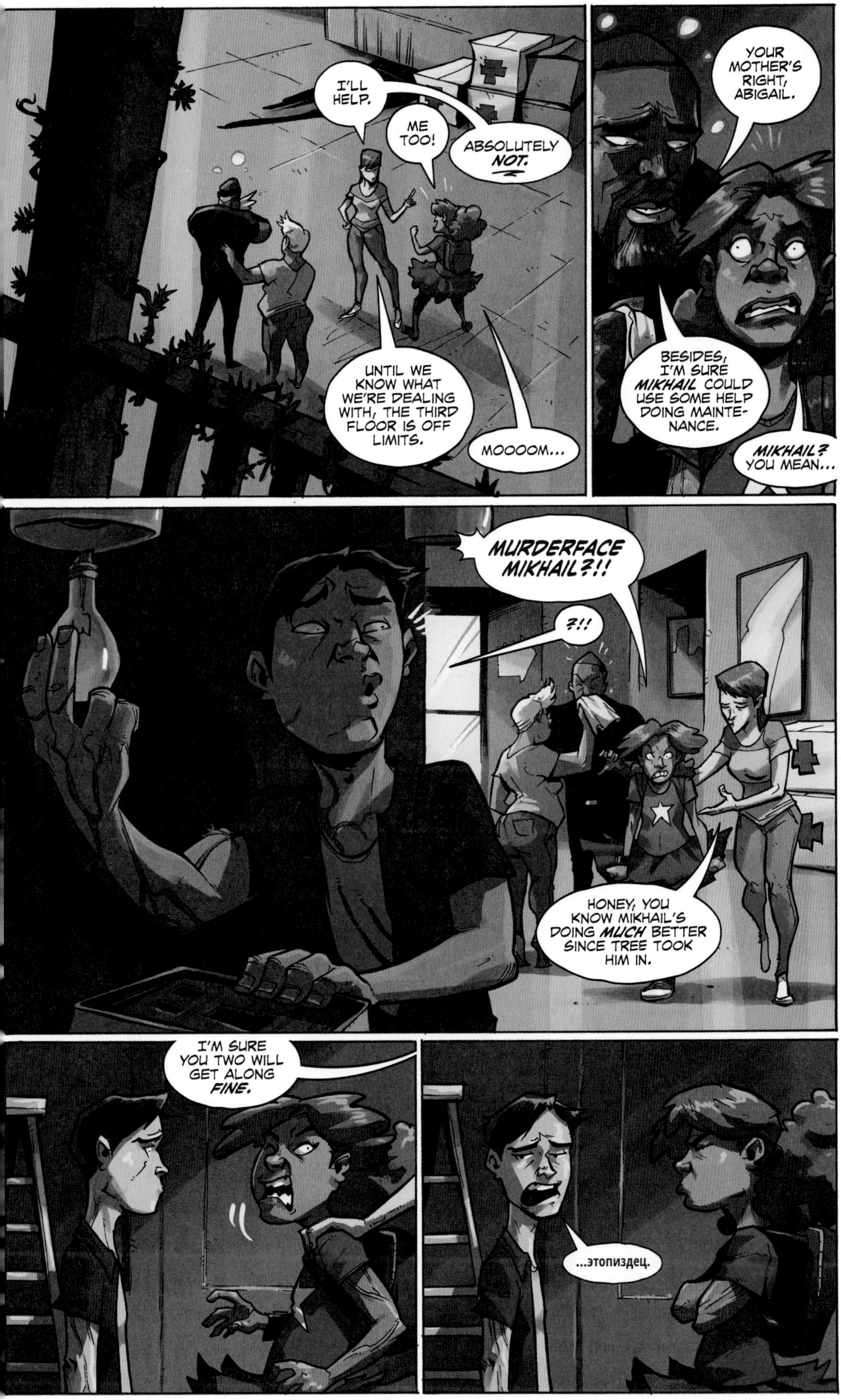
I'LL HELP.
ME TOO!
ABSOLUTELY NOT.
UNTIL WE KNOW WHAT WE'RE DEALING WITH, THE THIRD FLOOR IS OFF LIMITS.
MOOOOM...
YOUR MOTHER'S RIGHT, ABIGAIL.
BESIDES, I'M SURE MIKHAIL COULD USE SOME HELP DOING MAINTE-NANCE.
MIKHAIL? YOU MEAN...
MURDERFACE MIKHAIL?!!
?!!
HONEY, YOU KNOW MIKHAIL'S DOING MUCH BETTER SINCE TREE TOOK HIM IN.
I'M SURE YOU TWO WILL GET ALONG FINE.
...этопиздец.

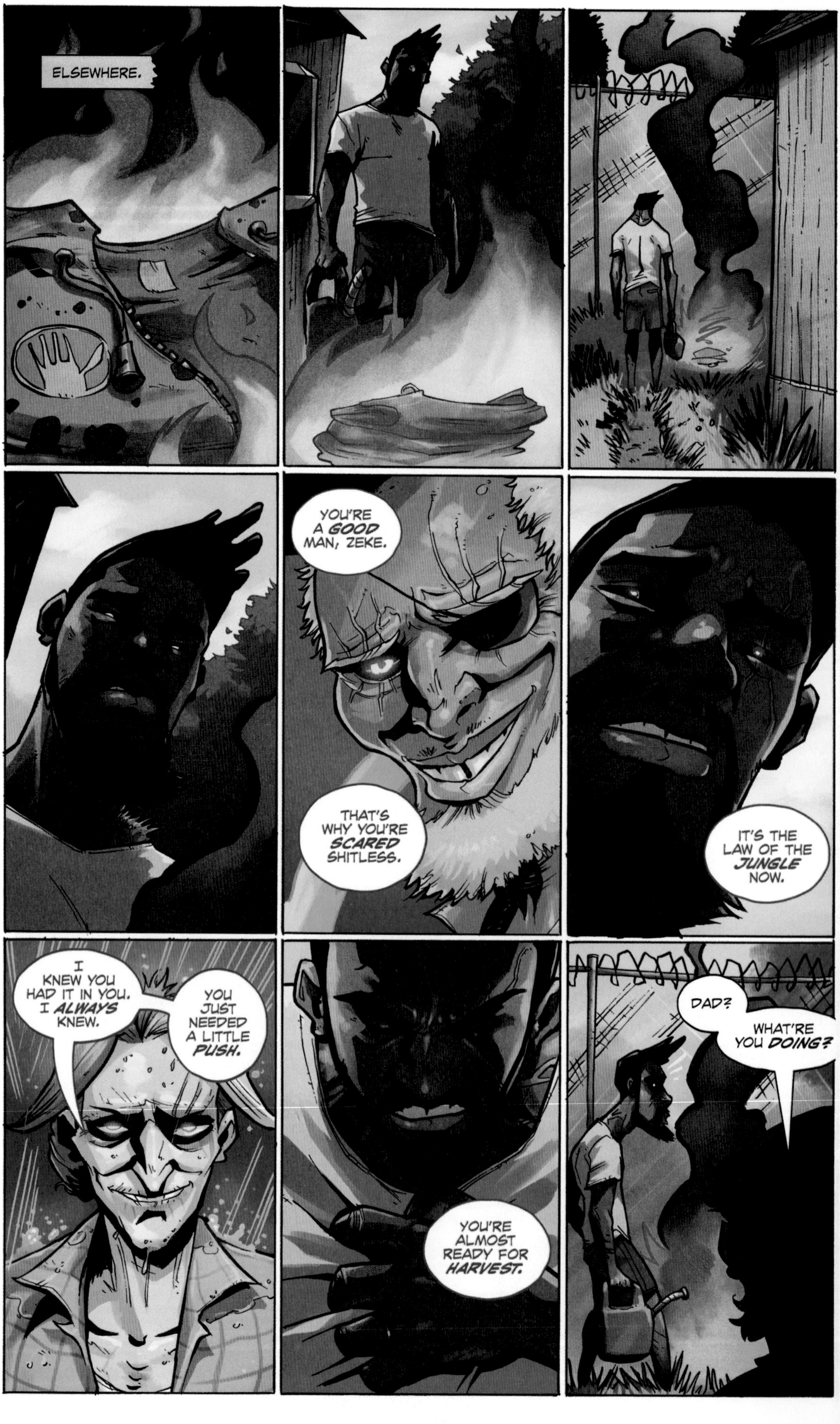
ELSEWHERE.
YOU'RE A GOOD MAN, ZEKE.
THAT'S WHY YOU'RE SCARED SHITLESS.
IT'S THE LAW OF THE JUNGLE NOW.
I KNEW YOU HAD IT IN YOU. I ALWAYS KNEW.
YOU JUST NEEDED A LITTLE PUSH.
YOU'RE ALMOST READY FOR HARVEST.
DAD?
WHAT'RE YOU DOING?

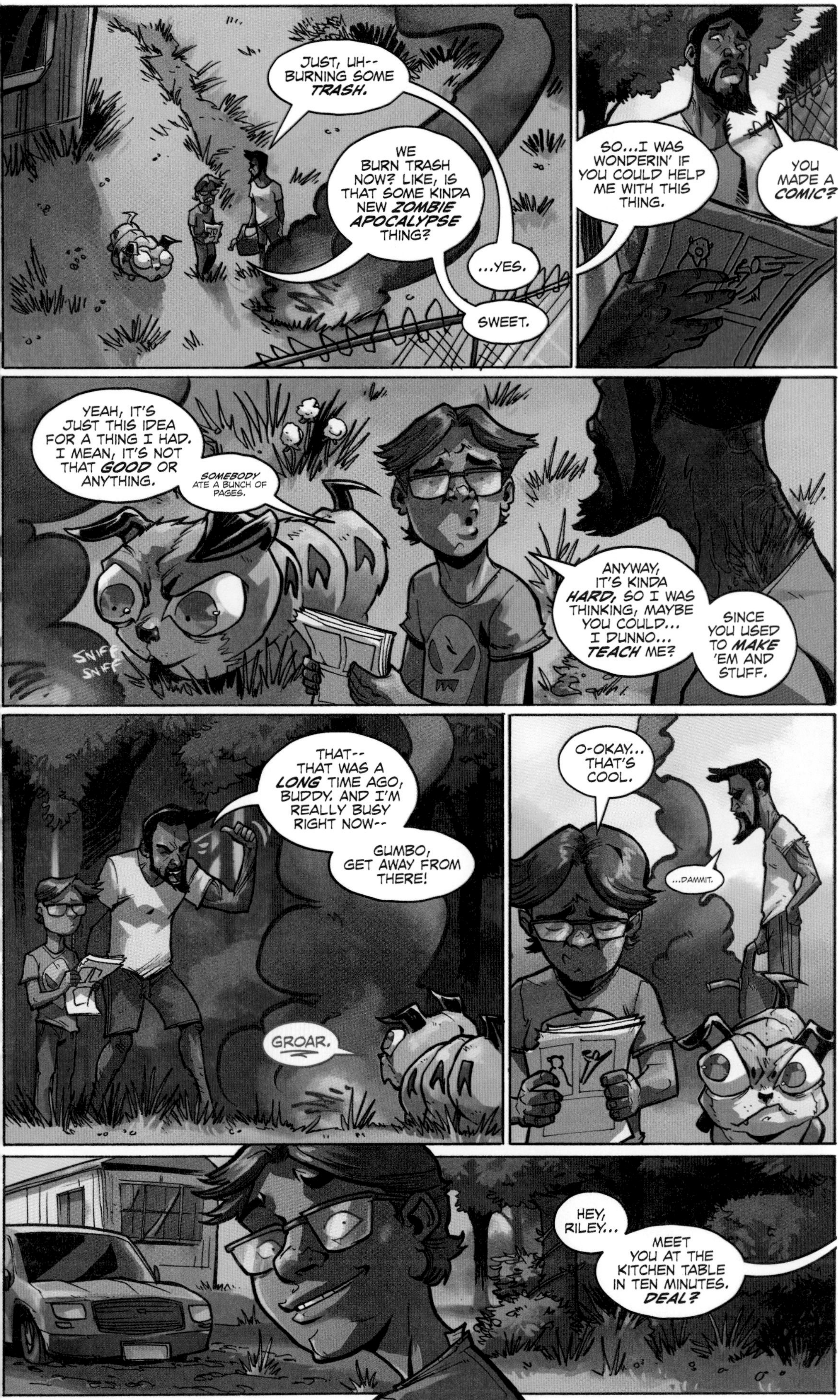
JUST, UH-- BURNING SOME *TRASH.*
WE BURN TRASH NOW? LIKE, IS THAT SOME KINDA NEW *ZOMBIE APOCALYPSE* THING?
...YES.
SWEET.
SO...I WAS WONDERIN' IF YOU COULD HELP ME WITH THIS THING.
YOU MADE A *COMIC?*
YEAH, IT'S JUST THIS IDEA FOR A THING I HAD. I MEAN, IT'S NOT THAT *GOOD* OR ANYTHING.
SOMEBODY ATE A BUNCH OF PAGES.
SNIFF SNIFF
ANYWAY, IT'S KINDA *HARD,* SO I WAS THINKING, MAYBE YOU COULD... I DUNNO... *TEACH* ME?
SINCE YOU USED TO *MAKE* 'EM AND STUFF.
THAT-- THAT WAS A *LONG* TIME AGO, BUDDY. AND I'M REALLY BUSY RIGHT NOW--
GUMBO, GET AWAY FROM THERE!
GROAR.
O-OKAY... THAT'S COOL.
...DAMMIT.
HEY, RILEY...
MEET YOU AT THE KITCHEN TABLE IN TEN MINUTES. *DEAL?*

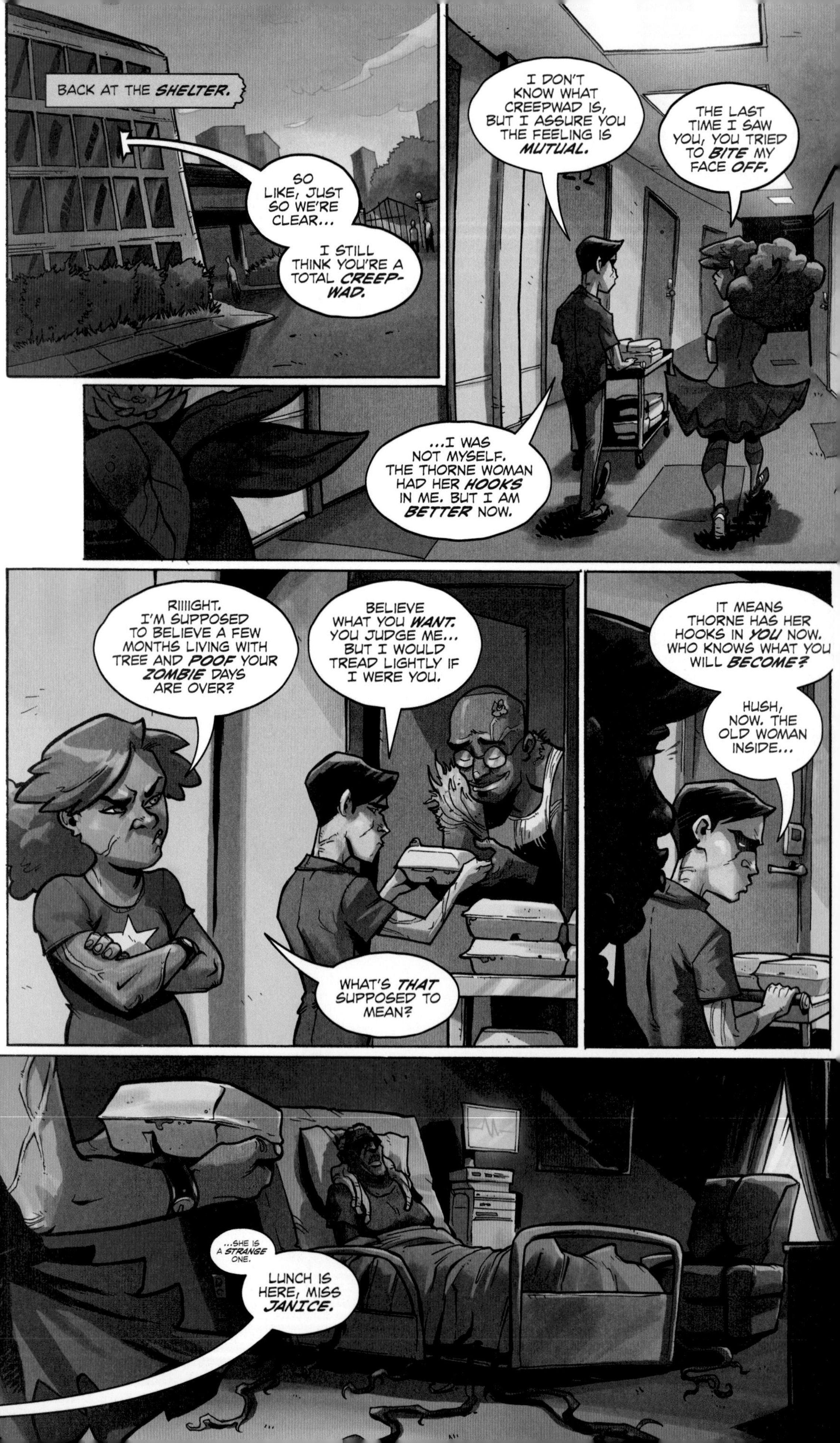
BACK AT THE SHELTER.
SO LIKE, JUST SO WE'RE CLEAR...
I STILL THINK YOU'RE A TOTAL CREEP-WAD.
I DON'T KNOW WHAT CREEPWAD IS, BUT I ASSURE YOU THE FEELING IS MUTUAL.
THE LAST TIME I SAW YOU, YOU TRIED TO BITE MY FACE OFF.
...I WAS NOT MYSELF. THE THORNE WOMAN HAD HER HOOKS IN ME. BUT I AM BETTER NOW.
RIIIIGHT. I'M SUPPOSED TO BELIEVE A FEW MONTHS LIVING WITH TREE AND POOF YOUR ZOMBIE DAYS ARE OVER?
BELIEVE WHAT YOU WANT. YOU JUDGE ME... BUT I WOULD TREAD LIGHTLY IF I WERE YOU.
WHAT'S THAT SUPPOSED TO MEAN?
IT MEANS THORNE HAS HER HOOKS IN YOU NOW. WHO KNOWS WHAT YOU WILL BECOME?
HUSH, NOW. THE OLD WOMAN INSIDE...
...SHE IS A STRANGE ONE.
LUNCH IS HERE, MISS JANICE.

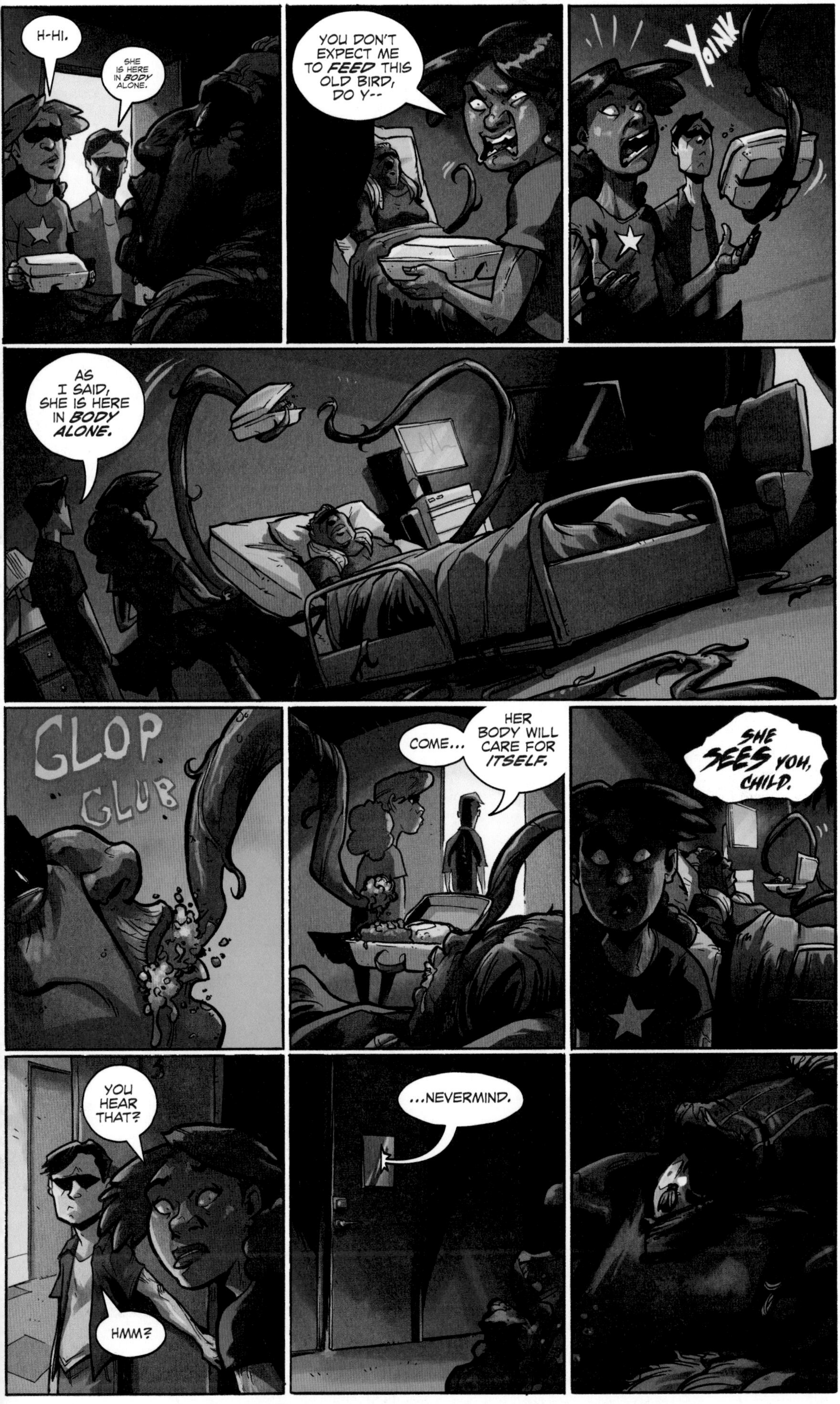
H-HI.
SHE IS HERE IN BODY ALONE.
YOU DON'T EXPECT ME TO FEED THIS OLD BIRD, DO Y--
YOINK
AS I SAID, SHE IS HERE IN BODY ALONE.
GLOP
GLUB
COME...
HER BODY WILL CARE FOR ITSELF.
SHE SEES YOU, CHILD.
YOU HEAR THAT?
HMM?
...NEVERMIND.

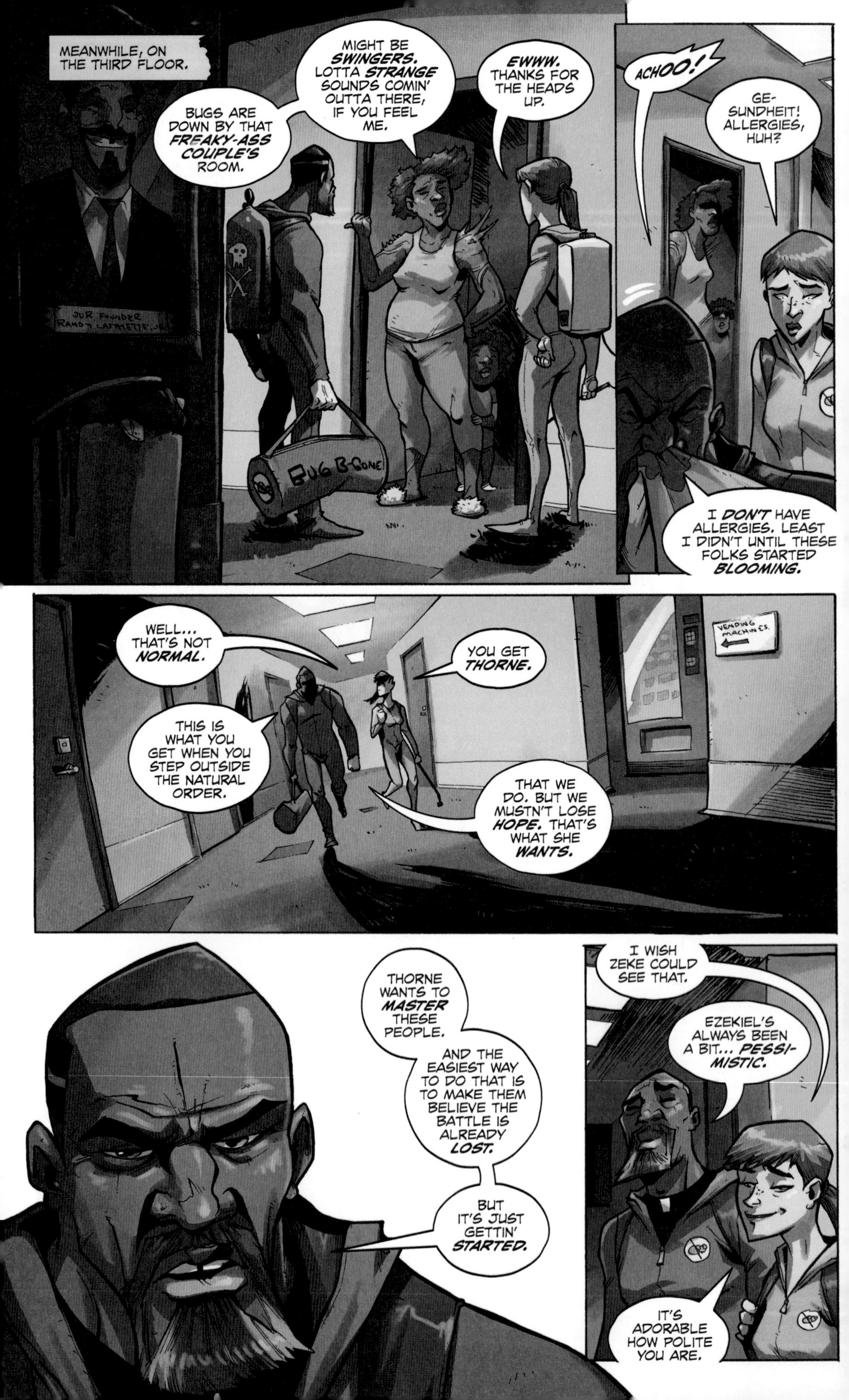
MEANWHILE, ON THE THIRD FLOOR.
BUGS ARE DOWN BY THAT FREAKY-ASS COUPLE'S ROOM.
MIGHT BE SWINGERS. LOTTA STRANGE SOUNDS COMIN' OUTTA THERE, IF YOU FEEL ME.
EWWW. THANKS FOR THE HEADS UP.
BUG B-GONE
ACHOO!
GE-SUNDHEIT! ALLERGIES, HUH?
I DON'T HAVE ALLERGIES. LEAST I DIDN'T UNTIL THESE FOLKS STARTED BLOOMING.
WELL... THAT'S NOT NORMAL.
YOU GET THORNE.
VENDING MACHINES
THIS IS WHAT YOU GET WHEN YOU STEP OUTSIDE THE NATURAL ORDER.
THAT WE DO. BUT WE MUSTN'T LOSE HOPE. THAT'S WHAT SHE WANTS.
THORNE WANTS TO MASTER THESE PEOPLE.
AND THE EASIEST WAY TO DO THAT IS TO MAKE THEM BELIEVE THE BATTLE IS ALREADY LOST.
BUT IT'S JUST GETTIN' STARTED.
I WISH ZEKE COULD SEE THAT.
EZEKIEL'S ALWAYS BEEN A BIT... PESSI-MISTIC.
IT'S ADORABLE HOW POLITE YOU ARE.

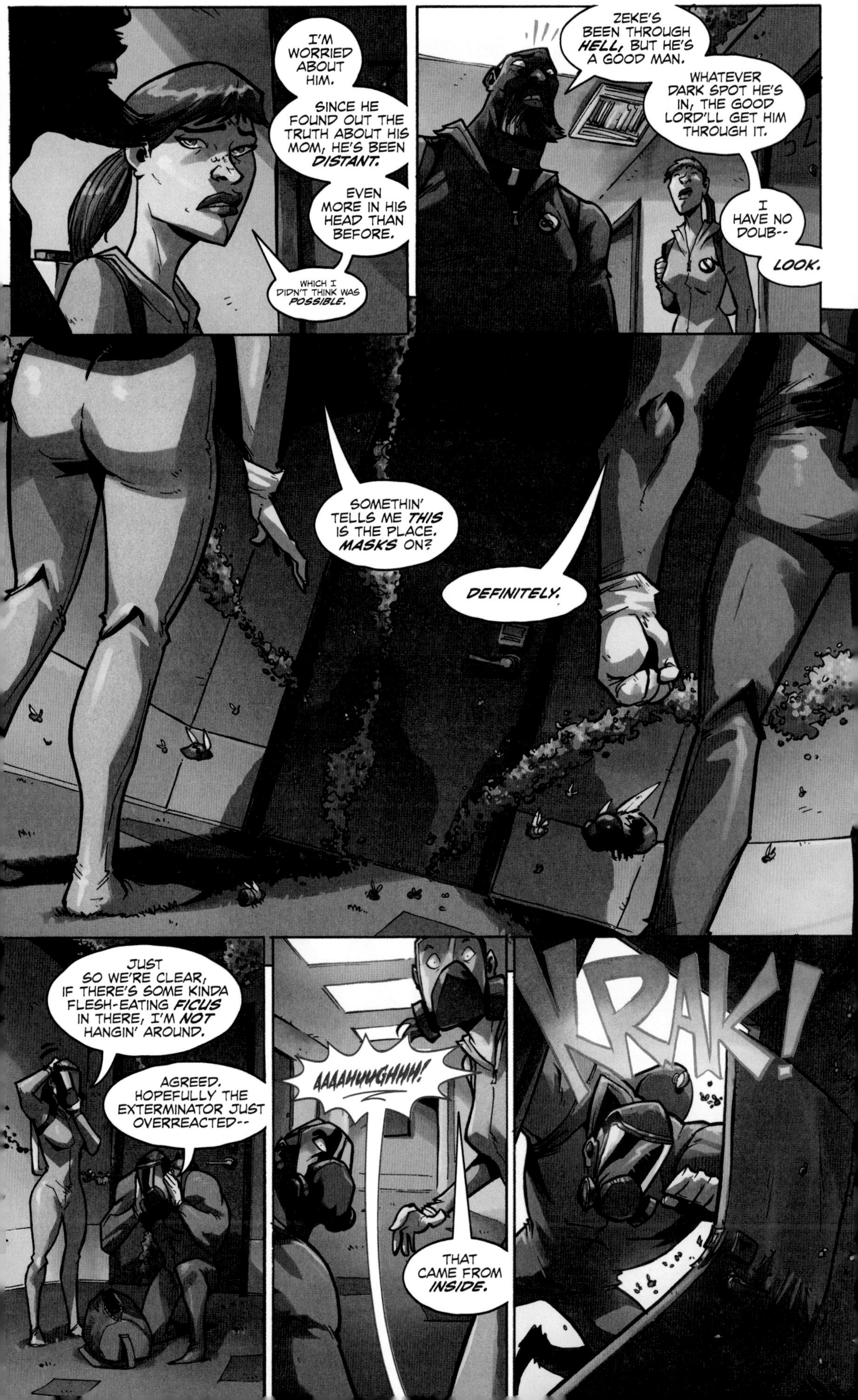
I'M WORRIED ABOUT HIM.
SINCE HE FOUND OUT THE TRUTH ABOUT HIS MOM, HE'S BEEN DISTANT.
EVEN MORE IN HIS HEAD THAN BEFORE.
WHICH I DIDN'T THINK WAS POSSIBLE.
ZEKE'S BEEN THROUGH HELL, BUT HE'S A GOOD MAN.
WHATEVER DARK SPOT HE'S IN, THE GOOD LORD'LL GET HIM THROUGH IT.
I HAVE NO DOUB--
LOOK.
SOMETHIN' TELLS ME THIS IS THE PLACE. MASKS ON?
DEFINITELY.
JUST SO WE'RE CLEAR, IF THERE'S SOME KINDA FLESH-EATING FICUS IN THERE, I'M NOT HANGIN' AROUND.
AGREED. HOPEFULLY THE EXTERMINATOR JUST OVERREACTED--
AAAAHUUGHHH!
THAT CAME FROM INSIDE.
KRAK!

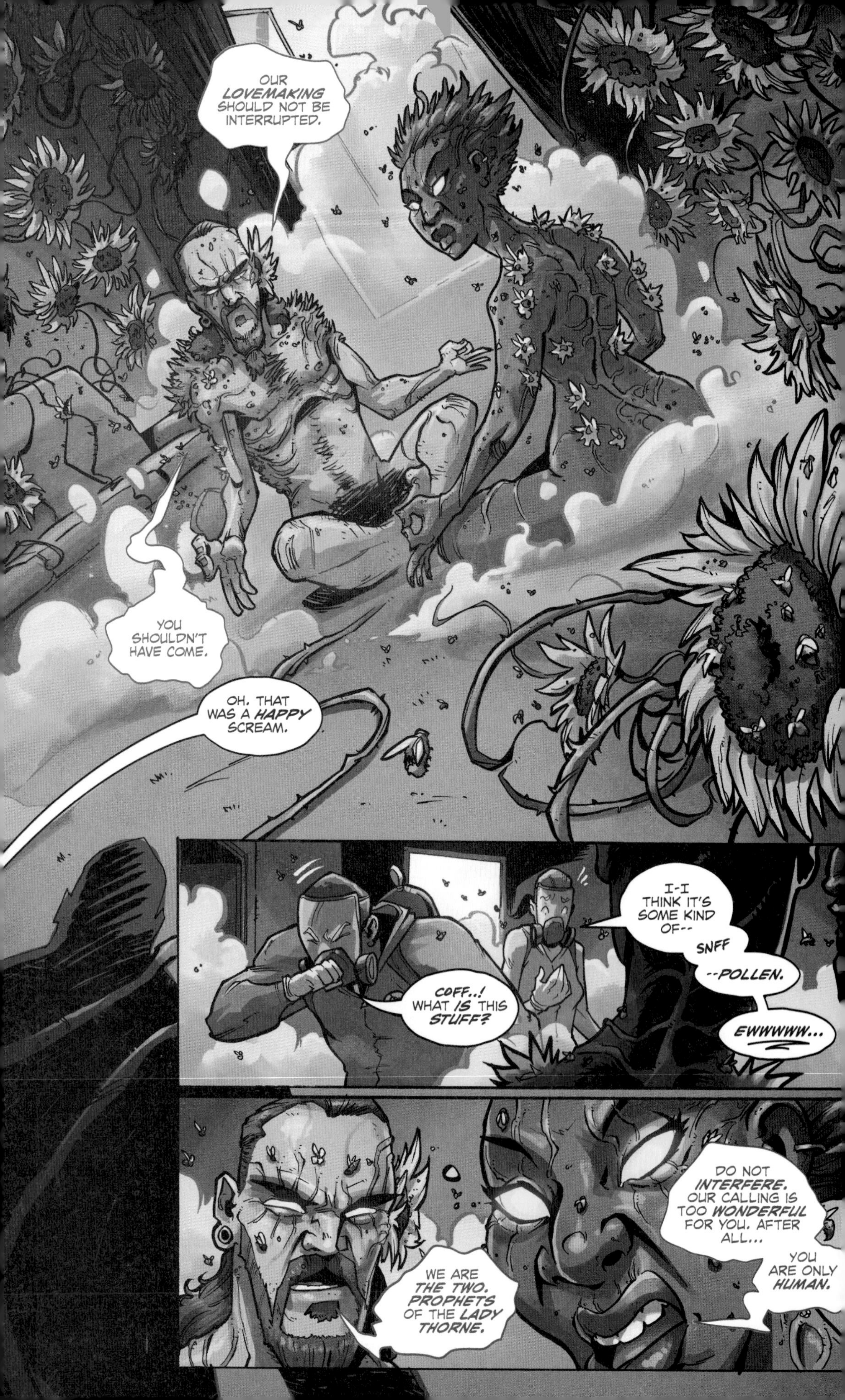
OUR LOVEMAKING SHOULD NOT BE INTERRUPTED.
YOU SHOULDN'T HAVE COME.
OH. THAT WAS A HAPPY SCREAM.
COFF..! WHAT IS THIS STUFF?
I-I THINK IT'S SOME KIND OF--
SNFF
--POLLEN.
EWWWWW...
WE ARE THE TWO. PROPHETS OF THE LADY THORNE.
DO NOT INTERFERE. OUR CALLING IS TOO WONDERFUL FOR YOU. AFTER ALL...
YOU ARE ONLY HUMAN.

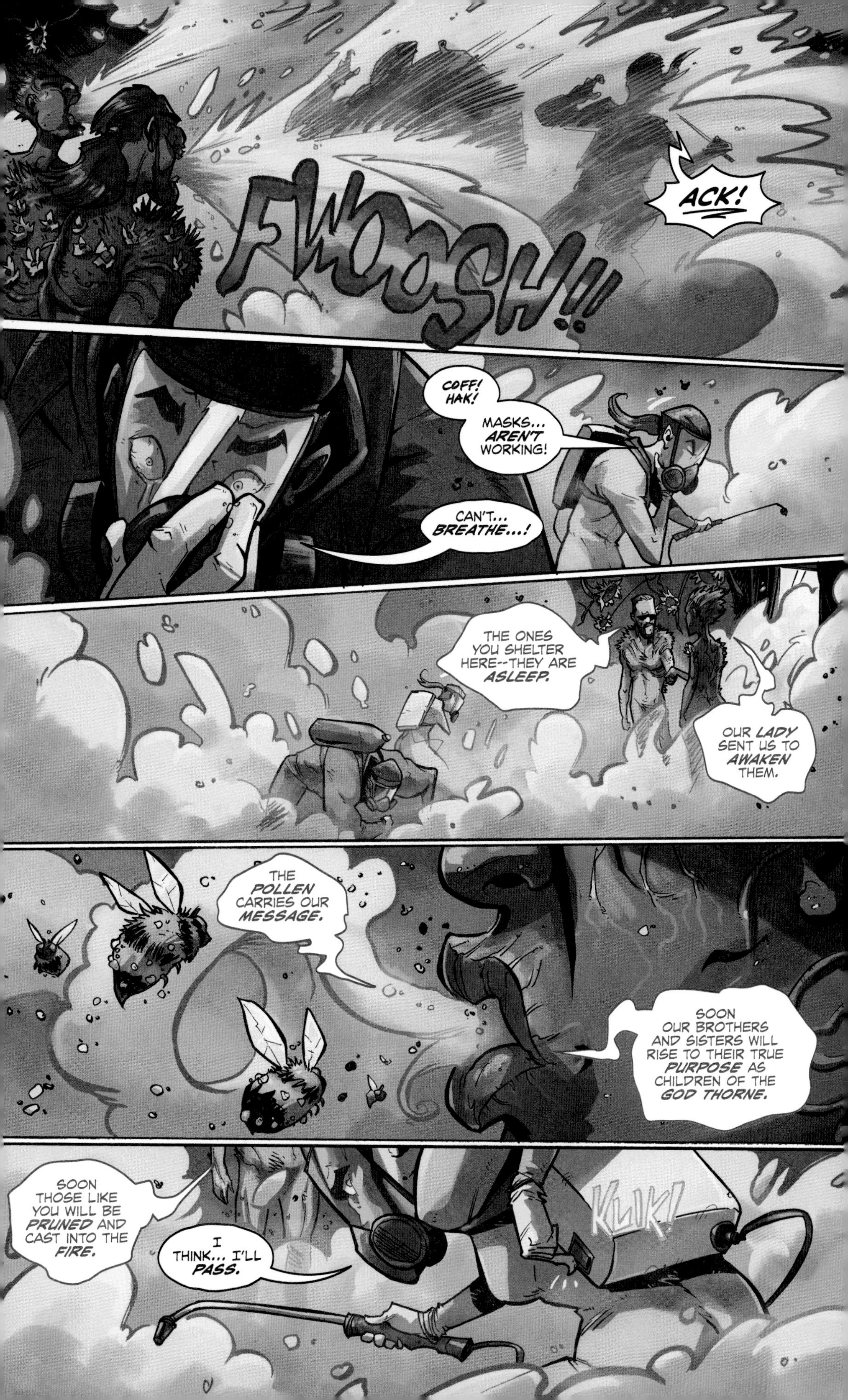
FWOOSH!!!
ACK!
COFF! HAK!
MASKS... AREN'T WORKING!
CAN'T... BREATHE...!
THE ONES YOU SHELTER HERE--THEY ARE ASLEEP.
OUR LADY SENT US TO AWAKEN THEM.
THE POLLEN CARRIES OUR MESSAGE.
SOON OUR BROTHERS AND SISTERS WILL RISE TO THEIR TRUE PURPOSE AS CHILDREN OF THE GOD THORNE.
SOON THOSE LIKE YOU WILL BE PRUNED AND CAST INTO THE FIRE.
I THINK... I'LL PASS.
KLIK!

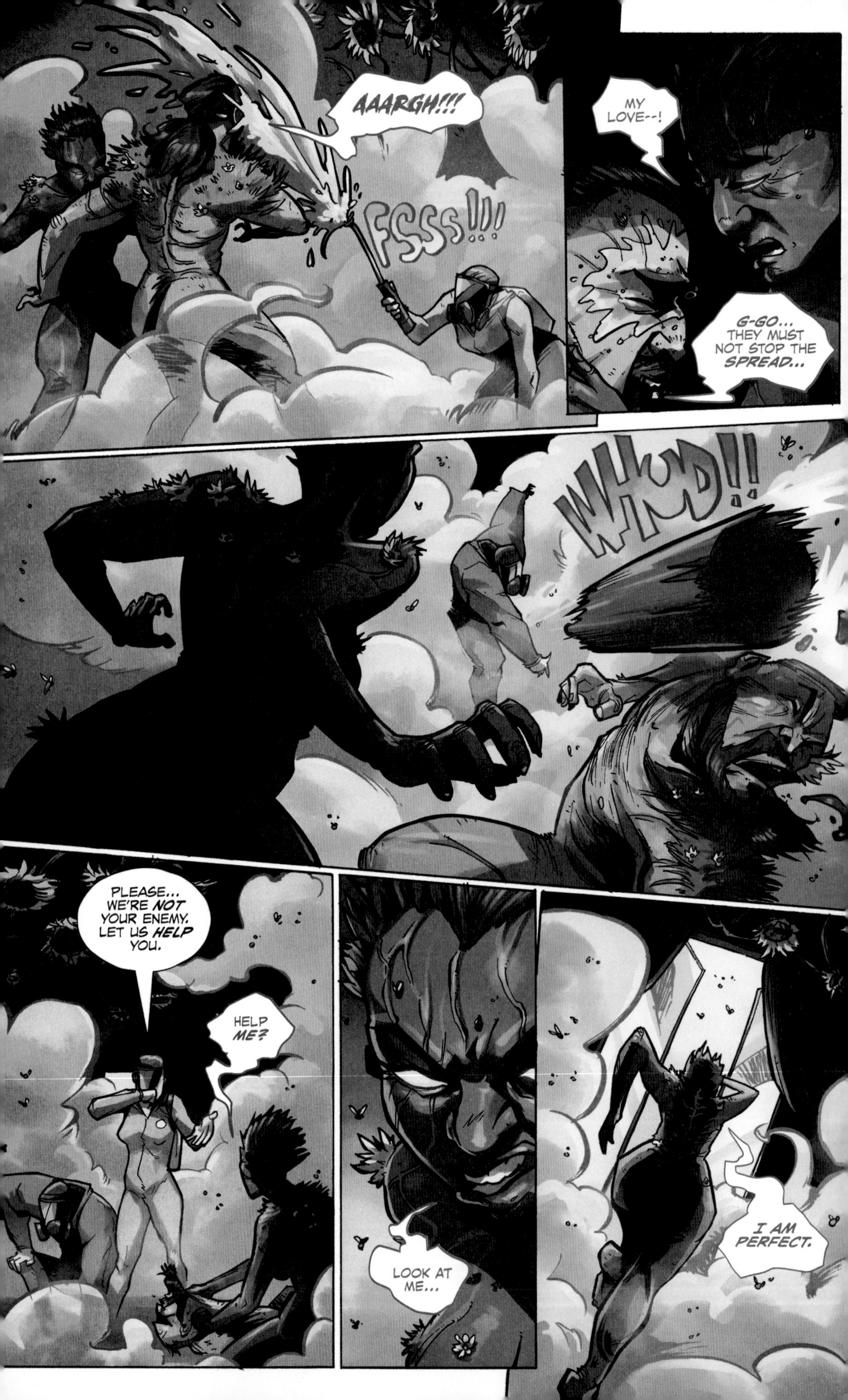
AAARGH!!!
FSSS!!!
MY LOVE--!
G-GO... THEY MUST NOT STOP THE SPREAD...
WHUD!!
PLEASE... WE'RE NOT YOUR ENEMY. LET US HELP YOU.
HELP ME?
LOOK AT ME...
I AM PERFECT.

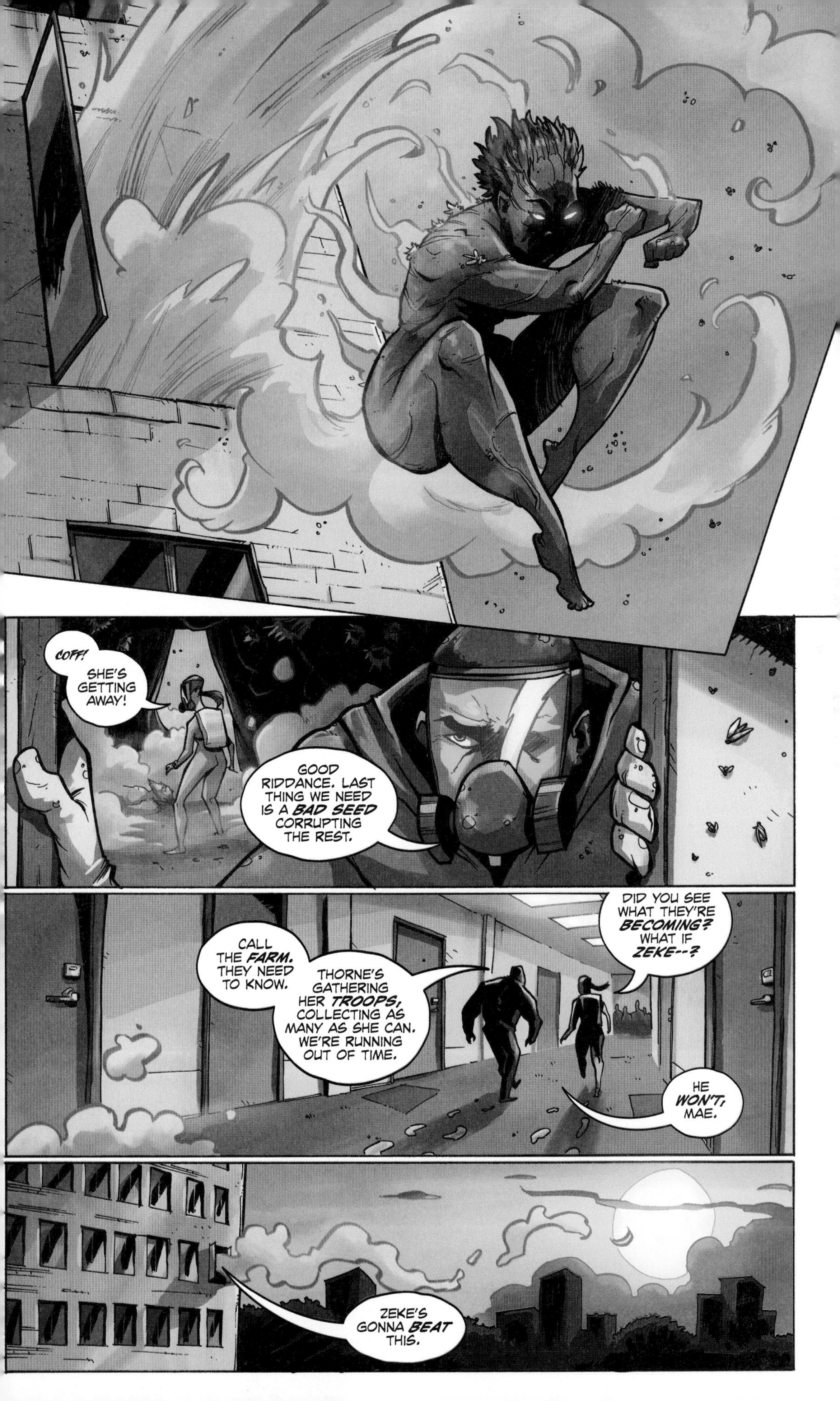
COFF!
SHE'S GETTING AWAY!
GOOD RIDDANCE. LAST THING WE NEED IS A BAD SEED CORRUPTING THE REST.
CALL THE FARM. THEY NEED TO KNOW.
THORNE'S GATHERING HER TROOPS, COLLECTING AS MANY AS SHE CAN. WE'RE RUNNING OUT OF TIME.
DID YOU SEE WHAT THEY'RE BECOMING? WHAT IF ZEKE--?
HE WON'T, MAE.
ZEKE'S GONNA BEAT THIS.

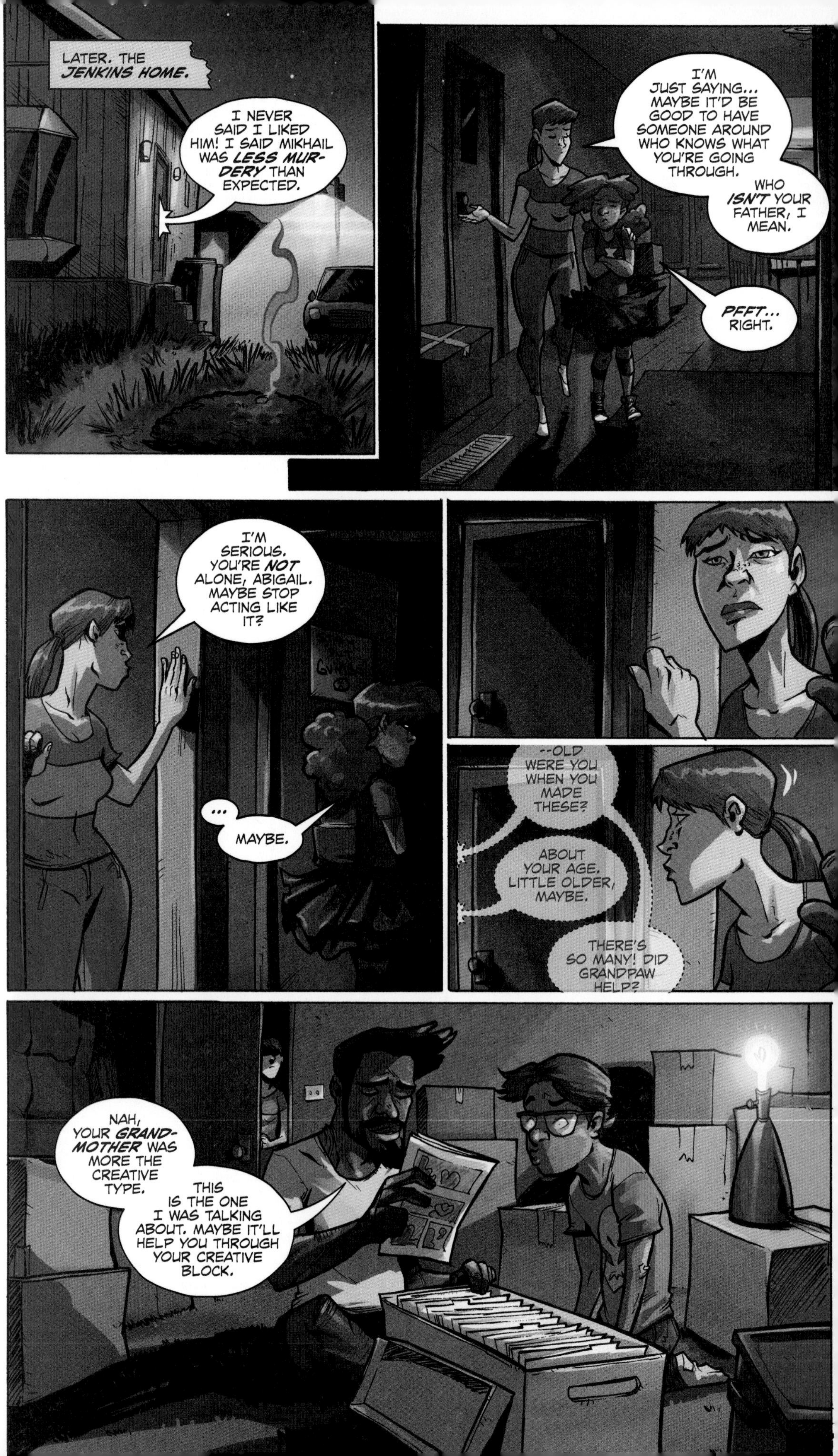
LATER. THE JENKINS HOME.
I NEVER SAID I LIKED HIM! I SAID MIKHAIL WAS LESS MURDERY THAN EXPECTED.
I'M JUST SAYING... MAYBE IT'D BE GOOD TO HAVE SOMEONE AROUND WHO KNOWS WHAT YOU'RE GOING THROUGH.
WHO ISN'T YOUR FATHER, I MEAN.
PFFT... RIGHT.
I'M SERIOUS. YOU'RE NOT ALONE, ABIGAIL. MAYBE STOP ACTING LIKE IT?
... MAYBE.
--OLD WERE YOU WHEN YOU MADE THESE?
ABOUT YOUR AGE. LITTLE OLDER, MAYBE.
THERE'S SO MANY! DID GRANDPAW HELP?
NAH, YOUR GRANDMOTHER WAS MORE THE CREATIVE TYPE.
THIS IS THE ONE I WAS TALKING ABOUT. MAYBE IT'LL HELP YOU THROUGH YOUR CREATIVE BLOCK.

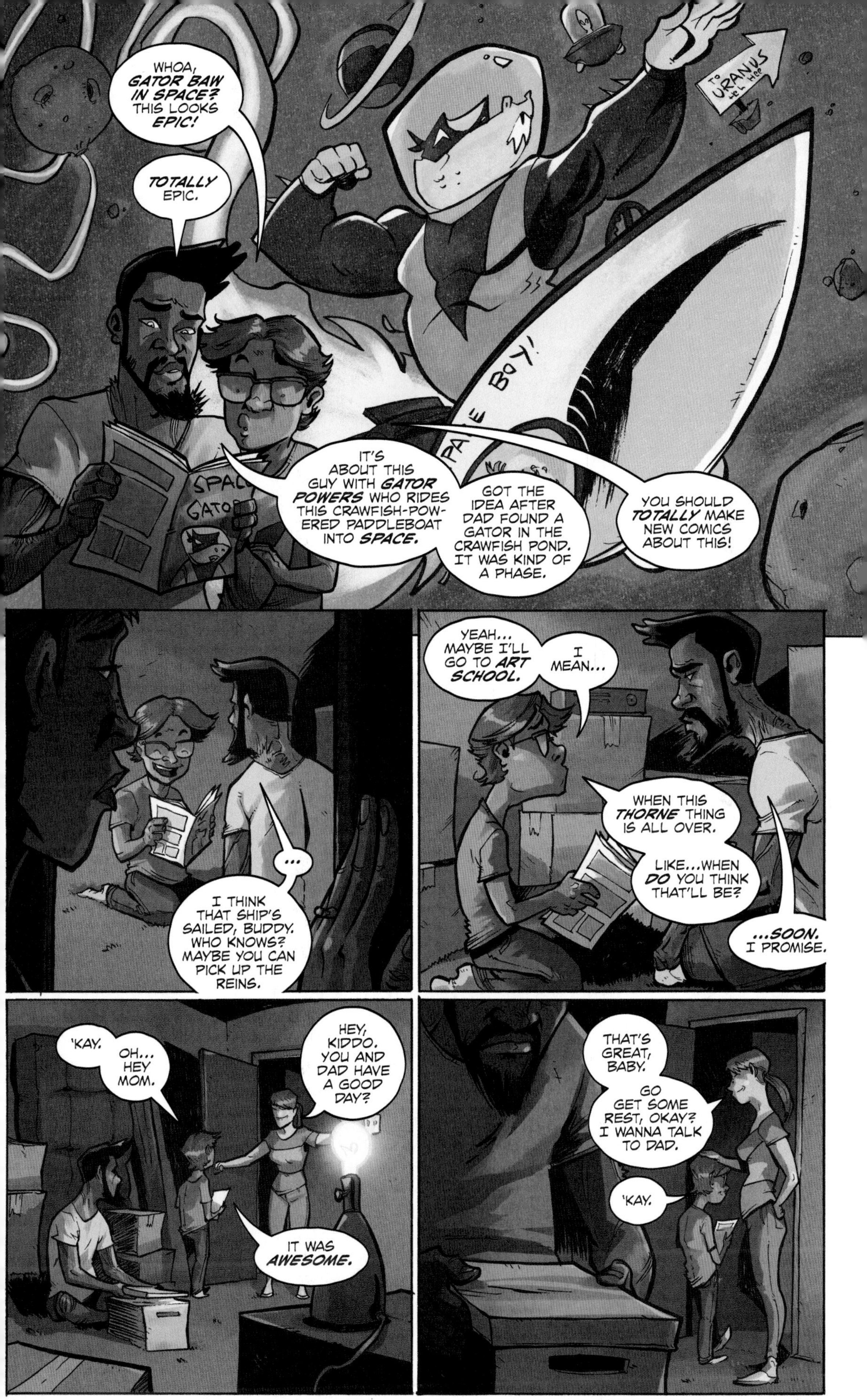
WHOA, GATOR BAW IN SPACE? THIS LOOKS EPIC!
TOTALLY EPIC.
TO URANUS
SPACE GATOR
PADDLE BOY!
IT'S ABOUT THIS GUY WITH GATOR POWERS WHO RIDES THIS CRAWFISH-POWERED PADDLEBOAT INTO SPACE.
GOT THE IDEA AFTER DAD FOUND A GATOR IN THE CRAWFISH POND. IT WAS KIND OF A PHASE.
YOU SHOULD TOTALLY MAKE NEW COMICS ABOUT THIS!
...
I THINK THAT SHIP'S SAILED, BUDDY. WHO KNOWS? MAYBE YOU CAN PICK UP THE REINS.
YEAH... MAYBE I'LL GO TO ART SCHOOL.
I MEAN...
WHEN THIS THORNE THING IS ALL OVER.
LIKE...WHEN DO YOU THINK THAT'LL BE?
...SOON. I PROMISE.
'KAY.
OH... HEY MOM.
HEY, KIDDO. YOU AND DAD HAVE A GOOD DAY?
IT WAS AWESOME.
THAT'S GREAT, BABY.
GO GET SOME REST, OKAY? I WANNA TALK TO DAD.
'KAY.

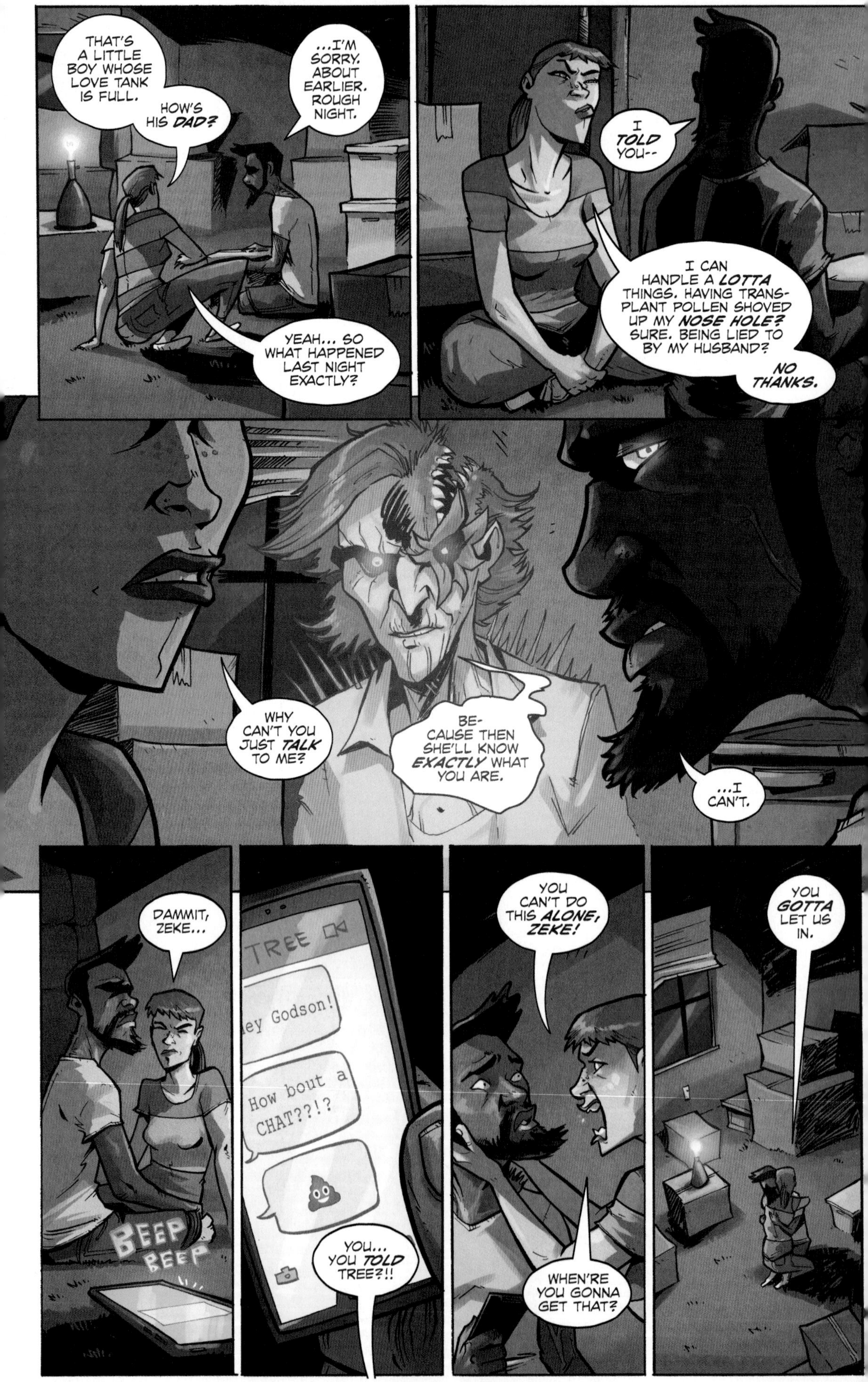
THAT'S A LITTLE BOY WHOSE LOVE TANK IS FULL.
HOW'S HIS DAD?
...I'M SORRY. ABOUT EARLIER. ROUGH NIGHT.
YEAH... SO WHAT HAPPENED LAST NIGHT EXACTLY?
I TOLD YOU--
I CAN HANDLE A LOTTA THINGS. HAVING TRANS-PLANT POLLEN SHOVED UP MY NOSE HOLE? SURE. BEING LIED TO BY MY HUSBAND?
NO THANKS.
WHY CAN'T YOU JUST TALK TO ME?
BE-CAUSE THEN SHE'LL KNOW EXACTLY WHAT YOU ARE.
...I CAN'T.
DAMMIT, ZEKE...
BEEP BEEP
TREE
Hey Godson!
How bout a CHAT??!?
YOU... YOU TOLD TREE?!!
YOU CAN'T DO THIS ALONE, ZEKE!
WHEN'RE YOU GONNA GET THAT?
YOU GOTTA LET US IN.

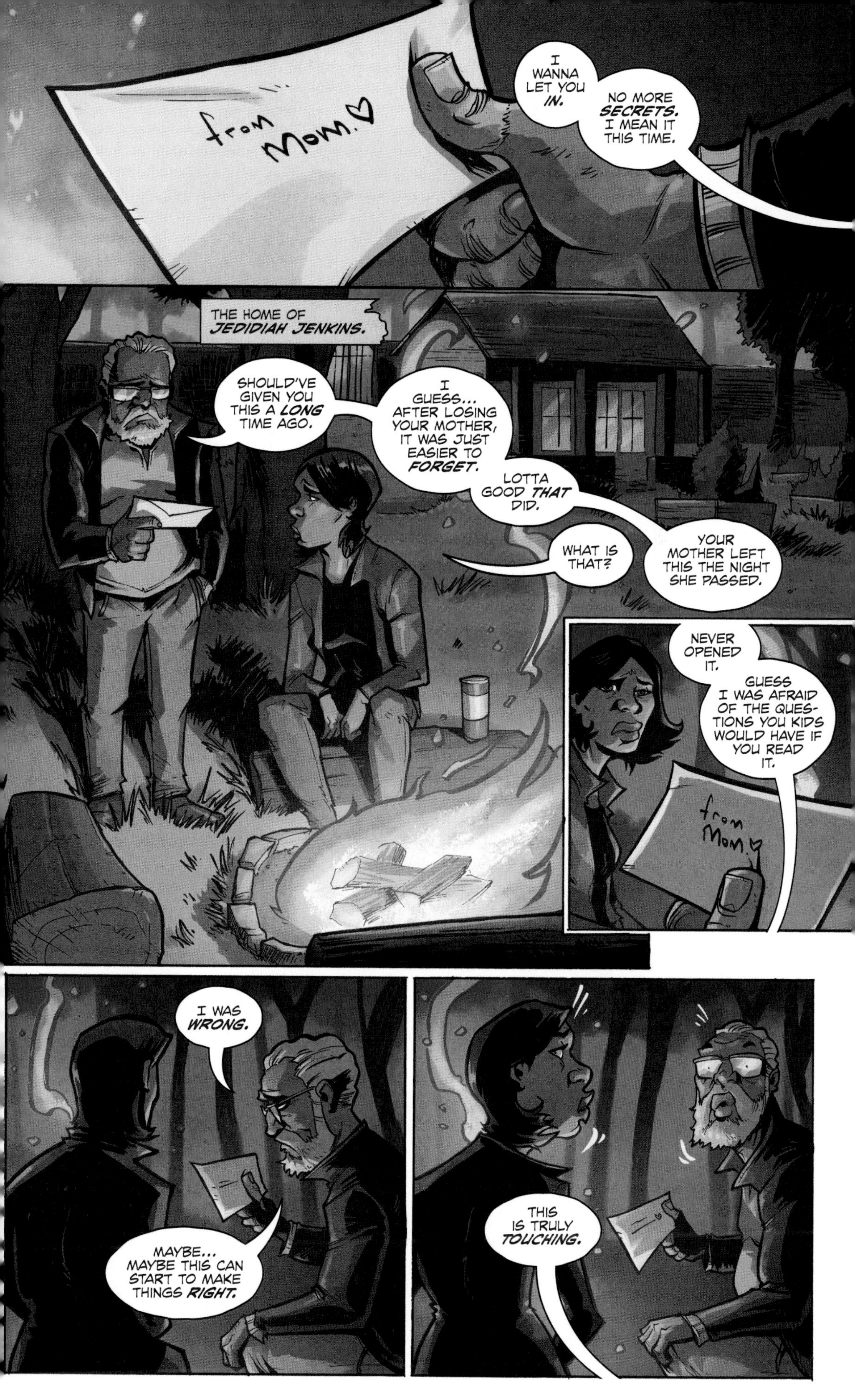
from Mom.
I WANNA LET YOU *IN.*
NO MORE *SECRETS.* I MEAN IT THIS TIME.
THE HOME OF *JEDIDIAH JENKINS.*
SHOULD'VE GIVEN YOU THIS A *LONG* TIME AGO.
I GUESS... AFTER LOSING YOUR MOTHER, IT WAS JUST EASIER TO *FORGET*.
LOTTA GOOD *THAT* DID.
WHAT IS THAT?
YOUR MOTHER LEFT THIS THE NIGHT SHE PASSED.
NEVER OPENED IT.
GUESS I WAS AFRAID OF THE QUESTIONS YOU KIDS WOULD HAVE IF YOU READ IT.
from Mom.
I WAS *WRONG.*
MAYBE... MAYBE THIS CAN START TO MAKE THINGS *RIGHT.*
THIS IS TRULY *TOUCHING.*

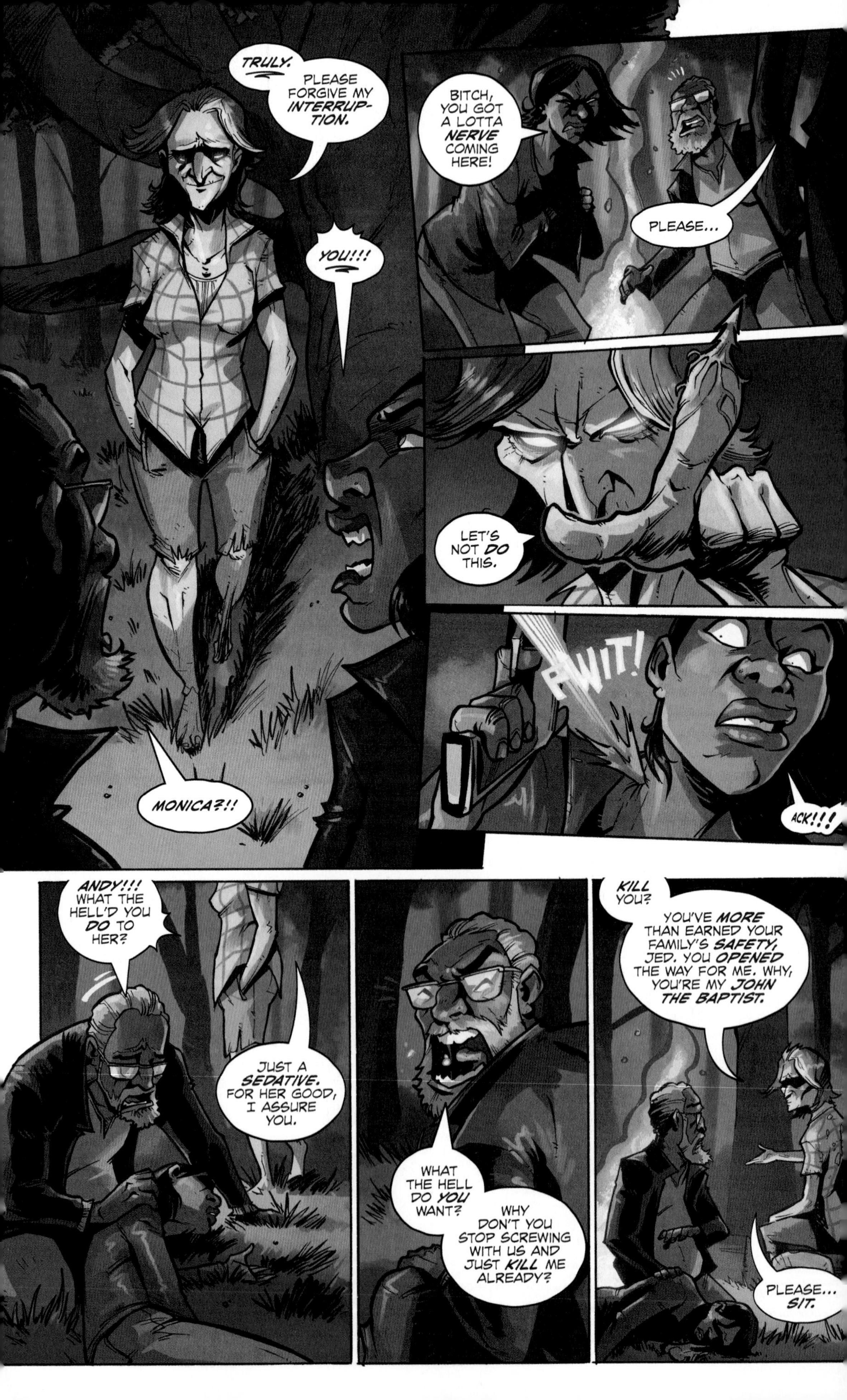
TRULY.
PLEASE FORGIVE MY INTERRUPTION.
YOU!!!
MONICA?!!
BITCH, YOU GOT A LOTTA NERVE COMING HERE!
PLEASE...
LET'S NOT DO THIS.
FWIT!
ACK!!!
ANDY!!! WHAT THE HELL'D YOU DO TO HER?
JUST A SEDATIVE. FOR HER GOOD, I ASSURE YOU.
WHAT THE HELL DO YOU WANT?
WHY DON'T YOU STOP SCREWING WITH US AND JUST KILL ME ALREADY?
KILL YOU?
YOU'VE MORE THAN EARNED YOUR FAMILY'S SAFETY, JED. YOU OPENED THE WAY FOR ME. WHY, YOU'RE MY JOHN THE BAPTIST.
PLEASE... SIT.

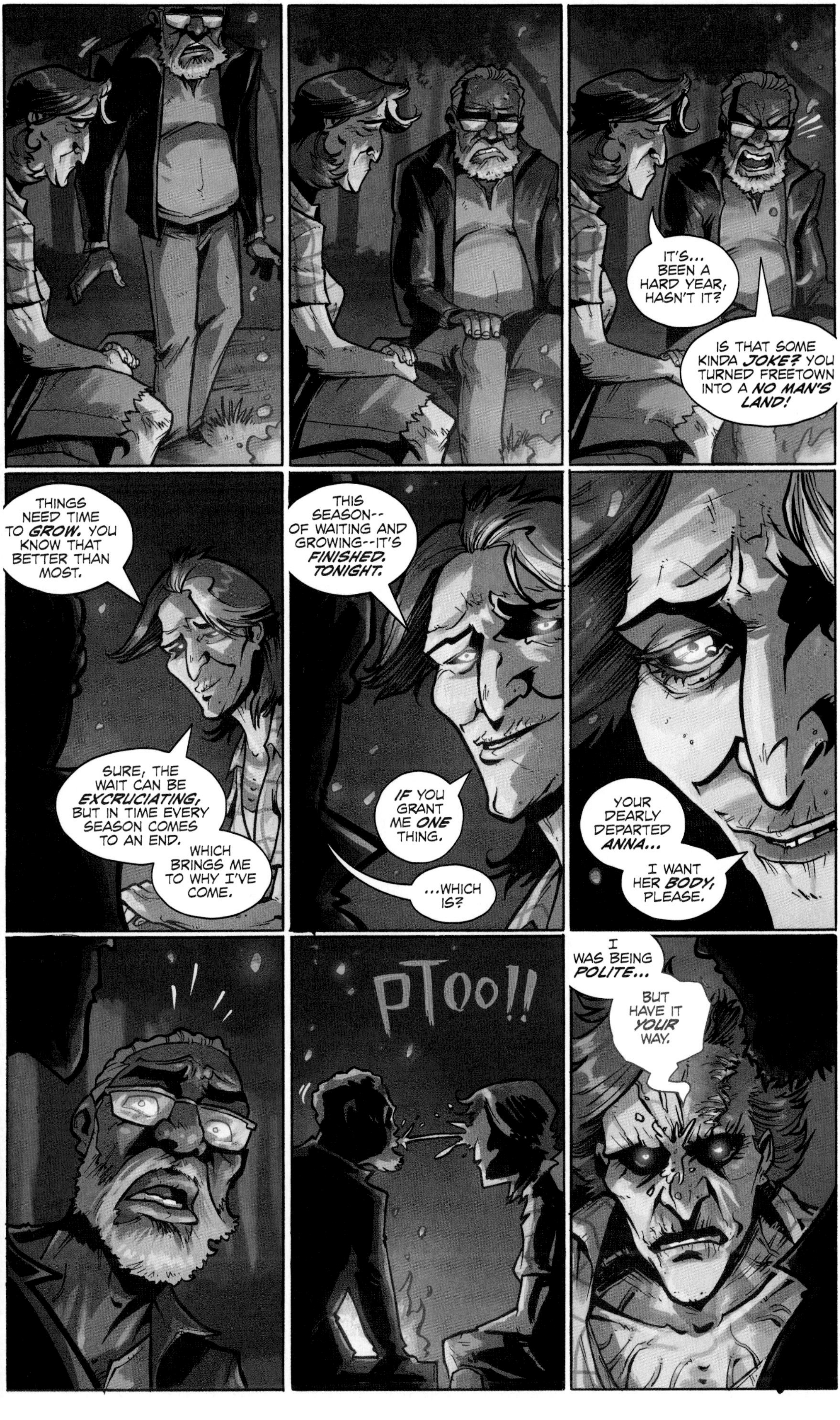
IT'S... BEEN A HARD YEAR, HASN'T IT?
IS THAT SOME KINDA JOKE? YOU TURNED FREETOWN INTO A NO MAN'S LAND!
THINGS NEED TIME TO GROW. YOU KNOW THAT BETTER THAN MOST.
SURE, THE WAIT CAN BE EXCRUCIATING, BUT IN TIME EVERY SEASON COMES TO AN END.
WHICH BRINGS ME TO WHY I'VE COME.
THIS SEASON--OF WAITING AND GROWING--IT'S FINISHED. TONIGHT.
IF YOU GRANT ME ONE THING.
...WHICH IS?
YOUR DEARLY DEPARTED ANNA...
I WANT HER BODY, PLEASE.
PTOO!!
I WAS BEING POLITE...
BUT HAVE IT YOUR WAY.

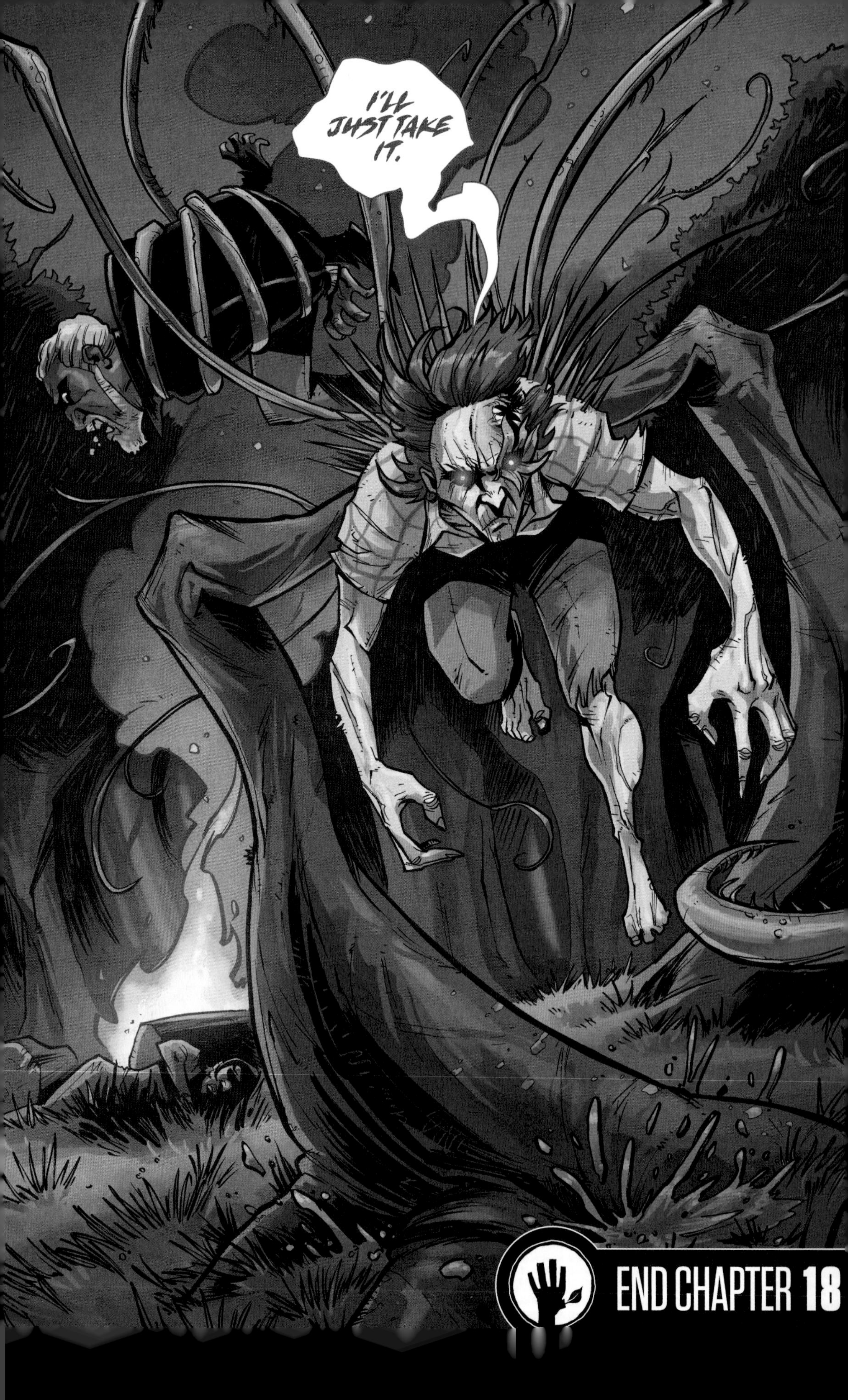
I'LL JUST TAKE IT.
END CHAPTER 18

CHAPTER 19

RoB!

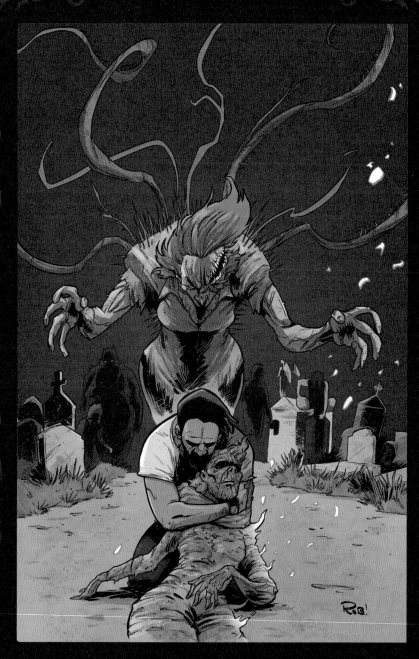

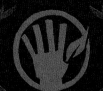

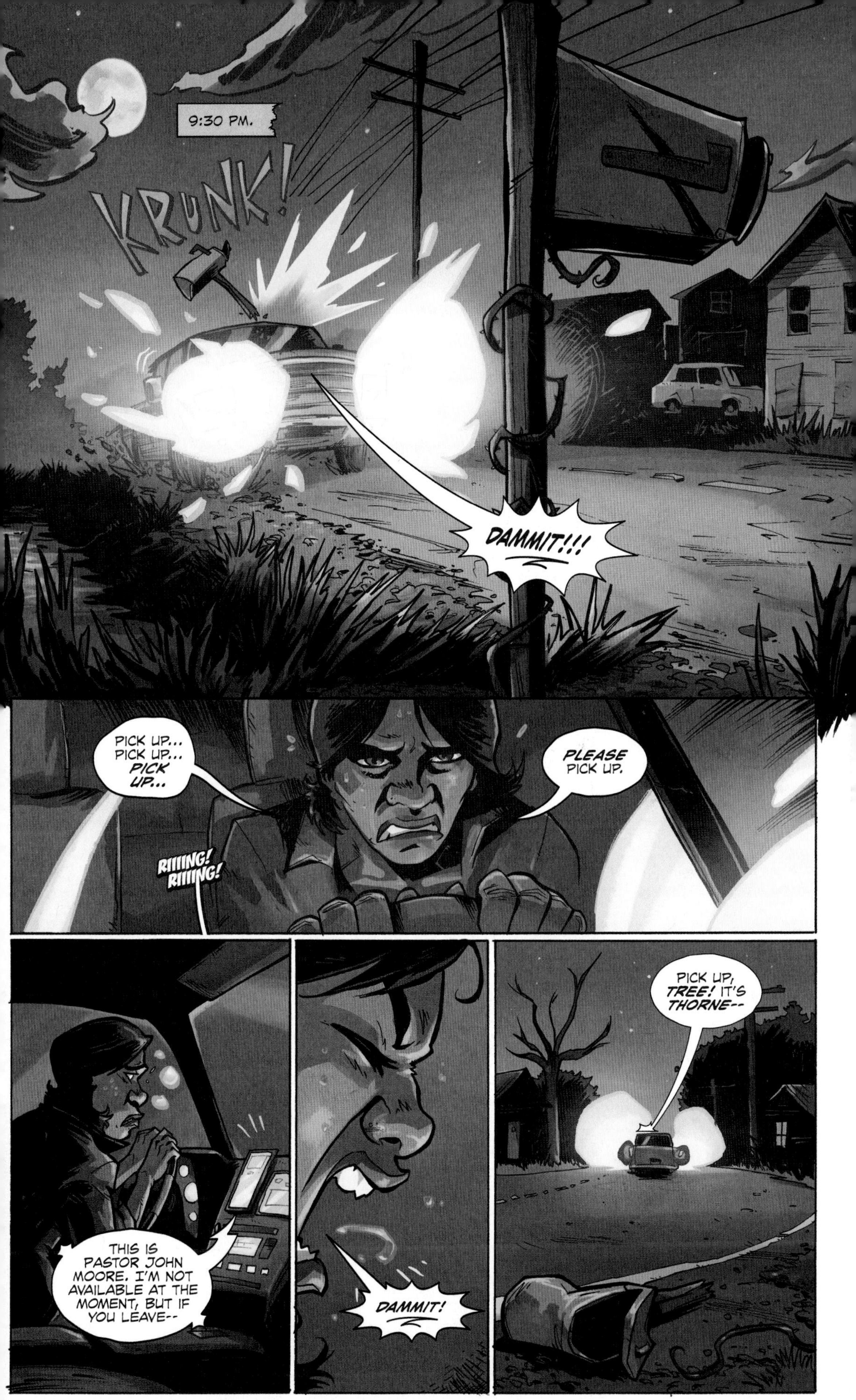
9:30 PM.
KRUNK!
DAMMIT!!!
PICK UP... PICK UP... PICK UP...
PLEASE PICK UP.
RIIIING! RIIIING!
THIS IS PASTOR JOHN MOORE. I'M NOT AVAILABLE AT THE MOMENT, BUT IF YOU LEAVE--
DAMMIT!
PICK UP, TREE! IT'S THORNE--

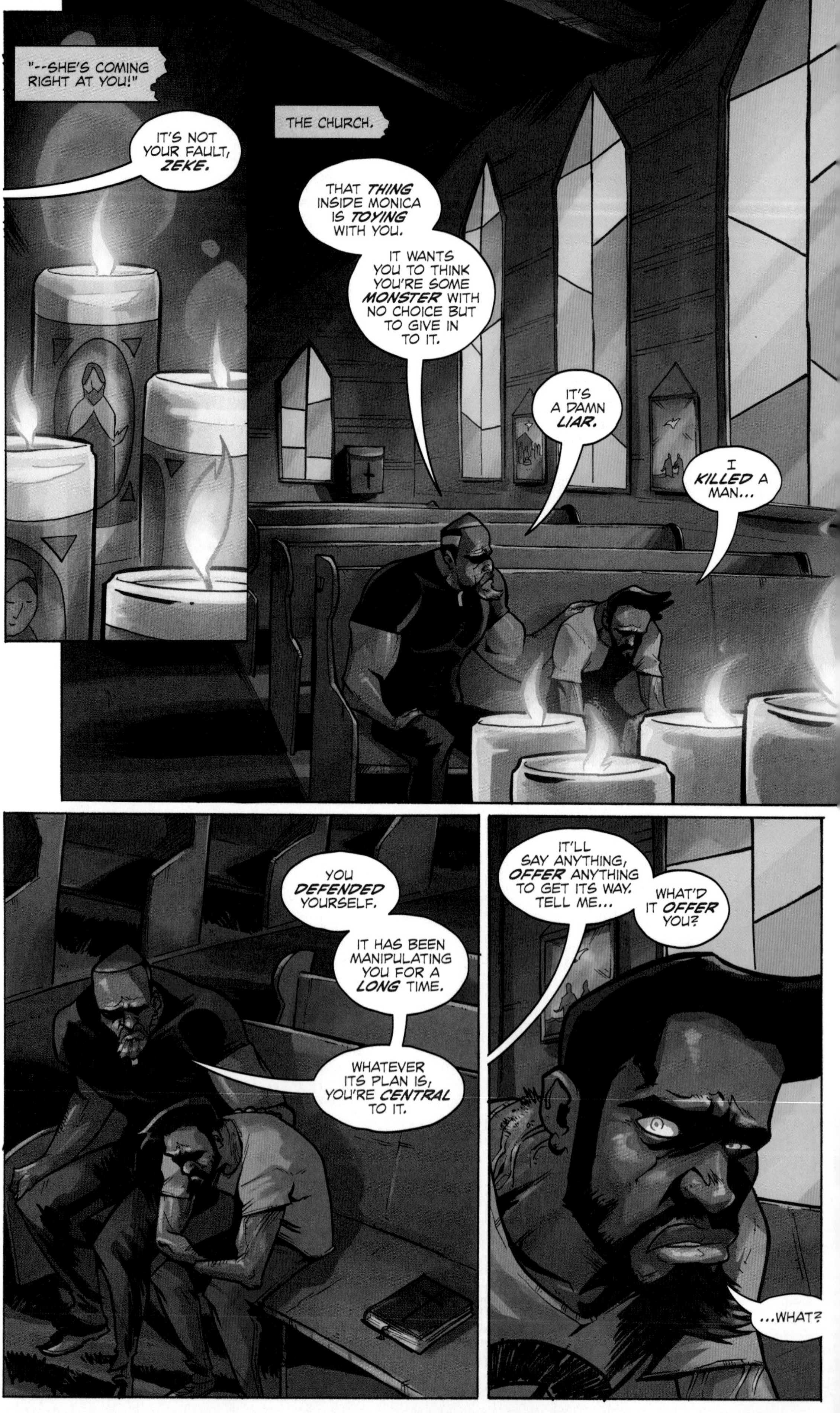
"--SHE'S COMING RIGHT AT YOU!"
THE CHURCH.
IT'S NOT YOUR FAULT, ZEKE.
THAT THING INSIDE MONICA IS TOYING WITH YOU.
IT WANTS YOU TO THINK YOU'RE SOME MONSTER WITH NO CHOICE BUT TO GIVE IN TO IT.
IT'S A DAMN LIAR.
I KILLED A MAN...
YOU DEFENDED YOURSELF.
IT HAS BEEN MANIPULATING YOU FOR A LONG TIME.
WHATEVER ITS PLAN IS, YOU'RE CENTRAL TO IT.
IT'LL SAY ANYTHING, OFFER ANYTHING TO GET ITS WAY. TELL ME...
WHAT'D IT OFFER YOU?
...WHAT?

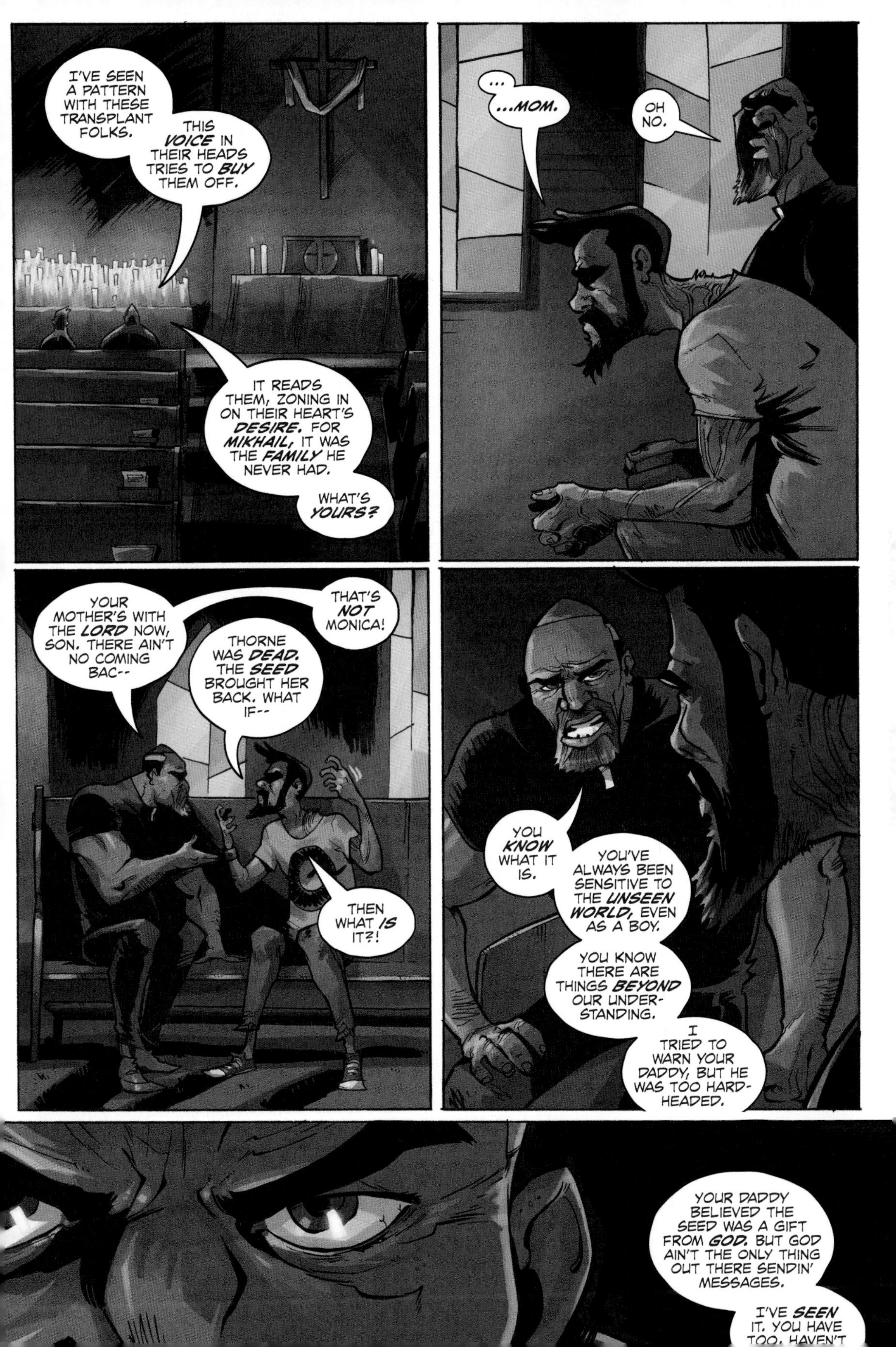

I'VE SEEN A PATTERN WITH THESE TRANSPLANT FOLKS.
THIS VOICE IN THEIR HEADS TRIES TO BUY THEM OFF.
IT READS THEM, ZONING IN ON THEIR HEART'S DESIRE. FOR MIKHAIL, IT WAS THE FAMILY HE NEVER HAD.
WHAT'S YOURS?
...
...MOM.
OH NO.
YOUR MOTHER'S WITH THE LORD NOW, SON. THERE AIN'T NO COMING BAC--
THAT'S NOT MONICA!
THORNE WAS DEAD. THE SEED BROUGHT HER BACK. WHAT IF--
THEN WHAT IS IT?!
YOU KNOW WHAT IT IS.
YOU'VE ALWAYS BEEN SENSITIVE TO THE UNSEEN WORLD, EVEN AS A BOY.
YOU KNOW THERE ARE THINGS BEYOND OUR UNDER-STANDING.
I TRIED TO WARN YOUR DADDY, BUT HE WAS TOO HARD-HEADED.
YOUR DADDY BELIEVED THE SEED WAS A GIFT FROM GOD. BUT GOD AIN'T THE ONLY THING OUT THERE SENDIN' MESSAGES.
I'VE SEEN IT. YOU HAVE TOO, HAVEN'T

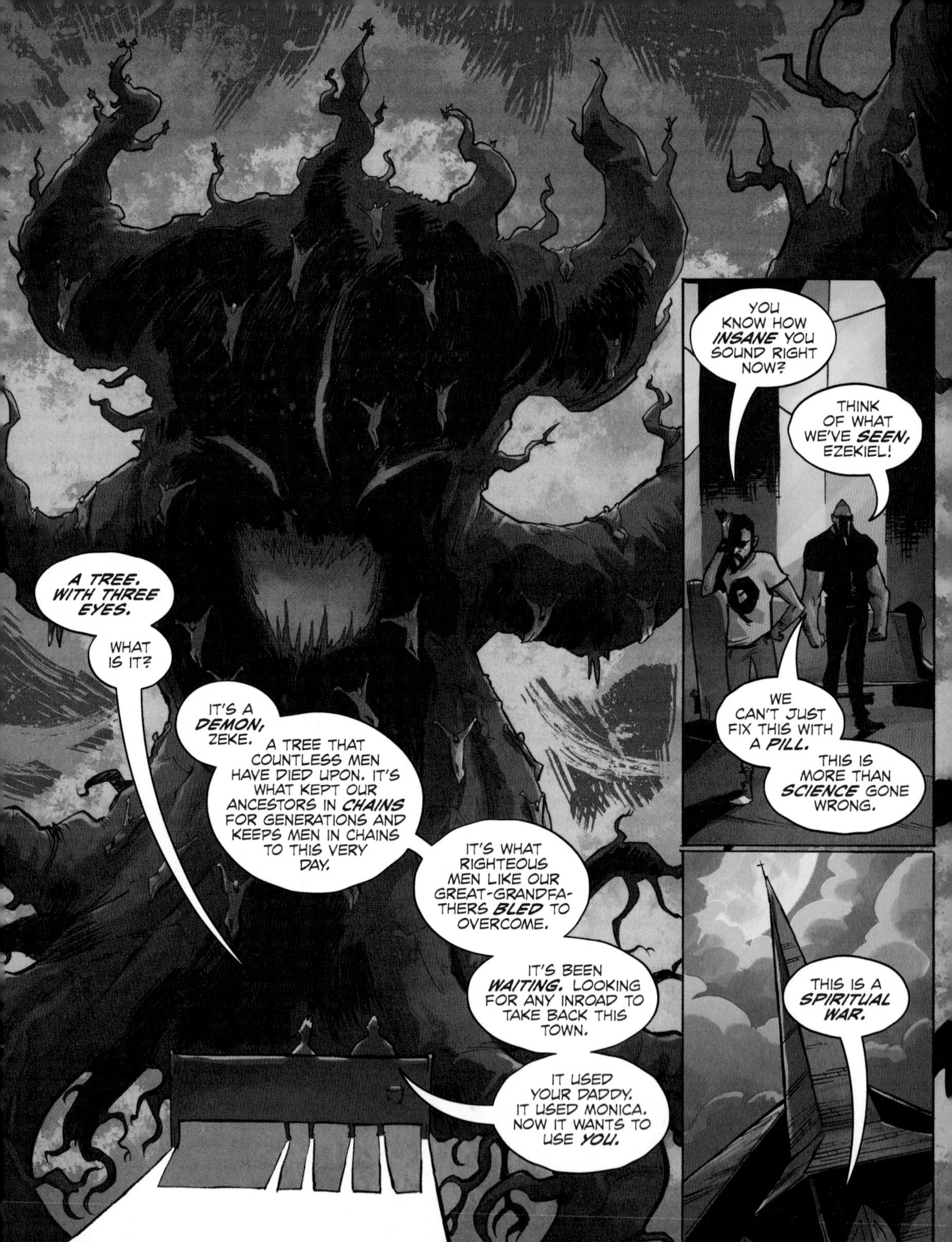
A TREE. WITH THREE EYES.
WHAT IS IT?
IT'S A DEMON, ZEKE.
A TREE THAT COUNTLESS MEN HAVE DIED UPON. IT'S WHAT KEPT OUR ANCESTORS IN CHAINS FOR GENERATIONS AND KEEPS MEN IN CHAINS TO THIS VERY DAY.
IT'S WHAT RIGHTEOUS MEN LIKE OUR GREAT-GRANDFA-THERS BLED TO OVERCOME.
IT'S BEEN WAITING. LOOKING FOR ANY INROAD TO TAKE BACK THIS TOWN.
IT USED YOUR DADDY. IT USED MONICA. NOW IT WANTS TO USE YOU.
YOU KNOW HOW INSANE YOU SOUND RIGHT NOW?
THINK OF WHAT WE'VE SEEN, EZEKIEL!
WE CAN'T JUST FIX THIS WITH A PILL.
THIS IS MORE THAN SCIENCE GONE WRONG.
THIS IS A SPIRITUAL WAR.

CHAPTER 19: MOMMA'S BONES.

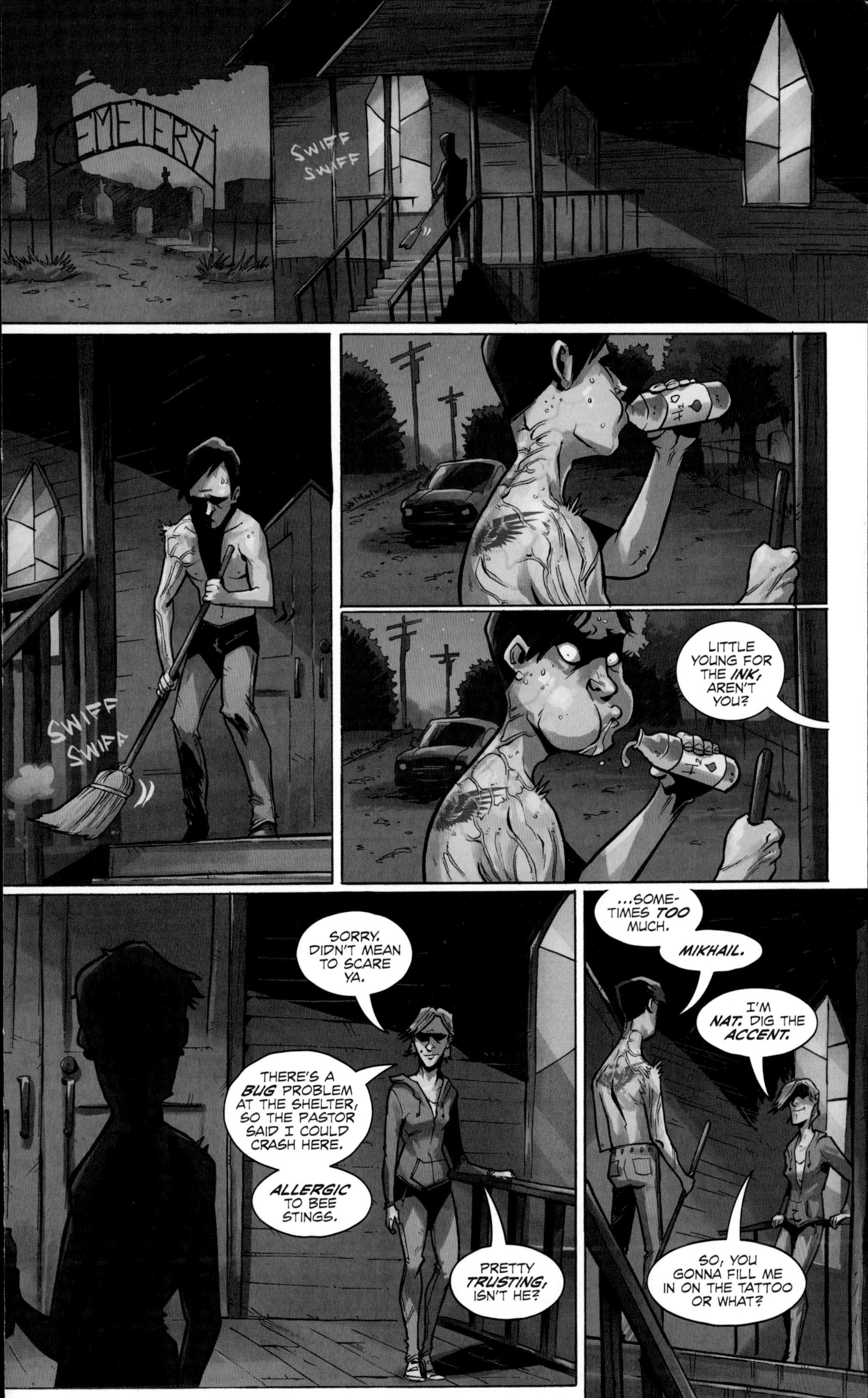
CEMETERY
SWIFF SWIFF
SWIFF SWIFF
LITTLE YOUNG FOR THE INK, AREN'T YOU?
SORRY. DIDN'T MEAN TO SCARE YA.
THERE'S A BUG PROBLEM AT THE SHELTER, SO THE PASTOR SAID I COULD CRASH HERE.
ALLERGIC TO BEE STINGS.
PRETTY TRUSTING, ISN'T HE?
...SOMETIMES TOO MUCH.
MIKHAIL.
I'M NAT. DIG THE ACCENT.
SO, YOU GONNA FILL ME IN ON THE TATTOO OR WHAT?

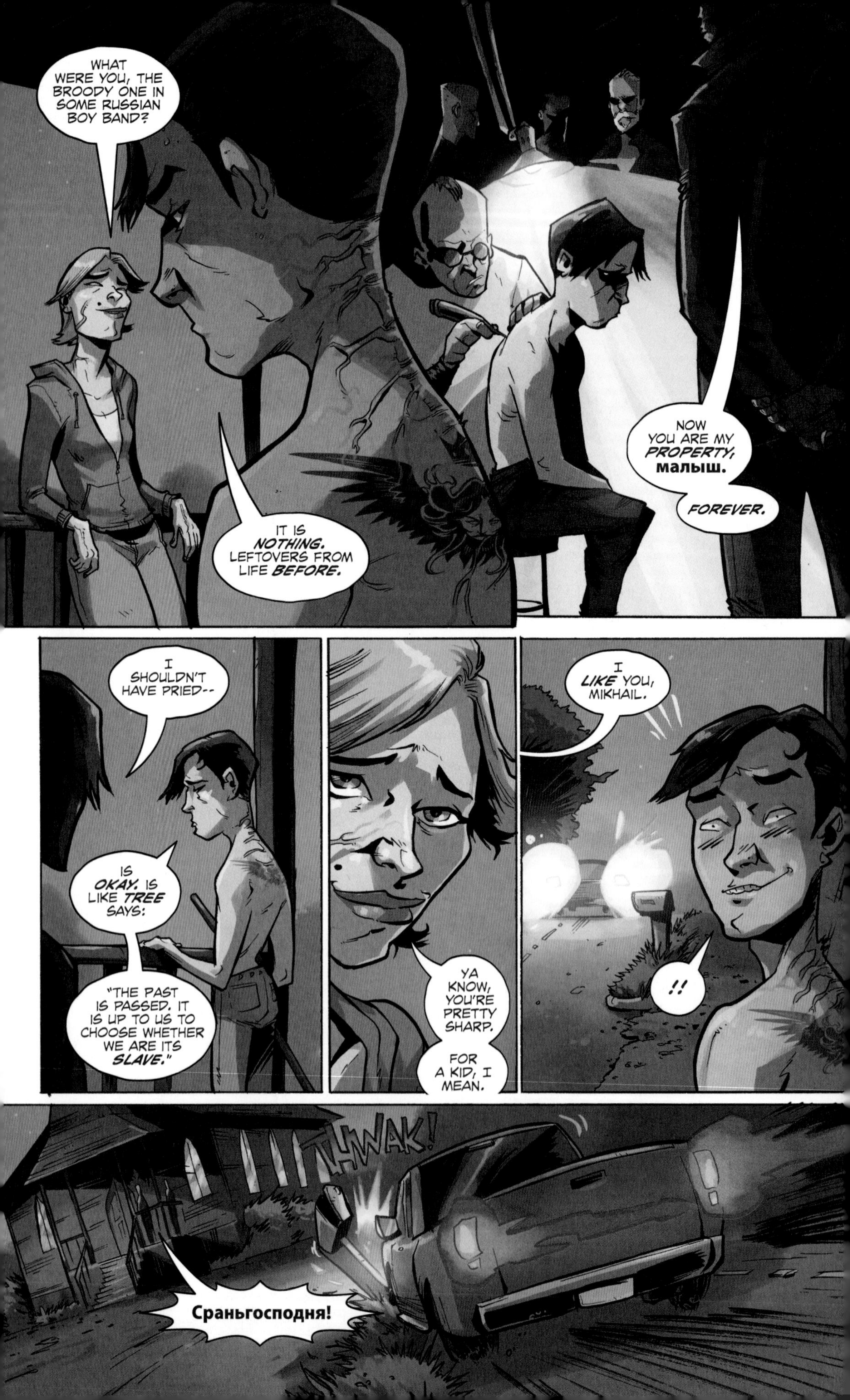
WHAT WERE YOU, THE BROODY ONE IN SOME RUSSIAN BOY BAND?
IT IS NOTHING. LEFTOVERS FROM LIFE BEFORE.
NOW YOU ARE MY PROPERTY, малыш.
FOREVER.
I SHOULDN'T HAVE PRIED--
IS OKAY. IS LIKE TREE SAYS:
"THE PAST IS PASSED. IT IS UP TO US TO CHOOSE WHETHER WE ARE ITS SLAVE."
YA KNOW, YOU'RE PRETTY SHARP.
FOR A KID, I MEAN.
I LIKE YOU, MIKHAIL.
!!
THWAK!
Сраньгосподня!

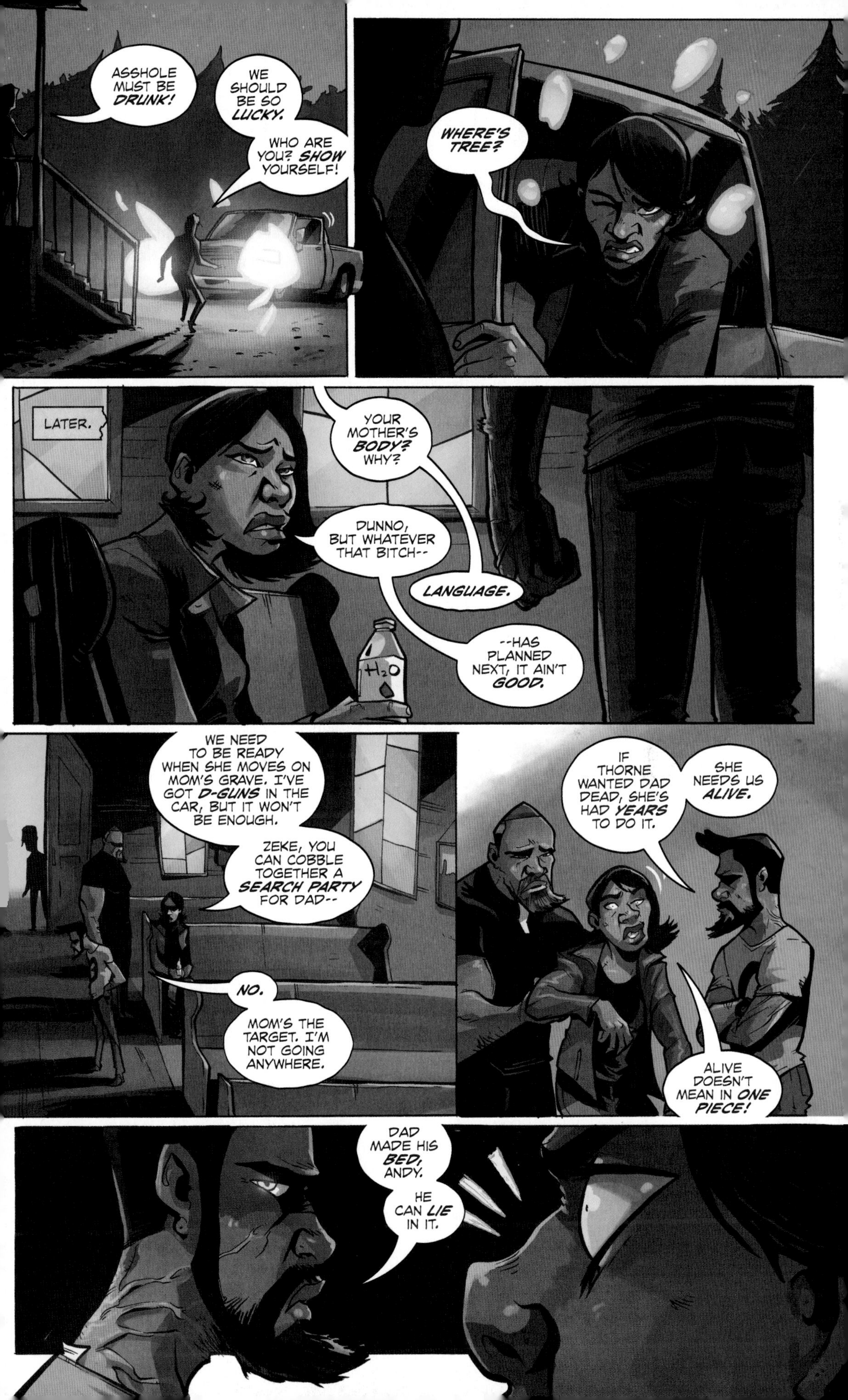

ASSHOLE MUST BE *DRUNK!*
WE SHOULD BE SO *LUCKY.*
WHO ARE YOU? *SHOW* YOURSELF!
WHERE'S TREE?
LATER.
YOUR MOTHER'S *BODY?* WHY?
DUNNO, BUT WHATEVER THAT BITCH--
LANGUAGE.
--HAS PLANNED NEXT, IT AIN'T *GOOD.*
H_2O
WE NEED TO BE READY WHEN SHE MOVES ON MOM'S GRAVE. I'VE GOT *D-GUNS* IN THE CAR, BUT IT WON'T BE ENOUGH.
ZEKE, YOU CAN COBBLE TOGETHER A *SEARCH PARTY* FOR DAD--
NO.
MOM'S THE TARGET. I'M NOT GOING ANYWHERE.
IF THORNE WANTED DAD DEAD, SHE'S HAD *YEARS* TO DO IT.
SHE NEEDS US *ALIVE.*
ALIVE DOESN'T MEAN IN *ONE PIECE!*
DAD MADE HIS *BED,* ANDY.
HE CAN *LIE* IN IT.

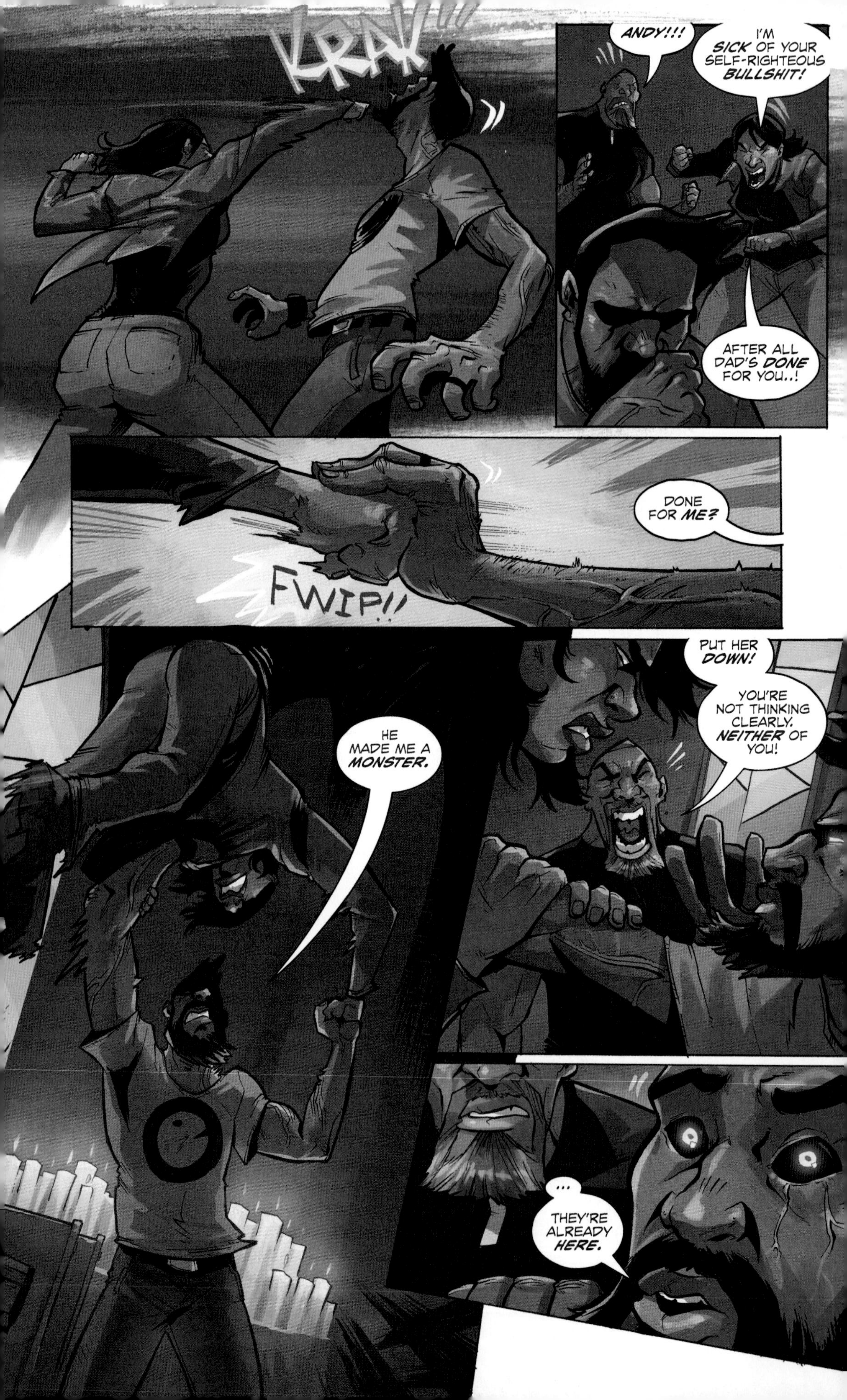
KRAK!!!
ANDY!!!
I'M SICK OF YOUR SELF-RIGHTEOUS BULLSHIT!
AFTER ALL DAD'S DONE FOR YOU..!
DONE FOR ME?
FWIP!!
HE MADE ME A MONSTER.
PUT HER DOWN!
YOU'RE NOT THINKING CLEARLY. NEITHER OF YOU!
...
THEY'RE ALREADY HERE.

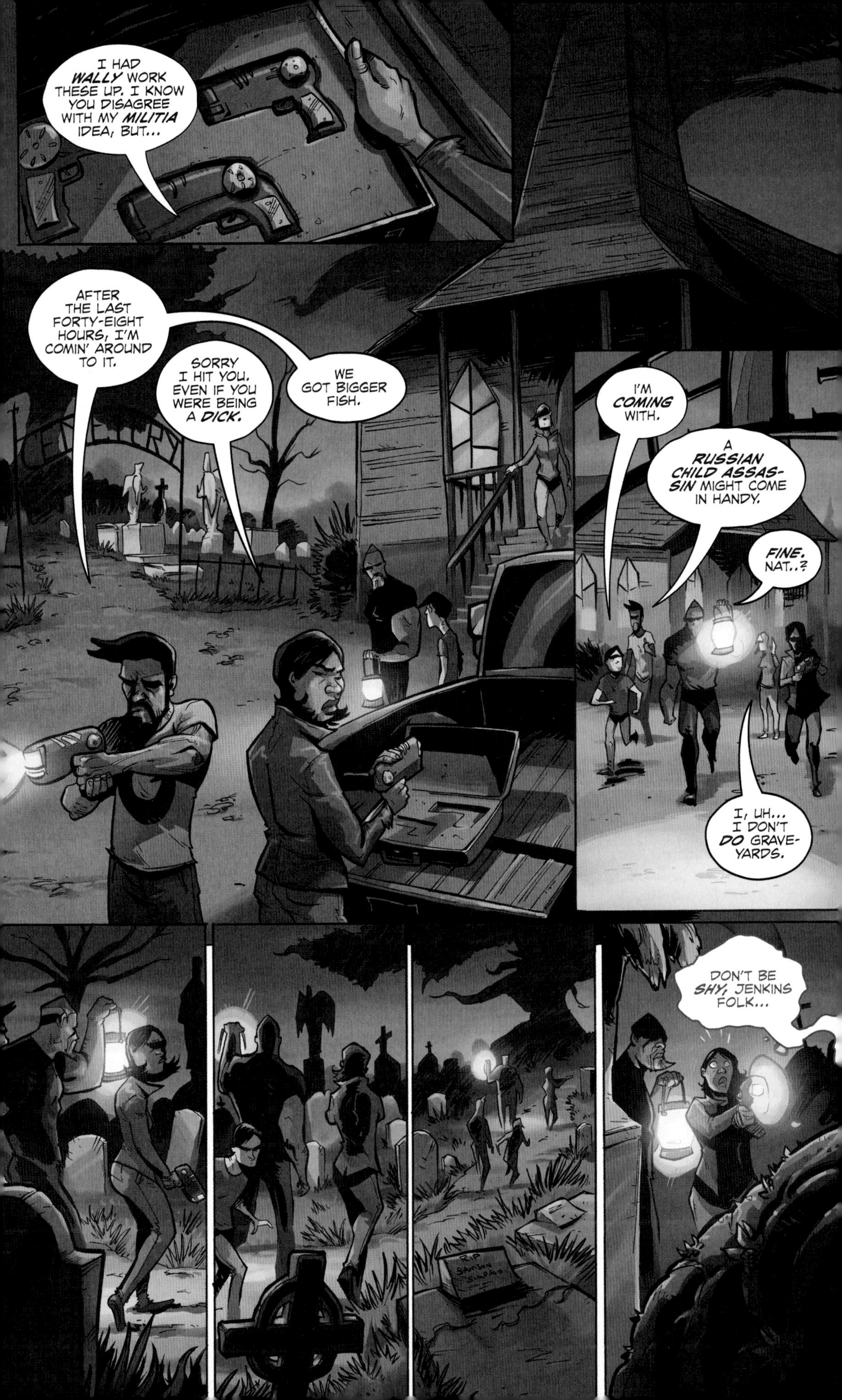
I HAD WALLY WORK THESE UP. I KNOW YOU DISAGREE WITH MY MILITIA IDEA, BUT...
AFTER THE LAST FORTY-EIGHT HOURS, I'M COMIN' AROUND TO IT.
SORRY I HIT YOU. EVEN IF YOU WERE BEING A DICK.
WE GOT BIGGER FISH.
I'M COMING WITH.
A RUSSIAN CHILD ASSAS-SIN MIGHT COME IN HANDY.
FINE. NAT..?
I, UH... I DON'T DO GRAVE-YARDS.
RIP SAMSON
DON'T BE SHY, JENKINS FOLK...

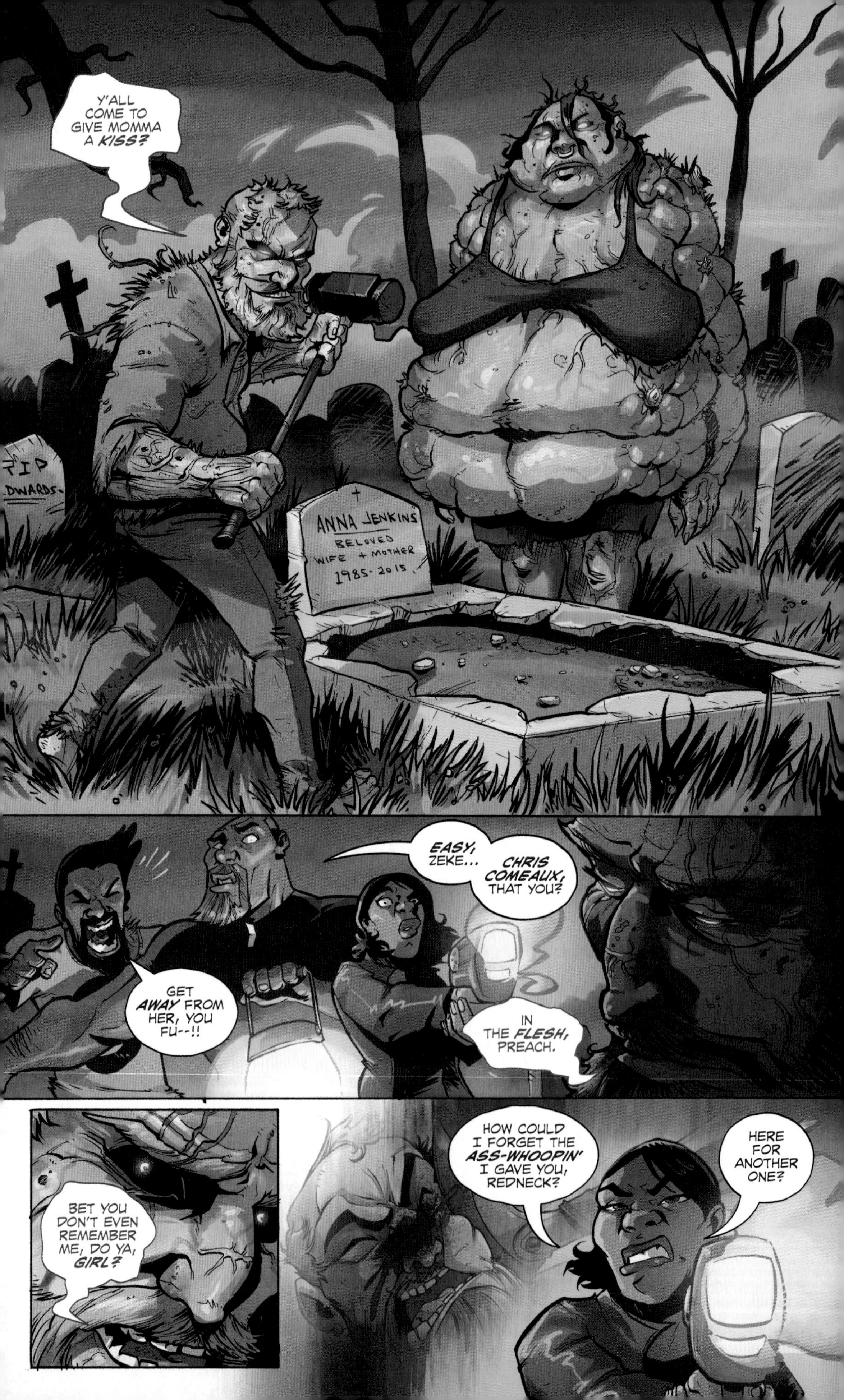
Y'ALL COME TO GIVE MOMMA A *KISS?*
RIP
DWARDS
ANNA JENKINS
BELOVED
WIFE + MOTHER
1985-2015
EASY, ZEKE... *CHRIS COMEAUX,* THAT YOU?
GET *AWAY* FROM HER, YOU FU--!!
IN THE *FLESH,* PREACH.
BET YOU DON'T EVEN REMEMBER ME, DO YA, *GIRL?*
HOW COULD I FORGET THE *ASS-WHOOPIN'* I GAVE YOU, REDNECK?
HERE FOR ANOTHER ONE?

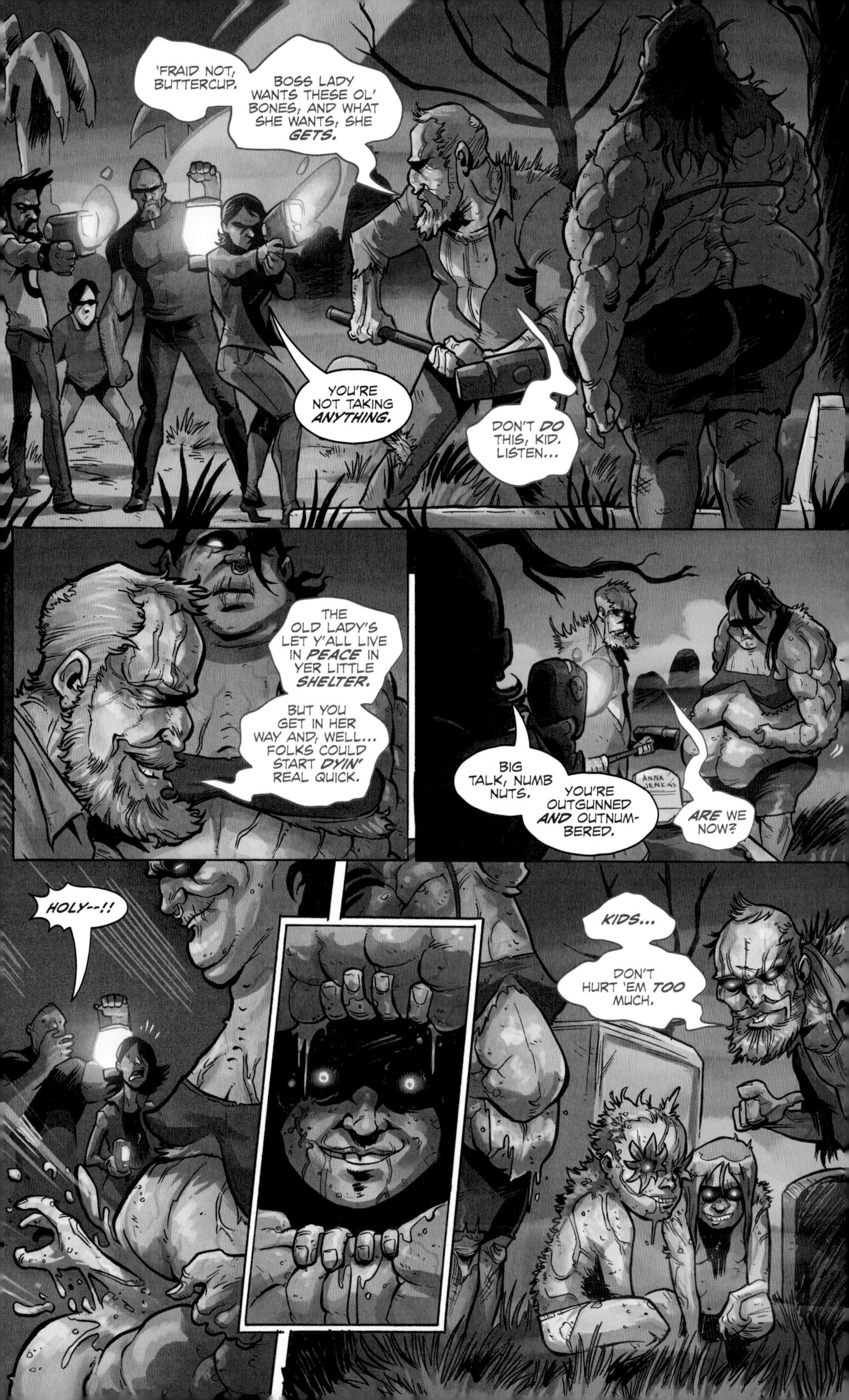
'FRAID NOT, BUTTERCUP.
BOSS LADY WANTS THESE OL' BONES, AND WHAT SHE WANTS, SHE *GETS.*
YOU'RE NOT TAKING *ANYTHING.*
DON'T *DO* THIS, KID. LISTEN...
THE OLD LADY'S LET Y'ALL LIVE IN *PEACE* IN YER LITTLE *SHELTER.*
BUT YOU GET IN HER WAY AND, WELL... FOLKS COULD START *DYIN'* REAL QUICK.
BIG TALK, NUMB NUTS.
YOU'RE OUTGUNNED *AND* OUTNUMBERED.
ANNA JENKINS
ARE WE NOW?
HOLY--!!
KIDS...
DON'T HURT 'EM *TOO* MUCH.

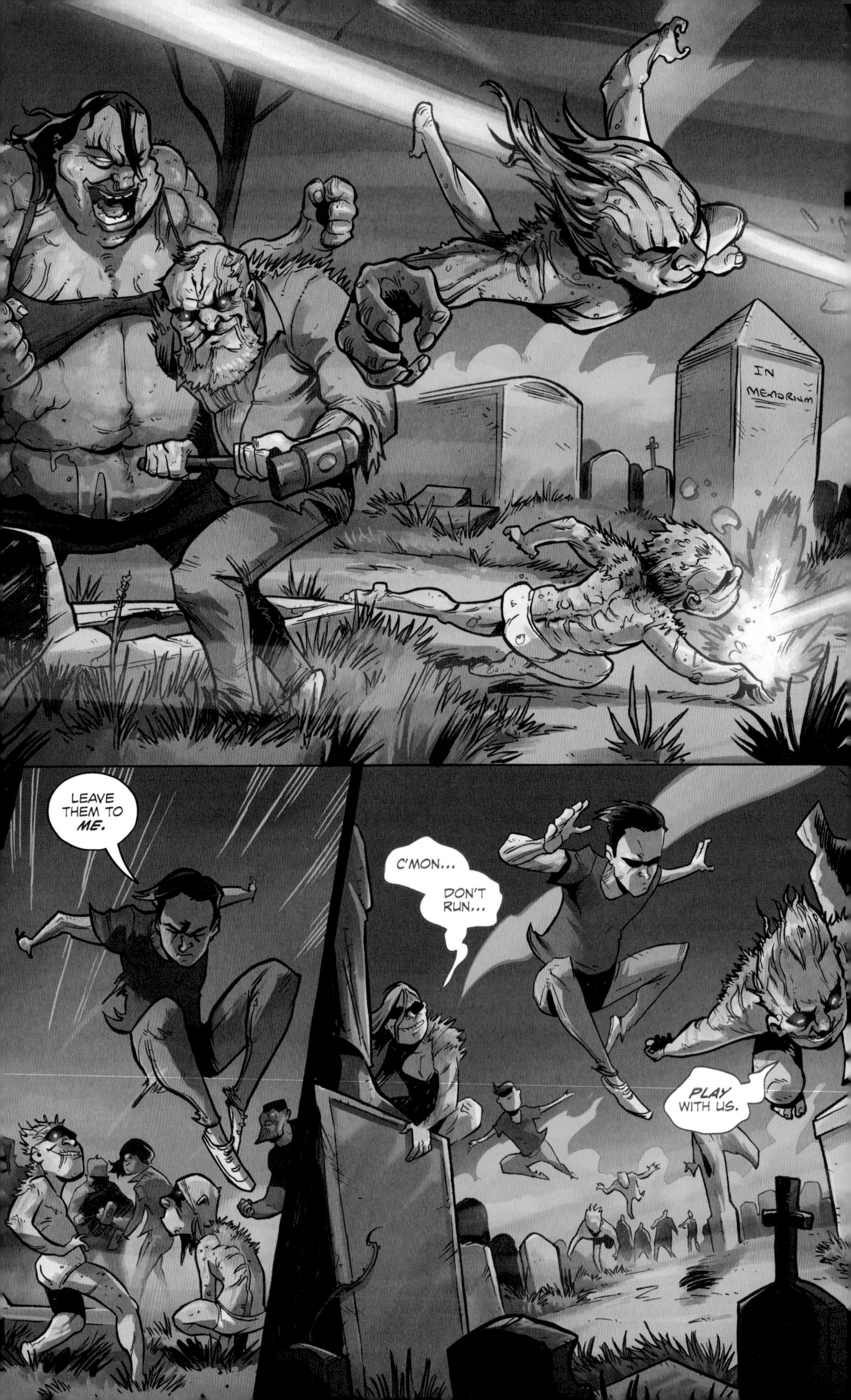
IN MEMORIUM
LEAVE THEM TO ME.
C'MON...
DON'T RUN...
PLAY WITH US.

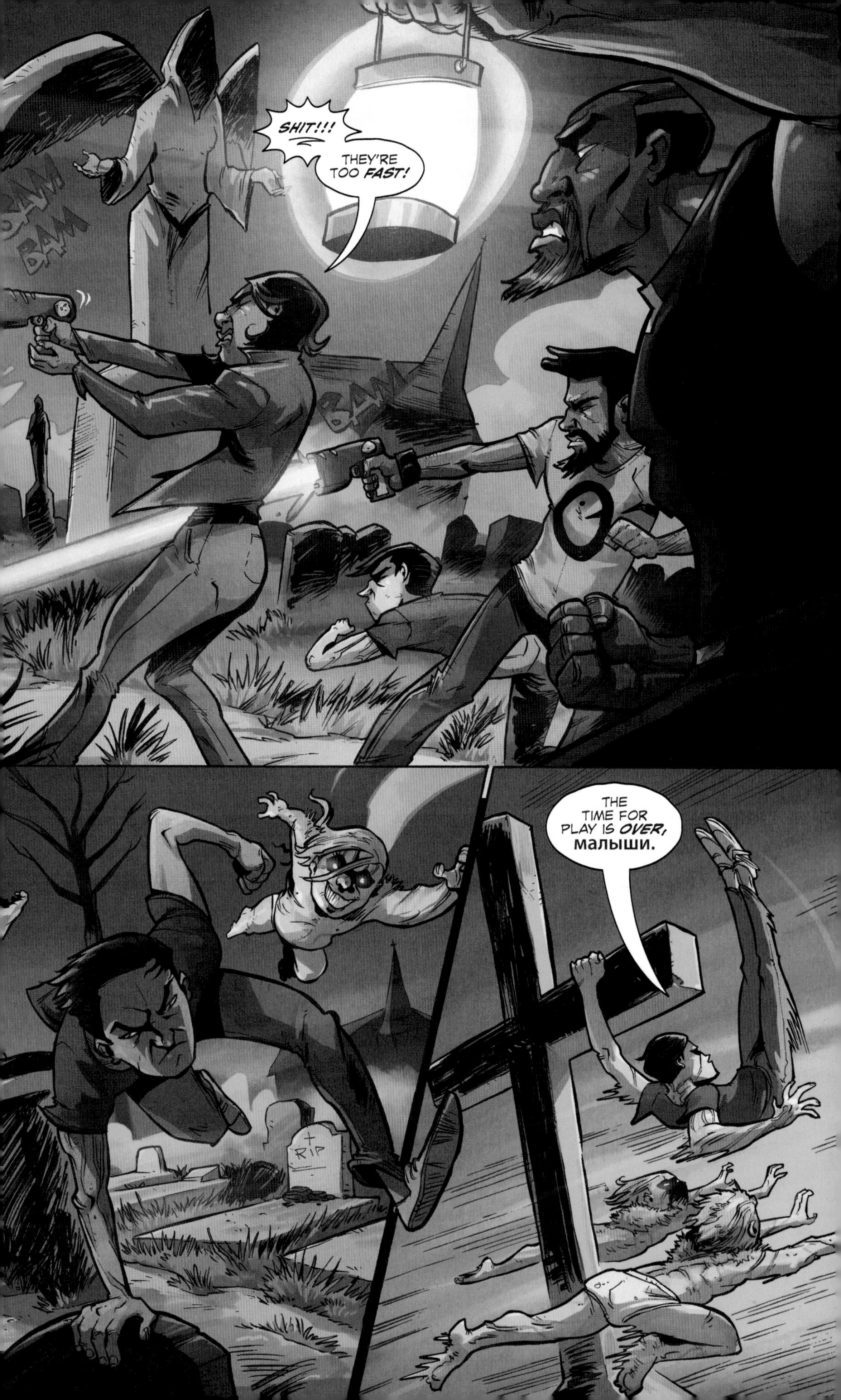
BAM BAM
BAM
SHIT!!!
THEY'RE TOO FAST!
THE TIME FOR PLAY IS OVER, малыши.
RIP

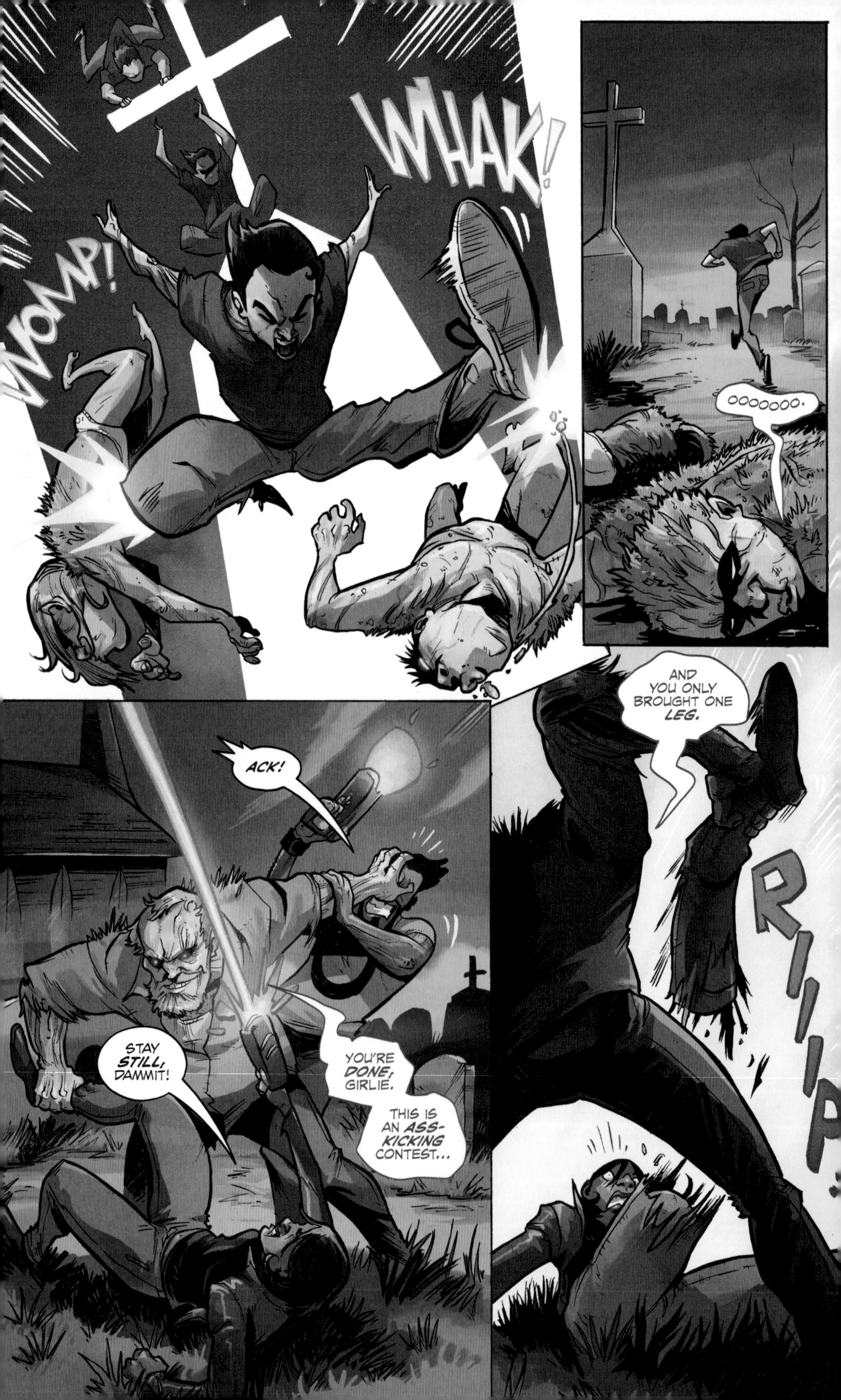

WHAK!
WOMP!
OOOOOOO.
AND YOU ONLY BROUGHT ONE LEG.
RIIIP
ACK!
STAY STILL, DAMMIT!
YOU'RE DONE, GIRLIE.
THIS IS AN ASS-KICKING CONTEST...

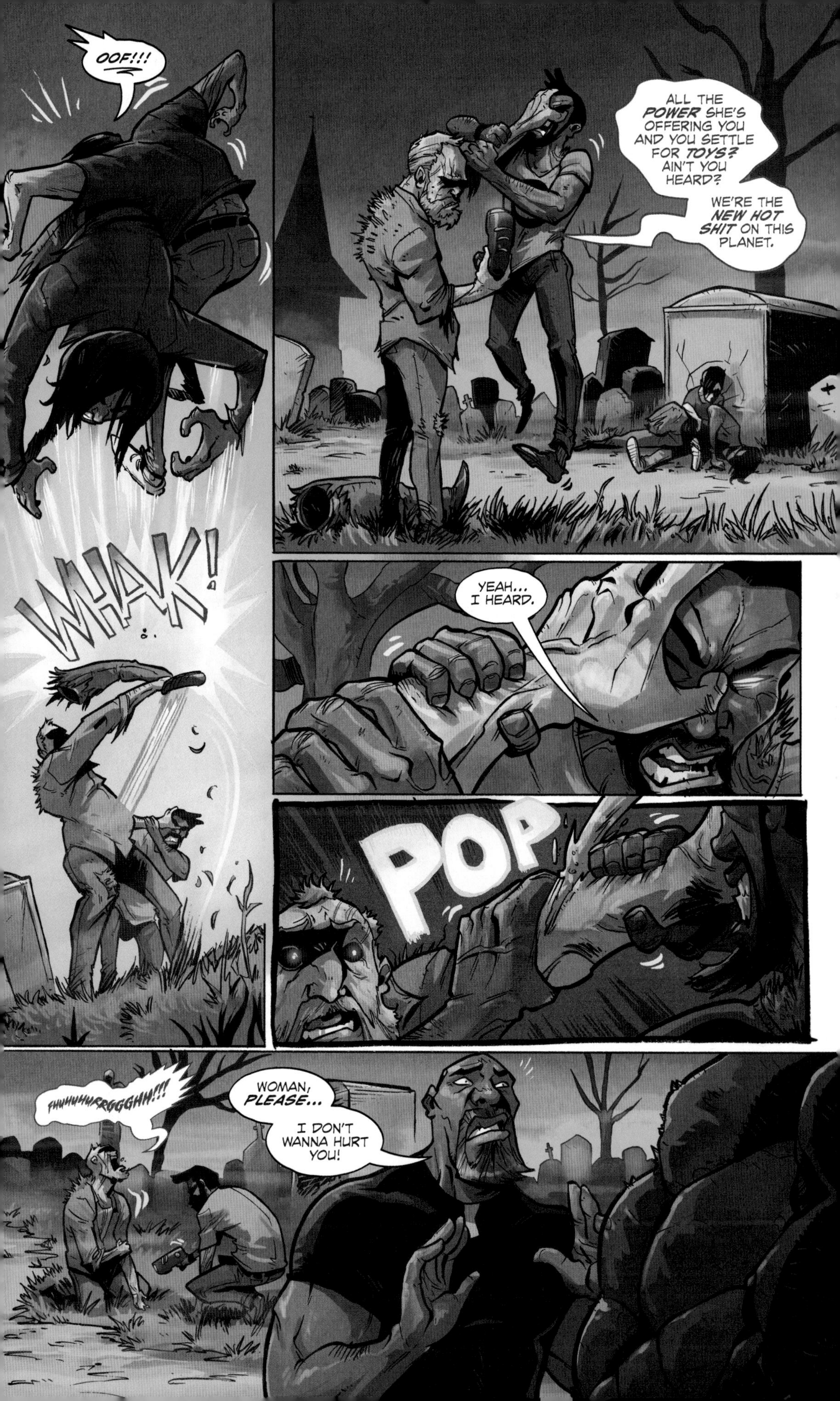
OOF!!!
ALL THE POWER SHE'S OFFERING YOU AND YOU SETTLE FOR TOYS? AIN'T YOU HEARD?
WE'RE THE NEW HOT SHIT ON THIS PLANET.
WHAK!
YEAH... I HEARD.
POP
FHUUUHURRGGGHH!!!
WOMAN, PLEASE...
I DON'T WANNA HURT YOU!

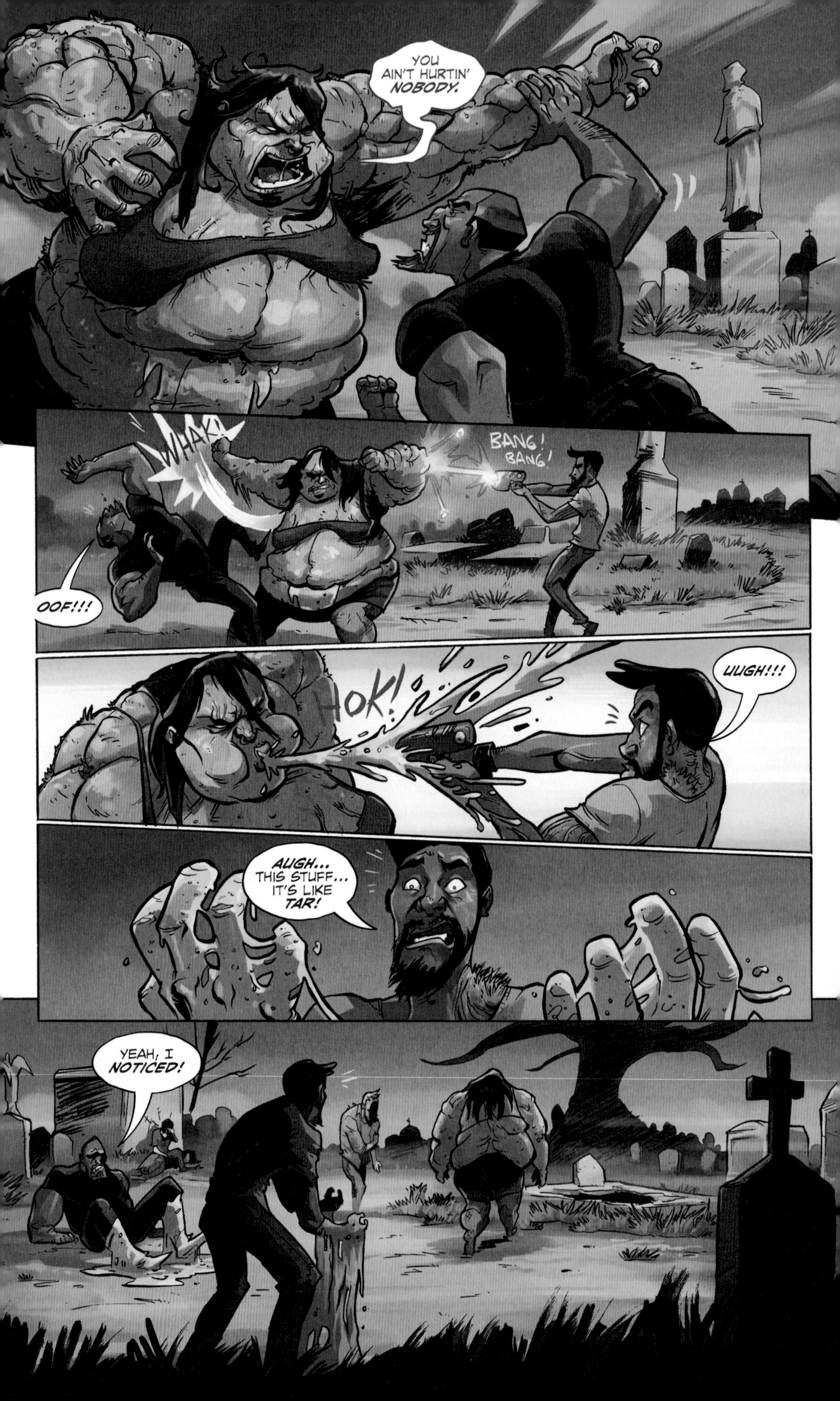
YOU AIN'T HURTIN' NOBODY.
WHAK!
BANG! BANG!
OOF!!!
HOK!
UUGH!!!
AUGH... THIS STUFF... IT'S LIKE TAR!
YEAH, I NOTICED!

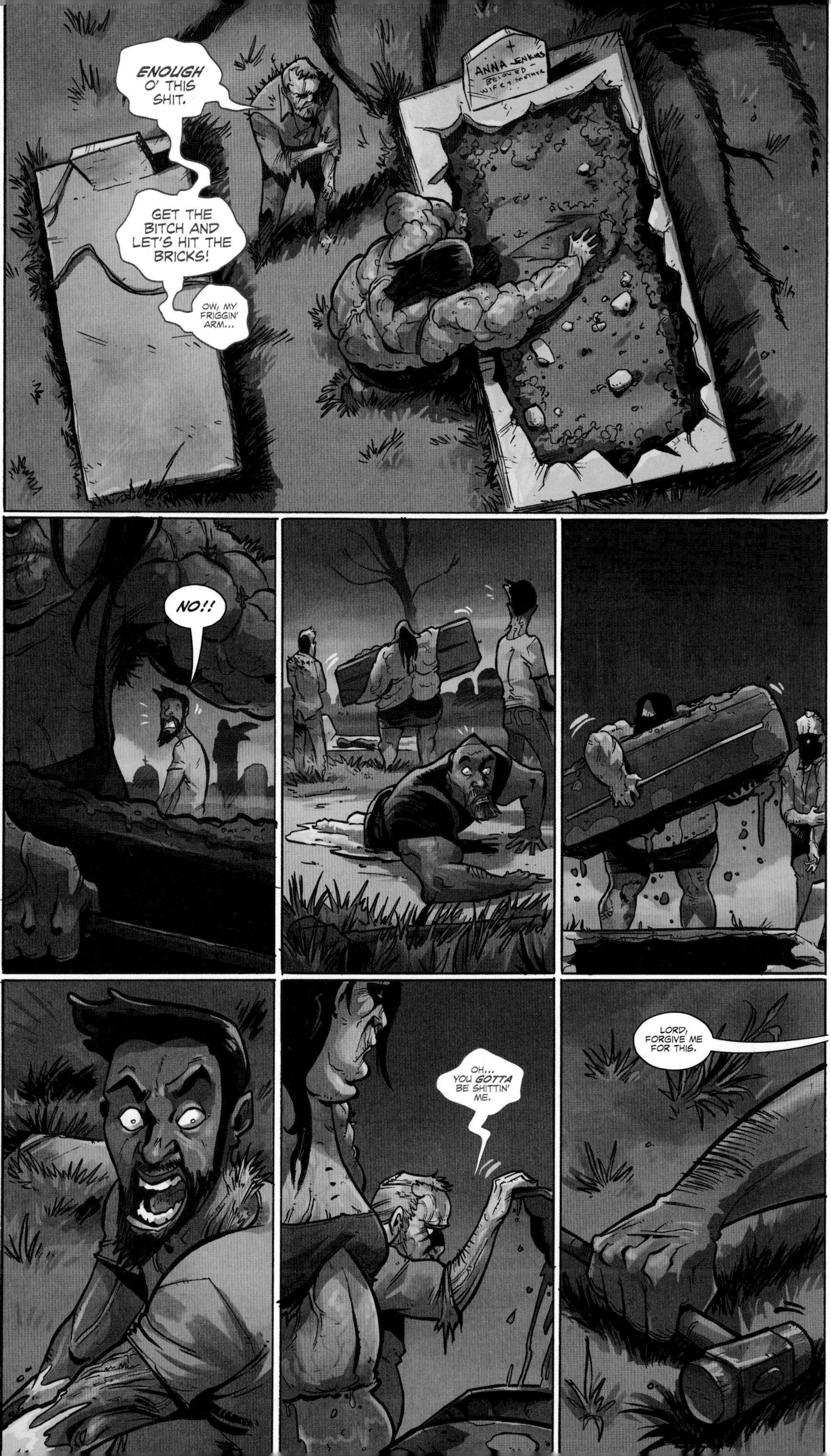
ENOUGH O' THIS SHIT.
GET THE BITCH AND LET'S HIT THE BRICKS!
OW, MY FRIGGIN' ARM...
ANNA JENKINS BELOVED WIFE & MOTHER
NO!!
OH... YOU GOTTA BE SHITTIN' ME.
LORD, FORGIVE ME FOR THIS.

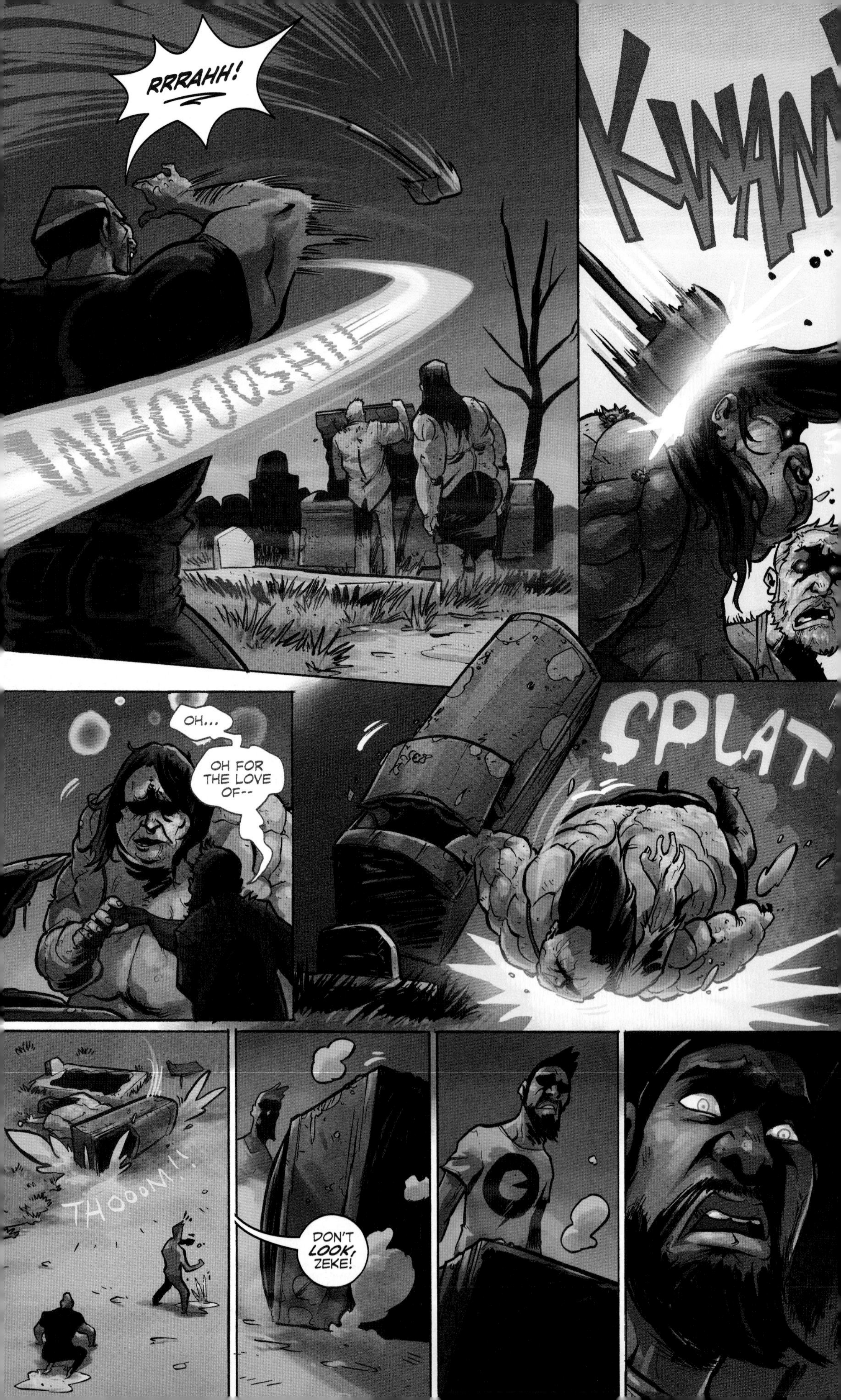
RRRAHH!
WHOOOSH!!
KWAM
OH...
OH FOR THE LOVE OF--
SPLAT
THOOOM!!
DON'T LOOK, ZEKE!

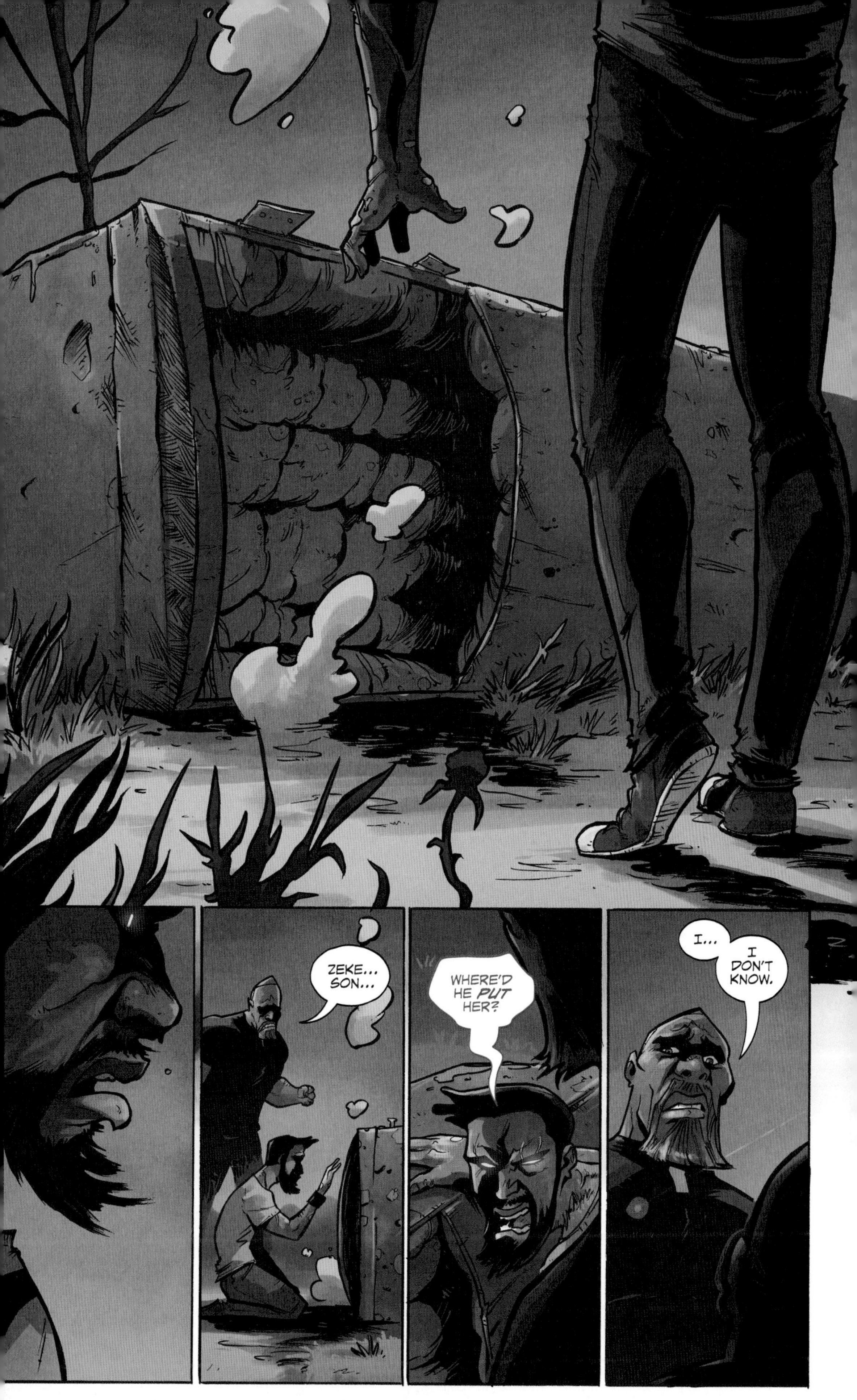
ZEKE... SON...
WHERE'D HE PUT HER?
I...
I DON'T KNOW.

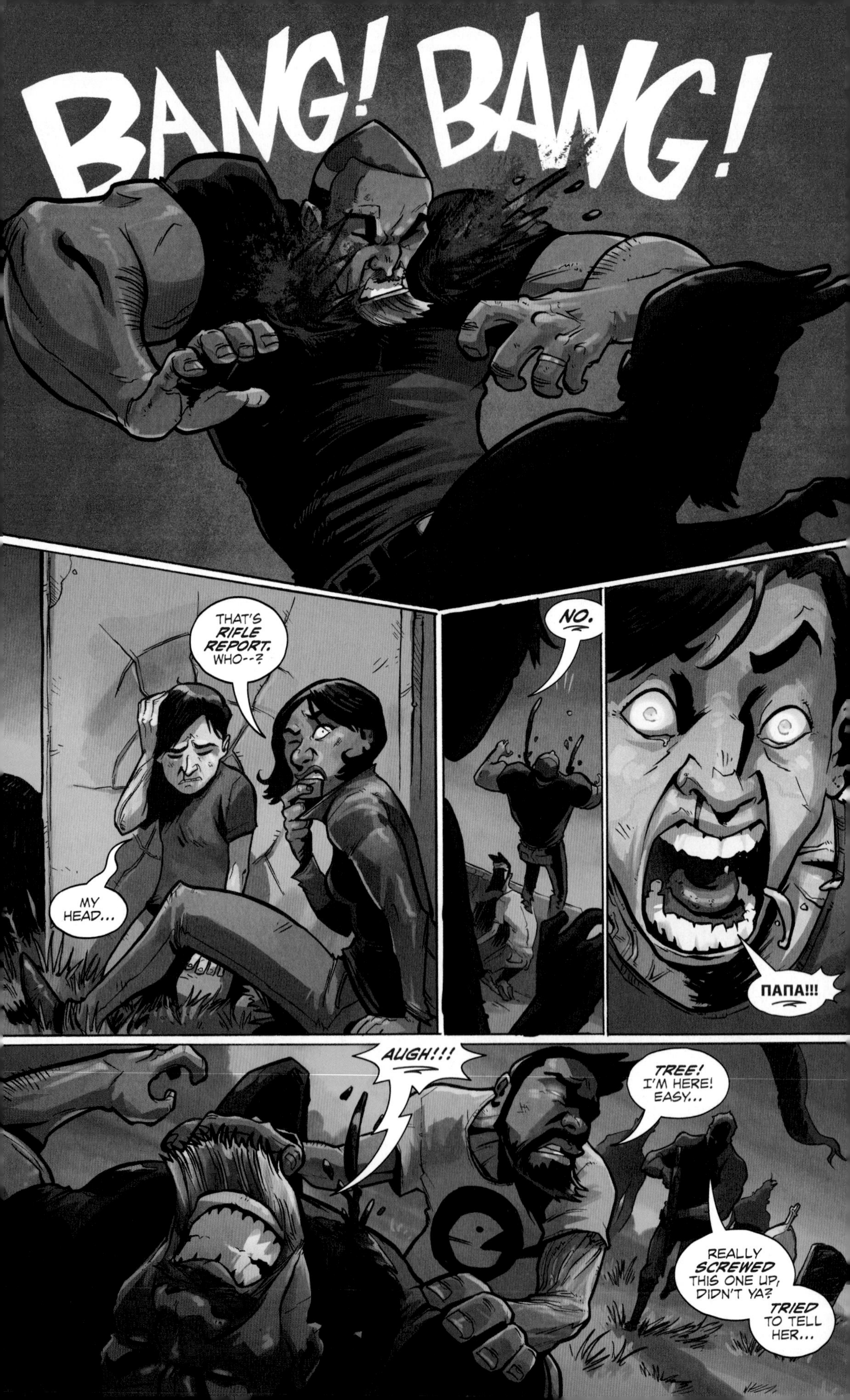
BANG! BANG!
THAT'S RIFLE REPORT. WHO--?
MY HEAD...
NO.
ПАПА!!!
AUGH!!!
TREE! I'M HERE! EASY...
REALLY SCREWED THIS ONE UP, DIDN'T YA?
TRIED TO TELL HER...

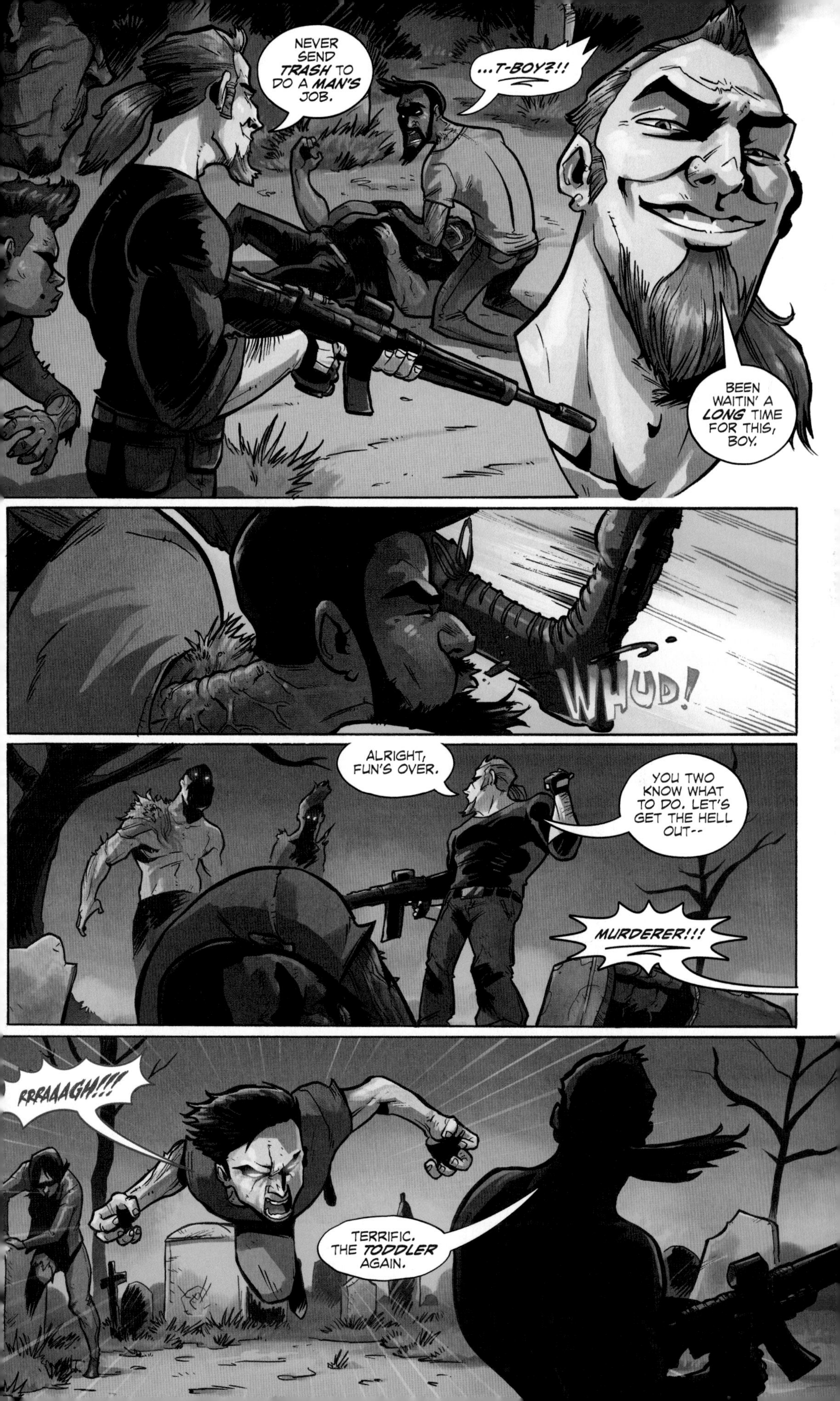
NEVER SEND TRASH TO DO A MAN'S JOB.
...T-BOY?!!
BEEN WAITIN' A LONG TIME FOR THIS, BOY.
WHUD!
ALRIGHT, FUN'S OVER.
YOU TWO KNOW WHAT TO DO. LET'S GET THE HELL OUT--
MURDERER!!!
RRRAAAGH!!!
TERRIFIC. THE TODDLER AGAIN.

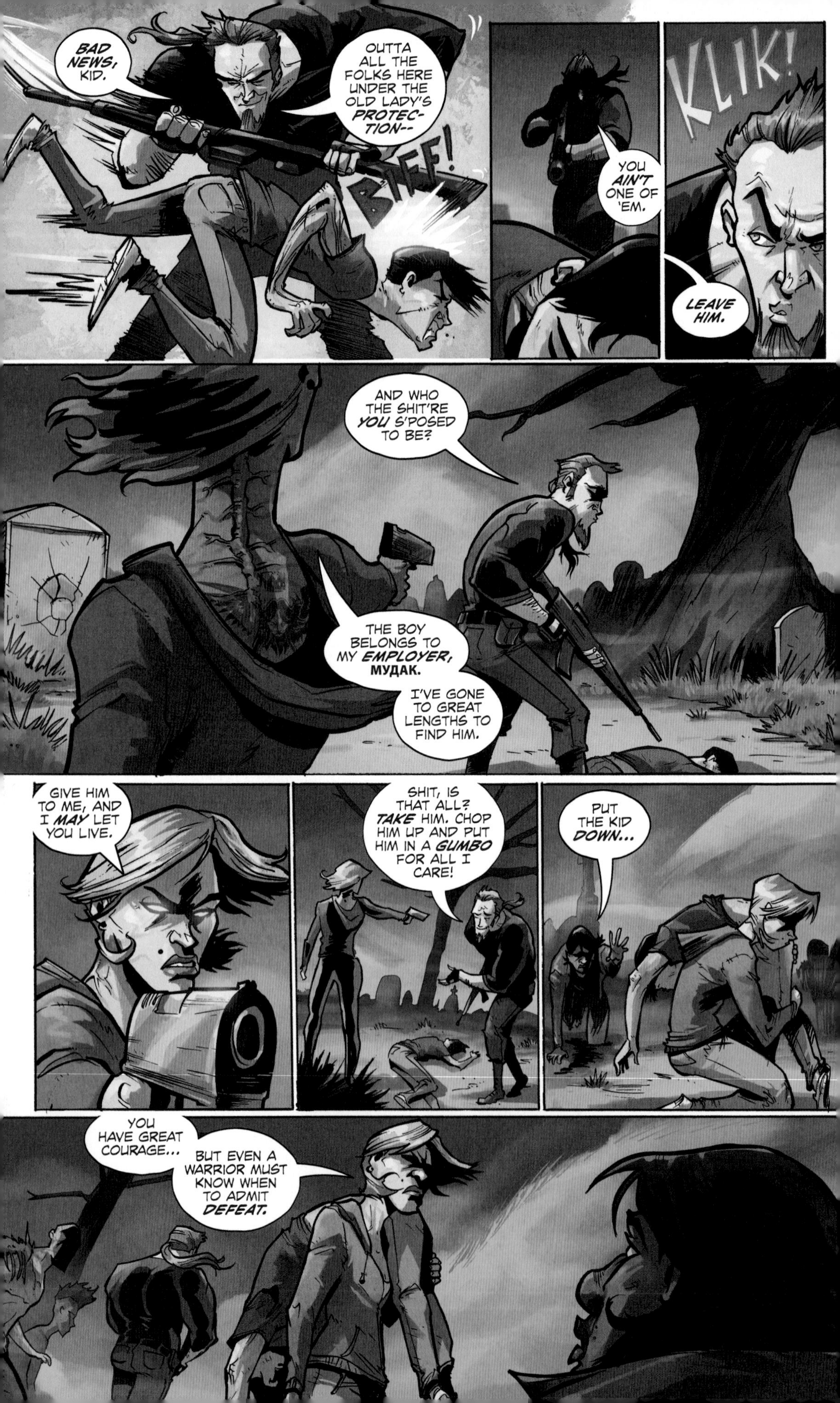
BAD NEWS, KID.
OUTTA ALL THE FOLKS HERE UNDER THE OLD LADY'S PROTECTION--
BIFF!
YOU AIN'T ONE OF 'EM.
KLIK!
LEAVE HIM.
AND WHO THE SHIT'RE YOU S'POSED TO BE?
THE BOY BELONGS TO MY EMPLOYER, МУДАК.
I'VE GONE TO GREAT LENGTHS TO FIND HIM.
GIVE HIM TO ME, AND I MAY LET YOU LIVE.
SHIT, IS THAT ALL? TAKE HIM. CHOP HIM UP AND PUT HIM IN A GUMBO FOR ALL I CARE!
PUT THE KID DOWN...
YOU HAVE GREAT COURAGE...
BUT EVEN A WARRIOR MUST KNOW WHEN TO ADMIT DEFEAT.

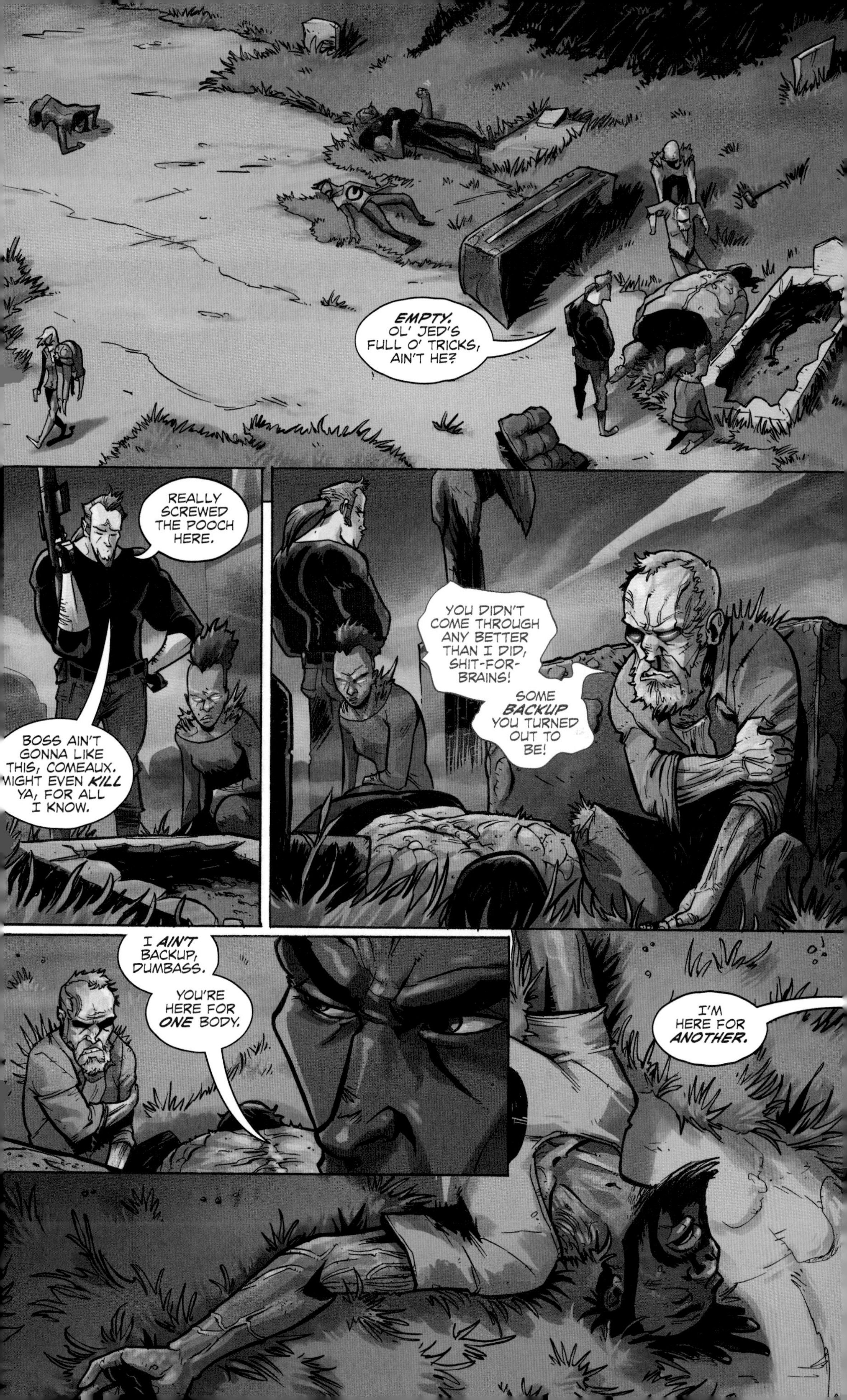
EMPTY. OL' JED'S FULL O' TRICKS, AIN'T HE?
REALLY SCREWED THE POOCH HERE.
BOSS AIN'T GONNA LIKE THIS, COMEAUX. MIGHT EVEN KILL YA, FOR ALL I KNOW.
YOU DIDN'T COME THROUGH ANY BETTER THAN I DID, SHIT-FOR-BRAINS!
SOME BACKUP YOU TURNED OUT TO BE!
I AIN'T BACKUP, DUMBASS.
YOU'RE HERE FOR ONE BODY.
I'M HERE FOR ANOTHER.

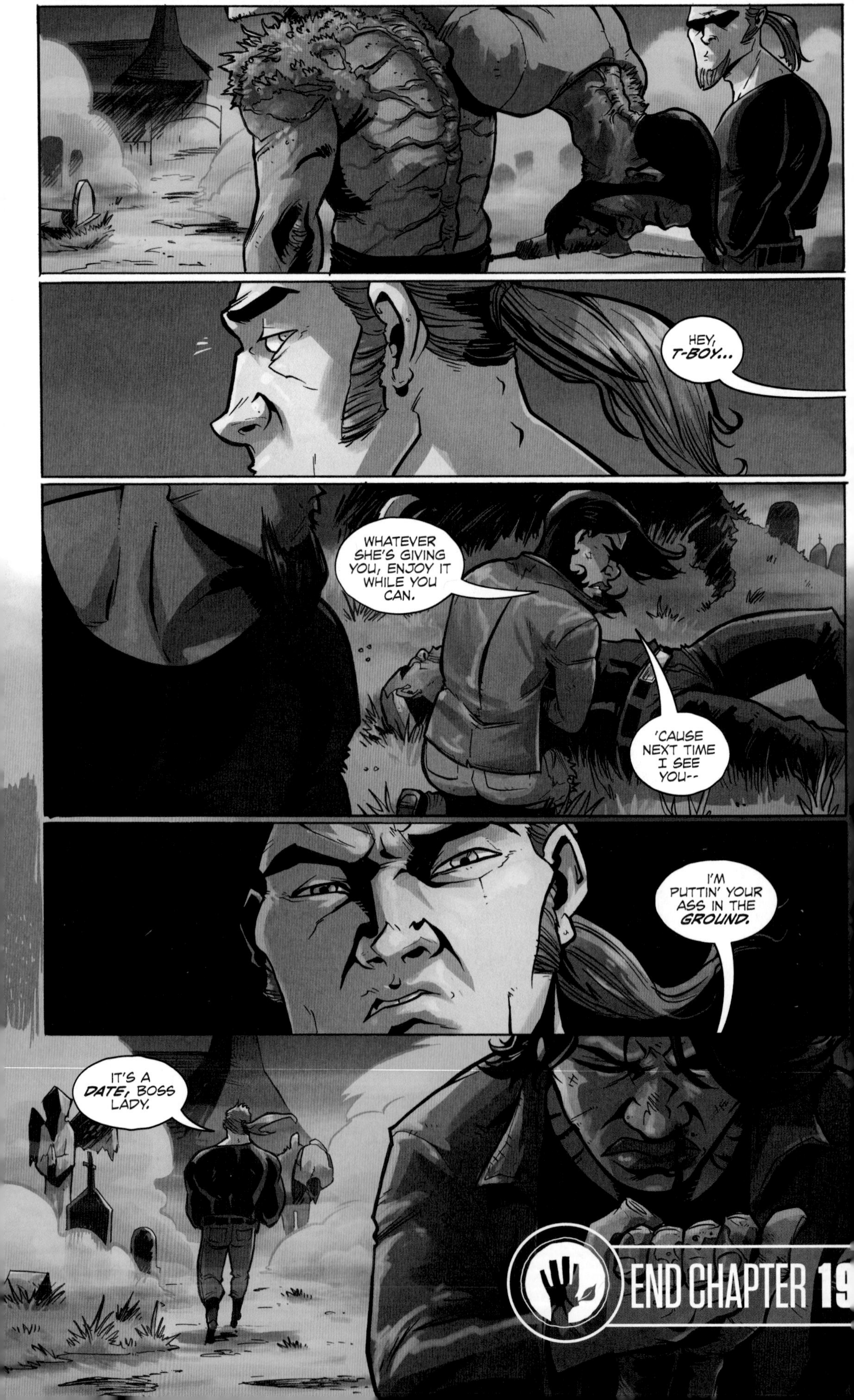
HEY, T-BOY...
WHATEVER SHE'S GIVING YOU, ENJOY IT WHILE YOU CAN.
'CAUSE NEXT TIME I SEE YOU--
I'M PUTTIN' YOUR ASS IN THE GROUND.
IT'S A DATE, BOSS LADY.
END CHAPTER 19

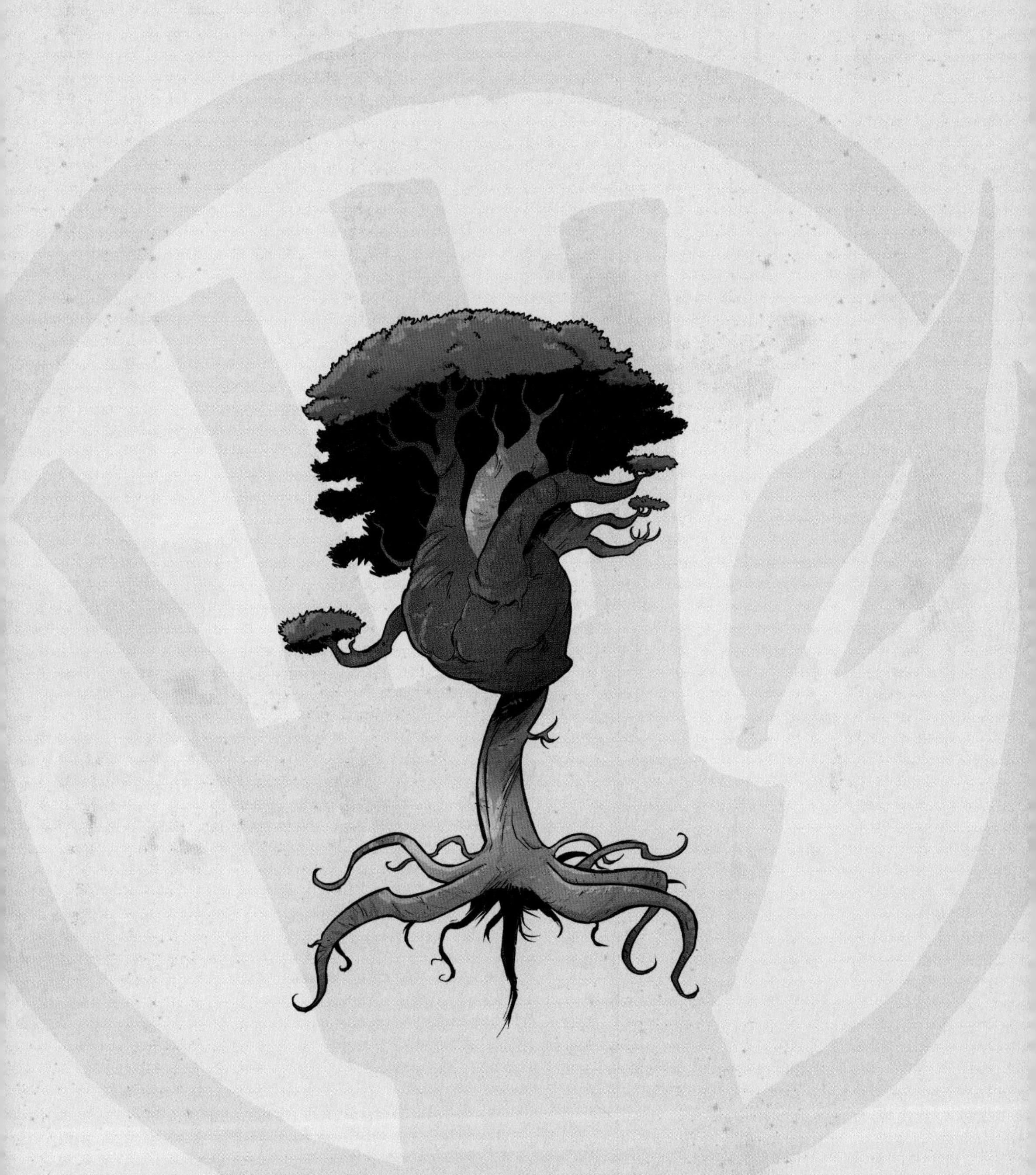

CHAPTER 20

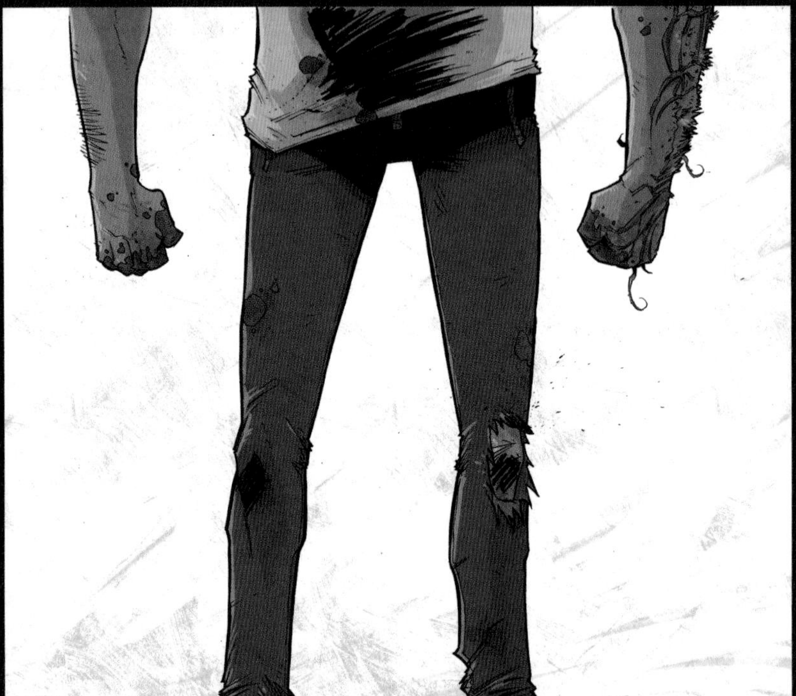

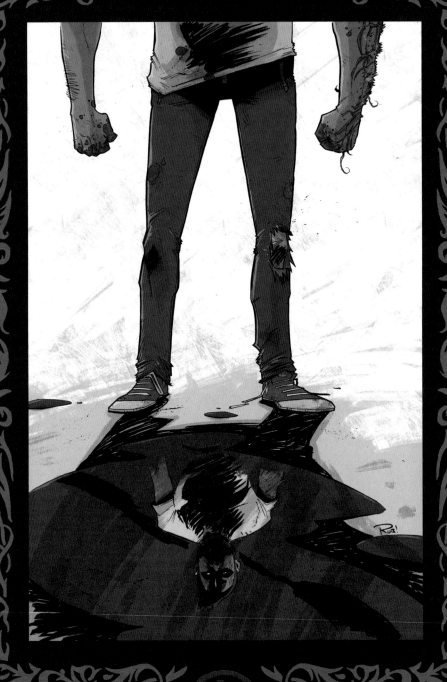

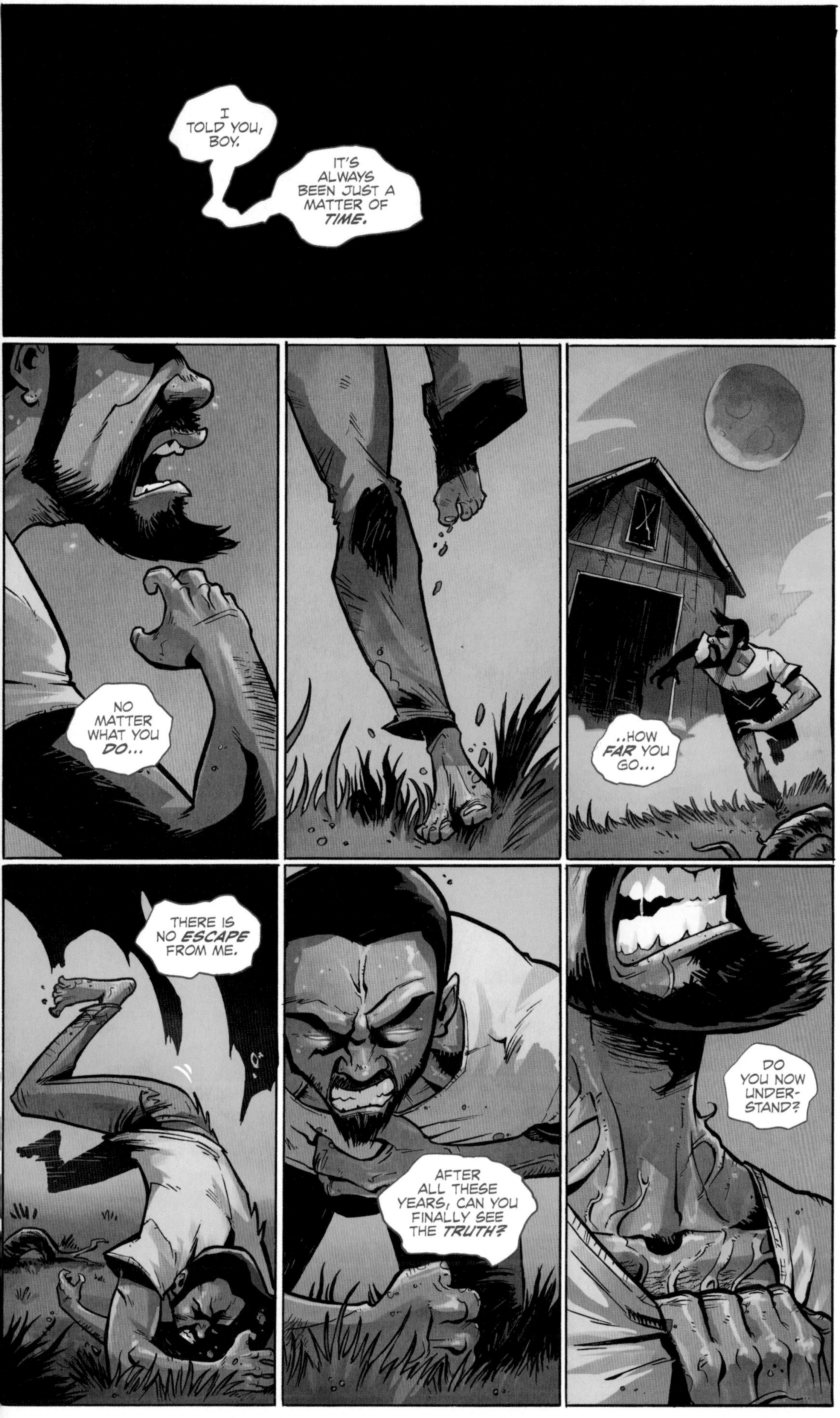
I TOLD YOU, BOY.
IT'S ALWAYS BEEN JUST A MATTER OF *TIME.*
NO MATTER WHAT YOU *DO*...
..HOW *FAR* YOU GO...
THERE IS NO *ESCAPE* FROM ME.
AFTER ALL THESE YEARS, CAN YOU FINALLY SEE THE *TRUTH?*
DO YOU NOW UNDER-STAND?

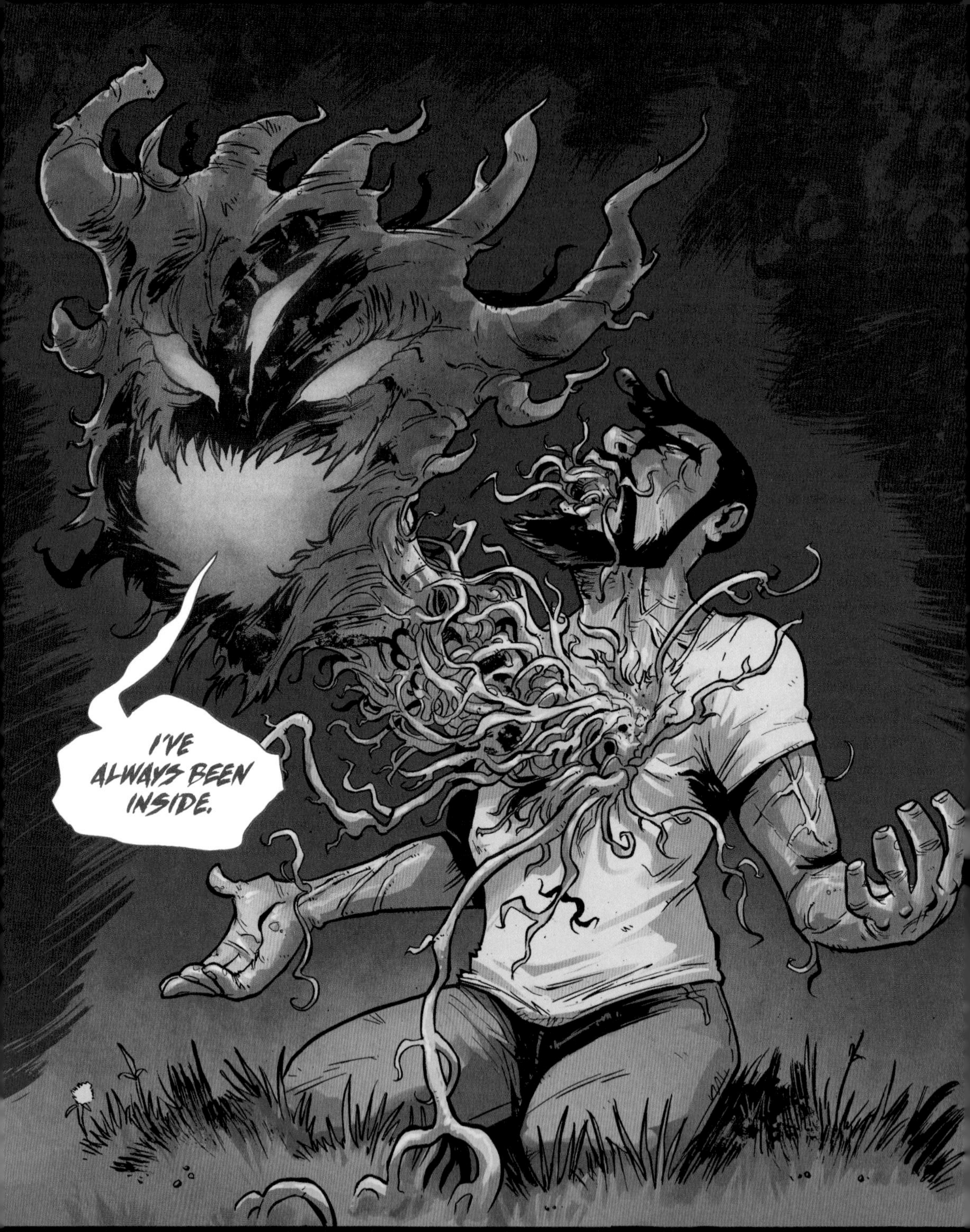
I'VE ALWAYS BEEN INSIDE.

CHAPTER 20: **THE PROVING GROUNDS.**

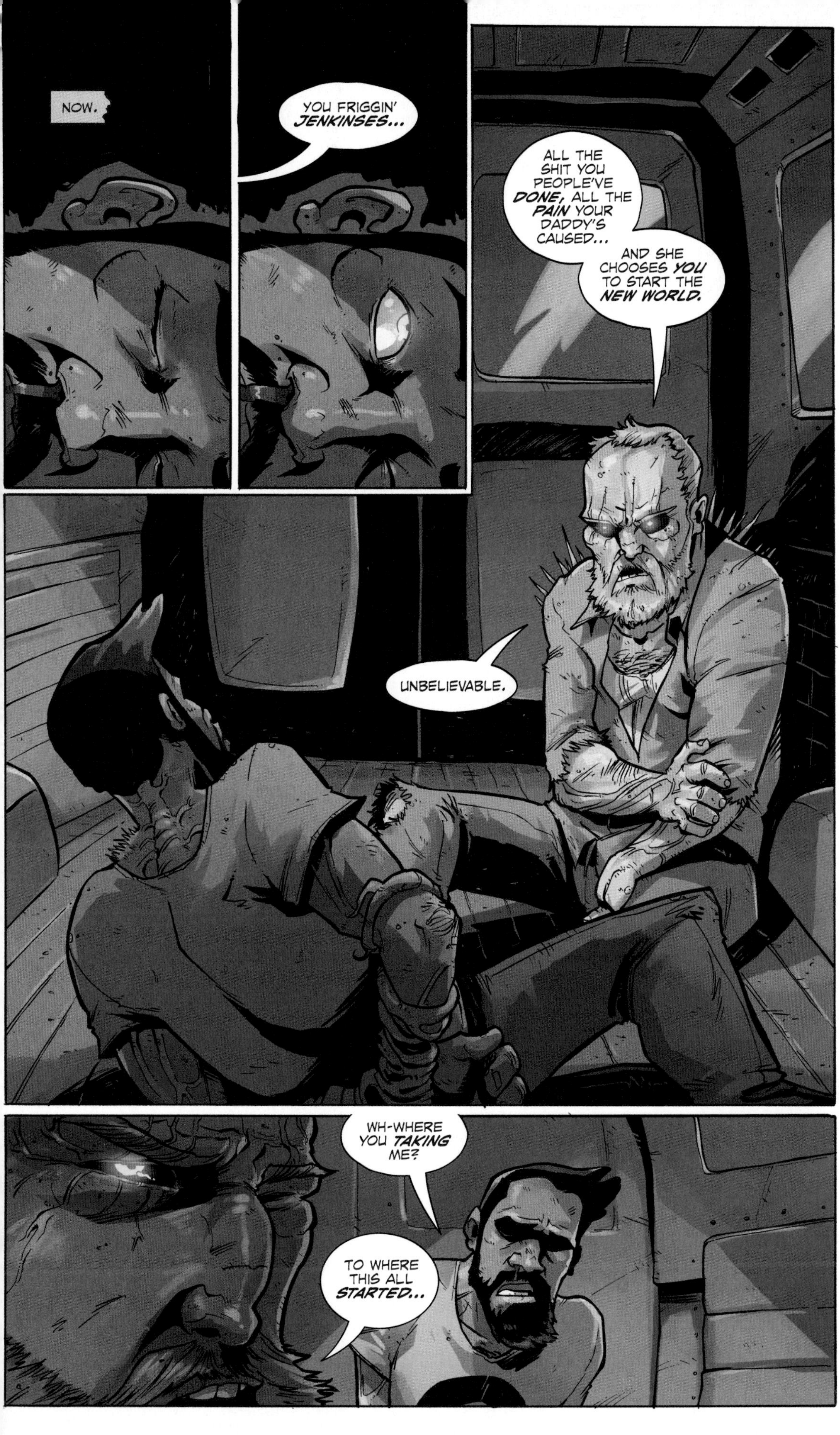
NOW.
YOU FRIGGIN' JENKINSES...
ALL THE SHIT YOU PEOPLE'VE DONE, ALL THE PAIN YOUR DADDY'S CAUSED...
AND SHE CHOOSES YOU TO START THE NEW WORLD.
UNBELIEVABLE.
WH-WHERE YOU TAKING ME?
TO WHERE THIS ALL STARTED...

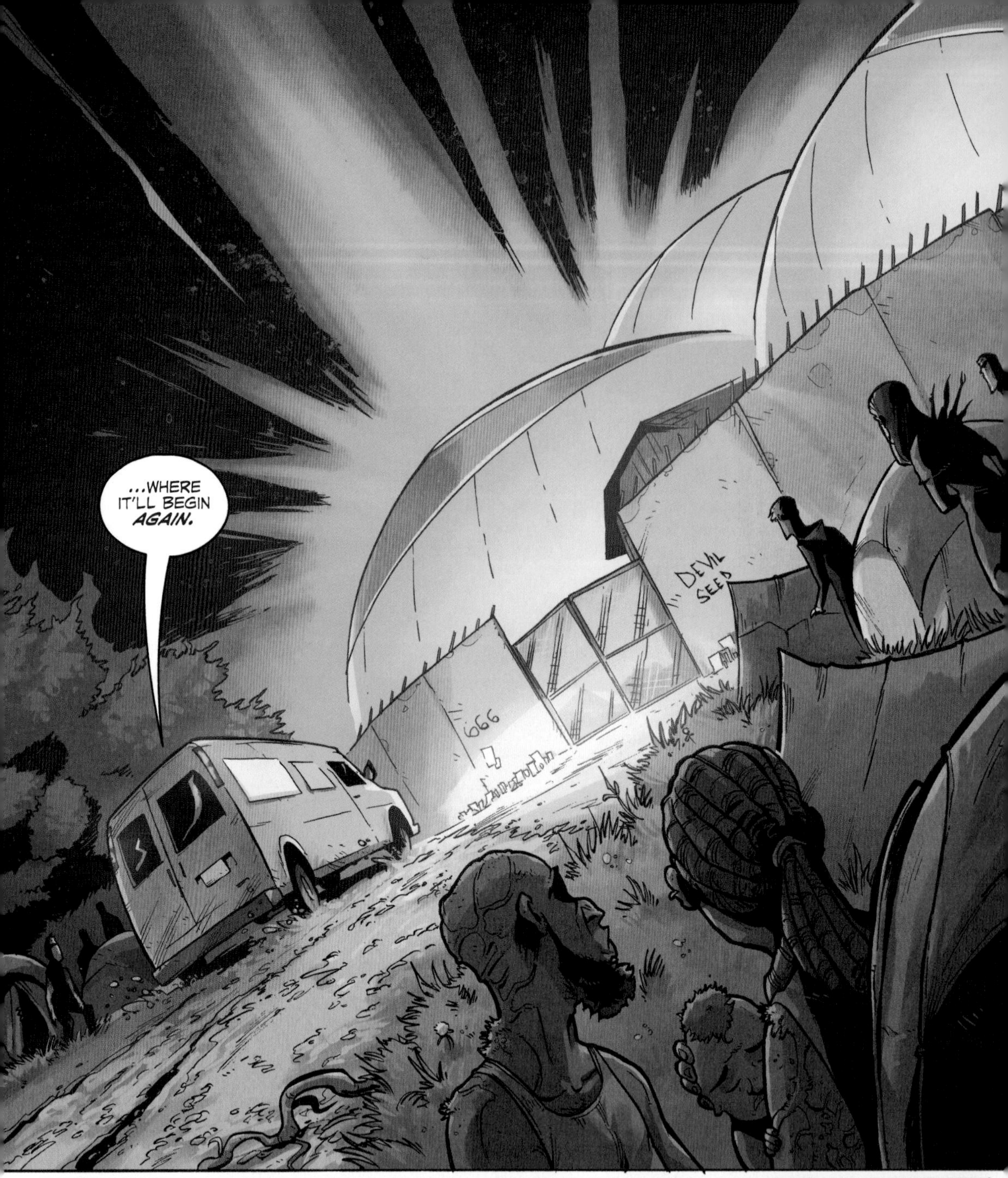
...WHERE IT'LL BEGIN AGAIN.
DEVIL SEED
666

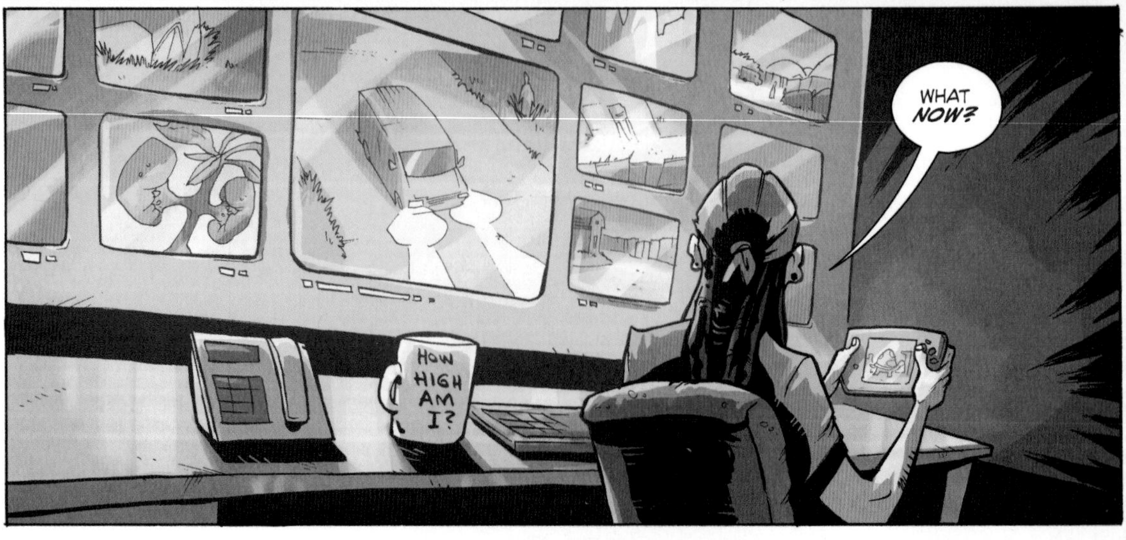
WHAT NOW?
HOW HIGH AM I?

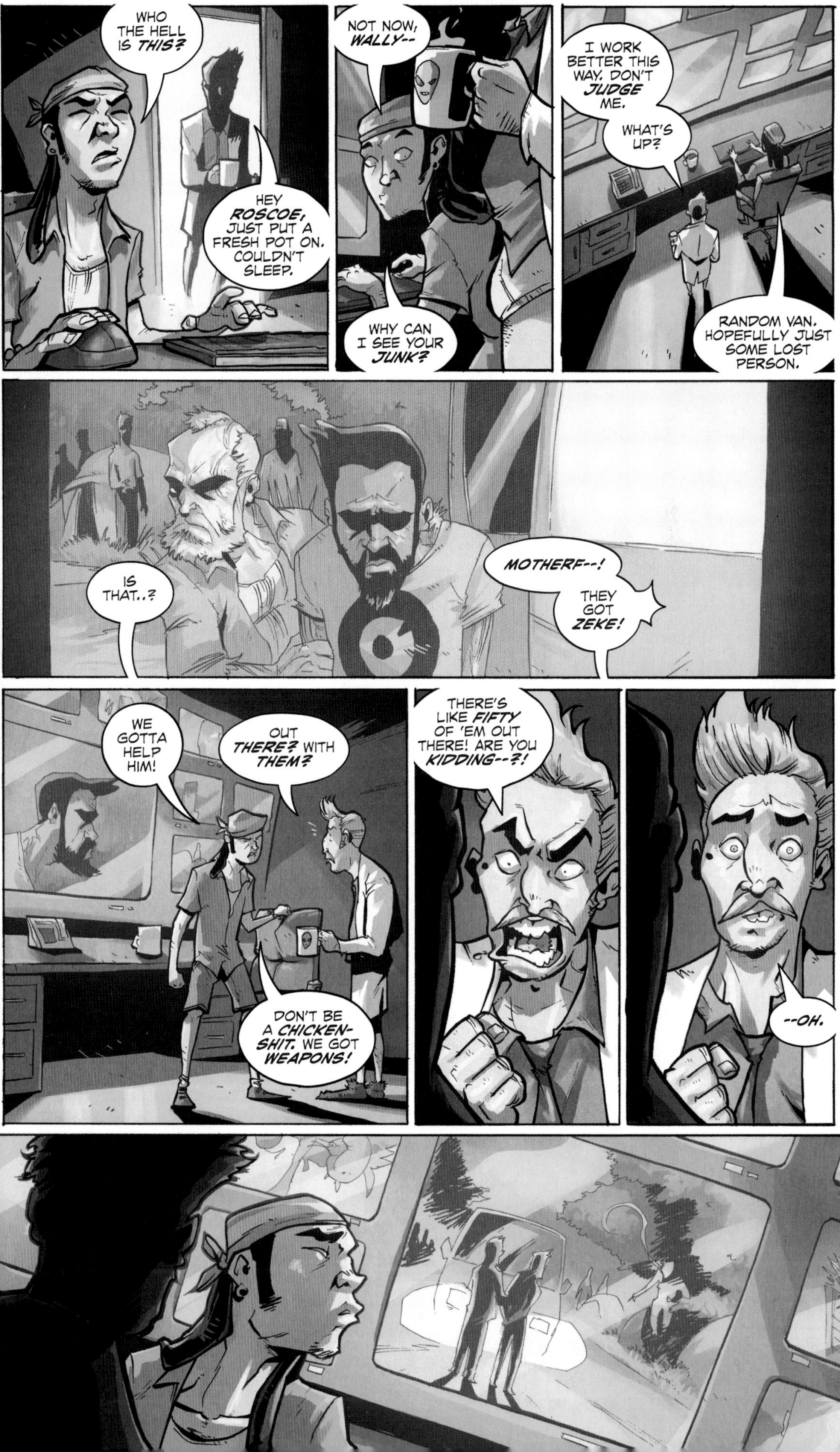
WHO THE HELL IS *THIS?*
HEY *ROSCOE,* JUST PUT A FRESH POT ON. COULDN'T SLEEP.
NOT NOW, *WALLY--*
WHY CAN I SEE YOUR *JUNK?*
I WORK BETTER THIS WAY. DON'T *JUDGE* ME.
WHAT'S UP?
RANDOM VAN. HOPEFULLY JUST SOME LOST PERSON.
IS THAT..?
MOTHERF--!
THEY GOT *ZEKE!*
WE GOTTA HELP HIM!
OUT *THERE?* WITH *THEM?*
DON'T BE A *CHICKEN-SHIT.* WE GOT *WEAPONS!*
THERE'S LIKE *FIFTY* OF 'EM OUT THERE! ARE YOU *KIDDING--?!*
--OH.

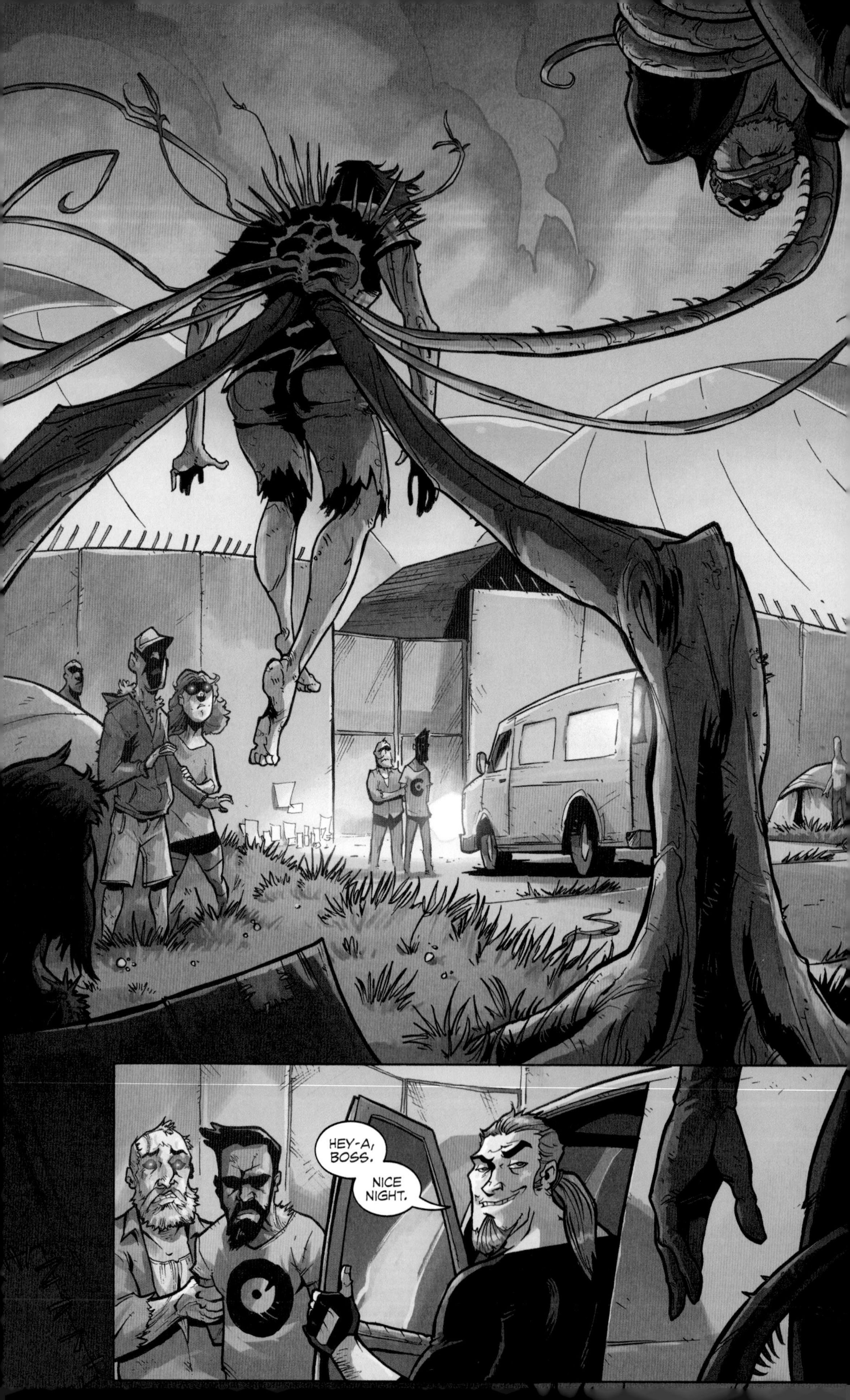
HEY-A, BOSS.
NICE NIGHT.

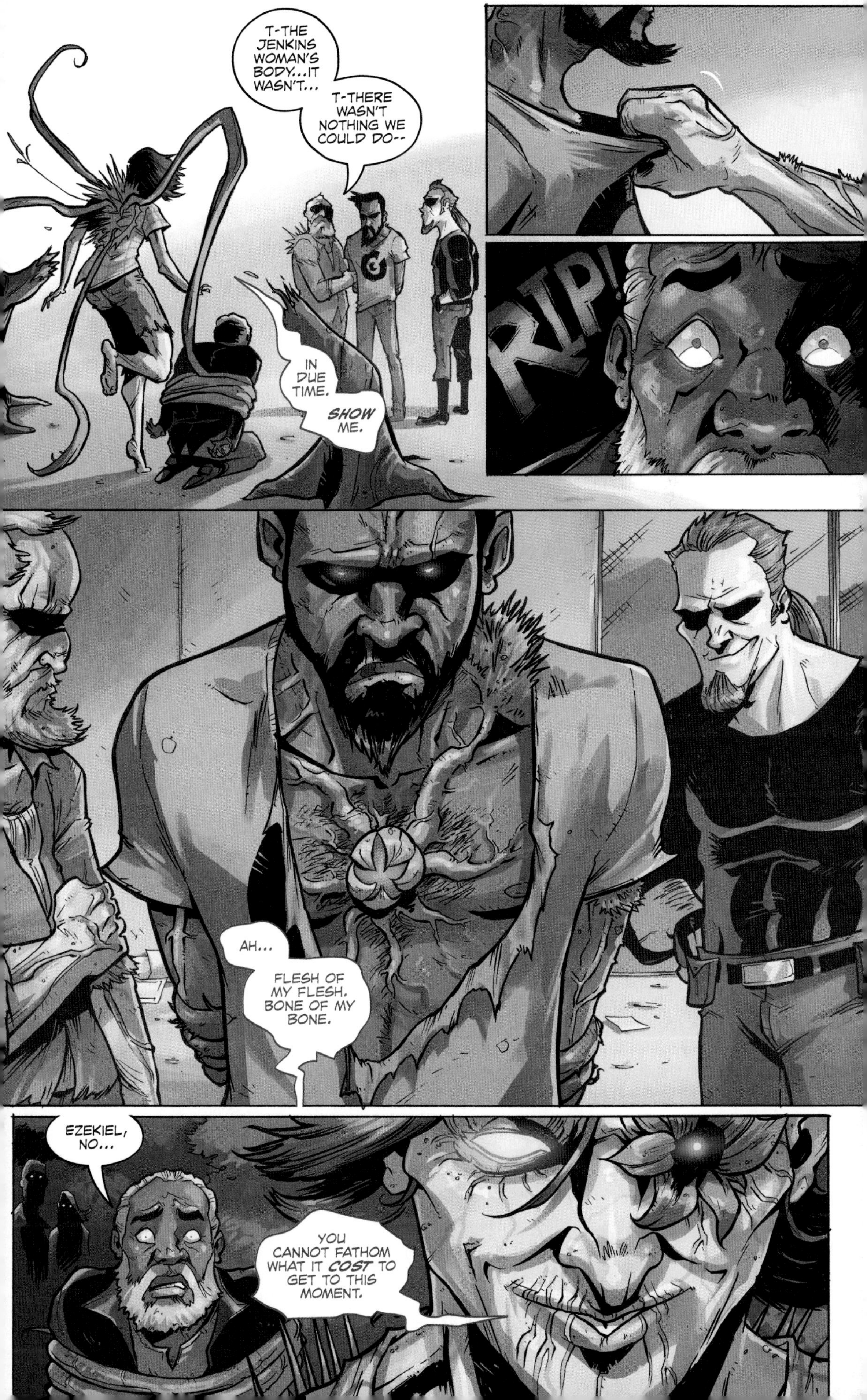
T-THE JENKINS WOMAN'S BODY...IT WASN'T...
T-THERE WASN'T NOTHING WE COULD DO--
IN DUE TIME.
SHOW ME.
RIP!
AH...
FLESH OF MY FLESH. BONE OF MY BONE.
EZEKIEL, NO...
YOU CANNOT FATHOM WHAT IT COST TO GET TO THIS MOMENT.

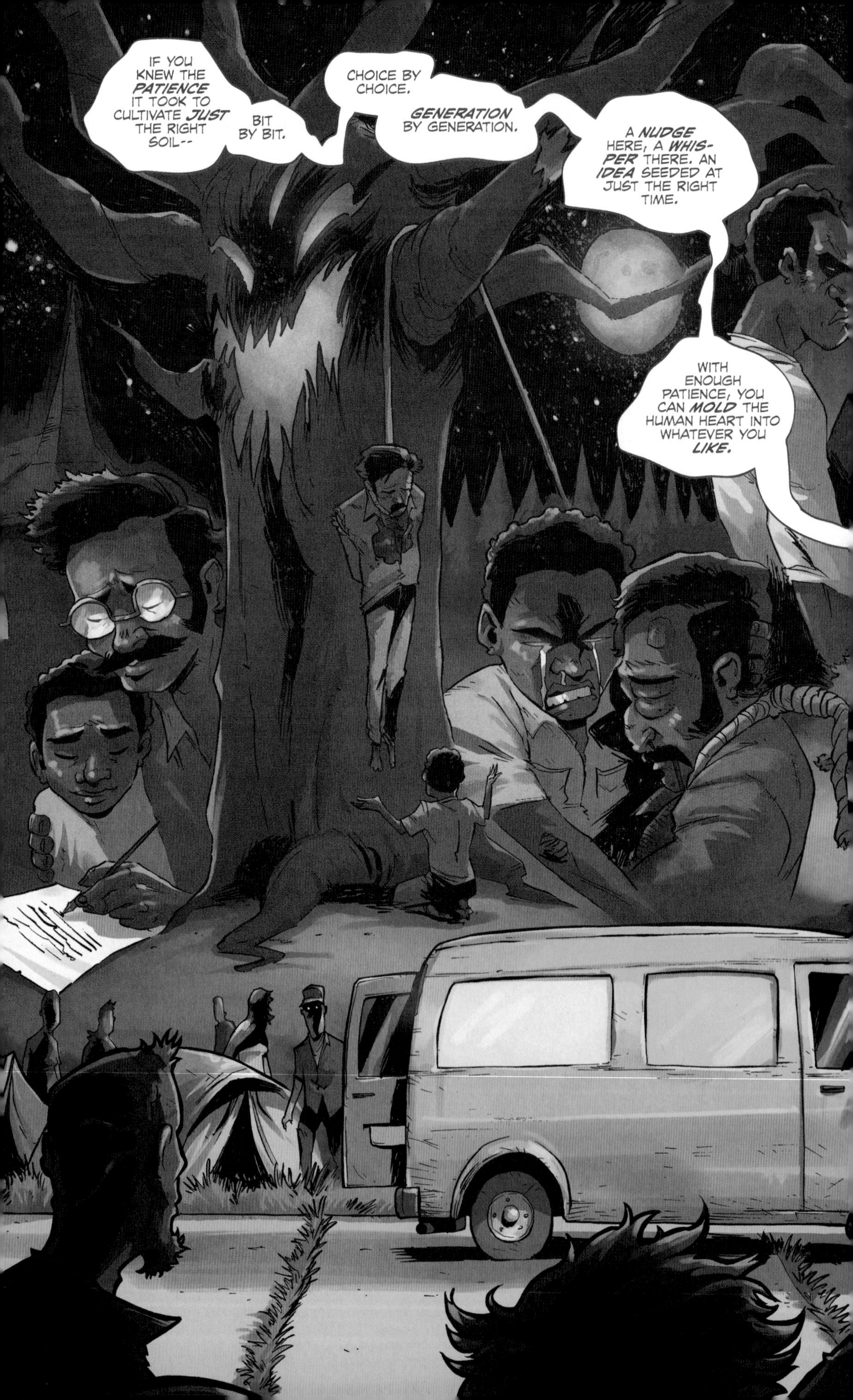
IF YOU KNEW THE PATIENCE IT TOOK TO CULTIVATE JUST THE RIGHT SOIL--
BIT BY BIT.
CHOICE BY CHOICE.
GENERATION BY GENERATION.
A NUDGE HERE, A WHISPER THERE. AN IDEA SEEDED AT JUST THE RIGHT TIME.
WITH ENOUGH PATIENCE, YOU CAN MOLD THE HUMAN HEART INTO WHATEVER YOU LIKE.

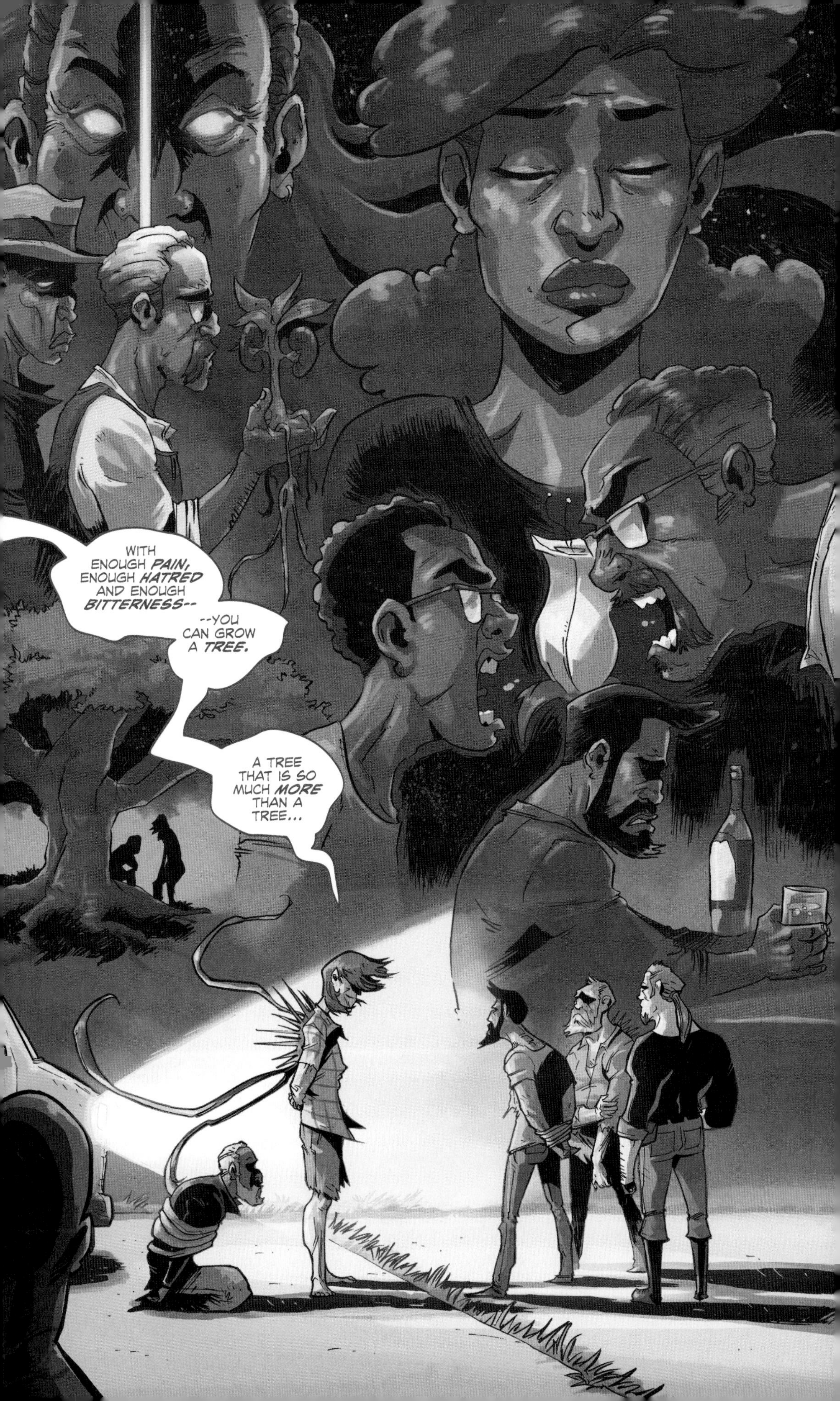
WITH ENOUGH *PAIN,* ENOUGH *HATRED* AND ENOUGH *BITTERNESS--*
--YOU CAN GROW A *TREE.*
A TREE THAT IS SO MUCH *MORE* THAN A TREE...

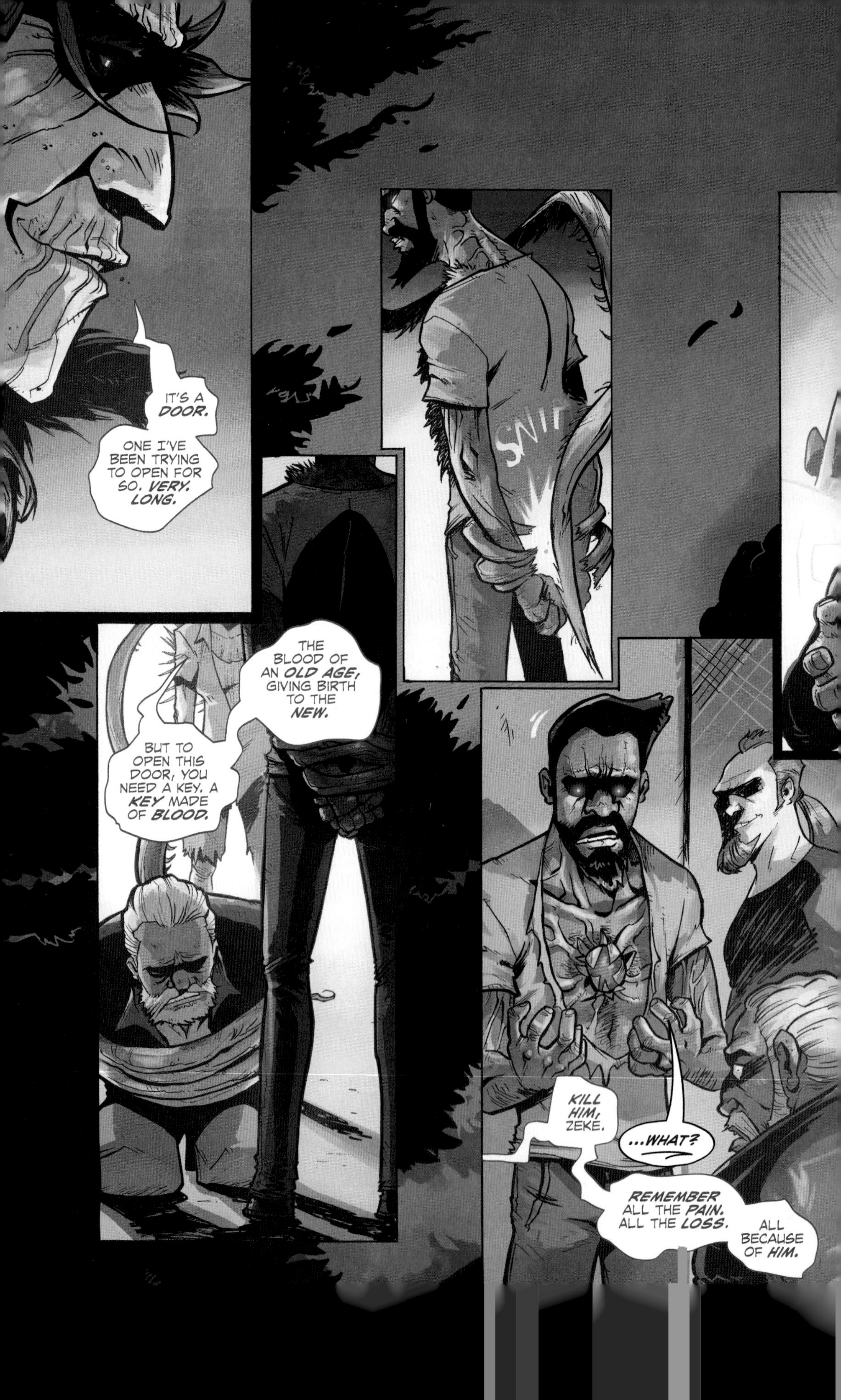

IT'S A DOOR.
ONE I'VE BEEN TRYING TO OPEN FOR SO. VERY. LONG.
THE BLOOD OF AN OLD AGE, GIVING BIRTH TO THE NEW.
BUT TO OPEN THIS DOOR, YOU NEED A KEY. A KEY MADE OF BLOOD.
KILL HIM, ZEKE.
...WHAT?
REMEMBER ALL THE PAIN. ALL THE LOSS.
ALL BECAUSE OF HIM.

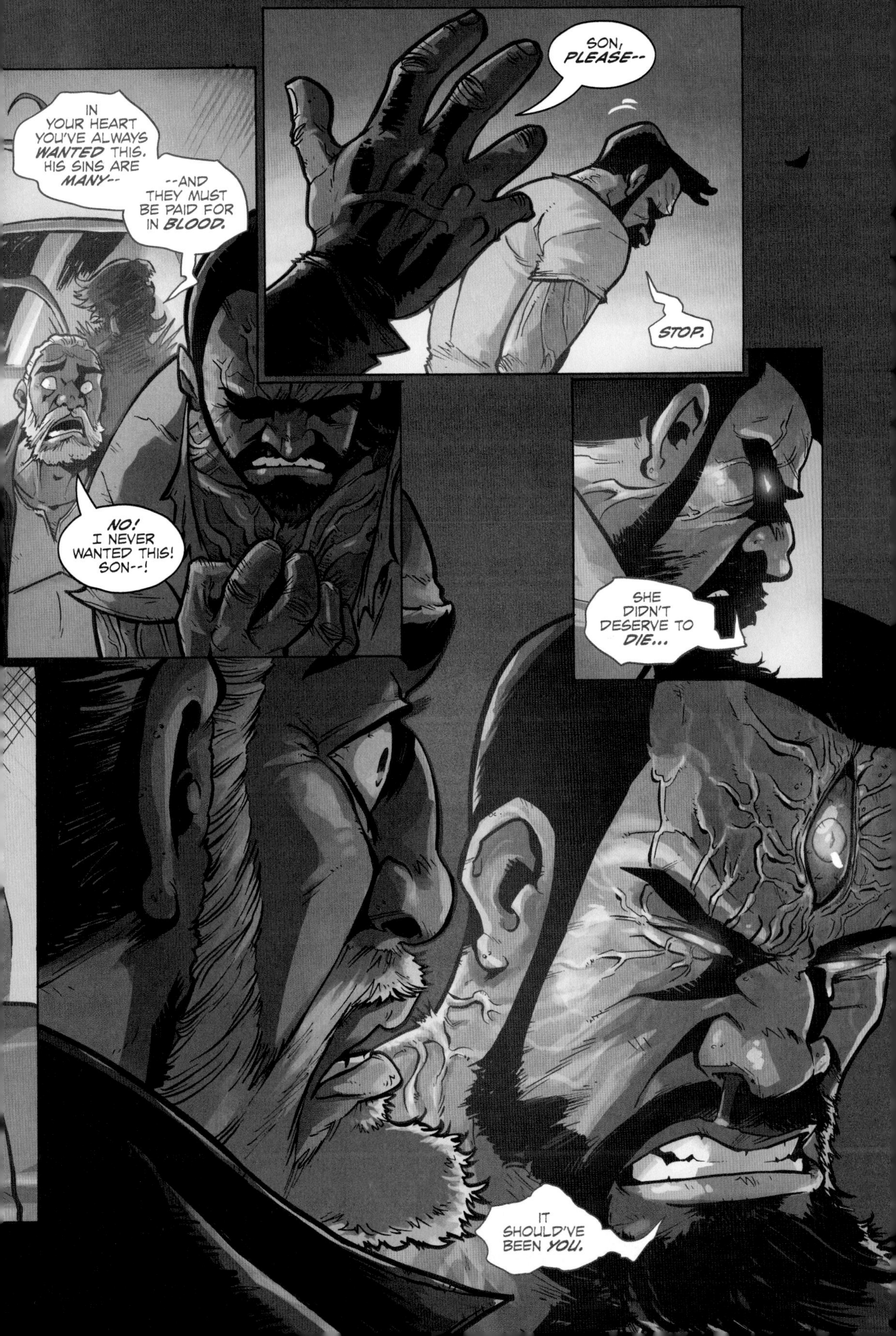
IN YOUR HEART YOU'VE ALWAYS WANTED THIS. HIS SINS ARE MANY--
--AND THEY MUST BE PAID FOR IN BLOOD.
NO! I NEVER WANTED THIS! SON--!
SON, PLEASE--
STOP.
SHE DIDN'T DESERVE TO DIE...
IT SHOULD'VE BEEN YOU.

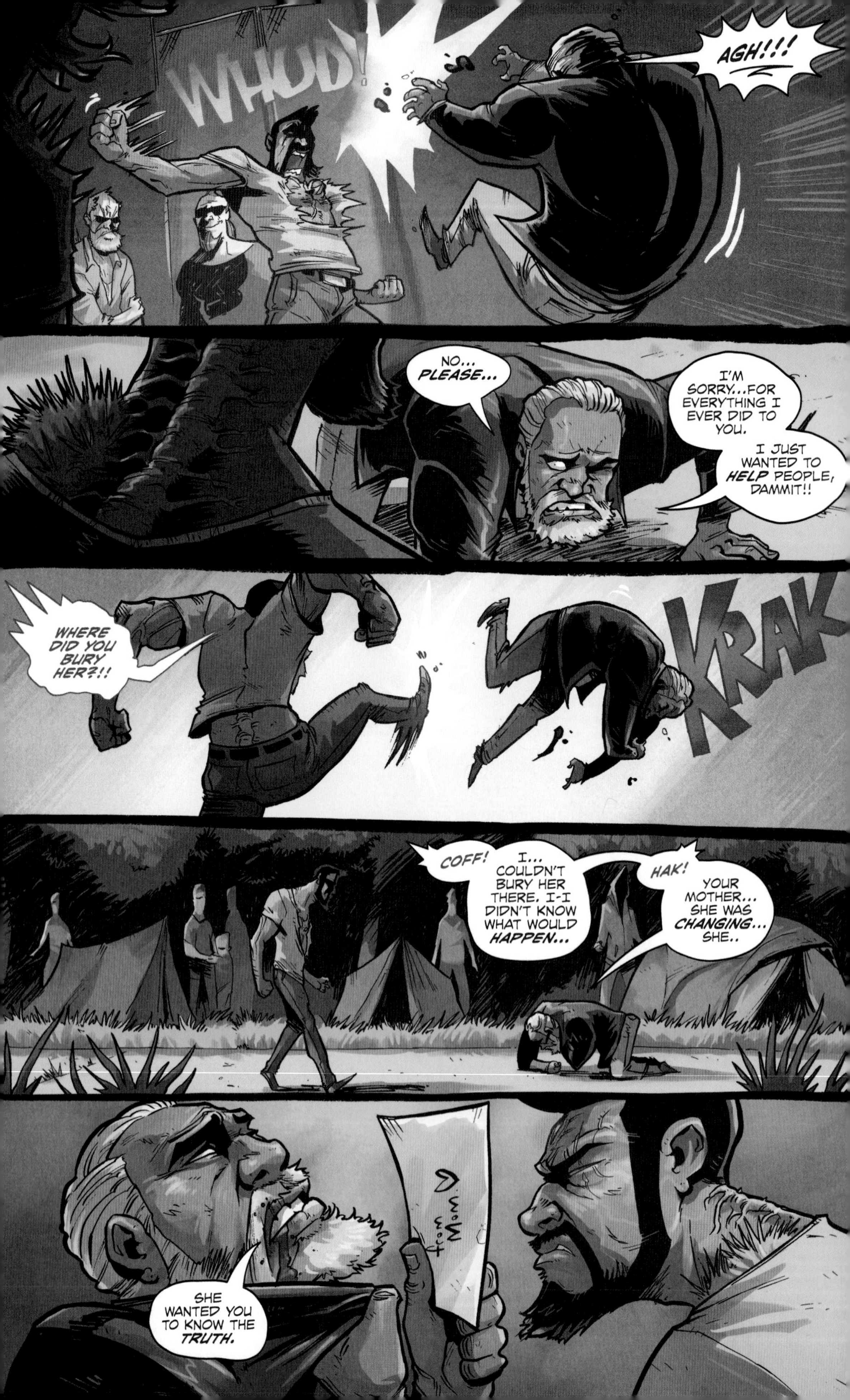
WHUD!
AGH!!!
NO... PLEASE...
I'M SORRY...FOR EVERYTHING I EVER DID TO YOU.
I JUST WANTED TO HELP PEOPLE, DAMMIT!!
WHERE DID YOU BURY HER?!!
KRAK
COFF!
I... COULDN'T BURY HER THERE. I-I DIDN'T KNOW WHAT WOULD HAPPEN...
HAK!
YOUR MOTHER... SHE WAS CHANGING... SHE..
SHE WANTED YOU TO KNOW THE TRUTH.

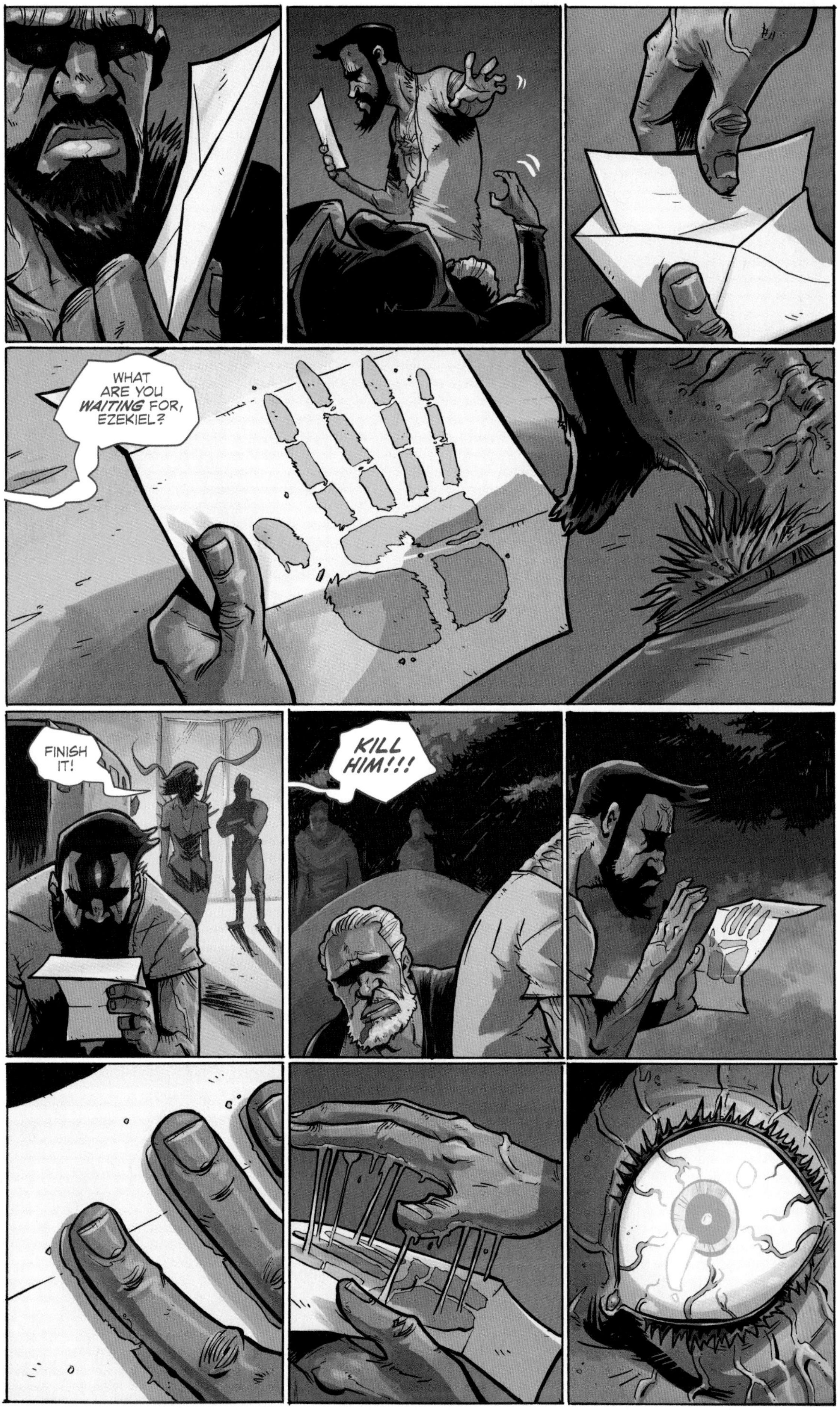
WHAT ARE YOU *WAITING* FOR, EZEKIEL?
FINISH IT!
KILL HIM!!!

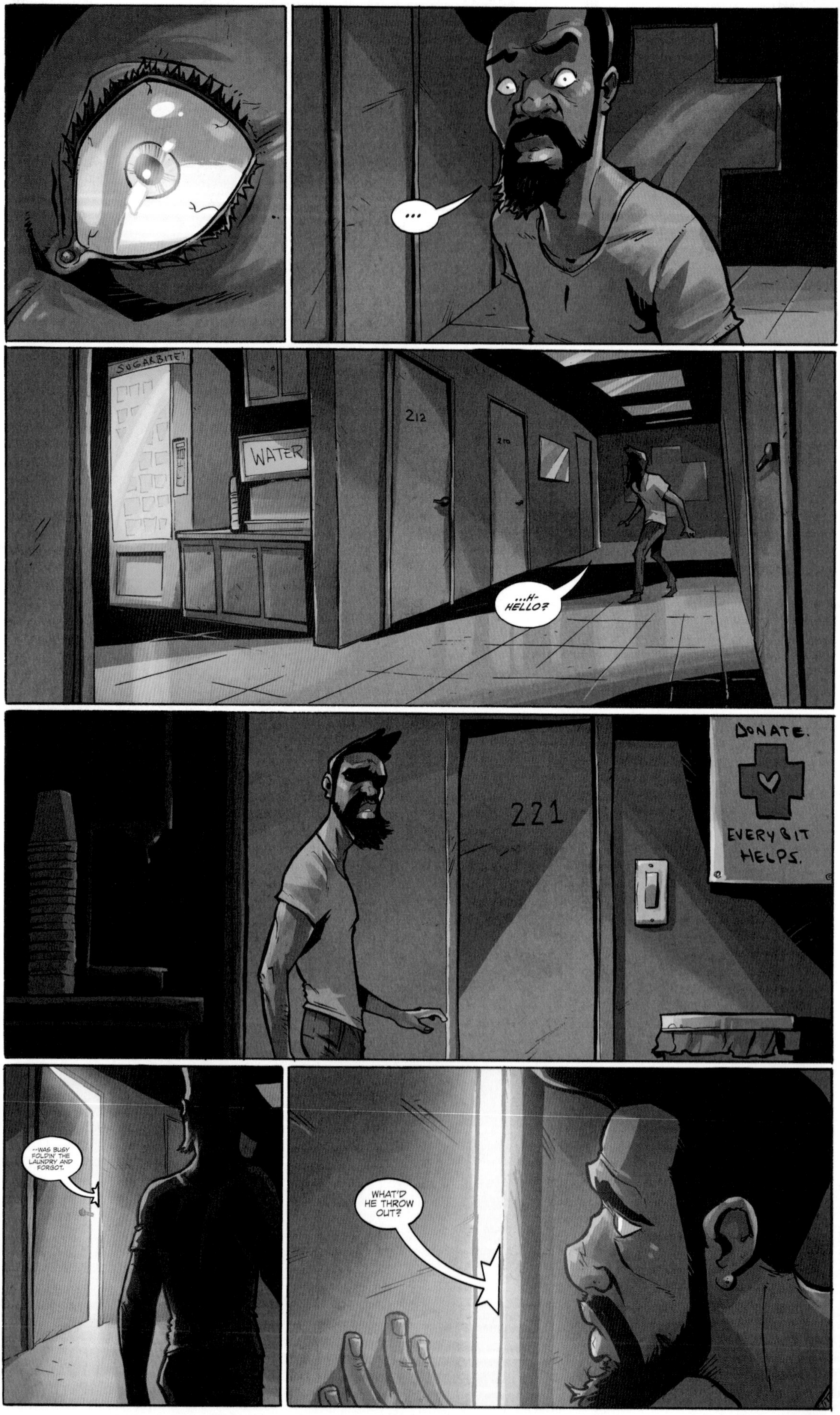
...
SUGARBITE!
WATER
212
...H-HELLO?
221
DONATE.
EVERY BIT HELPS.
--WAS BUSY FOLDIN' THE LAUNDRY AND FORGOT.
WHAT'D HE THROW OUT?

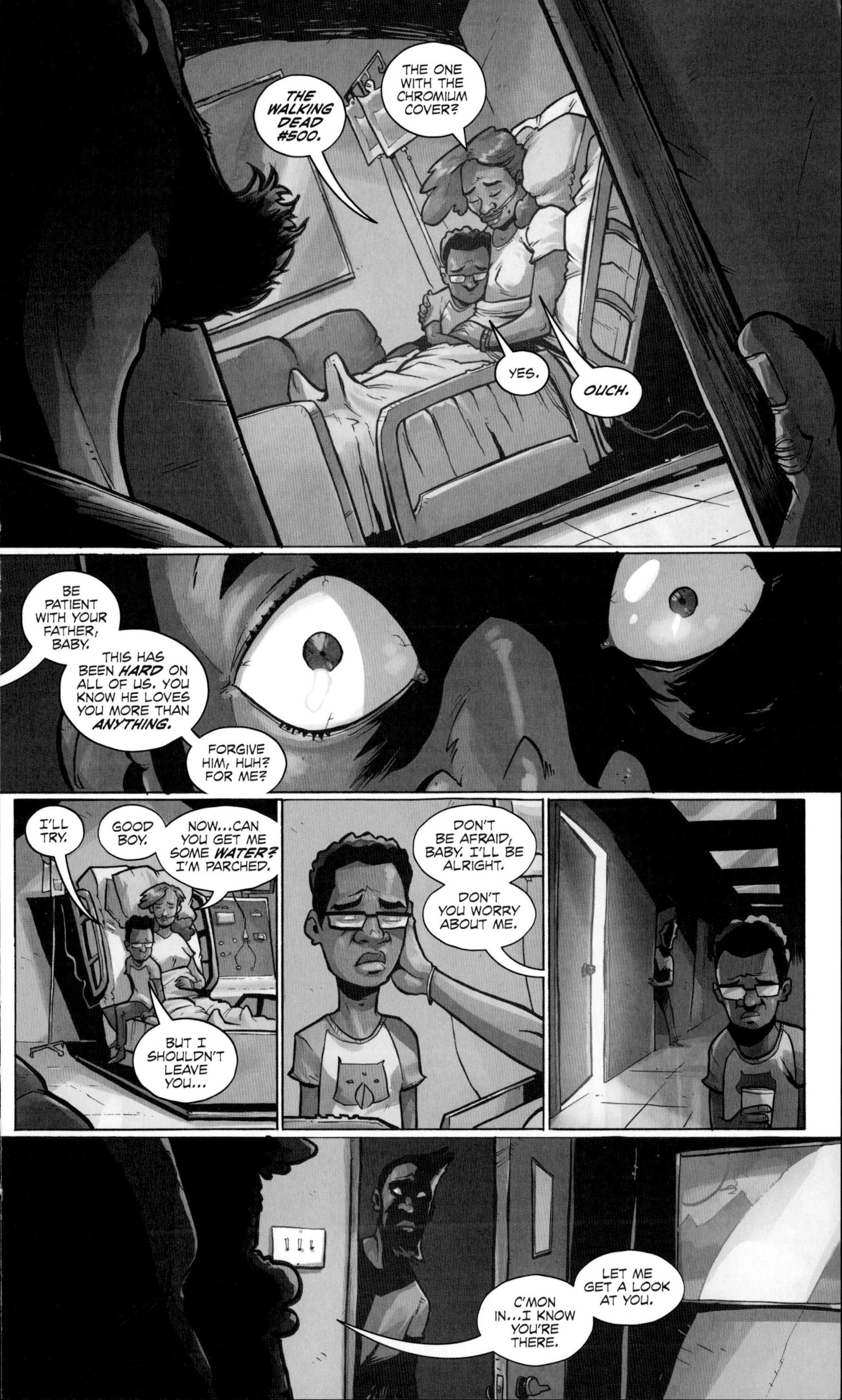
THE WALKING DEAD #500.
THE ONE WITH THE CHROMIUM COVER?
YES.
OUCH.
BE PATIENT WITH YOUR FATHER, BABY.
THIS HAS BEEN HARD ON ALL OF US. YOU KNOW HE LOVES YOU MORE THAN ANYTHING.
FORGIVE HIM, HUH? FOR ME?
I'LL TRY.
GOOD BOY.
NOW...CAN YOU GET ME SOME WATER? I'M PARCHED.
BUT I SHOULDN'T LEAVE YOU...
DON'T BE AFRAID, BABY. I'LL BE ALRIGHT.
DON'T YOU WORRY ABOUT ME.
LET ME GET A LOOK AT YOU.
C'MON IN...I KNOW YOU'RE THERE.

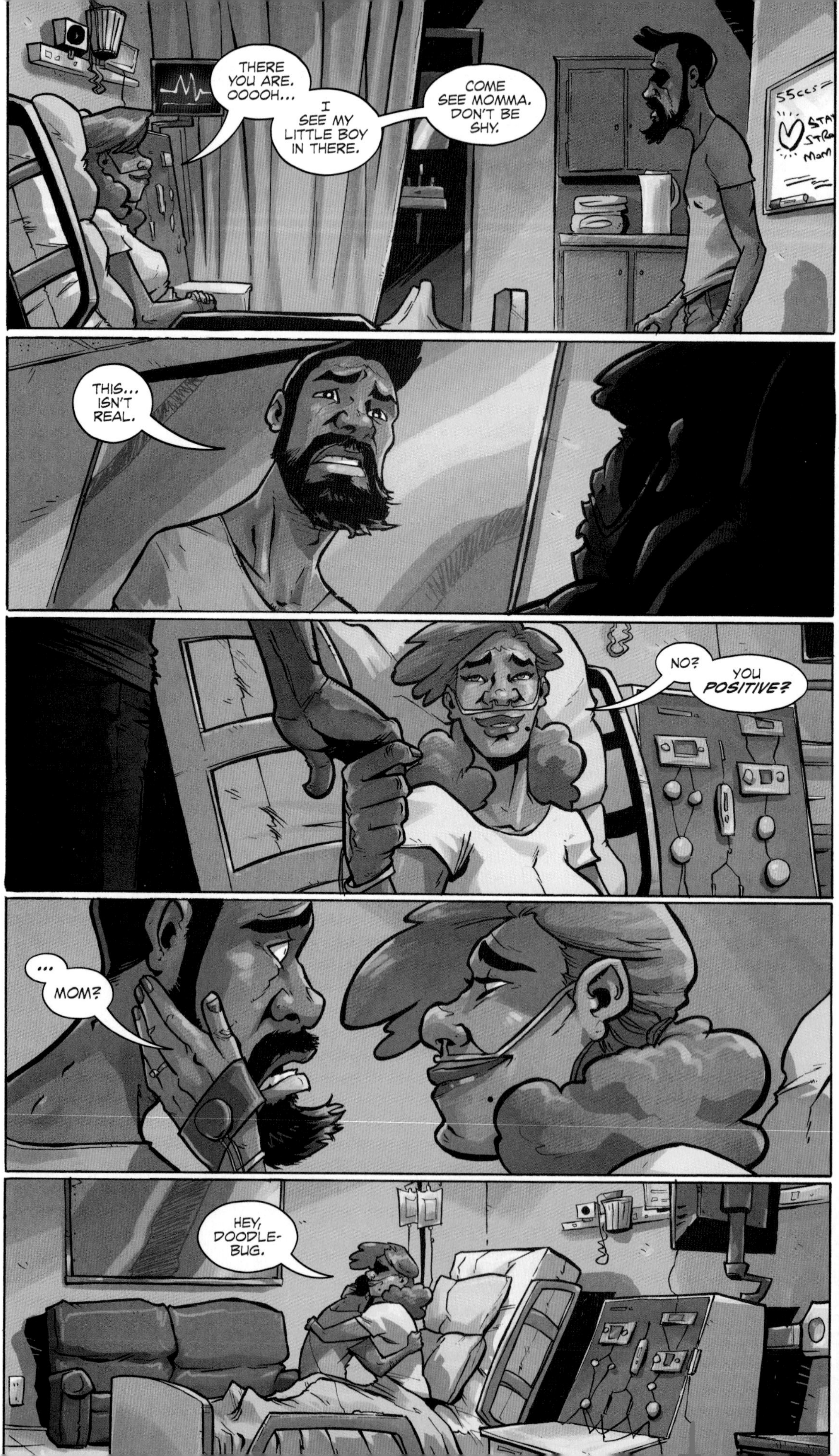
THERE YOU ARE. OOOOH...
I SEE MY LITTLE BOY IN THERE.
COME SEE MOMMA. DON'T BE SHY.
THIS... ISN'T REAL.
NO?
YOU *POSITIVE?*
...
MOM?
HEY, DOODLE-BUG.

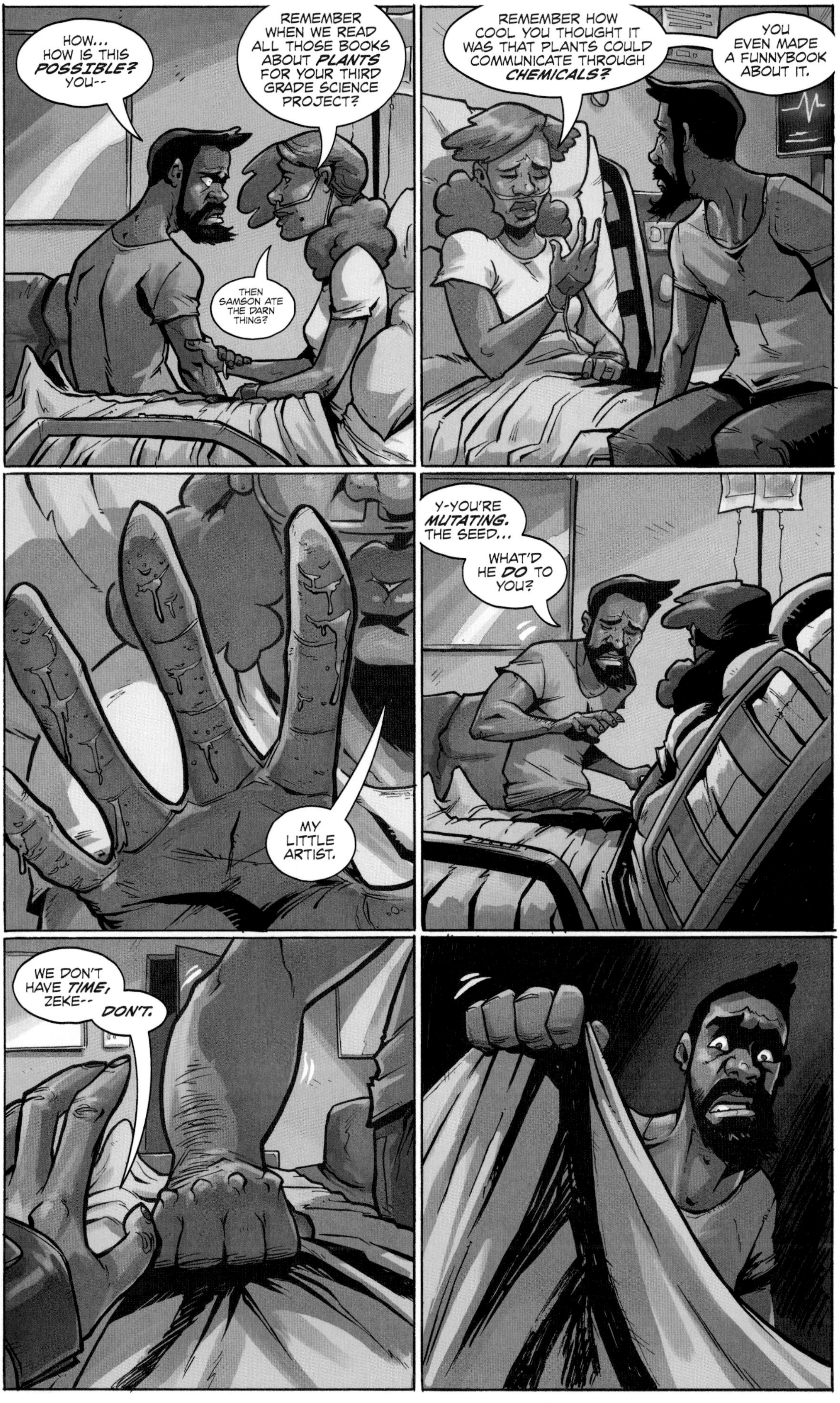
HOW... HOW IS THIS POSSIBLE? YOU--
REMEMBER WHEN WE READ ALL THOSE BOOKS ABOUT PLANTS FOR YOUR THIRD GRADE SCIENCE PROJECT?
THEN SAMSON ATE THE DARN THING?
REMEMBER HOW COOL YOU THOUGHT IT WAS THAT PLANTS COULD COMMUNICATE THROUGH CHEMICALS?
YOU EVEN MADE A FUNNYBOOK ABOUT IT.
MY LITTLE ARTIST.
Y-YOU'RE MUTATING. THE SEED...
WHAT'D HE DO TO YOU?
WE DON'T HAVE TIME, ZEKE--
DON'T.

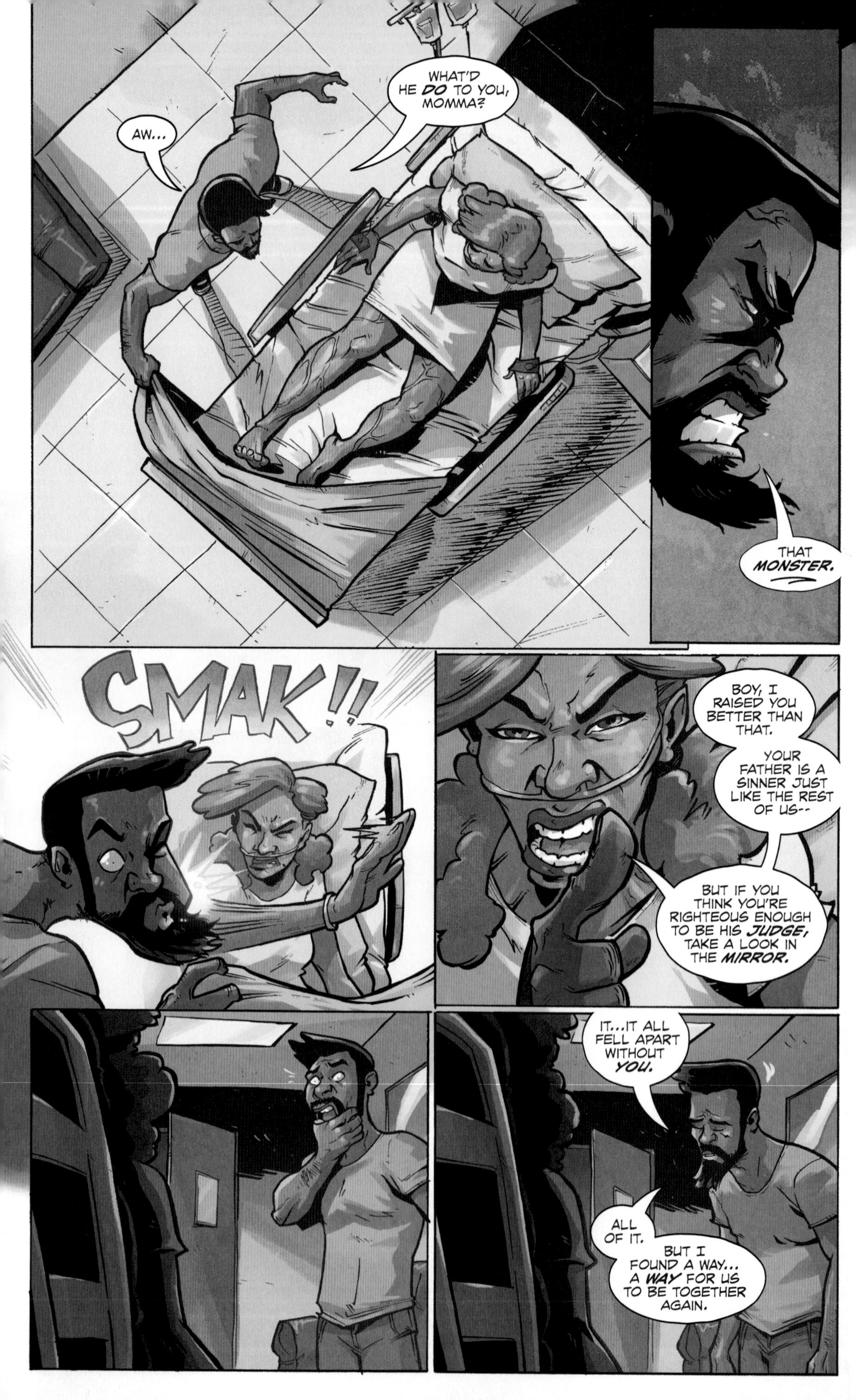
AW...
WHAT'D HE DO TO YOU, MOMMA?
THAT MONSTER.
SMAK!!
BOY, I RAISED YOU BETTER THAN THAT.
YOUR FATHER IS A SINNER JUST LIKE THE REST OF US--
BUT IF YOU THINK YOU'RE RIGHTEOUS ENOUGH TO BE HIS JUDGE, TAKE A LOOK IN THE MIRROR.
IT...IT ALL FELL APART WITHOUT YOU.
ALL OF IT.
BUT I FOUND A WAY... A WAY FOR US TO BE TOGETHER AGAIN.

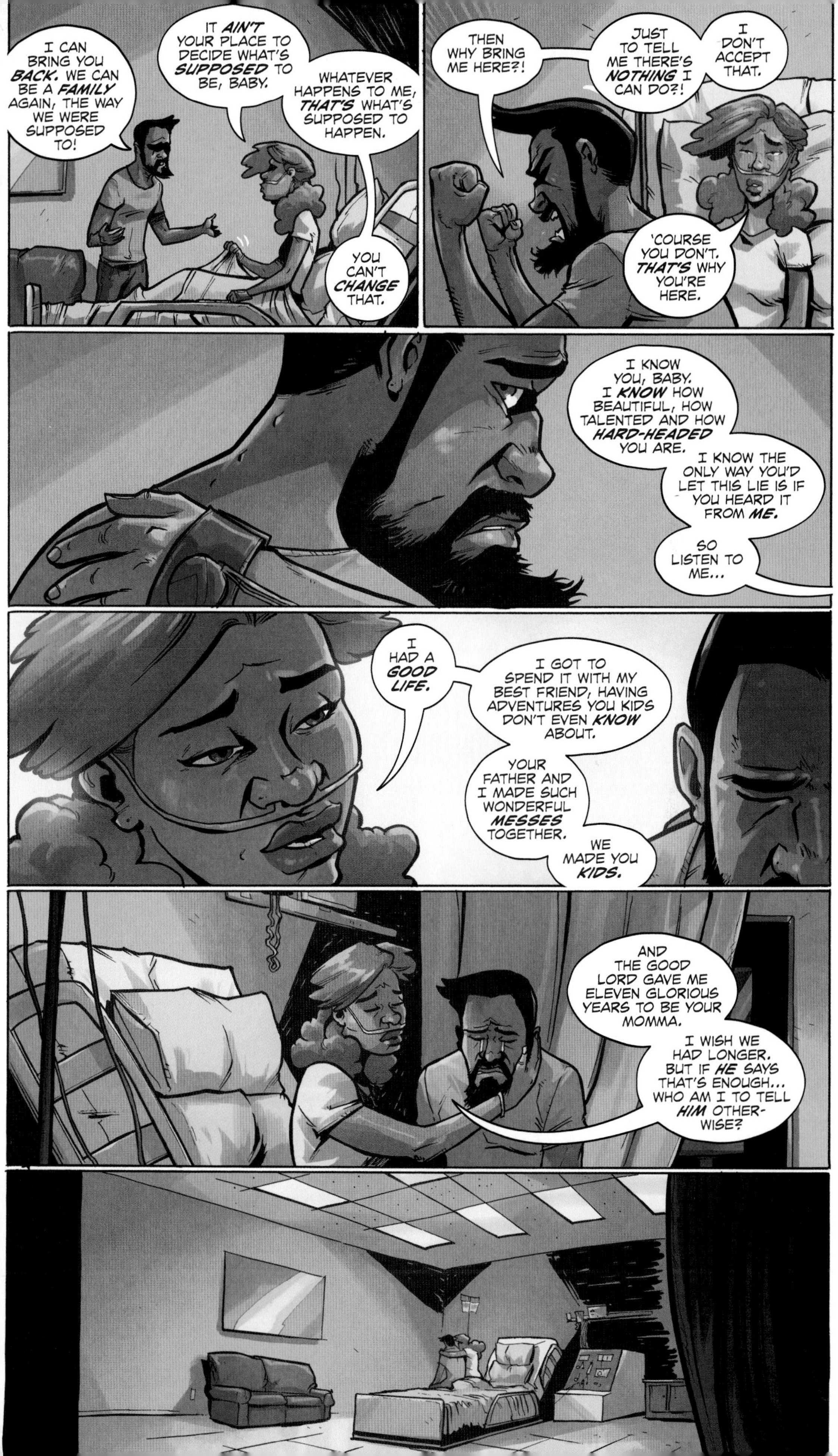

I CAN BRING YOU BACK. WE CAN BE A FAMILY AGAIN, THE WAY WE WERE SUPPOSED TO!
IT AIN'T YOUR PLACE TO DECIDE WHAT'S SUPPOSED TO BE, BABY.
WHATEVER HAPPENS TO ME, THAT'S WHAT'S SUPPOSED TO HAPPEN.
YOU CAN'T CHANGE THAT.
THEN WHY BRING ME HERE?!
JUST TO TELL ME THERE'S NOTHING I CAN DO?!
I DON'T ACCEPT THAT.
'COURSE YOU DON'T. THAT'S WHY YOU'RE HERE.
I KNOW YOU, BABY. I KNOW HOW BEAUTIFUL, HOW TALENTED AND HOW HARD-HEADED YOU ARE.
I KNOW THE ONLY WAY YOU'D LET THIS LIE IS IF YOU HEARD IT FROM ME.
SO LISTEN TO ME...
I HAD A GOOD LIFE.
I GOT TO SPEND IT WITH MY BEST FRIEND, HAVING ADVENTURES YOU KIDS DON'T EVEN KNOW ABOUT.
YOUR FATHER AND I MADE SUCH WONDERFUL MESSES TOGETHER.
WE MADE YOU KIDS.
AND THE GOOD LORD GAVE ME ELEVEN GLORIOUS YEARS TO BE YOUR MOMMA.
I WISH WE HAD LONGER. BUT IF HE SAYS THAT'S ENOUGH... WHO AM I TO TELL HIM OTHER-WISE?

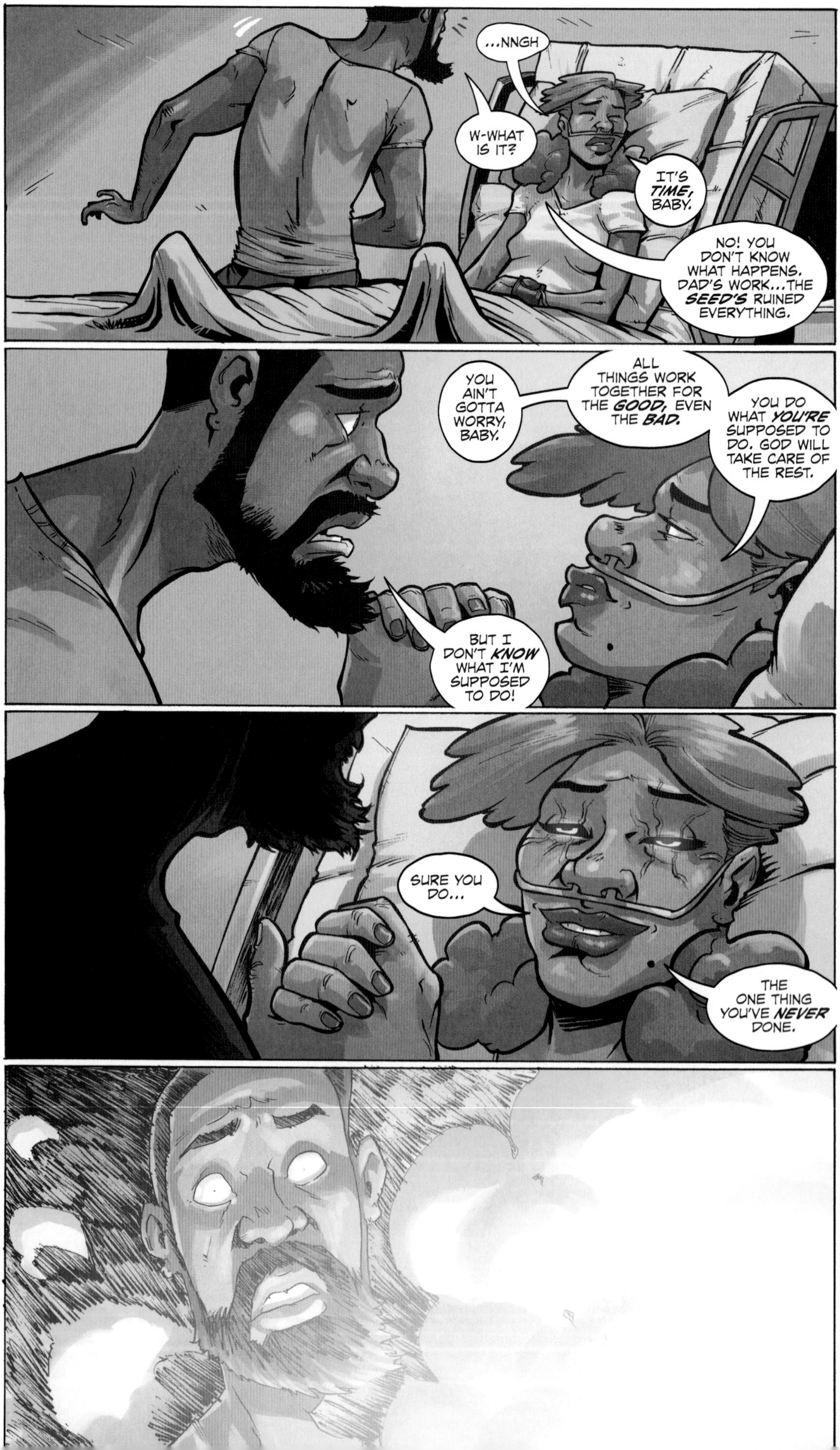
...NNGH
W-WHAT IS IT?
IT'S TIME, BABY.
NO! YOU DON'T KNOW WHAT HAPPENS. DAD'S WORK...THE SEED'S RUINED EVERYTHING.
YOU AIN'T GOTTA WORRY, BABY.
ALL THINGS WORK TOGETHER FOR THE GOOD, EVEN THE BAD.
YOU DO WHAT YOU'RE SUPPOSED TO DO. GOD WILL TAKE CARE OF THE REST.
BUT I DON'T KNOW WHAT I'M SUPPOSED TO DO!
SURE YOU DO...
THE ONE THING YOU'VE NEVER DONE.

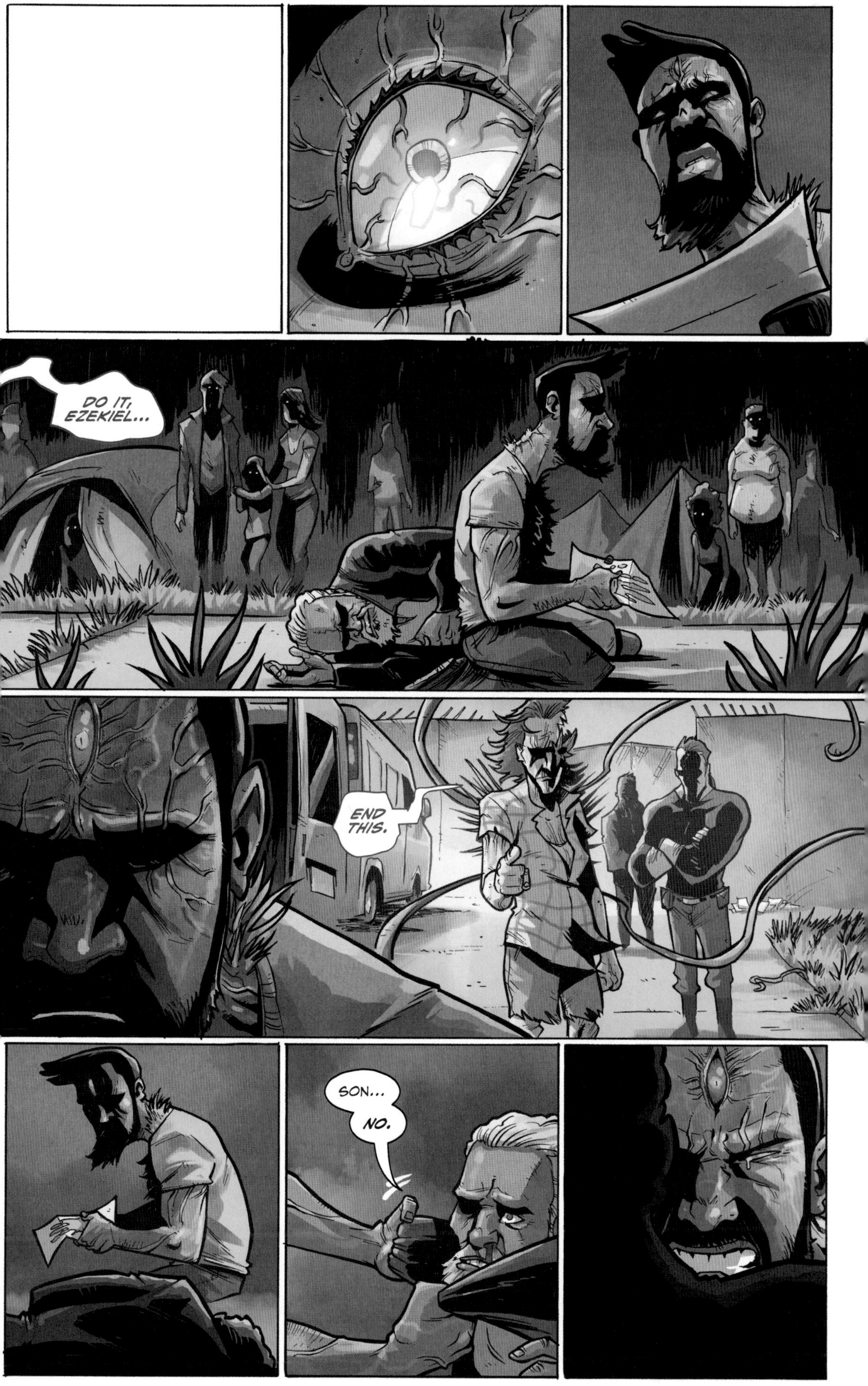
DO IT, EZEKIEL...
END THIS.
SON...
NO.

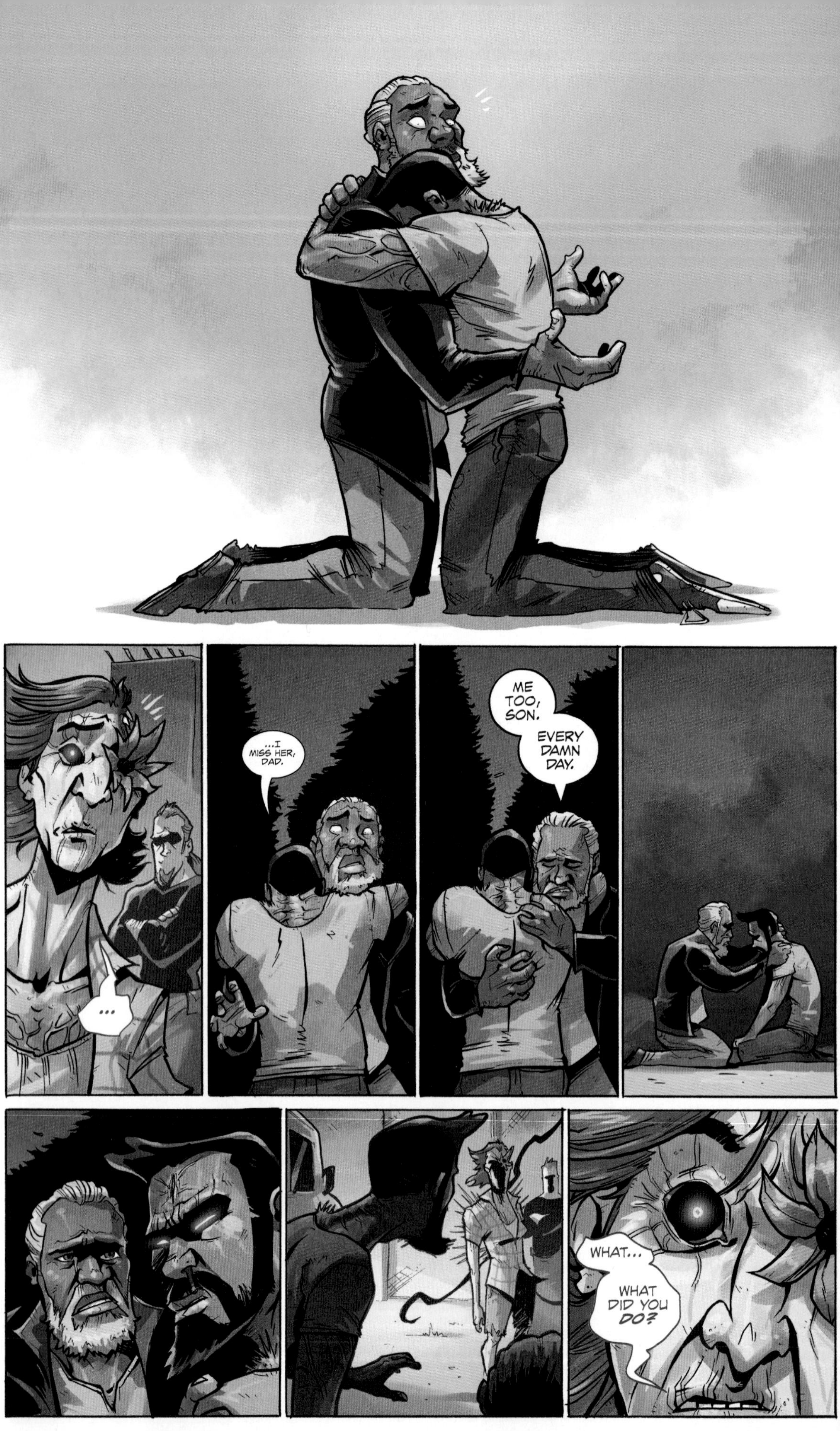
...
...I MISS HER, DAD.
ME TOO, SON.
EVERY DAMN DAY.
WHAT...
WHAT DID YOU DO?

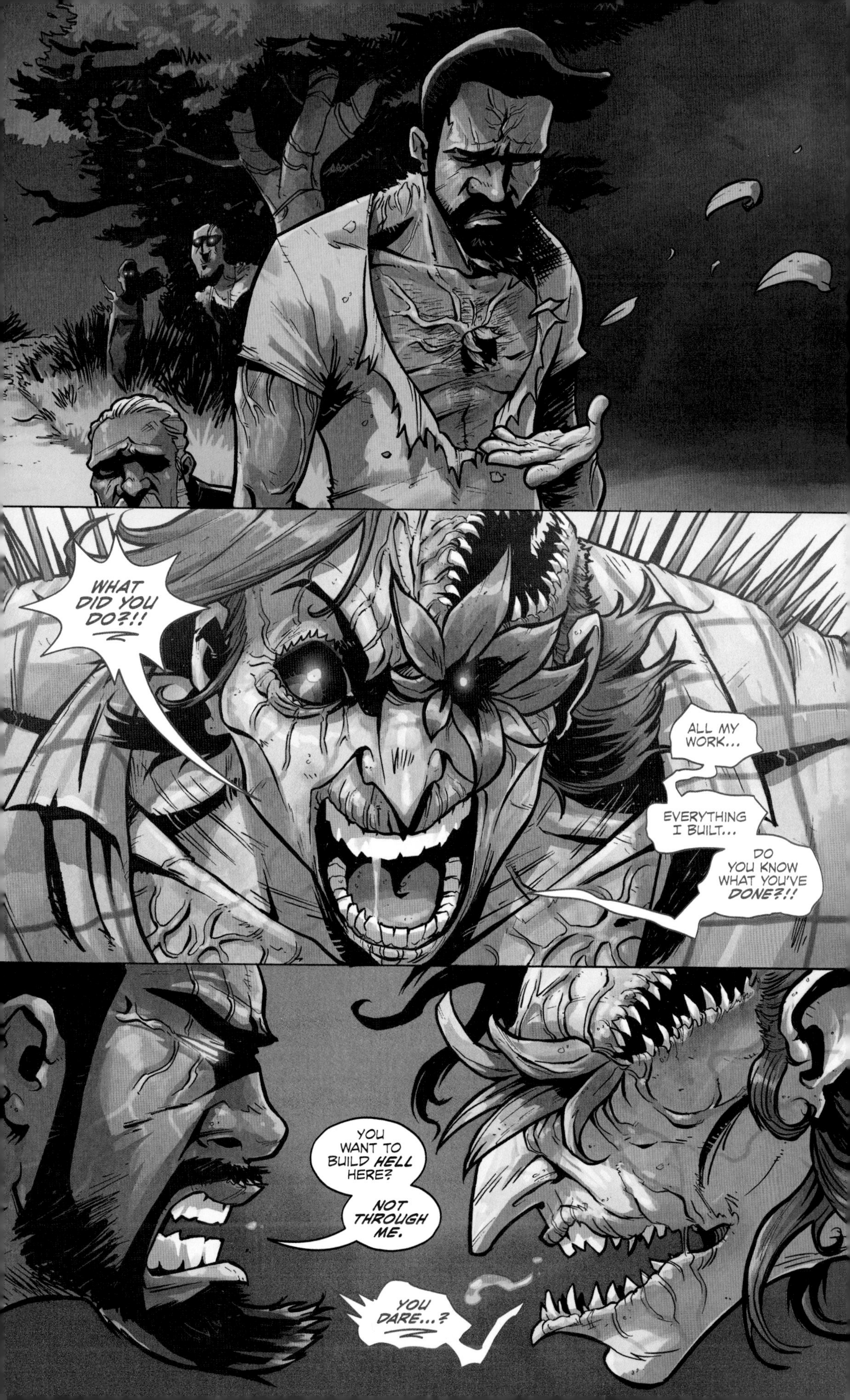
WHAT DID YOU DO?!!
ALL MY WORK...
EVERYTHING I BUILT...
DO YOU KNOW WHAT YOU'VE *DONE?!!*
YOU WANT TO BUILD *HELL* HERE?
NOT THROUGH ME.
YOU DARE...?

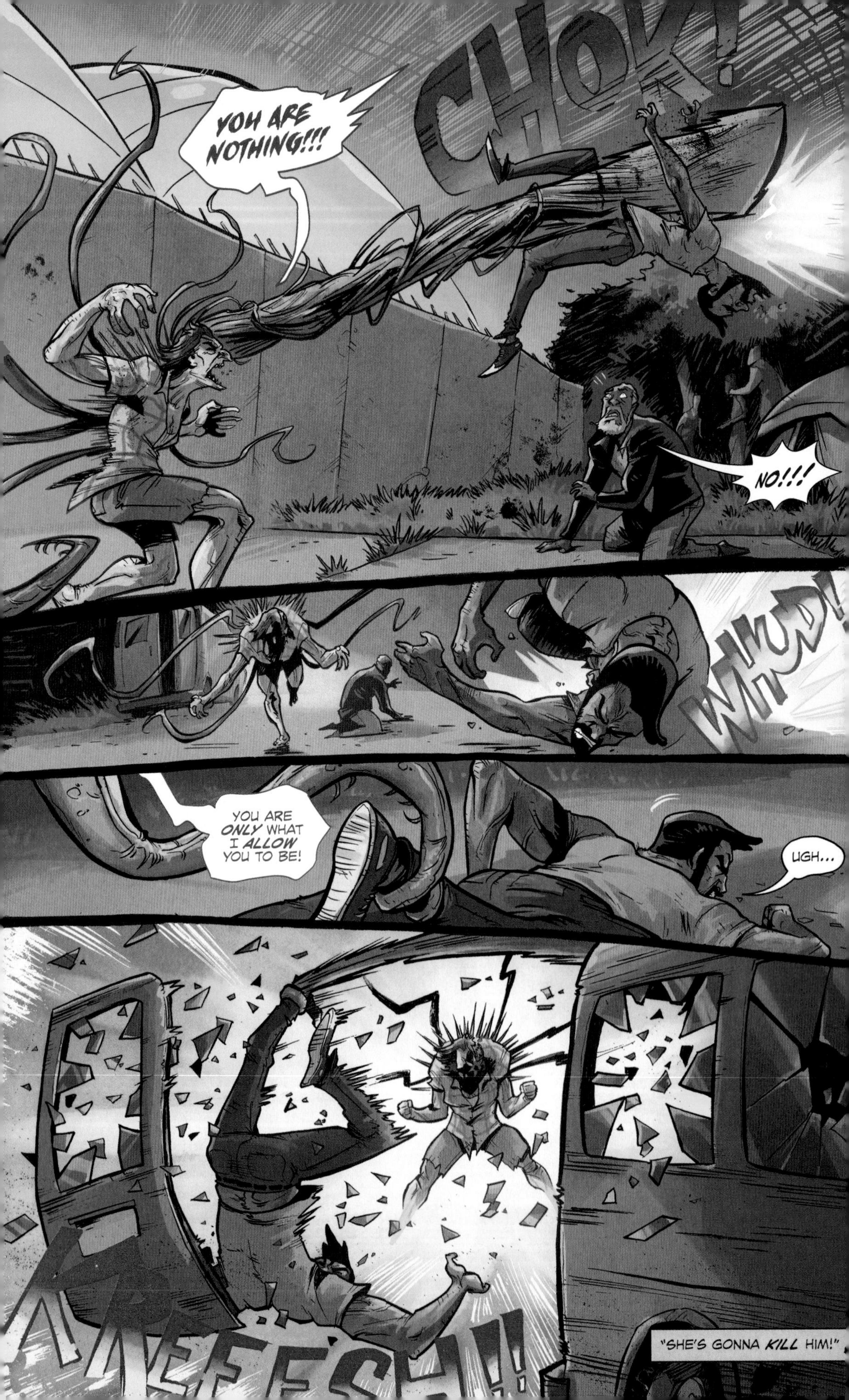
CHOK!
YOU ARE NOTHING!!!
NO!!!
WHUD!
YOU ARE ONLY WHAT I ALLOW YOU TO BE!
UGH...
"SHE'S GONNA KILL HIM!"

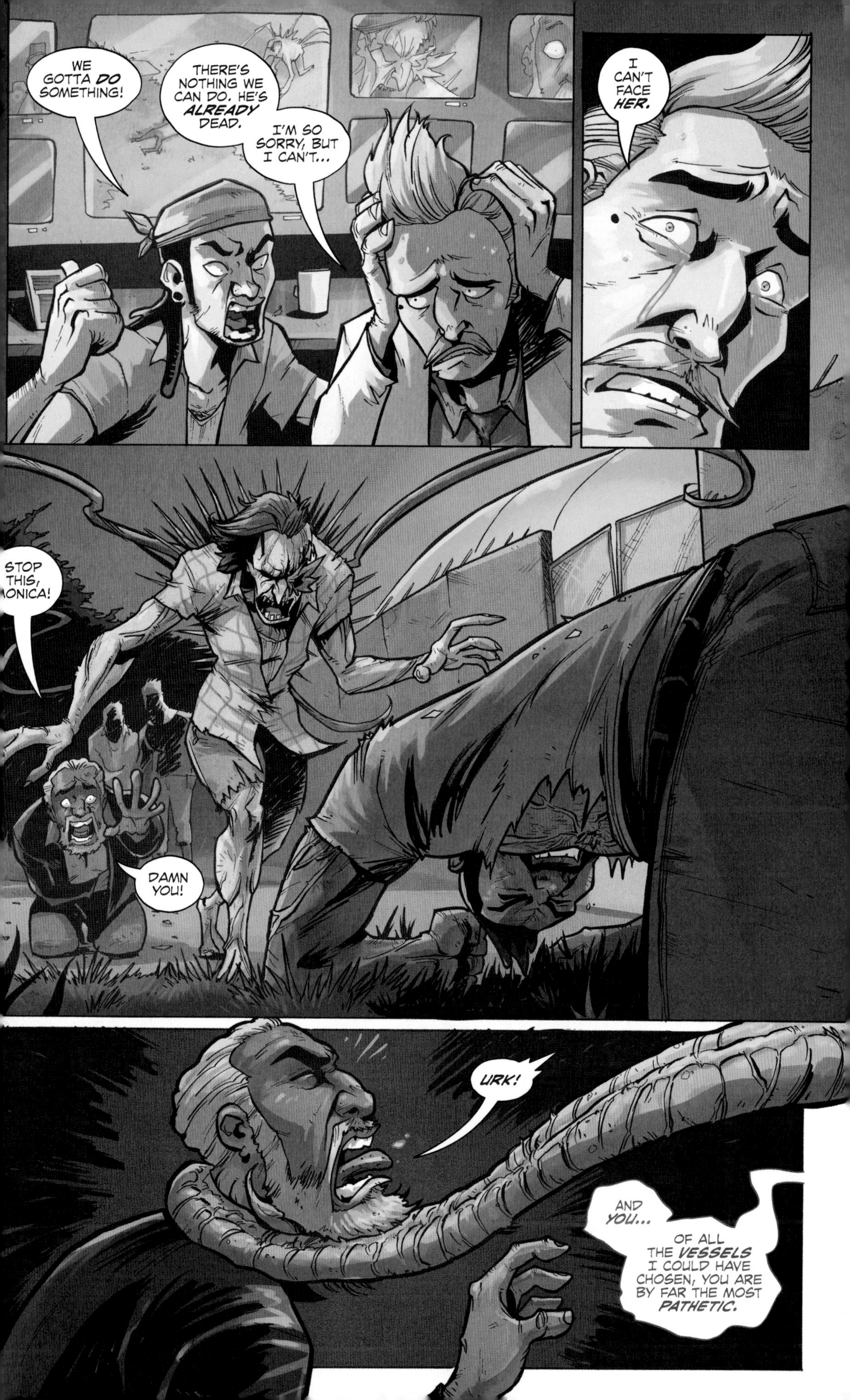
WE GOTTA DO SOMETHING!
THERE'S NOTHING WE CAN DO. HE'S ALREADY DEAD.
I'M SO SORRY, BUT I CAN'T...
I CAN'T FACE HER.
STOP THIS, ONICA!
DAMN YOU!
URK!
AND YOU...
OF ALL THE VESSELS I COULD HAVE CHOSEN, YOU ARE BY FAR THE MOST PATHETIC.

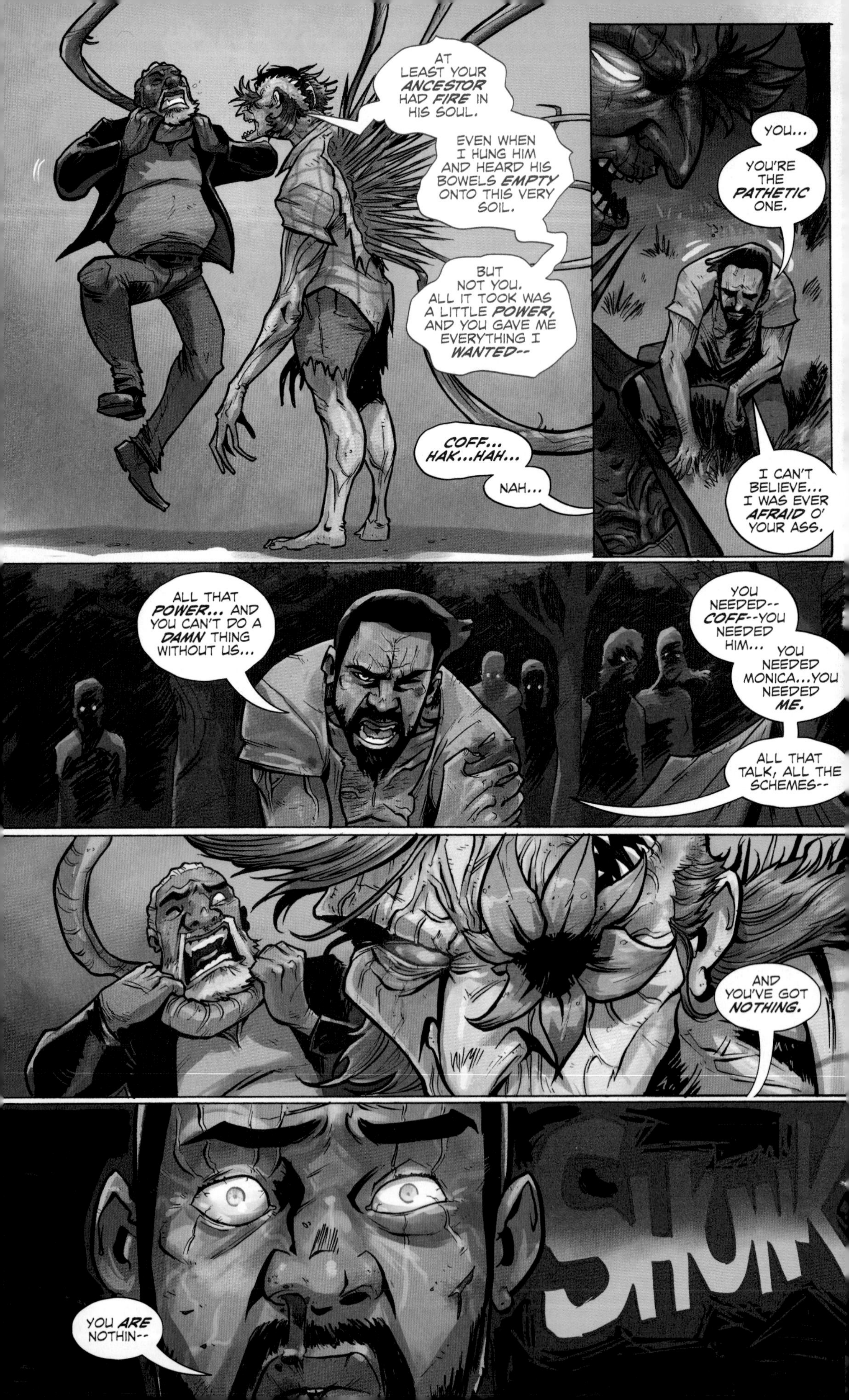

AT LEAST YOUR ANCESTOR HAD FIRE IN HIS SOUL.
EVEN WHEN I HUNG HIM AND HEARD HIS BOWELS EMPTY ONTO THIS VERY SOIL.
BUT NOT YOU. ALL IT TOOK WAS A LITTLE POWER, AND YOU GAVE ME EVERYTHING I WANTED--
COFF... HAK...HAH...
NAH...
YOU...
YOU'RE THE PATHETIC ONE.
I CAN'T BELIEVE... I WAS EVER AFRAID O' YOUR ASS.
ALL THAT POWER... AND YOU CAN'T DO A DAMN THING WITHOUT US...
YOU NEEDED-- COFF--YOU NEEDED HIM...
YOU NEEDED MONICA...YOU NEEDED ME.
ALL THAT TALK, ALL THE SCHEMES--
AND YOU'VE GOT NOTHING.
YOU ARE NOTHIN--
SHUNK

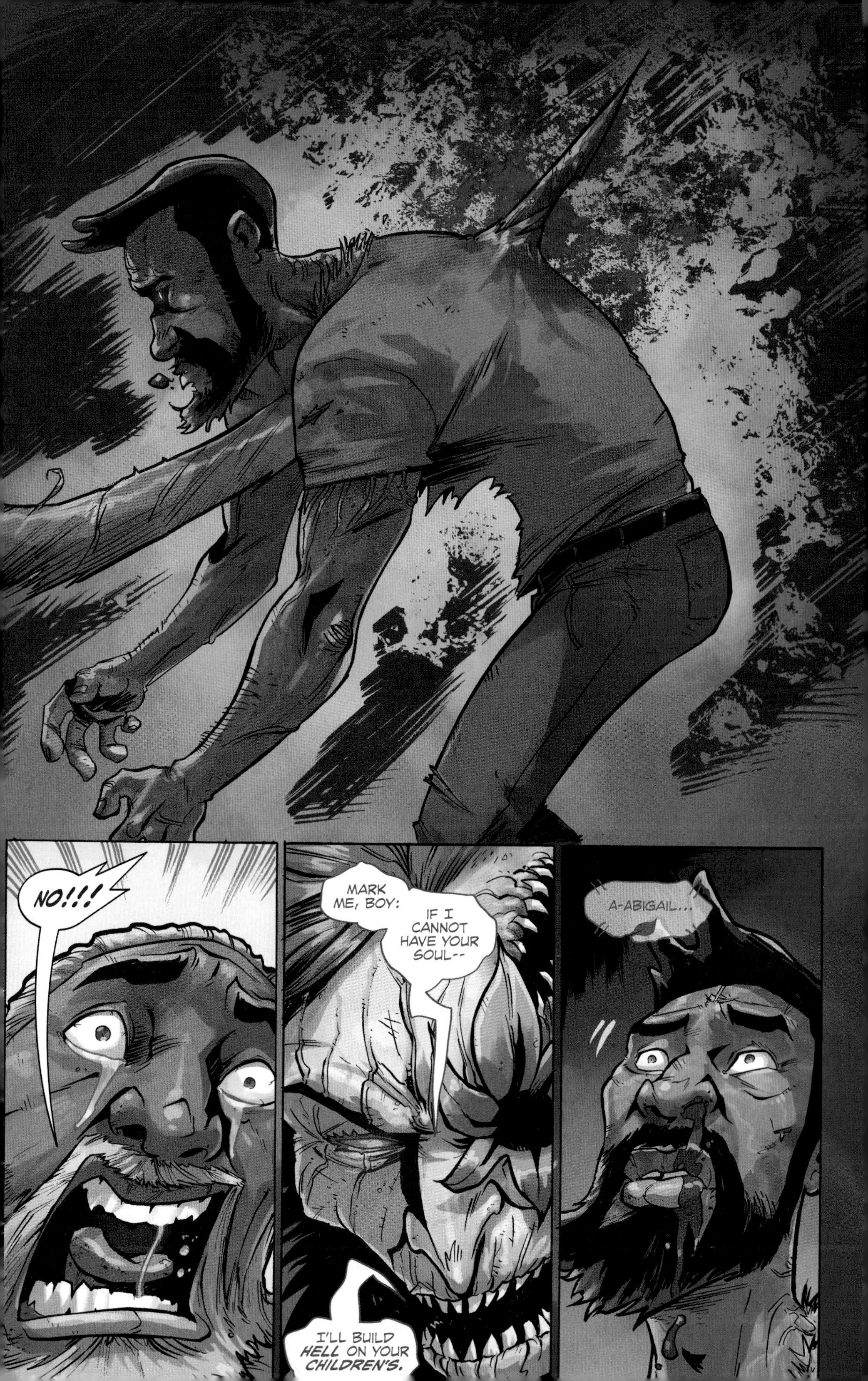
NO!!!
MARK ME, BOY:
IF I CANNOT HAVE YOUR SOUL--
I'LL BUILD *HELL* ON YOUR *CHILDREN'S.*
A-ABIGAIL...

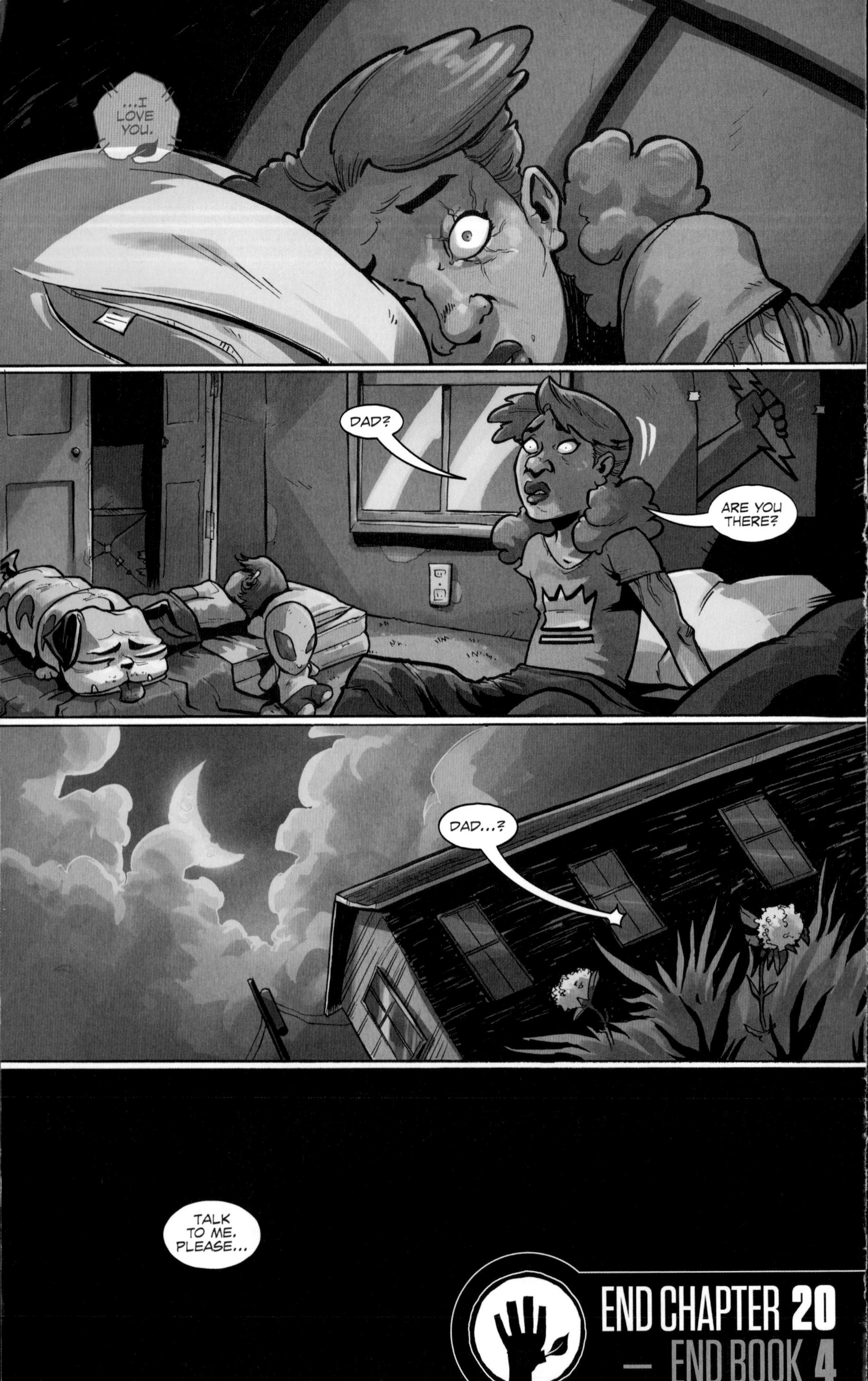
...I LOVE YOU.
DAD?
ARE YOU THERE?
DAD...?
TALK TO ME. PLEASE...
END CHAPTER 20
— END BOOK 4

To everything there is a season,

and a time for every purpose under heaven:

a time to be born and a time to die,

a time to plant and a time to uproot,

a time to kill and a time to heal,

a time to break down and a time to build,

a time to weep and a time to laugh,

a time to mourn and a time to dance,

a time to cast away stones and a time to gather stones together,

a time to embrace and a time to refrain from embracing,

a time to search and a time to count as lost,

a time to keep and a time to discard,

a time to tear and a time to mend,

a time to be silent and a time to speak,

a time to love and a time to hate,

a time for war and a time for peace.

Ecclesiastes 3:1-8

RobGuillory.com

Original Art + Merch + Signed Books

~~GRASSROOTS~~

The Official FARMHAND Letters Column!

Accepting fan mail, gardening tips, haiku poems and random pictures of your dog.

You can email letters to:
FARMHAND@robguillory.com

Or go the snail mail route:
FARMHAND | P.O. Box 304 | Scott, LA 70583

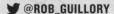 @ROB_GUILLORY    @ROB_GUILLORY   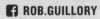 ROB.GUILLORY